She knew she had to tell him, but she also knew it would break his heart and destroy their love...

"Sara Jacobs."

Sara turned to face him. David only used her full name when he was worried.

"What is it?" he asked. "What is bothering you?"

She could only stare at him. She couldn't do it. She had to, she argued. *David, forgive me.* "David, I was sent here by my boss Simon. He isn't just a businessman. He's the head of the Mossad department assigned to a branch of internal security. More specifically, he is in charge of the investigation of the Falashian Sect." David stood up with a look that prompted Sara to hurry. "David, I work for—"

"*Wait!*" he shouted. "Sara, are you trying to tell me you are a—a—" He couldn't say it.

"David, I'm an agent with the Mossad. I was assigned—"

Again, he cut her off, only this time by walking over to the window where she was standing. The eyes she looked up at bore little resemblance to their dancing twins. Something in her responded negatively to the revulsion she believed she saw in them.

"I'm an agent, dammit, and a good one, at that. I won't apologize for doing my job. I would do anything to help our country. I also know you will do whatever it takes to save her. We are adults, David. Let's act like adults. Thousands of people are dying a horrible death. You may have the keys to save their lives. That's all that's important at this moment. We will have to worry about us later. There isn't time for that now. You have to hurry to the priest's home and talk to him. You do understand that, don't you? Every minute wasted another person gets infected, another person dies."

He didn't hear most of what she said. Only enough to figure out she had deceived him without explaining why. The pain in his chest grew in direct proportion to the coldness of her words—words without feeling.

During two mass immigrations from 1984 to 1991, thousands of Ethiopian Jews were permitted to flee persecution in their country and migrate to Israel. This is their story and how it could possibly save a nation from a plague.

Israeli coastal towns suddenly experience a rash of severe flu-like symptoms. As those infected become gravely ill and die at an alarming rate, it becomes apparent that this is more than an epidemic. The plague is identified as a variant of Anthrax, a deadly disease used in chemical warfare. The nation of Israel is faced with total annihilation.

With tens of thousands dead, and finding no antidote, the nation prays for a Messiah. The answer comes from a Falashian refugee named David Yasuda, who knows a secret: Hidden in a reclusive mountain valley in Ethiopia is a secret pool of miracle water. When the Mossad is refused admission into the country to search for it, a secret mission is launched. But someone knows they are coming and will stop at nothing to prevent the elite team from finding what they seek.

KUDOS for *The Messiah Drug*

In *The Messiah Drug* by E. Lessly Taylor, David Yasuda is a
"Black" or Ethiopian Jew who immigrated to Israel from Ethiopia. He works for the Israeli Government, acting as a liaison
between them and the rest of the Ethiopian immigrants and
helping the newcomers to find jobs and assimilate into Israeli
society. When David falls in love, he doesn't know that the
Mossad is investigating him and his love is an agent assigned
to seduce him to get information on the Ethiopians who have
immigrated into the country. Then an outbreak of deadly anthrax is instigated by an enemy country and Israelis start dying
by the thousands, all but the Ethiopians, who seem to have
some sort of immunity. Now David's girlfriend, Sara, is
tasked to get the secret out of David as to why he and the others aren't getting sick. This precipitates a secret mission into
Ethiopia to search for this mysterious cure. Taylor does a good
job of laying the foundation of the hate and prejudice that
cause the bio-terrorism, the plot is strong, and the characters
realistic and believable. It's a suspenseful and intriguing read.
~ *Taylor Jones, Reviewer*

The Messiah Drug by E. Lessly Taylor is the story of hate,
prejudice, and betrayal on the most basic level. Imagine how
you would feel if you suddenly discovered that the love of
your life was an intelligence agent who had been assigned to
seduce you for information. Well, that is exactly what happens
to our hero, David Yasuda. Not only has his lover been assigned to seduce him, she also has to confess that she has been
assigned to him and solicit his help to stop a ma-made plague,
regardless of how he might feel about it. Needless to say, he's
upset, but since people are dying, he agrees to help secure the
information as to why he and his fellow immigrants from
Ethiopian seem to be impervious to the anthrax that has been
foisted on Israel by an enemy. Talk about being torn between
doing what is right for your new country and wanting revenge
for being duped. Not an easy position to be in, I'm sure. *The
Messiah Drug* is a chilling tale of love, betrayal, terrorism, and
the damage this combination can cause in the lives of innocent

bystanders. It will catch and hold your interest from beginning to end. ~ *Regan Murphy, Reviewer*

ACKNOWLEDGEMENTS

I need to first thank my God for the opportunity to tell this story that he placed on my heart. I believe that, in everything you do, give thanks to God.

Next I would like to thank is my wonderful wife Carol, who has always encouraged me on this sometimes-frustrating journey. Her upbeat attitude was the strength I needed to continue writing.

I would like to thank a very talented crew of editors for their invaluable assistance and teaching. These gifted professionals often took me back to school.

Finally, I would like to thank my children, Stacie, Katie, and E. J., who share my love of writing. My kids are my life and the reason why I take a breath every day—something every loving parent understands.

THE

MESSIAH

DRUG

E. Lessly Taylor

A Black Opal Books Publication

GENRE: RELIGIOUS THRILLER/MYSTERY-DETECTIVE

THE MESSIAH DRUG
Copyright © 2016 by E. Lessly Taylor
Cover Design by Jackson Cover Designs with E. Lessly Taylor
All cover art copyright © 2016
All Rights Reserved
Print ISBN: 9781-626945-11-1

First Publication: AUGUST 2016

Published by Black Opal Books **http://www.blackopalbooks.com**

DEDICATION

I would like to dedicate my first novel to my wife Carol, a young woman who, when riding her bus to work, got off and walked past a total stranger holding a coffee in one hand and reading the morning newspaper in the other, and later told her girlfriend that she just saw the man she was going to marry. Thirty-five years of marriage later she is still capturing my heart.

Special thanks to my daughter Stacie, an amazing author, who has ranked number one in her particular genre and has published five highly ranked novels. We have often sounded off to each other about the characters close to our hearts we write about. Stacie's success gave weigh to her encouraging me to share the over a dozen novels that I have written. If I can enjoy a micron of the success and acclaim this best-selling author has obtained, it will be worth all the hard work.

CHAPTER 1

Haifa, Israel, April 1999:

D avid Yasuda took out his handkerchief and wiped the beads of salty sweat from his face. Leaning back against the wire fence, he studied his handiwork. "I hope she appreciates all this hard work," he mumbled knowing he did it as much for himself as for her.

The polished old van reflected his hard work from every angle. So clean it could pass for new with streak-free windows. Nothing annoyed him more than to be driving along, peering out a window, and spotting a flaw in his effort. Today, he'd spent more time on the van windows than usual. Finally, the van was clean inside and out, just in time, as the morning sun began to assert itself upon the day. A yellow orb in a cloudless sky, looking for victims to fry. Twice he had the unfortunate pleasure of tasting his own body salt as sweat-painted lines ran down his face. Soaked and dirty from his effort, he didn't allow that to sway him because this was a very important day, and he wanted everything perfect. Or as nearly perfect as he could manage.

The second coat of wax had given the old van the luster he desired. The shine was impressive but deceptive, belying the vehicle's true age. *Even if it doesn't impress Sara*, he thought, *at least it looks good*. A frown broke through his satisfied grin when, on his final walk-a-round, he spotted an imperfection hidden in the corner of the rear window.

"Not today," he vowed at fate's weak attempt to mar what was going to be a beautiful afternoon. One quick wipe at the small streak and David pronounced the van finished.

"Now to get showered and pick up Sara." Her name triggered that stunned and stupid grin men get when the woman that possessed their soul danced across their minds. Added to what he knew was a smitten expression, was a song he started singing by Hall & Oates, asking Sara to smile.

The last few months have sure been fantastic, David thought as he gathered up his cleaning supplies and placed them in the box he carried in the back of the van. Never in his dreams did he think he would meet someone like Sara. Snippets of their times together sidetracked him as he started to lock the rear doors of the van. Stopping, he stared out at the harbor and the calm Mediterranean Sea. Various ships passed before him unseen, the native fowl squawked overhead unheard, as he speculated about his life lately and its remarkable twist and turns.

Another set of eyes were watching David's idle musing from two streets over and taking careful notes. From that advantage point, he scrutinized his mark with complete privacy. Well, minus being annoyed by some loud kids kicking a soccer ball around in the street. For a moment, he relished in the idea of shooting a few of them and watching the others flee screaming in terror.

Raising his binoculars, he continued monitoring his subject for information gathered for possible future "close" encounters.

"Yes, that's him," the small microphone in his collar recorded. "He's about six feet one and, let's see, yes, about one hundred and eighty pounds. He was washing his van when I arrived but appears to be finished now." The observer tapped his collar shutting off the mike. "What are you up to Mr. Yasuda? I hope it's something interesting. All I get are the boring assignments. Maybe I should leave some incriminating evi-

dence in your van, or are you so well connected it might back-
fire on me? I better check you out first my brown friend."

A car driving past with a faulty muffler snapped David out
of his trance but that smile never left his face. Her cameo image was the air that lifted his spirits and gave wings to his feet.
He raced up the steps to his apartment and, just as he unlocked
the door, the phone rang. A trumpet blasting in his ear
couldn't have startled him more. Paralyzed, he weighed the
consequences of answering. All day he had struggled with the
taunting voices of doubt. In his labor of love, getting the van
ready for his date, he had sensed that the fingers of fate were
waiting in the shadows, mocking him, waiting to intercept his
prospects for happiness and detour his plans for the evening.
Just let it ring, he decided, but what if its Sara calling? That
possibility on the fourth ring triggered a mad rush for the
phone.

"Hello!"

"David?"

His heart leaped at the mention of his name. The voice was
soft and feminine—but not Sara's. Disappointed, he sighed
deeply and then put the traitorous phone back to his lips. "Yes,
this is David."

"David, this is Yael Tefera."

David closed his eyes and exhaled slowly. It wasn't the
caller that provoked that response but the picture of her troublesome brother that flavored David's frustration. No, there
was nothing wrong with the caller. Yael was a very sweet
young woman. It quickly became clear to both of them that
there could be something between them the first time their
eyes met.

She had adjusted quickly to living in Israel when her family arrived from Ethiopia. Yael was bright, fun to be with, and
very beautiful. He had often kicked himself for not following
up on the obvious openings she had given him. Every time he
made an effort to open that door, her foolish brother would do

or say something to screw it up. *Naw, it's too late now, anyway,* he mused. Sara had entered his life and Yael was now only a very pleasant memory.

"David, are you there?"

"Yes, Yael, I'm sorry, what can I do for you?"

"It's not for me…"

The long silence answered his question. He just waited for the painful confirmation.

"It's Yonatan. David, he's in trouble with the authorities. He needs your help—again—I'm sorry to say."

The pain in her voice reached through the phone and touched a familiar cord. Not today, David prayed silently. Please, not today.

"What's wrong this time, Yael?" Her reluctance to answer caused him to close his eyes and mumble to himself. He pounded his fist against the wall. "Look, Yael—" He had to ask, as his feelings for the petite winsome lass touched something in him. "I'm meeting someone in a few hours. Is there anything I can do to help?"

He knew it was a hollow and empty attempt at saving his date and that those special plans were shattered the moment he answered the phone.

"Thank you, David. I knew I could count on you for help. You're his only friend and I—" Silence again punctuated the air between them. She was careful to hide her feelings for the man on the other end of the line after having made it abundantly clear how she felt about him and received nothing but friendship in return. She valued that friendship but dreamed of much more. There wasn't an available woman in their synagogue who didn't want to catch him—a few, she giggled to herself, who weren't available but also whispered about being with him. Only her pride prevented her from opening that door wider, like some had vowed to do, and make her desires plain.

"The policeman at the station said he knew you and would release him into your custody. Can you help him, David? I promise never to bother you again. I told my brother this is the last time I'm going to try and help him out of the holes he jumps in."

The urge to say no lost its sting as the softness of her voice caressed his ear. "All right. Look, Yael, I'll go down to the station and do what I can. But I want to make something very clear. The last time he was arrested, I told Yonatan that, if he wouldn't listen to reason, not to call me anymore. I'm going to go down there and try to get him out. But I'm not doing it for him." The reason went unspoken but it was clear.

Her gentle song of thanks chimed in his ears long after she hung up. It was another minute of listening to the dial tone before he removed the phone from his ear and placed it in its cradle. There was nothing to be gained from throwing it against the wall, he finally reasoned, but he wanted to, so much.

Would he ever learn to say no to people? He scolded himself. They sure as hell knew how to say it to him. He wanted to berate himself further but knew that would only make him feel worse. Maybe he could deal with Yonatan's problems and still make it back in time to take Sara out like they planned. That possible likelihood put enough charge in his batteries to energize a dispirited David Yasuda.

"Don't hand me that," the prisoner said. "What do you know about how I'm feeling? You're one of the elite."

"Elite? That's the first time someone has called me that," David answered.

"You have everything but we common people have nothing," the angry man explained as he paced the cell room. A six-by-eight-foot-sized room that reeked of urine and something he was afraid to label. "They treat you better than they treat us. I don't want their token jobs. Why don't they train us to be a real part of this country? They save the good jobs for their own. We Black Jews are no better than the Arabs are to them. I've had enough of their condescending attitudes and derogatory comments. The last smart remark I heard was answered with my fist."

"That's great, and look where it got you. Yonatan, you're

wrong and you know it," David countered as he pushed him against the cell wall. "I've begged you to take the time to get to know the customs of this country, to find your place in this society. You have to want to be successful. You're complaining. Will that get it done? Sure, there are people who do not want you here. I recall there were plenty of people at home that did not want us there either. They didn't hurt our feeling with words, they were killing us. Look around you, Yonatan. Some of these people risked their lives to get you here. If they can risk everything, can you do any less to stay here?"

What, no snide comeback? David thought as he looked into the fiery eyes of his angry friend.

Yonatan's failure to answer him wasn't a complete surprise. It was the same argument he had used to deal with other dissidents. He always acknowledged their strength, and their right to their opinions, but never wavered on the need for their commitment to endure any and every obstacle. The significance of his argument was clear, even to the most impassioned, disgruntled, Falashian Jew. David backed off and tried to calm down.

Yonatan recovered quickly and pointed his finger at David. "You've changed."

"What do you mean by that?"

"You know what I mean." Having said that, Yonatan then walked to the far end of his cell and sat down.

Unfortunately, David did know. He had heard the whispers, the small talk. None of it was true, David thought. He was the same person. What was different was that he wasn't agreeing with any of their bull—

"I haven't changed," David said calmly to the man watching him and anyone else listening. Jewish jails were known for their hidden listening devices. "I'm still doing my job. I'm still battling for more aid for my people, for all peoples for that matter. I can't create jobs that aren't there. I'm doing the—"

"Then you're not doing enough!" Yonatan shouted at him as he stood up and again aimed a finger at his friend. He was sorry as soon as he said it. He knew plenty of people who David had gotten jobs for, good jobs. No one worked harder in the community to help their people and yet thousands remained out of work. Yonatan knew that wasn't David's fault. "Sorry, David," he forced himself to say and then pounded his fist on his leg. "That was unfair."

"Don't worry about it. Look, Yonatan, I will talk to the magistrate about getting you out of here. I've dealt with him before. He's tough, but fair."

Yonatan looked into the troubled face of his friend. The hurt hiding in those eyes was evident in the lack of the usual fire in David's voice. *Damn*, Yonatan swore. *This is the last time I will drag him down with my problems. David is a good friend,* he grudgingly admitted, and probably the only friend who would have come down here to help him.

They were the same age and liked the same sports, music, and food. That became a common ground for a friendship when David interviewed him upon Yonatan's arrival in Israel two years ago. Their friendship grew until they were like brothers to the rest of the community. But slowly, as many struggled to find work, Yonatan became discontented with the pace of change and started running with a more vocal group. The final straw in their friendship, he sadly remembered, was when he noticed David and his younger sister Yael becoming interested in each other. Every time they took a step toward some kind of relationship, Yonatan did or said something to put cold water on it. Only after David stopped coming around and he saw the loneness in his favorite sister's eyes did he realize, too late, that his jealousy had fueled his actions to keep them apart.

Yonatan walked over and hugged him. "Whatever you can do, I'd appreciate it. Thank you, my friend."

David shook his head, walked to the door, and signaled for the guard to let him out.

It's your job, he argued with himself as he drove down Jaffa Street. *You're paid to help these people and the problems they brought with them.* Those facts weren't the dilemma. The real reason for the funk he was in had more to do with what hadn't happened than what had. He was able to get the charges dropped, but Yonatan would spend the next three days in jail, with a promise from the magistrate to be twice as hard on Yonatan if he saw him again.

"Cheer up," Sara told him when he called from the jail with the bad news.

Besides, he thought, she did say she was free all day and night tomorrow…hmmmm, day *and* night. A big smile appeared on his face as he started scheming. Feeling better about his prospects, he became more reflective. As that loud American he'd met at the hospital would have said, "It's no big deal."

On the drive home, David stole glances at the orange ball setting in Haifa harbor. The sun's dying rays reflected off the shiny, dark water, highlighting ships, large and small, dotting the harbor. It was a common picture to him, noteworthy for its daily originality, a familiar sight bordering a changing seascape. The passing ships did little to distract the daydreaming man scanning the darkening port city.

Tomorrow, he conceded to his growing optimism, *will be my day. Tomorrow*. The word wrapped him in warm arms of expectation summed up in one word—Sara.

CHAPTER 2

The Mediterranean Sea, June 1999:

The water was choppy as the old freighter cut a slow path through the darkening sea while the diving sun's softening rays painted the final strokes to a seaman's day. Strips of thin clouds weaved an abstract pattern against a red/orange sky. It was sailor's weather.

Three exhausted seagulls landed on the rusted pilothouse of the old freighter and rested from their travels. A storm off the coast of Italy had battered them and separated the trio from the flock. The tired stowaways went unnoticed as they huddled together on the strange perch. Daybreak would give the gulls fresh wings and a new direction to their nesting area.

Again, the mighty sea had performed its seductive dance. Captain Ahmed Mohamedy shook off the trance his rocking ship had generated and, with it, the nagging questions that troubled his spirit. He took a deep breath and sat up, once again assuming command.

"All ahead one-third," he shouted above the din of the equipment and small talk in the pilothouse.

"All ahead one-third, sir," the helmsman answered.

The dryness the captain felt in his throat was a direct result of the seriousness of their mission. He had sailed the rusty old freighter—named Ondo, after a town in Nigeria—inconspicuously through the busy Mediterranean Sea. *It's ironic*, he thought, *that the sun should set just as we reached our waypoint. There's nothing to worry about in the coming darkness. It's our friend.* He understood the need for night to cloak and to protect them. Surreptitiously, he rubbed his hands against his pants, their dampness an embarrassment.

He had ordered the ship to slow down, lest they move too close to shore. These were very dangerous waters for any ship passing so near to the coast of the Jews. His ship, with its dangerous cargo, was like a burning match near a pool of gasoline. A sudden shift in wind direction, the fumes would find the match, and Boom! The startling image of angry Israeli planes, having gotten *wind* of their mission, screaming down at them out of a blue-black sky had shaken him awake out of a couple of nightmares. Had they an inkling of what he was transporting, he had little doubt that the nightmare would have become a deadly reality.

"Ah, check our perimeter again, Iman," he nervously ordered his radar operator.

"All's clear for over fifty miles, sir. There are two aircraft flying near the coast but they're headed in the opposite direction. No radar is illuminating in our direction. We are still out of range of the coastal radar stations."

"Allah be praised."

"Praise be to Allah," everyone in the pilothouse answered as one.

"Check every ten to twenty minutes, Iman, and stagger your search. Only go active sporadically so as not to tip off anyone that we are scanning the area."

"Yes, sir," the young ensign answered, hoping no one caught the implication in his voice. *We have only practiced this mission a hundred damn times,* he grumbled silently while searching the radar screen again.

He didn't know the exact mission, but they all knew it was very dangerous and, understanding their location, knew how important it was that they remain undiscovered.

Captain Mohamedy sensed the irritability of his crew. He was starting to become repetitive, he realized, and knew why.

Stay calm, he chastised himself, *this crew understands the danger in this insane voyage. After all, you trained them your-*

self. And they have no other choice. So relax. Trying to obey his own order, he got up from his captain's chair and walked out of the pilothouse. As expected, breathing the crisp sea air that greeted him when he stepped outside was a simple, but restful pleasure. He wasn't disappointed.

The first-mate watched his captain leave the bridge, immediately stepped forward, and took his position beside the command chair with the remnant of smoke from the captain's cigar camping around the chair like a protective phantom.

"You have got to keep it together for their sakes," Captain Mohamedy mumbled, now alone in the quiet night. "This is the only way you will ever see them again."

He took a deep drag of his Cuban cigar and blew the smoke high above his head, trying hard to resist the nagging feeling that his family was in grave danger. The effort failed. Trying again, he started walking around the gangway until he was standing in front of the pilothouse. He watched for a few minutes as the bow of the gangly ship cut into the wall of darkness. Pangs of anxiety gripped his gut as he longed to feel his wife in his arms again. Looking up at the night sky, he sought relief in the mass of stars. These were the same pin pricks of light he took comfort in as a boy, tending his father's sheep in the desert at night. These were the same friends he talked to then that guided his way now. Their vast number confirmed that it was a clear and crisp late spring night.

Captain Mohamedy walked to the port side and observed the fading dark blue of the horizon. The dim light of the retreating day was shrinking in from both sides, as if two hands were coming together to clap in its departure. He took the last sweet draws from his cigar, while watching the nightshade slide down, until the only separation between the night sky and the black sea was the sparkling blanket of stars and a blurry reflection. His only barometer now to direct him to where the sun actually set was his imagination. After all these years, he still felt the love and awe sailors have for the mysteries of the sea.

Suddenly, he felt an intrusion in his reflections. It was a beckoning that he couldn't deny. If the sunset was to his left, then the destination of their voyage loomed off to starboard. He looked intensely at the black wall that lay beyond the glare of the ship's lights. There was a quiet reverence to the ebony barrier that shielded the target of this *Jihad*. There, a little over fifty miles due east from their present position, was the temporary home of their despised adversary.

He tried to picture the enemy as some vicious ghoul, an immoral invader who killed ingenuous children, the ravisher of pure women, a vile drinker of alcohol, and the shedder of innocent blood. The attempt failed when only the darkness in his soul was reflected back at him.

As a devout Muslim, the captain understood it was his duty to commence the *Jihad* to drive the infidels from the land of his brothers. There was something, however, that troubled him. *Why,* he'd questioned over and over the last few months, *use such a cowardly method to destroy them?* It was his earlier questioning of this mission, he later decided, that prompted the president-for-life to insist that his family stay at the palace for their safety until the mission was completed. Captain Mohamedy came to understand that this overt act of kindness was a veiled threat should he again question his orders.

The thought of his two teenage sons and gentle wife Rini being held as glorified hostages angered him. He gripped the hand railing as he realized his helplessness. "I have never shied from obeying the will of Allah," the twenty-year veteran of the sea whispered in his confusion, "why would they feel threatened by me now?"

The heavy darkness offered no answers. Should this dangerous mission fail, he had no doubt as to their fate. For Allah, and his family's safety, he vowed that this mission must succeed.

After years of dealing with tough seaman, this veteran of the sea understood the importance of the chain of command and he knew how necessary it was for them to obey orders. He had threatened to physically throw a few disgruntled seamen overboard himself when they hesitated to do as ordered. There could only be one captain, regardless of the situation, and he was the captain of this ship—but not his country. He had definite orders and something in him, nurtured over many campaigns captaining ships, was repulsed at doing anything other than what was expected of him.

"Sorry," he whispered eastward toward the sleeping infidels.

This time, he didn't want to see the faces of the enemy, knowing the horrible monster he was about to unleash on them. The growing weight of his actions was troubling, as he stared out into the darkness, searching for a reason to justify not committing the heinous act he was about to commence—a reason to sacrifice his beloved family for complete strangers.

"It's you or my family," he apologetically lamented. "May Allah show you the mercy that I cannot."

Alone in the dark, he prayed. He was slow to recognize the growing compassion he was starting to feel for his lifetime enemy, a kind of brotherhood. For some reason, the rhetoric of hate, nurtured in him from a child, was subsiding. Then, standing out in the humid night air, he realized why. The same bloody Angel of Death was lurking over his beloved family as well as the unsuspecting Israelis.

"Captain, it is time," a voice announced from behind him, shattering his supplication.

Startled from his thoughts, Captain Mohamedy turned to face his first officer Rasul Kabal.

Rasul was a tall, gangly man who ate like a horse but never gained weight, a very able seaman who had served on each of the captain's last ten voyages. He was a man that the captain trusted implicitly.

"Yes, my friend," he counseled, while placing his hand on Rasul's shoulder, "it is time to make history."

"Allah be praised!" Rasul shouted as he raised his right hand to the heavens, turned, and marched into the pilothouse.

"Praise Allah," Captain Mohamedy answered mechanically.

He hesitated for a moment, collecting himself, took the last draw of his cigar, and then tossed it overboard and followed Rasul into the pilothouse. Three of the five scientists they had secretly taken on board were standing together, staring at him as he entered. This was his ship but they were in complete control of the secret weapon that he was commanded to carry to the coast of Israel.

"Gentlemen," Captain Mohamedy announced, pausing to look each of the scientists in the eye, "it is time to unleash 'Allah's Revenge' on the unbelievers."

The three men just nodded and walked out into the night without saying a word. A strange trio, the captain reasoned, as he watched them depart. The scientists had very little to say to anyone and kept mostly to themselves in their cabins during the voyage.

By their mannerisms, Captain Mohamedy knew they weren't really Arabs. Probably dark Russians or Serbians, he figured and, obviously, the source of the inhumane weapon they would be releasing on the sleeping Israelis. What troubled him more was why the president-for-life had omitted telling him about the infidel Russian general. He was sure that the general was the one who had supplied both the scientists and "Allah's Revenge."

The president had freely revealed everything about the very secret mission to him except the general's part in it, but why? Had the captain not returned to thank the president when he learned of the offer to watch over his family while he was gone, he never would have heard the general's distinctive raspy voice in the president's office. Something about that oversight triggered a vein of cynicism in him. Something was wrong. He sensed it, but he could not figure out what.

"Come left ninety degrees into the wind," the captain shouted, the change in orders bringing everyone in the pilothouse into action. "All ahead full! Rasul, when we reach full speed, signal the scientists that we are ready."

"Yes, Captain," Rasul answered sharply, an air of excitement painting his voice. Reading the gauges, he watched intently as the old ship labored to approach max speed. "Captain, we're up to fourteen knots," he announced in a voice tainted with consternation ten minutes later.

Captain Mohamedy nodded to his first mate. The new engine upgrades worked as predicted. Rasul raised a cover on the control panel and pressed a button. Somewhere deep in the rocking ship a horn sounded. Next a large metallic balloon floated free from its mooring and ascended rapidly into the night sky. Radar recorded the balloons eastward movement confirming the wind's direction as it had in the last two tests. Computing their course, the navigator entered the minor adjustments in their course, moving their track slightly north to maximize the wind direction.

I can still stop this, the captain reasoned as he stared at the radar screen. *This is my ship. Who are you trying to fool? The die is already cast. The time to stop this has passed.*

"All is ready, Captain."

For the first time in his career he was reluctant to follow orders. He could feel the strong negative vibes, warning him to stop the madness. Every eye was on him in the deathly still pilothouse. He could feel the fear emanating from the men there. They didn't know what was being released, but they knew that it was a weapon again their hated and very dangerous enemy, and that was enough to pucker their asses. He looked around at each of them before giving the order. Their dark eyes struggled to hide their apprehension. Only the first mate knew the depth of the evil they were about to unleash, but word had a way of getting out aboard a ship. If they didn't know precisely what it was, what was plain to everyone present was that their actions opened a new and deadly chapter in their *Jihad.*

"Give the command, First Mate, seal the pilothouse, and blacken the ship."

"Yes, sir."

The first three-horn blast warned anyone foolish enough to be on deck to get below. The second set, five minutes later, sealed the ship by increasing the cabin and ship pressure to prevent the weapon from seeping into the compartments. All lights outside where doused and the pilothouse lights were switched to red. Another five minutes later, a third continuous blast started the release of "Allah's Revenge."

Captain Mohamedy stood at the rear port and watched as a lone low-wattage lamp, aimed at the dispersal tanks, illuminated the red cloud as it was released into the air. He was amazed at how innocent the drifting red smoke looked. It was as if they were marking their spot or signaling someone for help. Somehow, death should not be so quiet, Captain Mohamedy decided as Rasul joined him.

The first officer also stood watching the red cloud depart. He secretly rejoiced but knew he had another job he had to do and that weighed down his enthusiasm. The captain had disobeyed a direct order by telling him everything about the secret mission. Rasul contemplated what to do about it as he watched the release. It pained him, but he would have to report that as instructed. This mission was far too important, the beloved president had carefully explained, to allow anyone to break the code of silence each person involved in this glorious quest had sworn to Allah. Who knew what spies could have infiltrated the ship's company, it was explained to him. Being discovered, each person in the inner circle clearly understood, meant a brutal and thorough response from the Israelis or their puppets in Washington.

Rasul looked out over the back of his captain as the red cloud was pumped from the two olive-gray, rail-car-sized tanks at the stern of the freighter. The mist rose from the tank nozzles into the trailing wind and drifted away from the stern of the ship in swirls of red smoke. *May Allah have mercy on you my friend*, the first officer entreated, as he squeezed his captain's shoulder.

The artificially colored cloud drifted away in the breeze, never rising much higher than the stern of the boat. The two men took note that it was performing exactly as they were told it would. As the last of Allah's Revenge was pumped into the cool night sky, one of the two men watching from the pilothouse rejoiced in the red death that floated off into the black night. The other sensed that once released, the monster could quickly turn on friend and foe alike.

"Allah be praised," Rasul shouted, the joy in his voice unmistakable. "Thank you for granting us this chance to do thy will. The world will soon take note of the truth of your wrath."

The other man only felt a growing weakness in the pit of

his stomach. He never knew death could look so serene. In the billowing red cloud, he imagined he could hear all of the horrible cries of the dying and the louder cries of the living, but soon to be dead. Hell was drifting slowly east on the night winds and nothing short of a divine miracle could stop it now. By morning, it would begin to infect those along the coast.

"If the winds remain true," the older scientist, and probably the only one who could speak Arabic, explained to the captain as they ate dinner in private, "the coastal breezes will have carried the red colored mist until it strikes land along the Israeli coast. The charged particles, unless blasted by very strong winds, will basically remain in a cloud like state until reaching land. But by then, it will have dispersed and become invisible. As the infidels' day begins," the scientist continued, "the unsuspecting masses will inhale it and carry it to schools and to their jobs, contaminating everyone they come in close contact with. Here's the good part," the white-haired man said, grinning and revealing, for all to see, a set of decaying brown teeth. "The agent is slow-acting. By the time they start to get ill, they will have already spread the bacteria to others. The quickly mushrooming circle of disease will expand until the country is reeling from what it thinks is an apparent outbreak of the flu. Brilliant, huh? We call it the Sverdlovsk Anthrax or, to be more specific, a special derivative of that bacterium that now makes it communicable. Then we combined it with an aerosol agent that is slightly heavier than air. The aerosol agent acts like a truck, transporting the bacterium across sea or land. The mixture is released as a cloud, dispersing very slowly. The aerosol agent has a life span of approximately forty-eight hours. After two days, the aerosol breaks down into separate chemical compounds. The brilliance of this combination of compounds is," the gaunt-looking scientist explained, his usually dour features now alive with interest, "that once the aerosol agent begins to dissipate, it will break down the molecular structure of the lethal anthrax, rendering it impotent and traceless. Each infected victim will have reproduced his or her own version of the bacterium and already passed it on to others. Thus, the plague can only be traced back to its initial victims. By then, their contaminator would have dissipated into the prevailing winds."

"What about those leaving the country? Won't they carry the virus with them to other countries?"

"A few might, but that is the gamble. The authorities will realize they are infected and quickly isolate them."

"You don't know that!"

"It is the gamble your leader wanted to take. Should I question him on his judgment?"

"No."

Captain Ahmed turned around slowly in the pilothouse and looked at Rasul. For a brief moment, he thought he saw remorse or concern on the tough bronze countenance of his first officer.

"Activate the automatic flush-cleaning."

"Yes, Captain."

Captain Mohamedy watched as two mechanical arms moved outward from a newly built storage compartment near the holding tanks. Once fully extended, they would begin a programmed cycle of foam spraying of the deck from different angles followed by a seawater rinse. This would be repeated five times as they sailed. Afterward, the tanks would be filled with sea water and then ejected and the decks flushed again.

"Well, Rasul, fate will determine the future now," the captain said, while still trying to read the strange look on Rasul's face as he followed him over toward the pilothouse.

"No, my Captain," Rasul answered. "Allah has already given us a great victory. By the time we return and sail into port, our enemy will be no more. Think of it, my Captain," Rasul continued, while walking confidently around the pilothouse, "we have finally rid the world of the infidels without harming a single blade of grass or blowing up the region. We will be the sword that Allah uses to unite the Arab world."

"How many of the Arab people will die with them until the red fog losses its bite?"

Rasul looked incredulously at his captain. The mention of the red fog, in the presence of the crew, was another treasonable act. His orders were to shoot him on the spot and assume command should he show any semblance of doubt in the mission.

Captain Mohamedy tried to relax but the look he had seen on his first officer's face continued to puzzle him. He turned and looked up at Rasul, now standing at his side. *What's going on in that head of yours, my friend?* he silently questioned. He was sure something was up.

Rasul slowly slid his hand into his right pocket until he felt the smooth hard metal of the gun handle. He hesitated for a moment when he realized the captain was staring at him. Was it gratitude, Rasul later wondered, for the long and rewarding friendship they nurtured that stayed his hand?

My God! Captain Mohanedy realized then smiled warmly up at his friend.

"Yes, my Captain," Rasul answered, judging the captain's sudden smile as reason enough to delay killing his long-time friend. "I know we may lose some brave soldiers in this fight, but victory is assured. How many lives have we already lost in the struggle?"

"Yes, yes, you're right of course, First Mate. Many brave young men and obedient women have given their all." Captain Mohamedy purposefully smiled even harder. He watched as Rasul slowly took his hand out of his pocket. "The price of victory is often high, but we know Paradise awaits those brave men," the captain continued and then leaned around Rasul and shouted an order. "Mohammet!"

"Yes, Captain," the radio operator answered quickly.

"Send this message to our home port: 'Allah be praised. Allah's blessing on his obedient servants. Allahu Akhbar!' Keep repeating it every ten minutes until you hear it repeated back to you twice, understand."

"Yes, Captain."

"Rasul, make sure everything is secured below. When we get farther out to sea, we'll flood the tanks with seawater and then dump them after we clear this area. Keep a close eye on our distinguished passengers," the captain advised, winking at his first officer.

"Yes, sir. I'll see to it that they all sleep like babies," Rasul answered, patting the small lump he felt in his pant pocket.

That confirmed Captain Mohamedy's suspicions that his friend was armed. Since only he, or someone of higher authority, could authorize the carrying of firearms on board a non-capital ship, the captain sadly realized what was going on. He was the captain of the Ondo, but he was not in command. The long arm of the president-for-life had touched him even hundreds of miles away at sea.

Three hours after dumping the chemical tanks, a small lifeboat was carefully and quietly lowered with the automatic winch from the side of the boat. A man slipped down the mooring line onto the lifeboat. The lone man was very fortunate tonight, as he unhooked the mooring lines, for, with the mission now completed, there wasn't anyone outside on watch. Truth was no one wanted to be outside or anywhere near where the tanks were stored.

He rowed away unseen. After what he thought was a safe distance, he pulled in the oars and slid down to the bottom of the small craft. He was more exhausted from the tension of the escape than the effort. He was now completely invisible in the dark water. He felt safe now, at least safe from discovery by anyone onboard ship. The freighter sailed off unaware of its loss.

He sat impassively in the rocking boat while his former life steamed off into the massive black of a sea at night. Smaller and smaller, the ship became until it was just another bright star in the low horizon. The thumping sound of its slightly warped number two-propeller shaft sang out to him, even at that great distance. It had always fascinated him how far sound could travel on a quiet sea.

As the lone passenger in the lifeboat quietly watched the lights from the receding ship as it moved slowly away, he knew he had taken a very serious gamble. His long and distinguished career was now over. Each minute that the ship sailed on, his faith in that gamble weakened. In the dark, he tried looking at his watch but he couldn't see the face. The sun would be rising soon. He figured it was no more than two hours ago, that he rowed away from the ship. Then, suddenly, the horizon blossomed—first white and then in many shades of red.

"Allah's mercy," he whispered as a burst of brilliant colors spread upward from the horizon, illuminating the night sky. It gave him just enough light to take a very fast inventory of the components of the lifeboat. Darkness quickly claimed his vision as it raced over him and sped toward the horizon. The red glow slowly darkened until the night crushed it into oblivion. In less than twenty minutes, the light on the horizon blinked out and he was alone on the dark ocean once again.

"I knew it!" he screamed into the blackness.

His faith in the treachery of the man he had sworn his allegiance to had borne fruit. However, that flash of light had painfully confirmed in his heart that his family was already dead. Former freighter Captain Ahmed Mohamedy pounded his fist on the bottom of the small craft. Every loose end, he had correctly deduced, would have to be tied. "Every possible door closed and locked," he screamed into the night. He was safe. No one could see or hear him now. "You couldn't allow anyone to live who could point the finger of blame, could you? No! That's why we painted and renamed the old freighter to look like a Nigerian ship. Let others take the fall for you if it was found. I abandoned my ship because I had to know," he cried, trying to explain to the souls of his brave men who went down with his ship. "I had to live long enough to see the treachery for myself. I didn't know how you would try to kill me, you coward, but I suspected you would. Rini, I'm so sorry I dragged you in to this!" he shouted up at the star-speckled sky as tears ran down his face.

He screamed at the heavens in anger as his hands reached out for the neck of the man responsible for the death of his wife and family. Guilt shredded his heart. Acknowledging his part in the horrible slaughter yet to come, he slipped slowly down to his knees in prayer.

"Allah, forgive me for what I've done," he prayed as the small craft bobbed about in the dark.

A voice spoke to the pain he felt. Captain Mohamedy knew what he must now do. When he stood up in the dark, the boat suddenly rocked under him. Blindly, he stuck out his arms to try steadying the small craft.

"What am I doing?" he shouted into the dark. Feeling around in the blackness, he found the bench and sat down. "I was going to drown myself, anyway. Does it really matter in the Book-of-Life," he asked, speaking more softly now, "if you fall in, or is it an honorable death only if you jump?"

Wiping away the tears in his eyes, he began to weigh his alternatives. *The Israelis are smart*, he reasoned. *Somehow they will figure out the outbreak was manmade and will be frantic to find out who perpetrated that despicable act.*

He spent the next few hours reviewing his life, from meeting Rini to the birth of their sons. Theirs was an arranged marriage by their parents. At the time, he protested because he was in love with another and avoided touching Rini for months, he now recalled with shame. He was twenty-two and had just graduated college and she was a skinny sixteen year old. He had to obey his parents, but they couldn't tell him where to work, so he joined the merchant marines and spent most of his time out to sea. Only after the woman he loved was given to another did he finally acquiesce and try to become a responsible husband. But by then, he had signed up to be a seaman and was gone for months on end. The faithfulness and kindness of his arranged wife, and her maturing into a beautiful woman, soon won him over and not a day went by afterward that he wasn't thankful for her. But he progressed quickly and was soon made an officer. He remained a seaman as their family grew. But his extended time in port was the source, she once teased him when he lamented having to leave her for weeks at a time, that produced their sons.

He formulated his escape when he realized he was the weak-link in the chain and the president would never allow that. The flash of light on the horizon had proven that. Now, as he sat on the bottom of the rocking boat, staring up at the night sky, he thought about who he was dealing with, and a plan started to form. It would be expected that he died with the others. The finger of blame would probably point east toward Iran or Iraq, not to the deranged lunatic who actually perpetrated this crime. Telling the world what the president had done, the captain reasoned, might free the country from the rule of those madmen.

They weren't true believers in Allah, but killers, vile men who were slowly dragging the country down into hell with them. *Yes*, he decided as he reached for the oars, *Allah will be praised and I will live on a little longer.*

As he rowed east, the picture of his dead sons' tortured faces weighed heavy with every stroke. Their sad eyes questioned why had he sacrificed them and so many other fathers' sons. He could think of nothing to say to appease them.

CHAPTER 3

Six days later:

The HH-60 Desert Hawk helicopter, bristling with the latest in electronic listening gear, skimmed a hundred feet over the dangerous dark waters of the Red Sea. Equipped with TMR—terrain mapping radar—the pilots were confident in avoiding any ships in the area. A sudden large rogue wave was something else. The peaks and valleys that could occur in rough weather could confuse the best terrain following radar into dipping too low to maintain a preset level. Tonight, however, they were blessed with a relatively calm sea.

Piloting this special insertion craft was Captain Benjamin "Benji" Mayer, thirty four, and his copilot and weapons operator, Captain Aaron "Shooter" Kennet, who was thirty two. The newest member of the crew was the navigator and radio operator, Lieutenant Eli Ben-Hon, twenty six. This Desert Hawk—the Israeli adaptation of the US Navy Seahawk helicopter—was redesigned to carry a smaller payload but with an increase in range to over four hundred miles.

In the hold was a cargo of ten battered souls. Seven of those were experienced commandos, accustomed to night flying in helicopters. They sat passively as the craft dipped, climbed, and jerked them around while trying to maintain what they knew were preset height restrictions. Major Yuri Steiner, twenty eight, was in charge of the commandos. The three other passengers were frightened civilians who clung tightly to their safety harnesses as the helicopter tossed them around. It took less than ten minutes into the fight before one of them grabbed for their barf bag.

Mossad Chief Agent Simon Levine, thirty nine, sat in the middle of the three civilians. He was in charge of the mission and held on just as tightly as the other two but with little concern for his own safety. He was wrestling with far greater fears. *If we fail,* Simon mused, as he inadvertently tightened his grip on the straps, *the death of Israel will be on our shoulders.*

Thoughts of the terrible disease attacking his homeland distracted him for a moment, and he was punished for his slothfulness as the copter swerved to the right, tossing him back hard against the bulkhead. *We can't fail,* he admonished the doubt creeping into his thoughts, *we can't.*

Simon leaned back and closed his eyes, but this time he held on tight as more vivid pictures of his dying homeland burst into his troubled consciousness. This dangerous mission was his idea, he reluctantly admitted. He was the one who sold the prime minister on the possibility that—that—We can't fail.

On Simon's left sat fellow Mossad agent Sara Jacobs, twenty six years old. On his immediate right was David Yasuda, twenty nine, considered by Simon to be the most important man in Israeli history since Moses.

Simon opened his eyes and looked over at Sara. "Are you all right?" he asked, leaning over and whispering in her ear.

Her nod was the only response she gave him. *You're a tough one, lady,* he told her silently, smiling. The smile lasted only long enough for him to turn to his right and look into the terror-filled eyes of David Yasuda. *Hang in there buddy,* he mentally encouraged by his squeezing of David's arm. David never opened his clenched lips, but he nodded.

The three civilians were dressed in the plain tan shirts and shorts common to the natives at the landing area. The commandos were wearing brown and green camouflage and were the only ones carrying weapons, but all ten wore Kevlar helmets with voice activated microphones and earplugs. Not a word was spoken, however, since they had flown off the *USS Seattle* on the final leg of their mission.

The position of that ship was one of the many random occurrences, Simon realized as they raced over the Red Sea toward the African coast, which contributed to the undertaking of this desperate mission. The *USS Seattle* had raced south at full speed to reach a position in the Red Sea where it could extend the range of their mission into Ethiopia. The *Seattle* was part of the US Navy fleet in the Red Sea on maneuvers. When the secret mission was hastily thrown together, the US Navy came to their rescue. Once again, the Americans were more than willing to extend a helping hand to Israel. *May the God of my Fathers bless America*, Simon prayed when he learned of their timely intervention.

The last leg of the trip was the hardest to arrange, Simon recalled, as the voices of opposition were quick to remind him of the distances involved in his plan.

"You can't make it that far by helicopter, Mr. Levine," General Assis shouted over the din in the conference room created when Simon revealed his scheme. "Our ports are closed off by the NATO blockade and you know none of the dark nations are going to let you land and refuel in Africa."

"You're right, General," Simon finally agreed as the crowed room quieted and every eye was on him. "That's one of many roadblocks I have to work out. If anyone has another idea, please offer it." No one answered. Simon looked around the room at the mute faces, using the delay to cement his suggestion. "The general is right," he volunteered as he walked over to a large wall map of the countries bordering the Red Sea. That's another problem we'll have to solve, and quickly. From our southernmost city of Elat," he acknowledged loud enough to quiet the rumblings behind him, "to the target area in Ethiopia is over twelve hundred miles, and there are no landing strips in the target area for planes, anyway. We have one ship in the Red Sea that we can use. It was away from port when the plague hit. I believe it's the *Gaza*." He looked at the naval commander he'd talked with earlier and received a nod. "The orders were already sent to move south to a waypoint about three hundred and fifty miles. It will take days for that ship to sail the remaining distance needed to launch after we land on it but, if we have no other options, that's what we are prepared to do. Helicopters are the only quick answer, and time is running out."

"Mr. Levine."

Simon looked from the still-fuming general to the up-until-then-quiet prime minister. "Yes, sir."

"You get the people you will need out to the *Gaza* and we will supply the additional logistic answers. I have a few favors owed to me that I think will make this happen. General, you will arrange whatever air transportation and Special Forces Mr. Levine will need."

"Yes, sir," General Assis answered and nodded yes to Simon.

The two of them remained in the room after the others left with the departed prime minister. Simon was curious, as they waited for the others to leave, which general he would have to deal with. The one who was adverse to his suggestions or the one who quickly acquiesced after the prime minister spoke.

"I have an idea, Simon, that might help," General Assis volunteered, breaking the silence and answering Simon's concerns. "I'll have a Desert Hawk helicopter stripped of everything but essential items and loaded with extra fuel tanks. That should improve your range. If you limit the passengers to a dozen or so, including the crew, I think you could get well over four hundred miles per trip."

"Thanks, General Assis, I was thinking about needing maybe a dozen, but we can cut that number to ten." Now it was Simon's turn to allow the military man to save face. "Do you have anyone in mind to accompany myself and Mr. Yasuda?"

Boy did he, the general thought, as he made a mental list of troublesome officers he would love to stick this hero with. They would eat him alive. But his strong devotion to duty won out.

"There are a few options. All are top-caliber soldiers. We can recruit the best of the army for this mission, but that would

take time. Time we don't have for them to learn to work together. The other option is a seasoned company, small and
deadly. Come to think of it, I know just the group you would
need. But let me warn you now, these men are averse to dealing with civilians. Yes, I know you more than just civilians,"
the general quickly added, confronting the coming rebuttal.
"You are highly trained in the Mossad, but they are a tight unit
trusting only in each other. They are the best of the best and
are accustomed to having a free hand to complete a mission
with any means that they decide are warranted."

Whose side are you on, General? Simon wondered as he
considered the choices. He was right about one thing—time
was the enemy. "Give me the data on the men. I'll decide
which course to take from there. I don't want to make a decision that important on a whim or because it's the easy way
out. And whichever option I choose, I will make any and all
decisions once we reach the destination. They will quickly
learn that."

General Assis was surprised by the boldness and the wisdom of this *civilian's* argument. Yes, he should take time to
weigh both points, but not long. "I will have both options on
your desk within the hour, Mr. Levine."

"Thank you, General."

It was the American Ambassador, Simon later learned, who
offered his help after a call from the prime minister. Orders
were secretly issued to move the US Sixth Fleet northward in
the Red Sea ASAP. From Elat, they flew over three hundred
miles south and landed on the Israeli Intel-gathering ship *Gaza.* On the *Gaza,* they sailed south at full speed. They also met
their pilots who would attempt to sneak them into Ethiopia on
their converted helicopter.

Four hours later, they took off and landed on the carrier
USS Lexington.

Only Jake Mazur, the captain of the great ship, knew the
truth of their mission. He told the crew that the helicopter was
trying to return home when it ran low on fuel and would be
isolated on deck until it was checked to insure everyone's
safety. Every warship in the Sixth Fleet was equipped to de-

fend itself from most chemical and biological weapons.

For over an hour, they were quarantined on the stern of the great ship until rigorous testing proved that they weren't carrying any chemical or biological hazards. The copter, and every piece of equipment and person on board, was checked over and over again as the mighty carrier group turned and raced south into the wind. Up until their departure, the team were isolated on the ship and retested. Every step was taken to prevent the crew from being exposed to any potential hazard. Everyone who was onboard the copter understood the precautions the captain of the huge ship was taking. Only after every test was negative were the ten team members of the mission allowed to move about freely, and only in assigned sections of the massive ship. The crew of the helicopter chose to stay aboard their craft and perform some checks of the systems.

"Mr. Levine," a young naval officer asked as he approached Simon sitting on one of the couches in the galley.

"Yes."

"The captain asked me to inquire if there is anything else your party might need?"

"No, no thank you. This is fine."

"Good, sir. Lunch is on the way, and the captain will join you shortly."

The mess room they were lodged in was large enough for triple their party. The commandos set up camp in one corner of the room and began another weapons check. The rhythmic sound of metal snapping together was almost musical. Simon and Sara were sitting on one of the couches occupying the area closest to the door. David sat alone at one of the tables. The separation actually made all three feel more comfortable.

Within minutes, two stewards entered the mess room and set up lunch along with three urns of hot coffee. Just as quickly, they departed, leaving the seven warriors and the three quiet, pensive civilians to fend for themselves.

"Well let's eat," Simon announced loud enough for everyone in the room to hear as he stood up and surveyed the repast. Without waiting for an answer from his brooding companions, he grabbed a plate and started filling it with "a taste of everything," as he called it. A line quickly formed behind him. Twenty minutes later, they had an important visitor.

"Mr. Levine, I'm Captain Mazur."

Simon stood up and walked toward the well-decorated naval officer. "Simon Levine, Captain," he said, shaking his hand. "Thank you for your help and kind hospitality. Tell the stewards the food was delicious."

"Our pleasure, sir. I hope this is comfortable enough for your party."

"More than enough, sir, thank you."

"What about the lady?" the handsome leader of this lethal war machine asked. "We have a special state room where she might want to freshen up."

Simon was impressed with the way the captain could change oceans so quickly. Simon turned to inquire of Sara, and she rewarded him with her no-thanks shake of her head. "Ah, I think she is happy just resting here, sir. Thank you for asking." From the look in her eyes, he had read her correctly. "This room is fine, sir. If it's all right with you, we'll just stay put. We have everything we need here."

"I just thought the lady might want a little privacy to stretch her legs a little," the captain answered, looking from Simon to Sara who, embarrassed by all the attention, just smiled her thank you.

Simon read her reluctance as his cue. "No thank you, sir. We'll be fine."

"Okay. As far as we can tell, we are on schedule and so is your next connection. I have to go and check on the refueling and with your flight crew about when they will be ready to take off. So relax if you can."

"Thank you, Captain," Simon answered.

They tried relaxing as they waited for the *USS Seattle* to sail closer to the outermost range of their helicopter. The game plan was to take off about midnight and land on the *Seattle's* deck about three a.m. The last refueling on the *Seattle* would take them within range of their destination in Ethiopia and allow their ride to return and land on the *Seattle*. Again, they would be quarantined when they arrived there until the ship's doctors were convinced they were not carrying anything harmful aboard.

When the captain returned this time Sara accepted the private room at Simon's insistence. At first, she feigned annoyance but then quickly acquiesced. *I have to be careful*, Simon reminded himself as he watched her depart, to keep Sara and David apart while making it look unintentional. He knew David's concentration might be critical to the success of this mission. It was his plea to the high priest of the Falashian sect in the city of Haifa that had gotten them the best guess as to where to search. In no way did he want another argument between the David and Sara interfering with this critical expedition. Any delay could cost the lives of thousands of Israelis.

Simon used his empty coffee cup as an excuse to walk over to where David was sitting. "Do you want a refill, David? This is great coffee, isn't it?"

"No and yes," David answered, taking the last sip from his cup, his words frozen behind a What-am-I-doing-here look on his face. *He's obviously still pissed*, Simon acknowledged. Apparently, the shock from Sara's confession wasn't a pill easily swallowed.

Sara is not handling this professionally either, Simon admitted as he filled his cup with the hot brew. He was convinced, although she would never admit it, that she had fallen in love with David. A picture formed in the calculating mind of the veteran agent. Simon made a mental note to remove Sara from all covert operations after this mission. She needed time off to deal with her feelings. Simon knew from experience that not being honest with your emotions was a springboard to disaster for an agent. One never knew when those hidden feeling would surface and cause an agent to momentarily question their orders or decisions. History had taught that usually occurred at the most inopportune and deadliest times.

Under the glare of floodlights, they boarded their copter and lifted off the deck of the *USS Lexington* at three minutes before midnight, climbed to about five hundred feet, and then headed west. As planned, they continued for ten minutes, then dropped below radar coverage, and continued west. The plan called for them to give the impression they were changing directions under the radar blanket. Three hours later, they were circling in the dark looking for the *USS Seattle*.

"Okay, we're here, where are they?" navigator Lieutenant Ben-Hon announced.

Both pilots noted, without comment, the nervousness in his voice. The veteran pilots knew Ben-Hon was one of the best navigators in the service. That was why he was aboard.

"Do another slow spin, Benji," the copilot suggested. "They're out there somewhere. We can't use our radar or radio unless absolutely necessary."

Benji put the helicopter in a slow 360. Nothing. They could be a few miles off and never spot them in this moonless night, he realized. "Shooter," Benji suggested, looking from his near-empty fuel gauge, "I think it might be time to illuminate the area."

As if on cue, a spotlight blinked on and off twice in the darkness.

"There! Over to your right at your four o'clock," Shooter blurted out.

"I see it, buddy. All right," the ecstatic pilot shouted. "Signal the ship."

They had reached the designated waypoint five gut-wrenching minutes before spotting the signal from the ship. Illuminated by a single beacon on her deck, the *USS Seattle* appeared out of the ink-black night. After hurriedly exchanging code names, they flew toward the ship and touched down on fumes.

At 3:08 a.m., they landed on the rear deck of the ship as it turned into the wind—an extra precaution necessary should there be any contamination. With the *Seattle* moving at full speed, the wind would help wash any residual airborne contaminates overboard. Their helo was washed in foam and disinfectant twice. Regardless of their passing inspection on their last stop, it would be another hour, they were informed, if they passed inspection, before they would be allowed to disembark. Mercifully, it only took half that long.

The lavishly prepared meal for the *Seattle's* important visitors did little to erase the tensions of the long flight. While openly courteous to each other, Simon noticed the rift between Sara and David widen. The silence between them shouted in its awkwardness. It was as if they could converse telepathically or trade angry epithets with a motion of their head or an odd movement of their bodies—painfully quiet words unspoken that were sensed by everyone around them.

Simon walked out into the crisp night air and stood alone on the windy forward deck of the *Seattle*, reviewing in his mind every detail of the mission. He heard footsteps approaching, but didn't turn around.

"Having some second thoughts?" a rather impressive deep voice inquired.

"Not really," Simon answered the leader of the commandos. "What other choices do we have?"

A head nod was the only answer he received, and the visitor joined him as he stared out into the darkness. Both had to hold on as the mighty ship plowed full speed toward their rendezvous, the sea breeze blowing over them like a cleansing agent.

Simon turned and studied the features of the career soldier—from the rock hard cut of his face to the square shoulders and rippling arm muscles protruding from his tight shirt. *This is a dangerous man,* Simon concluded.

"Why bring the girl?"

Again, Simon studied the man. "The agent? She's my ace-in-the-hole."

"That's what I figured," the veteran of many battles said. He was quiet for a minute then abruptly walked away.

"Wait a minute, Major Steiner." Simon moved toward him. "In the Mossad, when planning a mission, you learn to cover every angle. Better to have and not need than to need and not have, right? I'm sure the army does the same."

The commando leader gave the impression he wanted to say something before holding his thoughts, turning, and walking away.

'*Trust only in the facts.*' The words of old Dr. Abrams, one of Simon's instructors during his first year in the Mossad, echoed in his head as he watched the commando leave. He recalled the snicker that would appear on the man's wrinkled face as he added, *'As you see them.'*

Simon had used that reasoning in picking the commandos. Over a hundred bio folders were lying on his desk when he arrived at his office later that same afternoon after speaking with the general. Time again was the highlighter that colored his decision. These were the elite of the Israeli Army not infected. Given time this group would exceed his expectations, but he didn't have time. He chose the squad that General Assis had first suggested and read their bios.

They were led by Major Yuri Steiner, thirty-five, a fifteen-year veteran soldier who never married. He was a career soldier with only his college professor brother and his father still alive. His mother died six years earlier. From the many pages in his bio, Simon realized Major Steiner had been involved in numerous operations. Unfortunately, most were blacked out as top secret. From what Simon could gather from the information available there were quite a few insertions into enemy territory. It was just not clear from all of the blacked out sections of the report where that was.

Major Steiner received the highest marks possible for his leadership, courage, intelligence, marksmanship, and the handling of his men. He was a soldier's soldier, one personal evaluation from one of his commanding officer claimed. *But who are you really?* Simon wondered as he looked at a photo of the seasoned veteran. His blond head was shaved almost bald. He had clear blue eyes. Almost feminine in their clarity, though no man would be foolish enough to say that to him. Those same eyes seemed to look through you, Simon thought as he studied the portrait. Steiner had a hard face with muscles that spent little time smiling or laughing. He correctly came across as a very dangerous man.

From what Simon could piece together, they were down to a seven-man squad, having lost three in the last mission they were on two months ago. That would give them one shy of the ten the general recommended and Simon figured that he could take with him.

What made Simon an astute planner and organizer was his sixth sense that told him when he might have miscalculated or erred in his judgments. Sensing that, he would meticulously go over every aspect of a plan until that feeling subsided. His due diligence had favored him with success and repeatedly established his reputation among friend and foes alike.

The violent man staring back at him from the photo garnered some concern. Simon's plan was not to go to war in Ethiopia. The soldier with the cold blue eyes reflected another opinion.

"I don't have the resources or the time to be as practical with this mission as I would like," Simon said to those familiar feelings. "I don't expect to need a man with his skills, but what if I do? I would rather be looking at his back than his front." Simon slipped seven folders under his arm and headed for the door.

CHAPTER 4

At 3:55 a.m., they gathered in the *Seattle's* conference room for the final meeting before take-off. The *Seattle's* skipper, Captain Ed Taylor, was an amiable host as they sailed to their final embarkation point. With humorous stories about his children, he was very adept at relieving the obvious tension everyone was feeling. So much so, Sara kissed him goodbye when they boarded the helicopter, much to the dismay of an I'm-not-really-watching-you David.

By 4:30 a.m., they were lifting off the *USS Seattle* and skimming across the Red Sea toward the African coast. The *Seattle* would patrol near the coast, retrieve the returning helicopter, and remain on patrol for the next few days in international waters. She would defend herself against any aggressor while she waited on their successful return.

Simon noticed the veteran soldiers seated across from him in the helicopter were getting a little last-minute shut-eye as they raced toward the coast. Their confidence was infectious. Major Yuri Steiner and his commandos had spent the majority their time aboard the *USS Seattle* going over maps of the landing area before cleaning and rechecking their weapons. Now that they were under way again, they knew it was time to get all the rest they could before landing.

They don't seem worried about bouncing off of a wave and crashing, Simon noticed, as the majority of the soldiers sat with their eyes closed—save for one he noticed, a commando with the name tag Dog on his shirt. Each commando wore a squad nickname on their shirts, Simon assumed, as their only identification should they be killed or captured on a covert mission.

Dog felt a little empathy for the three civilians being tossed around across from him. He had won the bet in under the required ten minutes. The female did barf in under ten and lasted longer than Hawk had predicted at eight minutes and someone at fifteen, but he couldn't remember who that was. Snake, he recalled with a snicker, had bet the frightened-looking Black man would be first. He lost that bet.

There were some questions among the commandos about the Black man accompanying them. During their briefing, he was touted as the most important source for finding this miracle drug they needed to combat the plague killing their countrymen. Word quickly spread that he was one of the Black Jews rescued from Ethiopia, so his being there wasn't a big surprise when they learned where they were headed. The others quickly accepted him as Jewish, but Dog wasn't so sure about those people. The Ethiopian kept quiet and to himself, so if his coming along could help...

Dog, known as Ravid Rossman, was tired but he knew sleep would evade him. He was going to die on this mission and didn't want to waste another second of the life he had remaining by sleeping. With the same calm attitude he embarked on other missions, where their lives were at best a fifty-fifty gamble, he accepted what he believed fate had ordained. Dog had come to rely on that knowledge and, on more than a few occasions, guided himself and his buddies out of nearly impossible situations when all but him thought their number was up. Their number was up today, he sadly realized, for him and some of his squad.

When he got the call to join the others on this mission, he saw nothing that would indicate they were in any danger. Up until they boarded the copter—nothing. He looked in the mirror while in their barracks and only saw the reflection of a man tired from battles, a very nervous and concerned reflection.

Riding in the back of the truck transporting his squad to their embarkation site, he sensed the negative energies and, regardless of what he saw or didn't see on their faces, he knew for some of them their time was up. Once they were airborne, the confirmation came. It happened inadvertently when he saw his reflection on his canteen on the first leg of their trip. Later, while they were rechecking their equipment, he saw it on the faces of other commandos. Better to know late than not at all, he said to those who pulled the strings of fate. He had made peace with his Maker and prayed his death would have meaning for the Motherland. Then he settled back and relaxed. He was doing what he had been trained to do and do well. Dog took a deep breath, exhaled, and watched as the three civilians struggled with the bumpy ride.

Even observing the lovely woman barfing was something he enjoyed. She was very pretty and her shorts revealed she had nice legs. They had all agreed on that after they were first introduced to her and told of this desperate operation. Not the skinny legs of a fashion model but strong, muscular limbs of a woman obviously able to carry her own share of the load. These powerful men admired that in anyone.

She was feminine, he acknowledged, not like some women in the military who acted tough and manly. Just from the way she sat and crossed her legs, he could tell there was no "butch" in this woman. Just one look into her eyes and it was very obvious that one shouldn't mistake her femininity as a weakness. As with all citizens over eighteen she was conscripted to serve in the military for her two year term. It was almost three years for men. Although only fifty percent actually served. Others were rejected for various reasons, from poor health to religious exemptions. This was a well-trained former soldier and now a Mossad agent—with great legs. Dog grinned at that thought.

She sat across from him with her eyes closed. He could tell that she, like anyone unfamiliar with riding in helicopters, was struggling with nausea. So he was able to get a good look at her without being caught and maybe pissing her off. She would have slapped him—he snickered—if she knew he was imagining her sitting there naked. But she was probably the last woman, from his homeland anyway, he would get this close to, and he wanted to take that vision with him to wherever he was headed in the after-life, so he took full advantage of that freedom.

The clock was ticking and he was determined to enjoy each of the last few minutes life granted him.

Sara was her name, he recalled. Sara. He liked that name because he'd once dated a Sara for about six months until his constant unavailability for secret missions ended that. But he had very pleasant memories of that Sara. He looked at the Sara seated across from him, from her pretty head to her toes again, wondering if she was a tiger in bed like her namesake.

Knowing she was a highly trained Mossad agent, he wasn't about to ask. She wasn't as well trained in this particular mission as a commando, he boasted, but, as a Mossad agent, she was well schooled in weapons, hand-to-hand combat, and how to defend herself and kill if necessary. They all understood and respected anyone enduring the a two- to three-year difficult training course for a "Katsa," a field intelligence officer, at the Mossad Academy near the town of Herzliya.

Satisfied he had voyeuristically enjoyed every inch of the sweet flower weaving back and forth across from him, Dog stared down at the floor and the memories returned...

"Are you sure?" Michael Tomer, known as Whale, had asked when they were alone in the men's room after landing on the aircraft carrier. "Are you sure you saw me?"

Dog ignored the question. It didn't need an answer. Whale already knew the answer. Dog's psychic gift had been proven unfailing, even to him. They were going to die on this mission.

"Then I'm going to tell Yuri I've changed my mind. I'm not going any farther."

Dog ignored his friend and continued washing his hands.

That was until two angry hands grabbed him from behind and slammed him against the wall.

"Why do I have to die?" Whale screamed at his roommate. "I'm only twenty-four years old. I haven't lived yet."

When Dog failed to resist, even as his shirt was pulled up to his face, Whale let him go and stormed out of the restroom. *Don't blame Whale*, Dog scolded himself. Like he'd told him in the beginning, he didn't create it and couldn't change what he saw. Whale was angry about his short future, but who wouldn't be? Who really wanted to know when their time was up? But Whale no longer needed convincing. The last three dangerous missions had provided all the proof that Dog's words carried weight. Everyone Dog had told him he had seen dying had died, either on one of their missions into foreign territory or just catching the wrong bus. He didn't personally see every man who died when they were out on a mission, but those he did see died, and that was a certainty.

Now that it's my turn, who do I tell?" Dog debated. "Hey, Mom, Dad, it's your son—oh, and another thing, I'm about to die." Yeah, right. That would go over well with them. Dog looked up at the ceiling and sighed. "Why didn't I see this before we left? Then I could have said goodbye to them at least." He knew the answer to that question before he asked.

The picture of his little sister Becca came to mind. He had always been her hero, at least that was what she told him on his last leave home. The way she looked up to him had kept him out of trouble growing up. There was no way he would do anything to disappoint her.

His parents were good people, he admitted, but Becca—she was special. Dog felt a pain in his chest at the thought of never seeing his eighteen-year-old sister again. She had developed into a very pretty young woman. Opinionated, strong, intelligent, and in too big a hurry to follow in his footsteps and become a soldier. She would be a match for any young boy wooing her. He felt a half smile break out on his face at the picture of a nervous young man, trying to capture her attention. "I love you, Becca."

It was moments like this when he really felt alone. When

he was growing up, his parents were so busy with their careers in medicine that they had little time for their son. They loved him, he knew that, but showing emotions wasn't their strong suit and it was something he craved. The surprised birth of Becca fulfilled that need. She became his best friend and followed him around like a little puppy. He loved it. He would miss his parents but Becca...

Dog went in search of his friend. "Whale, don't forget I also saw myself dying," he later told the man, sulking and drinking a coffee alone in the corner of the large ship's galley. Dog decided not to mention who else he saw.

Whale just looked at his friend.

"I was thinking," Dog continued, "maybe we should say goodbye to our love ones while we can."

Whale looked confused. "How?"

"See that writing desk over in the corner."

"Then what, Dog, drop a letter in the mail? This is a secret mission. We aren't allowed to communicate with anyone. You know what? I'm not sure that is a good idea. It might seem like a letter from the grave to them when they learn about our deaths."

"Or a chance to hear we love them one more time."

"Say, you're right, how do we mail them?"

"I was thinking of giving them to her," he said and nodded toward their female passenger who had returned to the galley.

"Her, are you kidding, Dog?"

"Why not her? As a civilian they won't shoot her if she's captured."

"If she's captured, that would be the only thing they wouldn't do with her."

"Try thinking with your other head. Maybe we could give them to someone on this ship. They would eventually reach our loved ones."

"I don't know, Dog. If Birdman found out, he might shoot both of us."

Dog thought about it and realized Whale was probably right. Maybe letting his family remember him from the last time they were together was best. They did have a wonderful time together, a wonderful time. "You know, Whale, I've questioned all this many times, and I don't have any answers. But if it takes my life to save Israel on this mission, then so be it. But, my friend, remember this. When death calls, it doesn't matter where you are or what you're doing. I would rather be fighting to save Israel when it happens than a victim of some cowardly terrorist bomb or a stupid car accident."

Dog and Whale exchanged looks. The truth of those words didn't need defending or contradicting.

"Well, I can think of one other activity," Dog said, smiling and patting his friend on the shoulder. "I would rather death find me completing when my number is called."

Whale had been thinking the same thing ever since Dog told him his time was now measured in hours or days. He looked into the eyes of his friend, thinking about a certain young woman.

Whale watched as Dog walked over and started talking with some of the guys playing cards. He took a sip of his coffee and sat down on one of the couches. Watching Dog elicited the memory of the first time Whale learned about the man's visions. They were on a covert mission into Lebanon, observing an Arab town for night activity of some reported terrorists. The two of them were stationed on a ridge to the right of the main road leading out of town.

The night was warm, but after sweating from carrying all the gear they would need up to this lookout point, it was very tolerable. There was a cool breeze later after the sun set that made their location even more pleasant. Moving quickly, but without revealing their presence, they set up their listening and night vision equipment after making sure their area was secure.

"Hey, buddy, what's wrong?" Whale asked, after taking a refreshing drink from his canteen. Dog had seemed distracted to him during the climb and setup.

Dog took a deep breath while deciding how much he should share. "Remember when we were ambushed and I was seriously wounded that rainy night on patrol about six months ago just inside the Lebanese border?"

Sensing his partner's nervousness Whale leaned over and did another scan on the road below them with his infrared scope. The road was empty. He sat back, thought for a minute, and then nodded. He did remember Dog getting wounded in that crazy fire fight but Whale was too busy trying to shoot back as others rescued the casualties.

"Well, when they rushed me into surgery I was in bad shape. I knew I was dying," Dog explained. "They said my heart stopped three times on the operating table and each time was harder to restart. The last time they all thought I was finished because it took so long to bring me back. When I woke up, I was too weak even to talk. I learned from the nurses that I was unconscious for two weeks, and it was touch and go if I would ever wake up.

"While I was laying there unable to speak, I noticed something very strange. The faces of a few of the nurses on my floor turned dark one day. Well, it was more like they were gray. Then I didn't see them anymore. A week later when I was strong enough to talk, I asked two of the nurses in my room what happened to the three nurses who used to bathe or feed me. I thought they were either on vacation or on another floor—"

"Or just got tired of cleaning your smelly ass."

"Or just got tired of cleaning my smelly ass. Anyway, one nurse started crying. The other told me they had died when an Arab terrorist blew them and himself up in a restaurant where they were eating lunch."

"Damn!"

"Yeah, I also saw four or five other patients faces turn gray in the hospital while I was recovering from my wounds. Most of them were in their rooms, struggling to live, as I walked past. The next day or so their beds would be empty. I didn't have to ask. Once I was released, I saw others on the streets as I walked by. I had this weird idea. I stopped them and asked them their names as if I once knew them or one of their neighbors. Then for the next few days, I would read the obituaries. I was able to find each of their names printed usually within three days."

"Are you sure about all this, Dog? Maybe this is just a co-incidence and you're just guessing right when people are going to die."

"No, Whale. Believe me, I wish it was. I have seen a dozen people with that look on their face so far and each of them died within the three days." Dog shook his head. "I think something happened to me when I died one of those three times on that operating table. Something came back with me that wasn't meant to, maybe, but now that I see these things, what am I supposed to do with it? Do I tell strangers that I see they're going to die?"

"No! They will put you in the loony bin for sure," Whale emphatically replied. A little nervous about what Dog had revealed, Whale picked up his thermal glasses and scanned the town they were scouting. "I know you might think otherwise," he said while scanning, "but it could just be a very weird coincidence."

A vehicle driving out of town halted their conversation as they radioed its direction.

"I'm not sure I would want to know if I was going to die," Whale told him after thinking about his story. "And I would be careful telling anyone else about this."

"You are the only one I trust not to think I'm crazy."

"Oh I thought you were crazy when we first met. Remember that chick in that bar that you tried hitting on after she saw me. Now that was crazy."

"Thanks."

"You know what? Maybe I would want to know. Yes," Whale answered at the surprised look on his friend's face. "I would need that time to ask Jehovah God to forgive me for all the ladies hearts I've broken."

Dog ignored his laughing buddy. "Are you sure?"

Like the first drops of rain on a hot desert road, the humor quickly evaporated and Whale realized the seriousness of the moment. "If you see that ah look on me, tell me okay."

"Okay."

From that day on, it was their secret.

Whale became a reluctant believer after the third person

Dog fingered to him died within those three days. There was a two-week lull between Dog seeing the second and third victim. This raised false hopes that he was out from under "the curse," as he called it. When he drove past a school and looked at the kids running around and playing, his spirits were lifted by their innocence. That floating balloon was punctured when one little boy's face turned gray. Reluctantly, Dog asked him his name.

The next weekend Dog stood over the small grave, asking the departed child for forgiveness. Could that have been the one time he should have told someone? he questioned.

It took a week of mourning in his room before he was able to resume his military career.

Dog walked over to join his friend when he noticed him sitting alone on the couch.

"Look, Dog," Whale said after they were alone, "I'm ready to give my life for my country if I have to. Hell, I think we all decided that when we joined this hard luck outfit. With so many dying at home, at least I'm trying to do some good with my life. I just wish I would have done more before—you know what I mean. You remember me telling you about this one girl named Alia?"

"The one you said with the large—"

"Yes," Whale said, cutting him off and grinning at him. "We were just getting so close, I was going to ask her to be my girl."

"Wow, that is so cool buddy."

"I know. We weren't intimate yet because—" Michael stopped talking when the female of the three civilians they were transporting walked past them.

They watched her until she was out of the room. Dog shook his head and Whale grinned and nodded in agreement.

"Looking at her ass, now I know it was a mistake, but I figured we should wait until I returned from this mission, you know, so there wouldn't be any surprises, and I wouldn't leave her with that burden if I didn't make it back. Now I'm thinking maybe it would have been better for her if I did.

"No, Whale, it's never better to put a woman through that

with the child's father dead. This way, after mourning your death, she can start over again."

"Yeah, I guess you're right," Whale said after taking a deep breath and blowing it out. "Forget what I said. I'm ready to continue this crazy mission and give my life if I have to and save my Alia and our country."

Dog stood up and shouted out loud. "Anyone getting in the way of this group of killers had better beware."

Whale jumped up and they slapped hands. Then they joined their comrades when they noticed they were getting in line for another round of the delicious grub.

CHAPTER 5

A sudden movement, as the helicopter changed directions to confuse anyone trying to calculate their destination, threw Sara against Simon. He looked over at her in the semi-dark red glow of the combat-lights. He took note that her eyes were closed. She was either sleeping or pretending to be asleep. *This girl*, he decided, *is as cold as ice.* It was that virtue, he recalled, that had singled her out from the other female applicants who applied to work for the Mossad's Department of Internal Security. But he had to admit he was pleasantly surprised how quickly she fit in.

The growing pain in his head caused Simon to close his eyes for a moment. He knew the cause of the pain and accepted it. With the tension he had faced the last few days, a headache was the least of his obstacles. Pictures of the suffering and dying children in Israel were never far from his thoughts. Tens of thousands had died, and many thousands more were dying. The "plague," as he called it, was killing the fruit of Israel. This desperate mission was the only hope to save Zion.

The helicopter dipped again, drawing a small gasp from the woman next to him, but this time Simon never opened his eyes. The concern he felt for his country overcame any fear for their lives. Like most Israelis, the love of country was a powerful passion for him. Its survival was embedded deeply in his soul. He lived daily with the knowledge Israel was surrounded by her enemies who openly swore to kill all Israelis.

My God, Simon thought, who would do such a thing? Who

would sacrifice killing millions in the name of revenge, in the name of a god? He remembered the chilling words of the biological experts who blamed the outbreak on a terrorist plot. The plague, they discovered, had a biological make up strikingly similar to anthrax. But anthrax couldn't be spread by personal contact. It was either ingested in powder form or from eating food contaminated with the bacterium. For that reason it would be impossible, they argued, for it to spread so fast naturally.

The Mossad claimed it was probably a variant of anthrax created in the old Soviet Union labs, like the one located in the top-secret military town of Sverdlovsk. It was a poorly kept secret that the army base outside of town was a chemical and biological germ warfare testing facility. In 1979, spores of a germ they were experimenting with escaped their poorly ventilated buildings and was blown by the wind up to thirty miles away, infecting people and livestock. With the breakup of the Soviet Union, any number of high-ranking personnel could have access to the weapons and would gladly sell them on the black market for profit.

The general belief was that the biological agent was released near the coast and spread by the prevailing winds. There were reported outbreaks on ships that passed near their coast, giving weight to the theory that it was released near their shores. A change in the direction of that wind, the biological scientist reported, could have reaped terrible devastation on the heavily populated borders of Lebanon to the north or Egypt to the south. Simon twisted in his seat as the startling memories of the last few horrible days awakened painful emotions.

"Saul," he whispered under the constant whoop-whoop sound of the helicopter blades. He had frantically tried to call his brother when he received word of the outbreak of a strange sickness in the towns along the coast. Saul was married and had four of the sweetest kids Simon had ever known. They were special to him since he knew he could never have any of his own.

It was an unexpected medical discovery that had ended his

only attempt at getting married. Ava was right, he had decided over an empty bottle of Scotch. He was only half a man. When she left him, he vowed to marry his beloved country. He was never unfaithful to her. Even when he finally got through to Saul.

"Simon what is going on? There are emergency vehicles everywhere. The schools are closed and the hospitals overcrowded with the sick."

"I know, Saul, that's why I called. How is the family?" Silence. "Saul?"

"My youngest Breana is very ill, Simon. Thankfully a doctor is our neighbor or I don't know what I would do with the situation at the hospitals."

"The government is trying to get a vaccine for this plague, Saul."

"We hear that on the news. I would, people here would, just like some honest answers and not government bull. People are dying here."

"All I can say is we believe something is very suspicious about this outbreak. Brother, you call me if there is anything I can do for you or little Breana."

"I will."

"Bye, Saul."

Simon was heartbroken after hearing about Breana but he never left his post.

Even as he was giving his apologies for not being able to help his brother, Simon started thinking about who among his Arab contacts might have some information on the plague. Every door, he found out to his surprise, was closed on this one. Even the torture of some known terrorists had failed to break the ring of silence. As the deaths multiplied across the country, word was passed down through the Mossad that Prime Minister Eliab Shamir was considering retaliatory nuclear strikes.

There was little doubt that it was an enemy of Israel, but which one had orchestrated the outbreak? No one could find a clue as to who had perpetrated this atrocity. Yet the people, in their pain and loss, cried out for revenge. But neither they nor the heads of the government could decide on whose back it should be placed.

An American spy satellite did spot an unexplained explosion about a hundred miles off the coast of Israel, he had later learned. If it was a ship, it had sunk to the bottom of the Mediterranean Sea. Simon tried picturing the sunken ship, as if it might offer some sign of the nationality of the damnable vessel.

Is this the proverbial "End of the World" you read about in those cheap magazines? he wondered. Simon lowered his head and silently prayed that this was just another mountain they had to climb as a country. Then he remembered sitting in front of his TV, watching some boring program, when the news first broke. Several days later, the severity of the outbreak became clear.

"...ladies and gentleman," the news anchor said reading from the TelePrompTer, "the latest reports from the Ministry of Health are very frightening." The trembling voice of the reporter added fear to her every word. Gone was any premise of hope. She wasn't that good an actress. It was obvious that she was scared from the nervous way she continually looked at her notes. Also gone was the phony smile one got from reporters when the red light came on. Her heavy makeup couldn't hide the strain in her eyes and voice.

"It's been estimated that over thirty thousand have died across Israel in the last few days and numerous other hundreds of thousands either have the plague or have shown some symptoms of getting it. The Nation of Israel is under quarantine from the rest of the world. All of our borders are closed and guarded by soldiers from both sides. We have reports that our ships in any of the harbors in the world during the last week were forced to either return to Israel or be sunk. Two freighters were reportedly fired upon and sunk by the Italian navy after refusing to turn around and return to Israel. No one is being allowed to leave or enter the country. There are unconfirmed reports of shootings along both sides of the border with Jordan. All airports are closed and all ships are frozen in port. The American government has supplied special planes that are completely insulated against biological agents to fly in and unload medical supplies at the isolated end of the select runways.

"From unconfirmed reports, we learned that one of the first outbreaks was in the city of Nahariya along the northern coast. By noon, that city's hospitals were besieged with sick people. Schools reported over a third of the children were running fevers high enough to warrant notification of their parents or transportation to the nearest hospital.

"The Health Departments were either slow to respond to the emergency or just overwhelmed by the vastness of the outbreak. Then, like a swift storm, the epidemic raced inland. By the afternoon of the second day, there were reports coming in from the cities of Acre, Haifa, Shar Am, and Hadera. The authorities were convinced it was spreading inland without any sign of weakening. The cities of Tel Aviv, Bat Yam, and Holon were evacuated to the south but all reported major outbreaks of the sickness later that night.

"Like I've said, thousands are dead and dying across the country. Prime Minister Shamir, only a few hours ago at his news conference, stated that our scientists believe the plague is a variation of the lethal bacterium anthrax. Scientist are working feverishly—" She stopped and looked up from her notes, as if she had insulted someone with her choice of adjectives. She then continued. "—working hard to come up with a serum to halt the spread of the rampaging plague. There is speculation that—"

Suddenly the camera panned left to her co-anchor Elijah Humes.

"Excuse me Kayla, ladies, and gentlemen," he cut in, "we're going to patch in directly to one of our reporters, and I believe it is Joshua Ben Yorn standing outside a hospital in Haifa. We aren't permitted to say which hospital for security reasons, and we will honor that in this crisis."

Simon remembered watching his television in shock as this bizarre story took on flesh. The camera was now panning the grounds surrounding what he believed was the Rambam Medical Center. It was a disaster. People were running about in terror, seeking or administering what help they could. Panic was the wind that blew across the grass. It carried aloft the pungent smell of fear, death, and outrage. Desperate people in desperate situations were trying to find help wherever they could. The camera captured the gut-wrenching scene of hundreds of the sick and dying moaning in a chorus of agonies on the lawn in front of the overwhelmed hospital. The beleaguered medical staff was struggling to give aid as they ran from the dying to the very sick. The camera captured frantic parents, begging any and every one to help their sick children, while wandering from doctor to nurse. Fights broke out as beleaguered parents vied for the attention of the exhausted medical staff. Simon felt a knot in his throat as he watched their hopelessness.

This insidious malady attacked the children most frequently. It was reported that six out of ten infected were young children.

"As you can see from these pictures," an exhausted Joshua Ben Yorn said, looking wide-eyed and frantic into the camera, "the hospital is—is swamped with—with victims."

Simon felt the reporter's anguish as he turned and looked again at the horror occurring behind him. Suddenly, he jerked around and stared blankly at the camera. For an interminable moment, he just stood there, his dark eyes clearly seeing something—something beyond the camera lens. Then he must have realized he was still on the air because he ran his fingers through his hair and tried to gather himself. He looked down and wiped his mouth.

"Ah—ah the Ministry of Health—" The reporter, distracted again and again by the screams and wild chaos and confusion going on around him, struggled to read from his notes. "—is asking that you take the sick directly to the—to the—to the nearest school in your area for treatment. Don't come to the hospitals! I repeat, don't come to the hospitals. They're jammed with more patients than—than they can help. I repeat again, the authorities are pleading that you don't bring any more of the sick to the hospitals. Medical clinics are being setup in all the area schools to—"

Again a terrible scream from somewhere behind him stole his thoughts. He drifted off into a void, his face an emotionless mask, as if warding off the pandemonium unfolding around him. He turned to watch something that caught his attention. A moment later, he looked back into the camera, his face reflecting some terrible tragedy just beyond the camera lens.

"I hope everyone can see the massive magnitude of the problem," a voice from the studio said, trying to assist the shaken reporter. It appeared to work, as the reporter continued. "The seed—of—Israel is dying in the grass in front of me." His voice broke under the strain. "We could be witnessing the end of the nation of—of Israel. In less than two weeks, one of our scientists confided to me, at the rate it is spreading every Israeli could become infected. For that matter, this could be the beginning of the end for all of mankind if this accursed plague spreads across our borders."

Hearing the anguish in his last words, Simon was positive the reporter had also contracted the disease.

Again, the cameraman panned behind the distraught reporter at the crying, screaming, frightened mass of panic-driven humanity. There was no beginning or end to the confusion. People just stopped whoever was passing by and begged for help, many seeking assistance from others worse off than they were. The madness, having no center or reason, flowed from pleading, heartbroken parent to lost and suddenly orphaned crying children. The gift of the cameraman capturing it was in his desire to be true to the chaos.

As Simon struggled to watch, his spirit reeling from the utter pandemonium, the camera focused in on a pleasant-looking dark-haired woman about thirty, sitting on the ground, oblivious to the stampede around her. People raced past her, some kicking or bumping her as they sought their own deliverance. She just recoiled from the blows but did nothing to ward them off or protect herself, her dark eyes looking past the carnage at something only she could see. Her surrender made Simon gasp, as if her capitulation was the last straw for a camel that had long ago perished from a broken back.

The woman's head dropped down, signaling her surrender

to the forces of terror. Something in the slumped shoulders of the woman told Simon there was more to this scene than he wanted to know.

What's that in her—noooo! Simon tried to look away, but it was too late.

The camera panned down to reveal a small child in the slumped woman's lap. A motionless little girl lay quiet between her mother's pale arms. Her tiny face was looking up directly at the camera. In death, as in life, she was performing, as darling little princesses were apt to do. She wore a pretty flowered yellow dress that conflicted with the deathly paleness of her skin. Her black hair was matted to her head from the heat of the rampant fever that had ravaged her tiny body. The child was dead, yet her soft blue eyes reached through the TV screen to touch Simon's heart. A dark stain ran from the corner of her mouth down her chin. Simon tried to look away as the camera zoomed in closer on the young child. Her unspoken questions tormented him as he fixed his eyes on hers. Her soul looked up at him from wherever beautiful little girls go when they died and asked, "Why?"

Simon felt his tears swelling as he realized how much she looked like the little girl he had always pictured himself having.

Her fate was the same as the thousands who had already run the gambit from a very high fever and chills the first day, to nausea, vomiting, and severe diarrhea by the second. It was as though the body was trying to empty itself of all its fluids. Finally, by the third or fourth day, the deadly toxins released from the anthrax bacterium suffocated its victims as their lungs filled with fluid.

Simon had watched the many deaths of his countrymen with the same anger and hatred now shared by everyone in Israel. The pictures of the dead and dying were seared into his memory, even as their desperate mission winged its way through the pitch-black night over the Red Sea. That dead baby's blank, pale face would be the inspiration he would use to find the source of David Yasuda's "Messiah Drug." At least that was what he now swore to her memory.

The Messiah Drug, the small portions of holy water David was able to secure from his priest, had proven to be the only antidote for the plague. Nothing their scientist, or the brilliant doctors at the CDC in Atlanta, tried was able to combat the exploding plague. But David's miracle water proved one hundred percent effective and, after seeing children with one foot in the grave rebound within hours as if they had merely taken a nap, was the one thing that had restored his faith in Jehovah God, Simon realized.

All of the coincidences that led to its discovery, he reasoned as he added up all the fortuitous actions of the last few months, were more than just chance, more than a toss of the dice. He was positive that a Higher Power had a hand in all of this. What if Sara and David had never met? Rather, what if he, Simon, hadn't assigned her to get close to him and learn what his sect might be up to? Was the untimely death of her parents—was it untimely, or a part of this puzzle? He shook his head as the many notes that fate can play with the music of one's life baffled him.

One of the main reasons he chose Sara from a group of like-qualified female agents, he remembered, was because she needed an easy assignment after the deaths of her parents in that bloody Arab bombing of the bus in Tel Aviv.

The balance of life was far too fragile, the planner of this mission decided. *Think of all the incidents that had to take place,* he mused as his chariot winged its way toward the east coast of Africa, *for us to be at this point in time, at this place.*

Or was it all by chance?

CHAPTER 6

Three months earlier:

Simon was sitting behind his desk, trying to read some other meaning to the orders he was given from his boss, when there was a knocked on his office door.

"Come in."

"You sent for me, sir?" a somber-looking young female agent asked, walking into Simon's office.

She was conservatively dressed in a gray business suit covering the typical white blouse worn by most of the women in the office. Because of the poor air conditioning in the building, she was carrying her jacket. Her utilitarian white blouse was buttoned up to her neck. Her hair had a healthy glossy black sheen and she pinned it back in a tight bun, which was popular with the females in the office. It was believed by the men in his department, spoken in privacy, it was the females attempt at reducing their sex appeal. Even so, she carried a strong feminine presence.

"Yes I did, Sara. Close the door and take a seat please," he offered, standing and pointing to a chair in front of his desk.

She closed the door and walked over to the chair, never once looking up at her commanding officer in this section of the Mossad. He had to admit he was very concerned about her. The awful death of her family from those Arab suicide bombers was evident on her face and in her actions lately. Her eyes were distant, reflecting bits of the lasting pain of their passing, and gone was the dance in her step. She was always quick to smile, Simon remembered. Now she just seemed to be passing time at work.

She was never what Simon would have called his type, but he had to admit she was very nice looking. She had a kind of young woman innocence that Simon couldn't warm up to. His thoughts were detoured for a moment by the image of a couple of worldly looking agents up on the fifth floor who could really stir his coffee.

Was it in the neatness of her hair and her clean tanned skin that had once made her appealing to the men in this division? he wondered. She was always included in the underground male listing of the top ten sexiest women in the building. Whatever it was she had, it seemed lacking today. The woman with her legs crossed sitting in front of him seemed stuck in neutral.

He remembered spending most of the night revisiting an earlier decision to pick her for this assignment. After reading his orders again the next morning over toast and eggs, he was convinced it was the perfect job for her.

"Sara—" Simon hesitated as a light scent of her perfume drifted across his desk and threatened to rob him of his thoughts. "I have a new assignment for you," he continued, "if you're ready to get back to field work."

"Sir, I'm more than ready," she said as she sat up, now more alert. "The last two weeks I've spent saying good-bye to my parents. You didn't get a chance to meet them, did you, sir? They were special people. My father was a strong-willed individual and my mother even stronger. They would have wanted me to get on with my life."

He studied her closely as she stopped to take a deep breath. There were no signs of stress or nervousness in her voice. Her chest rose and fell, obviously expelling a deeply painful breath.

"They were always so proud of the work we do to help strengthen our beloved country," she added as the silence started to make her nervous. "It will help me, I think, if I can give as much of myself as they have."

That last statement set off all kind of warnings that Simon ignored. He really wanted to believe that she would be okay. He tossed her a manila folder. As Sara opened it, Simon started explaining her next assignment. The first page, she saw, contained the picture of a young man.

"His name is David Yasuda," Simon commented before she could ask. "He's an Ethiopian Jew who came into our country as a boy in the early '80s. He is working for the Immigration Services to help the Falashian Jews we liberated from that hell hole in Ethiopia melt into Israeli society. He's in charge of the Haifa absorption centers. He appears to be a fine young man with no record of any criminal activities. From the information we've gathered monitoring his activities, he's very dedicated to his job."

Sara sensed the man sitting on the other side of the desk was baiting her, but she refused to nibble. *He has that snicker on his face he gets when he thinks he's clever*, she deduced. *What are you up to, boss?* Her boss was dressed in his customary turtleneck under a suit jacket. Sara couldn't remember the last time she saw him in anything else. The tie she brought him for his birthday her first year here was probably still in the box.

"I know what you're going to ask," he felt driven to say as the silence between them grew. "Why then do we want you to get close to this man? We believe he is a door that will enable you to infiltrate the Falashian sect. Every leader in the sect respects this young man. If there's any insurrection growing, he'll be one of the first to know. As I'm sure you've seen in the news, some of the transitions are not going very smoothly with some of our dark Jewish brothers. Through no fault of this young man, some hotheads don't think enough opportunities are coming their way. I'm sure they are somewhat correct, but we can't allow protest to escalate into violence. In some quarters of government, I fear they're overly concerned that some of these poor souls might protest too loudly or join some of our more out-spoken Arab brothers, know what I mean?"

She looked closely at the additional photographs without answering. The man pictured was talking to some kids of high school age in a couple of the photos, and it was obvious he was genuinely interested in what they were saying. The teenagers seemed to be enjoying his company. Sara smiled at that. Some of the photos were covertly taken as he was washing his van and working out in his yard. Each caught him in only shorts, revealing a very muscular, toned body and nice abs. He was handsome for an Ethiopian. '*Wait a minute, Sara*, she chided herself, *you sound like a bigot. This is a good-looking man period.*' She looked at his eyes in one of the close-ups. Eyes were a reliable door into a person's soul, she believed. He had large, round eyes, which she would later learn, separated most Ethiopians from the other peoples of Africa.

As she was trained to do, Sara carefully studied the photograph until she had a mental picture of the man called David Yasuda. He wasn't really a black man, she determined. His complexion was closer to tan. There were white Israeli officers, she knew, who tanned deeper than this man was. Ummm, his bios listed him as six feet one inch tall, weighing about one hundred and eighty pounds. He had a very warm, trusting smile in most of the photos. He had no bad habits listed, she noticed, reading more of his bio. '*Let's see, likes women but isn't dating any one woman, thank God for that. It just might be an interesting assignment after all,*' Sara decided while leafing through more of his folder.

She knew Simon had personally rescued many of the Black Jews from Ethiopia himself. Some self-serving friends warned her that if she joined his department, she might have to work with "those people." All of the assignments concerning the Falashian, she later learned, were passed down to Simon's department and he gladly accepted them. Many people in the Mossad admired him for that. Those who sought to degrade him for it—only added to the legend.

"Do we have any real evidence that there is any trouble brewing with the Habash?" she asked, getting into her new assignment.

He struggled to hide his enjoyment. She was sitting up in her seat, showing real interest in this assignment. She had always possessed dancing eyes. When you looked into them they quickly captivated you with their energy. She would smile, those dimples would appear, and you just wanted to be a part of her life.

"Someone upstairs passed down these orders," he told her. "I don't know if it's motivated by past prejudices toward our dark brothers or genuine information from other sources. The word came down to this desk and the assignment fell to you."

Sara leafed through the folder as Simon waited for any additional preliminary questions she might have before she began to study in-depth all the information written on this case. He twitched in his seat as she started to open the sealed ROE. folder. Every assignment had clearly defined restrictions about what an agent could do and how far they could go to complete that mission. Her orders were to use whatever means available to infiltrate the Falashian sect and one David Yasuda, in particular.

Sara read that page and then looked up at Simon as if she was offended by what was written between the lines. She looked deep into his eyes until he turned away. *It still works*, she thought when he looked down and pretended to be straightening the papers on his desk. She continued reading the "rules of engagement" for this assignment.

Those "rules" were like a run-in-their-stocking to most female agents and a touchy issue with their superiors. The female agents used their advantage to make their nervous commanding officers understand that they hated being expected to freely use their bodies in the line of duty. It was an expectation that the rookie agents learned in the first week of training. The instructors were at first adamant in their defense of personal rights. No one should be forced to do anything, they preached, that their conscience disagreed with. Unspoken was the fact that you were required, no demanded, to get results in any manner possible if you wanted to be a field agent. It was something students had to come to grips with that first week or head for home.

It was an unspoken rule that everyone understood might be required of him or her. Sex was just another tool, a very powerful tool, that every agent male and female was expected to use if it got results, and history had confirmed those overwhelming successful results.

"Everything appears in order, sir," she admitted as she placed the papers back in the folder and put the folder under her arm.

"Good," he answered, obviously relieved. "Is there anything to prevent you from getting started on this right away?"

Ah ha, the question. She decided to just let him stew on that for a while. She reopened the folder and pretended to scan the documents, as if she might have forgotten something important, before looking up. "No, boss. Is there a rush on this?"

"Not that I know of. In fact, be careful not to rush it. I've had him under surveillance for weeks and, from those reports, he is a very dedicated young man. He is respected by everyone we talked with and has a spotless record. You might discover he's very bright."

"All men are very bright, sir, that's why they're so easy. They're too smart to fall for a stupid female," she commented, grinning back at him.

Yes! She was back, he remembered thinking. They shook hands and Sara walked out of his office. No, walked wasn't quite the word. She had that attitude back in her step. Her hips moved as if she was dancing across the floor and not walking. Then he remembered why the men in this department were so taken by her.

He sat back in his chair and relaxed for the first time in days. He loved it when he was able to solve two problems with one solution. Seeing the old fire in Sara's eyes again was refreshing. With a nod of his head and a grin on his face, he decided David Yasuda would be the vein that pumped life back into one of his favorite young agents.

He had faith in her ability. There weren't a lot of things, he reasoned, looking back on his life, that he still had faith in. For most of his life, his faith in Jehovah was all but unshakable. But years ago in the dirty, filthy, disease-riddled refugee camps of the forgotten in the Sudan, he lost that faith.

Under the most demanding of circumstances, he would soon need that conviction again.

Chapter 7

Seven years earlier:

Mossad Agents Simon Levine and Abe Rohm walked slowly to their weathered vehicle. It had to be well over a hundred degrees as the heat, and bugs battled for which would torment them the most. Their jeep was parked behind the largest of the UN relief tents in one of the many Sudanese refugee camps hastily set up to receive the thousands of Ethiopians fleeing their country. This camp near Umm Rekuba was the largest and the last of the camps they planned to visit. Neither spoke a word as they climbed into the hot, dusty jeep. Abe got behind the wheel and slumped back in his seat. He stared out the dust-caked windows at the unbelievable scene they had just witnessed.

Simon just lowered his head. Those terrible images were already burned into his heart and mind. None of his own nightmares could ever paint the depth of sorrow and utter helplessness he carried after forcing himself to visit these camps. He wasn't pressured by anyone to come here, so he had no one to blame. If he had searched deeper into his soul, he would have realized he was driven to be here. Driven by the pain he saw in the faces of the dying Ethiopian children, driven by the lack of concern from the host Sudanese government, the United Nations, and worst of all, the so-called Ethiopian government.

"I—don't—I don't—believe what I'm seeing," Abe said,

struggling to put words to his anguish. "It's still going on, isn't it?"

"It's never stopped," Simon answered as he pounded his fist against his thigh in disgust. "We evacuated over twelve thousand of the Falashian Ethiopians to Israel, and the government of Ethiopia turns their back on the remaining Beta-Israel in their country."

"Beta-Israel?"

"Yes Abe, that's what the Ethiopian Falashian call themselves. As you know, they believe they are direct descendants of King Solomon. As Orthodox Jews look for the coming of the Messiah, they look for the day when they will depart Ethiopia for Israel as our forefathers did from Egypt."

Abe started up the jeep and headed west out of the camp. Neither man spoke for a long while as the suffering they'd seen consumed their thoughts.

"Well, Simon," Abe finally said, after taking a deep breath, "the message I will take back to the Knesset is that the sad situation of our fellow Jews in Ethiopia is worse than it was in 1984. It's more than just the famine in Africa that is killing our brothers."

"Yeah, it's that timeless curse of being called a Jew," Simon swore through clenched teeth, "that has engendered such hatred and disregard for human life. I'm sure the old politicians haven't forgotten what that kind of hate is like."

"Simon, I've made my flight arrangements. We'll drive to Khartoum where I'll board a flight to Cairo before going on to Tel Aviv."

Simon nodded. "Good, and I'll join up with the Mossad underground in the capital and make my way back into Ethiopia."

Simon was part of a covert network that the Mossad had first set up in April of 1983 to help those trying to immigrate to Israel from Ethiopia and had already saved several hundred lives. They led small groups of ten or more on horseback, on foot, or by truck across the closely guarded Ethiopian/Sudanese border and boarded whatever planes they could rent, borrow, or steal, to get out of the Sudan to Athens and

Rome, which were the stops used most frequently. From there they were quietly flown by El Al airlines into Israel. It was these same brave, emancipated, Mossad agents who had daily risked their lives to save their dark brothers who finally influenced the politicians—when they returned home and told their stories—to once again help the displaced Jews of Africa.

Simon had led numerous groups of desperate Falashians on the arduous, exhausting, and very dangerous treks across the beautiful Ethiopian plateaus to the hot, dry desert of Eastern Sudan. Because of the dangers involved, they restricted their groups to small parties, much easier to hide in the desert. In 1984, the government of Ethiopia permitted the savagely persecuted Falashian sect to immigrate freely to Israel. That act permitted Simon to arrive openly with a contingent of Mossad agents to weed out the true Beta-Israel from those who sought immigration for other reasons.

When the Ethiopian government suddenly and unexpectedly halted the airlifts in early '85, over twelve thousand Black Jews had immigrated to Israel. Simon wasn't surprised when he was then expelled along with most of the foreigners in the country. Torn by the memories of those left behind, he volunteered to lead a group of agents back into Ethiopia and set up an underground network to clandestinely liberate as many fellow Jews as possible.

This elite group bribed officials, soldiers and anyone they could to build a solid underground unit that continued to rescue the Habash Jews. By the time the airlifts resumed in '89, Simon had seen the depths of despair men could sink to and the heights of courage an abandoned people could obtain. It was after one of many such missions into Ethiopia that his resolve was tested.

Ethiopia, despite the famine and hunger that was devastating the poor and needy, was a very beautiful country. The center of the country was one massive plateau that was split in half by the Great Rift Valley, a deep gorge that ran from the Middle East to southeastern Africa. It was formed millions of years ago by an upheaval in the Earth's crust during massive earthquakes. Ethiopia was blessed with high plateaus and ridges that suddenly plunged down thousands of feet into lush, dark gorges and valleys with swift rivers and green pastures.

The larger species of African wildlife were native to most parts of the country. Ethiopia was home to the giraffe, leopard, hippo, lion, elephant, and many varieties of antelopes. Even the mighty rhino abounded here. The southern section of Ethiopia was made up of lowlands. These lowlands suffered the worst of the famines of the '80s.

The northern sections of Ethiopia were made up of hot, arid desert. The Danakil Depression, a triangular shaped desert near the coast, was three hundred feet below sea level and recorded some of the highest temperatures in the world.

The north was also home to the majority of the Falashian Sect that once numbered in the hundreds of thousands. Exposed to a different brand of "ethnic cleansing," they were reduced to less than forty thousand by 1987. The majority of those "cleansed" were murdered or starved to death under the cruel hand of a succession of Christian rulers who were zealously determined to convert them.

Despite the murders, beatings, and cruelties, they continued to maintain that they were Jews and direct descendants of King Solomon. The word Falashian in Ethiopian meant "exiles" or "without land." Because of their refusal to convert to Christianity, they were barred from ever owning land. Ethiopian Christians abhorred them, believing they were the direct descendants of the killers of Jesus. Many believed that the Falashians could turn themselves into hyenas at night and would devour Christian women and use their blood for perverted Jewish rituals.

Despite the abuse suffered at the hands of their countrymen, it was their thirst to immigrate to Israel that stirred them to risk death at the hands of soldiers, thieves, or just the imposing task of crossing the treacherous desert of the Sudan. From small settlements to frightened families, they sold what little they had and paid Sudanese guides to lead them through the scorching hot desert. Some made it, but the majority were either killed or captured and returned by Ethiopian soldiers patrolling the border. Other groups fell victim to marauding bandits called Shifta's. Those who made it across the border were often arrested and placed in one of many filthy refugee camps like the one near Umm Rekuba.

Simon, and three other Mossad agents, stumbled upon one of these pitiful groups making the crossing, while sneaking back into Ethiopia from a mission...

CHAPTER 8

*W**e are at least moving in the right direction*, a tired, sweaty, and exhausted Simon tried to assure himself as his group meandered along in the intense heat. How could they lose, rather he lose, the only compass they had? It must have happened during their hard ride to avoid being seen by those damn bandits. *On the bright side*, he reasoned, *we were able to get another seventeen Falashian Jews out of their Ethiopian hellhole*. With the fairly reliable contacts they were able to make in the Sudan, he was sure that the Azariah Bobala family and friends would make it safely to Israel.

"Hold up," Simon said, motioning to his companions by raising his right hand. He then climbed wearily down off the sweating horse he was riding. "Let's give the mounts a rest." His real need was to get his sore butt off his "damn nag."

The desert sun was setting over their shoulder, so he knew they were headed east. *Bring a spare compass along next time stupid*, he scolded himself, *they're far too valuable to lose when you're in this wasteland*. Simon looked in the direction he believed was east, hoping to see the Simyem Mountain range through the evening haze. The rolling hills of the Sudanese desert continued on into the horizon.

"We should be close enough to see the mountains soon," he told whoever was listening.

There were no comments. Simon turned to face his comrades. "Yank" Koppel was busy watering his horse with water in his hat and seemed oblivious to Simon. But that was just Yank's way. Simon knew he heard every word he said. Yank stood six foot two inches tall and weighed about two hundred and twenty pounds. He was a quiet man who taught hand-to-hand combat in the Mossad before joining Simon in Ethiopia. Yank's quick reactions, during the times they had to fight their way out of trouble, had saved their necks on more than a few occasions. Yank picked up that nickname the minute he stood up in army training school and said, "My name is Ted Koppel."

Yank's family resided in Ashqelon and, as he was quick to tell you, in an expensive beachfront home. Yank's natural love of animals and keen sense for picking out the good horses, from the sick or drugged ones they were constantly being offered, was invaluable. It was Yank's nod and patting of his horse that signaled to Simon their need to rest them. Airy and Joshua made up the rest of the group.

Simon wiped the sweat off his face and took inventory of his crew. Joshua Cohn, the devout biblical scholar of the group, as he was wont to tell everyone he met, was spread out on the ground, resting from their hard ride. Joshua would say if asked, that he was resting up in case he was needed again to save them from those marauding thieves.

Although physically a non-entity in a fight at five foot four and around one hundred and forty-five pounds, he was one of the bravest men Simon had ever known. From their first day in Ethiopia, he proudly recalled, Joshua had volunteered for every mission and never complained about the inhuman conditions they were forced, at times, to endure.

Joshua was with Simon during the big airlift of Jews from Ethiopia in '84. He also "volunteered" to stay behind and rescue the people they had to leave there when the crooked, inhumane, anti-Semitic government of Ethiopia suddenly canceled the immigration.

Many believed, but never asked Joshua, if he felt a religious responsibility to be in Ethiopia helping the Falashians because of his famous biblical namesake who led the children of Israel to the promised land. The truth was—he never told anyone but Simon—he believed that the Falashians were the true progeny of King Solomon. After growing up with the stories of how the world had turned its back on the European Jews and allowed them to be murdered in cruel and inhuman ways, he felt a bond with the plight of the Beta-Israel. Simon knew that it was also one of the reasons that fueled his own decision to return. It was too late to kill Nazis, but there were other ways to defeat hate.

While rubbing his sore ass, Simon looked around but didn't see Airy. Airy Moshe, the fourth member of the group who was riding point, was out of sight. Riding point, Airy would first scout around their position in a complete circle before feeling confident enough to join his friends when they stopped to eat or rest. Simon eventually spotted him with his binoculars lying on top of a sand dune about two hundred yards away. It was obvious he was observing something on the other side of the dune. Simon pointed out Airy to Yank, took the reins to his horse, climbed on, and rode toward him. Airy had already started crawling back down the sand dune as Simon approached.

"Airy, what's going on?" Simon whispered after climbing down off "the nag" and walking quietly up to him.

From the look on Airy's face, Simon knew something was very wrong on the other side of that dune.

"There's a group of people being robbed and terrorized by what looks like the same group of Shifta bandits we eluded."

Airy led Simon carefully back up the dune. Removing his hat Simon slowly looked over the mound of hot sand. What he saw triggered the anger that he constantly struggled to contain in this crazy country. There, about one hundred yards away, was a group of twenty armed men on horseback surrounding a ragged band of five people. The five appeared to be unarmed and posed no threat but Simon couldn't be sure at that distance. Airy nudged him and pointed to something going on off to their far right. Simon took a deep breath. The scene unfolding before him was a common one. The strong was taking advantage of the weak. From the wrestling matches going on down there, the women were being attacked.

Simon slid down out of sight and pondered their next move. What to do now? They are greatly outnumbered. Without question, he knew what Airy was thinking. "Let's go back and get our horses and charge them firing our weapon as we ride." Airy was their John Wayne, Simon often confided to the others. Every military or police department had one. He was in Ethiopia because, "That's where the action is," Airy confessed.

Simon had once made the mistake of questioning the depth of Airy's commitment. In a very emotionally draining confrontation, Airy tearfully explained. "I'm going to fight the enemies of Jews wherever I found them, Simon, I am. If these dark people were really Jews, then I will die if I have to in order to rescue them. No more!" Airy screamed at him. "No more will this Jew stand still and let others grind us into the dirt. No more!"

Simon remembered how they somehow found common ground and hugged each other warmly that day and had been close friends ever since. He even grew to enjoy the constant inquiries of "You two brothers?"

With both of them standing six feet tall and about the same weight, they did have a lot in common. But what sealed it was when Airy grew his beard. That black curly haired beard was an exact copy of Simon's. A fact that, though vociferously denied, pleased both of them.

Again, Airy nudged Simon. Without asking why, he looked over at the horsemen and was surprised to see the rapists were rejoining the rest of their pack, indicating the assault on the women was over. The bandits had made the decision for him. He and Airy were unable to hear what they were saying as they rode around the frightened victims while mocking their impending deaths. It obviously was some final insult, some degrading threat to prolong their agony. The two men watched in silence as the bandits rode through the group kicking some of the men to the ground and then finally riding off to the south. They had taken what worth they had.

Four of the victims couldn't wait until the horsemen disappeared behind the sand dunes. Ignoring the potential threat from their adversaries, they ran to the three still prone targets of the Shiftas' savagery. The fifth one just stood there watching the others minister to the battered women. Simon recognized him immediately as their leader. That look of blame a leader had to bear when things went horribly wrong was obvious to Simon, even at that distance. Neither Simon nor Airy breathed until they saw that the three females were moving, apparently still alive.

"Let's go," Simon ordered, standing up and running down the dune toward the horses.

Noah had outrun the others and reached the victims first. From her tattered clothes, he recognized the crying figure curled up in the sand. He knelt down and carefully picked up the bruised head of his wife Elishva. There was genuine concern for her in his heart but his passive face reflected her suffering as just another grain of sand on what had become, for them, a beach. Somehow, his love for her found the spark that was buried beneath the despair, and he gently spoke of his heartfelt sorrow for what had happened to her and that he would always love her. Once this painful memory subsided, those words would forever seal her love for him.

Abban Masala, the elder and leader of the attempted *aliyah* stood alone as the others raced to help the three unfortunate women. He shared the pain and shame he knew they endured. Noah was his son and the gentle Elishva, his daughter-in-law. From the moment they decided to leave for the Sudan and the storied evacuations to the Holy Land they heard was possible there, they had experienced nothing but death, misery, and heartache.

Abban didn't question the reality or validity of his lifelong dream of migrating to Israel. That was the whole reason for living, or lately dying, for every member of Beta-Israel. He only questioned his ability to lead them out of this unforgiving desert. The painful memory of the two children they lost, while wandering around in this parched oven, was an unyielding yoke around his neck. He could only watch as the women were helped up from the hot sand.

He had made no promises to any of them, he told the voices of guilt that mocked his efforts. Never promised he could find the way across this hot, barren land. When their guide took off and never returned, Abban only said that he was determined to continue or die trying, and now this atrocity. He lowered his head in prayer. This setback, added to the despair of losing the little children, had stretched his faith to the limit.

Abban felt the heavy weight of their abysmal situation cause his legs to weaken. "This is the end of my strength, oh Lord," he prayed.

His supplication was halted when he heard his wife scream at him. He looked over at her. She was very agitated and was pointing nervously at something behind him. He turned around and saw four men on horseback riding slowly toward him. Abban's heart sank as he all but questioned his God's sense of fair play. *How much more must we endure?*

His spirits soared when he turned to warn the others and saw they were standing defiantly in front of the three women. Their actions said all he needed to know. They would die, here and now, before they would permit anyone to hurt them again.

Simon signaled his men to stop short of the old man. He got off his horse and handed the reins to Joshua. Slowly, and with his head bowed, so as not to appear threatening, he walked up to the old man. As he got closer, he could see the elder's bruised face. His nose had a trickle of dried blood running down to his lip. The old man's face was a battered icon of the assault they had all endured. He was dressed in a ragged white shamma that Simon recognized as the favorite local dress of the Falashians. A jolt of excitement tickled Simon's spine as he thought they might be Jews.

"*Ayhoud,*" Simon said, pointing at himself.

The pain and anger on the bruised face of the old man melted like ice cream in the summer sun. His round, startling dark eyes, clouded over as hope spilled down his cheeks in the form of tears. So use to negativity, he had to—

What did the young stranger say? Abban wondered, questioning his hearing. His head was still spinning from the beating he had taken. Did he say he was a Jew?

"*Ayhoud*," Abban managed to say, pointing at himself in answer to the puzzling young man staring at him.

Simon walked up to the elder and hugged him, their embrace hiding the tears in his own eyes from his men. Joshua, watching the surprised embrace, lowered his weapon, climbed off his horse, and led the group up to Simon. He sensed he might be needed, judging his knowledge of the Amharic language to be more profound than Simon's.

A frightened Rachel watched in astonishment as her husband passionately hugged the stranger. Her old legs betrayed her as she flopped down on the hot sand ignoring the pain to her knees. *Finally, a friend in this cruel land.* Lovingly, the battered younger women helped their matriarch to her feet. Rachel straightened her garment and cheerfully thanked the women.

They set up camp in a nearby gorge that would shield their small propane fire from the curious. Simon asked Yank and Airy, who had medical training and their few medical supplies, to help the wounded as much as they would permit. The women were beaten and bruised but, fortunately, without any lasting physical problems. Emotionally? Only time would tell how deep their scars were.

The four Mossad agents sat down with the Falashian men as Rachel Masala, Abban's wife and the only woman who was spared the assault—their attackers thought her too old—sat a distance away with the women. As they shared some of the water they carried, Abban told them of their plight.

"The man seated on Abban's right," Joshua interpreted, "is his only son Noah Masala. Ah…his wife's name is Elishva. The man to Noah's right is Abban's best friend Zechariah Bengala. His family includes Yoni, his wife, Yakir, his only son, and Yakir's wife, Alita." Joshua stopped and took a drink as Abban continued talking. "Noah and his wife have lost their only child in the desert as has Yakir Bengala." Joshua looked at the young mothers, the sadness of their loss written on their faces. "Both children," Joshua interpreted, "had wandered off and found what they probably thought was a drinking pond. With their throats parched, both children must have drunk from the filthy, smelly water in the pond."

"They had the fever for two days," Noah inserted into Abban's recounting, "then died minutes apart."

Abban reached over, hugged his son, and then continued.

"Their guide rode off to check on a distant fire they spotted," Joshua translated. "That was two nights ago and he never returned. They could have found their way back into Ethiopia."

"We determined—" The elder stood up, raised a clinched fist into the air, and emphatically said in the little Hebrew he knew, "—complete *ailyah.*"

Each member nodded in agreement with the persuasive herdsman as Joshua sat mute and surprised.

"After the guide left—" Joshua continued translating when the elder sat down and directed his words at him. "—they wandered through the hot land for two days before they were attacked by the robbers."

A cold silence fell over the talkative leader.

"Can we help you get home?" Joshua asked Abban first in Hebrew then in Amharic.

Noah raised his hand to silence his increasingly animated father. He then lowered his head, as if to gain the strength to say what was on his mind. "Are you going to take us to Israel?"

His father smiled proudly, displaying the few teeth remaining in his mouth at his lamenting son's answer. He was very proud of him. Even the pain of losing his only child and watching his wife raped by robbers didn't dilute Noah's hunger to complete the *ailyah.*

Yank told Joshua to ask them how they contemplated making it to Sudan after they were robbed of everything. Abban listened to the question for a minute then he answered him.

"*B'ezrat hashem,*" Abban said, looking from Yank to Joshua.

Yank recognized the answer was directed at him. He motioned to Joshua for an interpretation. The blank look he saw on Joshua's face in the flickering light of the fire gave him his answer.

"*B'ezrat hashem*," Joshua explained, "means something like, *with the help of God.*"

Their conversation was halted temporarily when Abban struggled to stand up. The group of men waited on another emotional diatribe about his determination to cross the barren wasteland but instead he motioned for the women to join them. The Falashian men had made camp for them a discreet distance from where the Israeli Mossad agents were camped. In the tradition of the Falashians, the women were isolated when strangers were present. Abban's act was a sign of friendship.

"Abban, permit us to share our food with you," Simon offered as the women sat down beside their men.

The old man stared at the Israeli.

Reading his silence as possibly an affront, Joshua stood up and diverted attention.

"It's a custom of the people of Israel, Abban," Joshua quickly clarified, "to share with fellow travelers when passing through their lands. Simon's offer is part of our—your new customs."

The old man thought about those words and then smiled.

Joshua volunteered to be the cook. His mastering of their language permitted him to offer up amusing anecdotes about his friends that endeared him to his Falashian audience. The laughter melted what apprehension remained, as the Africans felt at home with their white Jewish brothers.

Rested, fed, and feeling safe, the conversation returned to Israel. The members of Beta-Israel listened excitedly as Joshua spoke of his homeland. His, and the stories he interpreted from his comrades, beguiled even the starchy Abban. Joshua was relieved when Abban finally put a halt to the verbal onslaught and led his group to their encampment.

"Airy, there's got to be a way to talk them into going back to Ethiopia until we can find passage for them."

"They seem determined to cross this desert or die trying. And if they're that determined, what can we do?"

Simon spent most of the evening wondering how he could convince Abban and his band to return with them to Ethiopia until they could find safe passage into the Sudan. It would take about a week, he figured, to tie everything together. Attempting to sneak them in now would only lead to them getting captured and placed in one of those awful refugee camps.

Airy climbed the highest dune nearby to stand first watch. Joshua was to relieve him in four hours with Simon taking the last watch. Yank was in charge of cleaning up. Simon took one last look around the camp, lay down on his sleeping mat, and tried closing his eyes. The day's events made that a wasted effort. Staring up at the stars, he tried again to find a weakness in Abban's arguments that he could use to persuade the determined old man. It was a fruitless battle that sleep finally overcame.

Joshua sighed. One of the wonders of the desert at night was the lack of sound. When the breeze died down you could hear your heartbeat. The stars were out in abundance in the cloudless sky. So many, they illuminated the ground, much like the moonlight did. He felt confident he could see well enough without his night vision goggles to spot anyone approaching the camp.

Later, Joshua slid down the steep sand dune on his butt, dusting himself off as he walked toward camp. It was two hours past Simon's turn to stand watch. Joshua had already decided to tell Simon he couldn't sleep anyway so he took most of his watch for him. *He'll probably think I fell asleep while on guard*, Joshua mused as he kicked the sand. The truth was he couldn't sleep. The picture of a certain redhead with unforgettable green eyes and an endearing smile named Adriana invigorated his tired body.

All the dumb things he had said to her before he left came flashing back into his mind. This mission had robbed him of the opportunity to give her roses and an apology. Yes, she was high strung and high-maintenance, but she was very intelligent, driven, and she loved him.

"Look, Adriana, it's what I do. It's what I was doing when we first met."

"That's fine for you, Joshua, but not for me."

"I understand that, but I have made a commitment."

"If I didn't care for you, it wouldn't matter. Now it does and you can't see why."

She was right about that. They had been seeing each other off and on, whenever their schedules allowed. It had been wonderful. No commitments to discolor what they had. Each being free to be who they were, and then that changed—and he didn't know why.

Was she more than he had expected? Yes. She was a whirlwind of energy and emotions and he loved that about her. One minute she was cooking a special dinner for him and the next making passionate love to him standing against the wall as that dinner burned. Was he stupid for not wanting to give it a try? Yes. But leaving the Special Forces was a lot to ask. He loved what he was doing—he loved it. Was he glad to be here for the right reasons or was it just to get away from her, from committing to something? He knew what the answer to that question was—and that troubled him most of the night.

The clear night air did make him long for home so much he got caught up in that memory of her and forgot about the time. The early morning rays of sunlight became his alarm clock.

As Joshua neared the camp, he could see that the dark Jews were gathering up their few belongings in preparation for an early departure. He spotted Simon sleeping off to his left and headed in that direction. On the third nudge with his boot, Simon sat up.

"What? Is it time for my watch already?" a groggy voice asked of the man he recognized standing over him.

"It's two hours past your watch," Joshua explained to his boss. "You were so tired I let you sleep a few hours longer."

"Thank you, Josh. I sure needed it."

"You are welcome, but that's not why I'm here." Joshua looked Simon in the eye and then pointed toward the Falashian camp. Slowly Simon stood up and looked in that direction. "I believe our Black brothers are preparing to leave."

"What?" Simon shouted loud enough he woke up the others.

The weapons of the two waking commandos were aimed in a quick circle before they inquired what was going on. Their trained quick response pleased their leader but he was off without saying another word.

"What's going on?" Airy asked as he jumped up and replaced his gun back in his belt.

"Our company appears to be leaving," Joshua volunteered as he turned and followed Simon.

Airy motioned to a bewildered Yank and hurried to catch up with Joshua.

Noah saw their new friends approaching and told his father. Abban nodded acceptance of his son's observation as he continued to put their meager rations in a sack. He finished and advised his gathering flock to be strong and courageous. Joshua heard that part of the speech as they approached. They stopped short of the Beta-Israel camp in respect for the women in the group.

"Abban, good day to you," Simon said as calmly as he could. "Are you breaking camp already?"

The elderly man may not have understood those words but his blood-shot eyes spoke all the answer needed.

"Yes," Joshua translated when the old man finally spoke. Yank and Airy arrived in time to listen to the exchange. "It is better to get an early start before the angry sun gets too high in the sky," Joshua translated.

"That is true, my friend. It is the best time to move about in the desert. Where, may I ask, are you headed?"

Abban closed his eyes, after hearing the translation, and wrapped his arms over his chest as if lost in another place, another time. His eyes suddenly popped open and he gazed at Simon. Through Joshua he said, "We are going to the promise land, we are going to Israel."

Those words triggered a murmur of joy from the beleaguered members rallying around their leader, but only concern from the four men watching this rag-tag group prepare to walk across this scorched stretch of death-land.

"Abban, on foot it's a two- or three-day journey, at best, to cross the Sudanese desert," Simon argued. "Even if, by some miracle, you make it, the border is patrolled by guards from the Sudan and they will arrest you. They're putting hundreds of your people in squalid camps full of suffering and death."

"These things you say are probably true, my friend," Abban said to Simon. He then slowly turned and started walking away. "But we will see the Holy Land of our Fathers or..." His last words strangled by the now gusting breeze.

Simon's mind raced to find the words to stay their departure. He looked at his men for their help and was only greeted with shrugs. Simon started walking toward the elder and was cut off by his son Noah. Simon thought about tossing him aside but, only thought about it.

"Abban," Simon shouted above the gusting winds, "come with us back to Ethiopia until we can get a plane to fly you out of here. I promise I'll get you to Israel."

The old man never turned around to answer him. Noah put his hand on Simon's shoulder, gave him a nod that seemed to say thanks, and then turned to follow the last of their party up the dune. After a couple of steps, he turned and walked back to Simon. "We can't look back at Sodom," Noah said. "If we do we'll turn into a pillar of salt."

Simon was going to argue the insanity of that, but the glazed looked in the eyes of the author of that statement cancelled that.

Noah shook the hand of each of the men, thanking each of them for their help. Simon watched him as he hurried to rejoin his family. The rag-tag band stopped and waited at the crest of the dune for Noah and then waved good-bye to the men below. Long after they cleared the crest, the four men stood there as if awaiting their return.

"Well," Yank said to Simon, "you tried your best to stop them."

"That's right," each concurred as they patted Simon on the back.

Nothing they said could temper the feeling of dread that seemed to permeate the air around him.

Two hours later, after finishing breakfast and caring for their horses, they prepared to leave. All evidence of their camp was brushed over by dragging blankets in the loose sand. They knew from experience that the blowing wind would erase the remaining prints as they climbed up the side of the dune. Their actions, like the long breakfast, were planned to delay their departure as long as possible.

The sun was painfully bright and the day already smothering as they mounted up to leave. Simon hadn't said much as they broke camp. For some reason, he was having a world of trouble saddling up his horse correctly. Each man understood how deeply he was committed to rescuing as many of the Jews of Ethiopia as they possibly could. Riding off and letting these people die in the hot, foreboding desert wasn't his way of doing things. His saddle problem, very un-Simon like, was correctly interpreted as giving the brave but foolish Falashian travelers yet another chance to return. When Simon finally said what was bugging him, no one was surprised.

"Guys, I can't leave another group of people to wander around and probably die in this burning coffin," he explained, looking at each of them. "I couldn't find out last night how much food and water they had. It can't be very much. When I asked Noah, all he said was enough. Hell, enough for what, enough to die of thirst? As a professional, I know what I'm about to do is foolish. And as sure as camels stink, I'm going to regret this."

"No, we'll probably regret following you," Yank scolded his leader.

"No, guys, I can't ask you to go with me."

"Who said anything about you asking? It's a free desert the last time I looked," Airy added. "Besides, do you think we would let you get all the credit?"

"Am I the only reasonable swinging you-know-what here?" Joshua asked. "We don't have time to race off looking for anyone. Has everyone forgotten there are over fifty people waiting for us at the staging point in Ethiopia? If we're not back on time, I can guarantee they will also strike out on their own. And what about that old devil Tamarat? He and his people agreed, very reluctantly I might add, to meet us at Wad Medan. They have the transportation to move the fifty into

Khartoum by truck. The way the Sudanese government is cracking down, they won't wait for us, and I can't blame them."

"Joshua is right, Simon," Yank added.

Airy nodded in agreement.

"I know he is. That's why I'm going alone. The three of you can get those people out of Ethiopia and safely across the desert without me. I don't think Abban can."

With that said, Simon climbed up on "Old Nag," saluted his comrades, turned, and trotted off in pursuit of the Falashians. Three men, torn between what they wanted to do and what they should, watched him ride up a dune and out of sight. The grunting of their anxious horses were the only sounds as they mounted and rode toward the morning sun.

This is crazy, Joshua thought as he led his companions toward the Ethiopian border. *We have to stick to our plans or work in chaos.* He nudged his horse in the side and set off in a trot. The others followed suit.

An hour later, a lost and irritable Joshua stopped to get a fix on their course over the changing sand hills. It had been Simon's thankless job until now. Joshua was checking their route on the map when he noticed his horse looking around behind them. The third time it looked back, he knew something was wrong.

"Damn," he swore, "something isn't right, I can feel it."

The others only looked at him and then turned their horses around and waited for Joshua's lead.

"Yes," he shouted as he did the same and galloped past them.

They raced past their morning encampment, ignoring the message it sent. At the top of a dune, winded and sweating from the long ride, they stopped to scan the area. There wasn't any sign of life anywhere. To these desert travelers, that wasn't surprising. They knew that, to survive, animal or man had to seek shelter in the heat of the day. The three men carefully scoured the parched desert in search of their friend.

After battling the desert's harsh environment the last few years, they understood all too well the difficulty of tracking

someone here. They had used that bitter lesson to avoid countless patrols out looking for them. Now they were trying to
overcome that reality before it was too late.

Each day the dunes, carved by hot, gusting dry winds, produced new hills and valleys that could easily obscure someone
from view. As they rode up the side of one dune, they knew
that Simon could be resting behind another.

At Joshua's suggestion, they spread out as far as they could
and remain in visual contact. Joshua was stationed in the middle with Airy, and Yank, three hundred yards to each side. For
twenty minutes, they rode due west without seeing any sign of
Simon or the Falashians.

"Simon, where the hell are you?" Joshua whispered
through the bandana that covered his mouth.

The nagging thought that they might have missed him
found new urgency. Joshua waved to Airy and Yank to join up
with him. As they approached, Joshua surveyed the dunes, his
mind made up to turn north in search of their friend. Suddenly,
there he was. It was as if he just appeared from another dimen-
sion. He was about two hundred yards away at the top of a flat
section of desert, slumped over on his horse, with his back to
them. Sensing something was amiss, Joshua waited for the
others to get close then signaled for them to approach Simon
from the three directions.

Cautiously, with weapons drawn, they rode up to Simon.
Each man, as they neared the crest of the dune, was astonished
to see their leader sitting on his horse quietly sobbing. Airy,
Yank, and Joshua exchanged puzzled stares, then panned their
weapons around as they looked for the source of Simon's
grief. Yank motioned to Joshua and Airy to stay with Simon
while he scouted the area around them.

The dune slid down into a deep ravine directly in front of
them then snaked around to the left and dropped out of sight.
Yank rode down the steep plane, wondering why he stuck his
neck out so far. Caught out in the open like this, he mused—
while cautiously eyeing the tops of distant mounds—could be
suicidal.

At the bottom of the ravine, he follow what appeared to be

a dry riverbed around several bends. Seeing nothing out of the ordinary, he questioned what Simon found that upset—

Yank spotted something in the rocks up ahead. "My God," he groaned.

There, tossed between the rocks, were the bloodied bodies of Abban and the other men. Yank slipped his Uzi from his shoulder and looked around cautiously before approaching. The slightest movement overhead would precipitate an instant response and a "Who goes there?" later. His experience told him to retreat. Anyone hiding above held all the cards. Remembering the sight of Simon, just sitting on his horse sobbing, told him the killers were probably gone.

Slowly he rode up to the scene of the slaughter. The first body confirmed his suspicions. It was Abban Masala. He was lying on his back with a small hole in the center of his forehead. Only a trickle of blood ran down his wrinkled face, indicating to Yank that his death was quick. From the clothes of the man at his side, he recognized Noah, Abban's son. The two other men were Zechariah and Yakir Bengala. A burst of automatic weapon fire had rendered their facial appearance almost unrecognizable. They must have fought back.

But where were the women? he wondered. Yank couldn't shake the feeling that this gruesome scene would only get worse as he looked around for them. He studied the tracks in the riverbed. The harder surfaces resisted the blowing wind and yielded some clear hoof prints that led off farther down the riverbed. The wisdom in going on alone started to lose its appeal. He turned and realized he was out of line of sight from his friends. Again, a voice whispered for him to return for help, and again he resisted the advice. Uzi in hand, Yank swept the top of the dunes. Any head popping up would be cut off in a hail of lead. Nothing moved. Cautiously, he nudged his horse forward. It didn't take long to find evidence the women had passed this way. Scattered in between the hoof prints of the horses were a few human footprints. Their size confirmed Yank's worse suspicions. The narrow valley he was in continued forward another four hundred feet then appeared to open up. Yank climbed off his horse and walked quietly up to a wall of sand blocking the next turn in the riverbed. The footprints clearly led around the bend.

Oh God, Yank sighed as he leaned back against the sun-baked mound and closed his eyes. His heart was pounding in his chest. Each breath was labored as he fought the rising feeling of dread. *Maybe it's not too late to return and get the guys*, he argued. Something about the quiet signaled it was already too late.

It was as if the Angel of Death was just on the other side—waiting for Yank to stick his head around into his cold, dead, waiting hands—as an anxious Yank tried controlling his breathing, *Is this where I punch out?* he wondered. He could sense the presence of death around the curve of the dune. He hesitated. He listened. Death, he had come to learn, had no respect for people. Accepting all who walked boldly or stumbled blindly into his dead, lifeless arms.

Come on, Yank scolded himself. *They might need your help*. Suddenly his weapon felt very heavy in his hands. *The attackers could still be there*, his fear told him, *waiting in ambush*. He listened to the loud silence.

He took a deep breath then poked his head quickly around the bend of the dune and back again. Nothing moved that he could see and no one shot at him. He held his breath and listened. Only the sound of the wind disturbed the silence. Then Yank jumped. He was startled when his horse whinnied in his ear. Another time, another place, he would have laughed at himself. Not this time.

He crouched down and looked around the dune, this time on his knees. A high shot might buy him time, he figured. Very slowly, he peeked around the dune, straining to see danger before it spotted him. First one then another body came into view lying on the hot sand. There was no sign of life—and no killers. A deep sigh punctuated the silence when he spotted all of the women lying on the sand. He inhaled deeply, as his hand moved up and covered his mouth. He was lucky this time. The hot, burning bile that quickly rose up his throat only reached the base of his mouth. Only by force of will did he resist the urge to vomit. Tears ran down his face as he walked up to four naked, bloody, horse trampled bodies, lying immorally open on the hot sand. He noticed they didn't spare the old woman this time.

Yank finally succumbed to the horror and slid down to one knee, lowering his head in his hands. "God, thank you," he prayed. "They deserve to be together in Heaven as they were on this cruel Earth." There was no acrimony in his voice. In this brutal land, a farmer learned quickly to call a mound of camel shit fertilizer.

Later that day, the four agents made their final camp within view of the blue Simyem Mountains in the distance. That placed them less than a day from the Gonder region of Ethiopia and their base camp. Simon was almost himself again, if that was possible. Every now and then, he would look off into space until someone said something to him. Yank never told him that he had also found the women dead after painfully recalling hearing Simon praying for their safety when he returned. As long as Simon believed they were alive somewhere, he might not blame himself for all eight deaths.

Simon had meekly obeyed their suggestion to stand lookout at the top of the dunes for robbers while they buried the men and, without his knowledge, the women together. After saying a prayer over the graves, they sat down for a breather.

"I can't believe Simon took it so hard," Airy said, as he tried in vain to wipe all the sweat from his face while sitting under the burning sun. "It wasn't his fault they left. Why shoot, he tried to talk them out of it didn't he?"

"Airy," Joshua said. "The hurt Simon felt wasn't just for the Abban and his unfortunate family. Six months ago, he ran into another group of Falashians trying to find their way across the desert. That time he was returning to Ethiopia alone and was following orders to make contact with some Mossad agents in the Ethiopian capital, top priority. The Falashians he encountered asked for his help crossing the desert and he was forced to turn them down. He knew it would take a miracle for them to make it across alone.

"There was no chance he could make that very important meeting in time and deal with a bunch of lost refugees. Knowing Simon as we do, you know that was a very tough decision for him. No one cares more for these people than he does, but orders are orders. He risked his own life by giving them all his food and most of his water. He then instructed them to follow the setting sun to the border. The weary band of ten adults and seven children thanked him as he rode off.

"Near the Ethiopian border Simon was almost captured when he ran into a group of Ethiopian soldiers who were patrolling their side of the border looking for refugees. He realized he would never make that appointment with the border guarded so closely. The only detour route was days away. Then he remembered the lost group of Beta-Israel he passed in the desert. Carefully, he avoided the soldiers and doubled back to try and locate the Falashians.

"The next day he stumbled upon them. Or I should say one of them—a baby boy who was being picked apart by ten or more vultures. What was left of him wasn't worth burying. Throughout the rest of the day, he found four or five more bodies of children. The ones who weren't attacked by wild animals gave evidence they were brutally stabbed to death. Their abductors were cruelly slaughtering the children as they moved south toward Kenya. It became clear to him that the children were expendable. To Simon, this had the smell of slave traders. They are well known to dispose of the children because they aren't worth enough to them alive. If they become a problem and can't keep up, they slaughter them.

"Filled with anger and riding as hard as he could, he couldn't overtake them. He knew there were no straight roads in the desert. They could be headed in any direction. Near fatigue and barely able to stay on his sweating, exhausted horse, he told me he had finally given up. But a final heartbreak awaited him. Just before he turned to leave, he spotted vultures that were circling not too far from where he stopped. He climbed down off his horse, knowing that it was in worse shape than he was. Struggling to walk in the hot sand, he battled his way toward the flying marauders.

"What he saw as he cleared the next rise sickened him. A small dog was fighting off over thirty vultures from a very still, small body. The poor dog was bleeding from the pecking it received from the determined birds. Each one was bigger than the brave animal but he continued charging into them as they approached the child. Simon said he ran wildly down the sand dune screaming at the birds. Caught up in their blood lust, they ignored him. It wasn't until he was almost upon them that they gave up and flew off. The brave little dog hobbled over to the obviously dead child and plopped down beside it, exhausted. Simon realized later that the dog never made a sound as he approached after fighting off the vultures.

"Very slowly he walked up to the dog, all the while talking softly to the now whimpering animal. The little dog was common to the poor Ethiopian towns, a mixture of every dog in the area. This one was white with black spots all over it. It weakly wagged its tail as Simon approached. From the deep wounds in the throat of the little girl he could see that there was no hope for her. Simon said he wanted to save this brave little dog in the worse way. It was as if its life would atone for the deaths of the children he didn't help.

"Simon buried the child and gave the dog the last of his water. He held it in his arms as he climbed up on his horse and tried to find some shelter from the heat of the day. The dog didn't protest as he buried the child nor did it resist when Simon picked it up. He told me he never really knew when the dog died. But for some reason, as he rode through the desert, he started to weep. He rode on for hours as the tears ran down his face never once looking down again at the dog he was holding. That night he buried the brave little animal and swore an oath to Jehovah that he would never again turn his back on Beta-Israel."

"What the—" Airy suddenly blurted out as he spotted Simon riding down in the valley toward them. The others stood up, also surprised to see their friend.

"If you're finished, we had better get going before it gets dark," Simon suggested.

Over the next year, they smuggled out over three hundred people from the hell that was Ethiopia.

CHAPTER 9

June 1999:

Sara wasn't really sleeping. The buffeting from the helicopter made that nearly impossible. She wondered, in an absentminded moment, how long before she could wear a bikini again from the imagined bruises she had on her butt. She sat with her eyes closed to avoid looking at the commandos seated across from her and one in particular who met her eye for eye every time she opened them. *Who are you trying to fool, girl? It's not their eyes you are avoiding, but David's.* His disappointment and hurtful gaze had augmented the remorse she was feeling. Never before had she permitted any client to penetrate her hard, professional veneer. She must have hurt him very much, she reasoned, as evidenced by his continued negative reactions. What really surprised her was that she felt bad about that. In this line of business, she remembered her instructors ranting over and over, one could never allow sentiment or personal feelings to surface and color ones judgment or you were in the wrong business. Those who did, he explained graphically, were either soon found dead or missing and presumed dead.

Sara drifted off for a moment as pictures of their better times together overcame her attempts to dismiss them and painted her thoughts.

Stop it! You don't love him. Don't mistake pity for—he's an Ethiopian Falashian whom you were ordered to seduce in any manner necessary to infiltrate their sect. You were only obeying the direct edict of your government, like a good soldier. It's no different, she argued with herself, *than a soldier risking his life to protect our borders. They stand guard, willing to sacrifice their lives, if necessary, to protect our nation. What you were asked to sacrifice was very precious, but not life threatening. Who are you kidding?* She squeezed her knees together until they hurt. *This is different.* For one, it was the first time she had gone to those extreme means to seduce a client, although she thoroughly enjoyed the sacrificial part.

That memory caused Sara to sneak a peek past Simon at David. He was facing forward as his head rocked with the motion of the bouncing helicopter. She felt a longing in her chest as she watched him. If it wasn't love, it was the next best thing, she decided. Her mouth formed the words she wanted to say but she couldn't say them. Their argument, earlier today, flavored her reluctance…

"What do you want?" he had asked when he opened his hotel room door and saw the person who was knocking.

His harsh words did little, openly, to deter her. Inwardly, they cut deep, but she didn't answer him. She just stood arrogantly in the doorway awaiting an invitation to enter his hotel room. This was her attempt to smooth over any hurt feelings from earlier today when she revealed he was her assignment.

Her pride was something he both admired and disliked about Sara. Her silence gave him a chance to search her face for a reason. Not trusting in what he saw in her eyes, he finally took notice of how she was dressed. Everything about the way she looked was an unspoken apology. Her thick black hair hung down over her shoulders in glossy waves. The practical bun she usually wore was missing, as was her basic outfit of jeans and a T-shirt. The woman standing in his doorway was everything that David had dreamed she could be. Gawd, she looked good, he candidly acknowledged as her striking appearance momentarily tempered his ire. From her glossy black hair that he had always loved running his hands through, to the soft yellow V-neck cashmere sweater that highlighted her sculptured figure, she was dressed to capture his eye if not his heart.

Sara was portraying the woman she knew he saw or wanted in her. The form-fitting black skirt completed the outfit, if not its main highlight. It was enough to silence him. Seeing she had created the desired effect, Sara ignored the lack of a verbal invitation and sauntered past him into the warm hotel room.

The scent of her perfume, as she purposefully brushed past, swirled around him, awakening unforgettable memories of their wonderful times together and lured his eyes downward to the shapely body that had created those endearing recollections.

He turned away quickly before she could catch him in his weakness. David stared out into the empty hallway. He wanted to be strong, to be able to say the harsh words he had practiced for most of the day. Her allure had changed his mind before when he grasped an opinion that differed from hers. Then he judged the pleasure of her persuasion greater than the importance of his opinion. Not this time, he vowed.

During moments of quiet reflection together, he had asked her, no urged her, to look inside herself and see the real person hidden there. She obviously choose rather to search out his strengths and weaknesses, he realized. The woman who entered his room this evening was spawned from those weaknesses.

When he turned around, he imagined, she would be standing there with her head tilted to one side and her hands crossed in front of her. She could look so innocent sometimes. He knew he was drawn to the little girl in her like the little boy in some strong men captivated some women.

Tell her it won't work and to get out, his conscience demanded of him as he started to close his door. *Throw her out on her callous butt*. David inhaled slowly and turned to face Sara. The will to throw her out just wasn't there. He knew the lovely woman standing in the middle of his room had become the center of his universe. Her soft, red, full lips didn't have to speak to command his heart. Her voice was the music he heard in his loneliness. He was smitten by her and knew it. But it was the "nothing has changed" look on her face that shook him from his malaise. *Is she that blind?* he wondered. *Or maybe she just doesn't give a damn.* That question was the breeze that fanned to life the embers of his anger.

Sara watched him as he slowly turned around. At first glance, she saw the look of love written in the wide-eyed gaze on his face. A look she had grown to depend upon and that he always struggled to hide from her. The hours of preparation worked, she decided, as she hid her victory behind a frozen face. A victory she quickly realized was short lived when his eyes suddenly glared down at her. A wave of uneasiness passed through her, and Sara smiled innocuously at him. Usually that was enough to assuage his bad moods, she recalled. *After all*, she'd decided a few hours earlier while creating herself in her mirror, *he is just a man*. She had laughed at that overused truth as she finished applying her makeup. This time, however, she had underestimated the color of his pain.

"David, listen to me," Sara pleaded softly when she realized her less-than-subtle attempt at enticement had only momentarily distracted him, "I was assigned to you by the Mossad. It was my job to infiltrate, if I can use that harsh word, the Falashians to ensure they weren't planning any insurrections. What started out as only another assignment turned into a warm respect for you and your people."

"Spare me your warm respect for my people. That's bullshit, Sara," David said, slamming the door closed and not noticing her startled reaction. "What I want to know is why you deceived me?"

Sara sighed when she saw the wet in his eyes. He was a strong and confident man who had often demonstrated a fierce love for his people, hell, for all people. A man accustomed to fighting for what he believed. A man scarred from both victories and defeats. The depth of his acuity was one of the things she most admired in him. He was a man of great vision who was blindsided by his own heart. Sara began to realize for the first time that she had injured his soul, and at the same time, maybe derailed his life's work.

"David, listen to me," she demanded, taking a step toward him. "I never doubted your love for your people. Don't diminish the depth of my affection for mine. And you're an Israeli now, remember?" She tossed her head and wagged her finger at him. "I was only obeying my orders like I was commanded to do," she rationalized, as she walked up to him and poked a finger in his chest. "No one is above the security of our homeland, no one!"

David moved toward her and Sara took a step back. He noticed the concern on her face and stopped. Her hazel eyes momentary flashed a look of apprehension.

"I'm not going to argue your duty to investigate every faction in Israel," David continued. "What bothers me is that I'm—I thought we—what about us? I opened up to you. I let you into my life. I was always honest with you about everything. Now I find out you only thought of me as an assignment, and don't bother to say otherwise."

"David—"

"You don't understand, Sara," he said cutting her off. "The time I spent with you helped me to heal. I had grown embittered after hearing shocking story after story about the plight of the true Sons of Solomon. The memories of their suffering in Ethiopia had scarred me. I was very upset about all the stupid delays in getting them out. They had endured such great hardships and many died needlessly because few cared, or cared enough."

Sara listened respectfully as he talked. She knew and honored his strong devotion to his people. Those beautiful dark eyes would dance as he talked for hours about his plans for them.

"I—I had blamed those senseless delays on all white Jews," he continued, as he walked over to the window and looked out, "for not caring enough about their Black kinsmen dying in the scorched deserts of the Sudan. You helped me get through that wall of hate I created and to see all people for what they are. Our chance meeting—oh my God!" He spun around so quickly it alarmed Sara. "That wasn't by chance, was it? No, I guess not," David said, throwing her an ugly glare as he answered his own question.

This new revelation caused him to look dejectedly down at the floor, while shaking his head at his gullibility. All of the beauty and freshness of their relationship was an act, he sadly realized. She hadn't been happy to see him when he came over. She was just happy he was so gullible. David's shoulders slumped as he understood, for the first time, that the special-ness of their innocent infatuation was contrived.

While dating Sara, David had had an epiphany. He was never afraid of dying, he realized, until he met her. Death, his faith taught him, was just the door into a better life, free of hate and pain. Sara changed that philosophy. She became a reason to live. Heaven can wait, became more than a movie he liked. It was the daily chant he irreligiously but silently advo-cated after she touched him to the depth of his soul.

The defeated look on his face was what disturbed Sara the most. He had seen so much pain and misery and yet it never seemed to put a crack in that eternal smile of his when they were together. His smile was like the eternal flame—with it, rainy days became sunshine, a bumpy road a smooth inter-state. Yet, the face of the man who slowly walked past her and opened his door, a clear suggestion that she should leave, looked crushed and broken. Sara started for the door resigned that any further attempt at reconciliation was futile. She slowed her stride as she neared him, in some vain hope he would reach out and grab her into his arms. Either in anger or love—it wouldn't have mattered. If he would touch her, she was somehow convinced, she could heal his hurt.

The moment for healing came and went as she stepped out the door. She looked down the hallway toward the elevators. Voices battled within her to confess how she really felt about him. *It wouldn't make a difference. Of course, it would,* they argued. The clicking of the door latch behind her quieted the mental argument. Hearing the door lock, Sara tilted her head back defiantly, as she was wont to do, and walked abruptly toward the elevators.

David closed the door slowly behind her. He was relieved, in part, that her departure wasn't uglier because they would have to work together. Simon had asked for both their help in finding the "Pond of God."

There's little time left for self-pity. David changed into the clothes Simon had delivered to his room. There was a job to do.

Minutes before Sara had knocked on his door he was forced to turn off the television to avoid the misery being shown to the world. His adopted country was dying right before his eyes. What little hope they had was hidden on a mountainside in Ethiopia. Today, they would be leaving this hotel and attempting to sneak out of the country. By morning, they would be walking through the jungles of Ethiopia in search of the "Messiah Drug."

CHAPTER 10

S imon struggled to gather his thoughts, but the loud noise of the copter blades, combined with the closeness of the people and equipment, distracted him. This crazy mission was his idea, he wearily confessed. He closed his eyes and concentrated. Did he miss anything? For the umpteenth time, he reviewed from the start the actions that led up to their racing across the Red Sea, at wave-top level, in the dark of night...

During the days of early June, the nation of Israel was buckling under the terrible weight of the killing disease ravaging the innocent. Thousands had died. Ten times that many were now infected, and most of those would die within days without a cure. When the top scientists in the country, and the Center for Disease Control in Atlanta, sadly admitted they could find no cure or antidote for the plague, Simon went into action. Sara's last report on the Falashian she was assigned to monitor stated that David had acknowledged to her a startling revelation. None of the Falashian that he knew of had contracted the plague. In the chaos occurring around him, Simon had ignored that figuring it was inaccurate. Even if it was true, what did a few healthy people have to do with this crazy country-wide outbreak?

The speed in which the bacterium was killing and ravaging the countryside gave impetus to every suggestion. Hope was a withering flower in Israel with no sign of rain. The finding of a path through this hell-storm, however remote, triggered the beleaguered Israeli government, and Prime Minister Shamir, to vociferously support any valid suggestions.

Stepping out on a very thin limb when all other branches broke off, Simon ordered Sara to reveal who she was to David and seek his help in discovering why the Falashian he knew had escaped the plague. Simon then presented the shocking report to his boss, General Amin Hoie.

In the beginning, when David's assumptions were proven correct, Israeli scientists believed that a serum could be extracted from the blood of those healthy dark Jews who must have had some mysterious resistance to the plague. That hope quickly died. Whatever it was in the healthy bodies they had tested it resisted every attempt by scientists to isolate it.

Even blood transfusions failed. At first, the sick showed a marked improvement then, hours later, the bacteria started multiplying again in the transfused blood of the new host. Hope once again teased the dying nation of Israel and then floated just outside its desperate reach.

By the tenth day, the death toll reached over fifty thousand in Israel alone. The nation of Jordan belatedly reported that the plague had crossed its borders three days ago and now thousands were sick and dying there also.

Now in the helicopter hoping from ship to ship with David, Sara, and the commandos, Simon recalled that it was a miracle they were even able to find out about this Messiah Drug. Grabbing hold of his safety harness, he turned to his right and squeezed David's leg. His gesture was met by a poor excuse for a smile from his friend. Simon felt a genuine respect for this man. "Hang in there."

The humanity of this brown man had already changed the lives of thousands of his people. It was that abiding, sincere humanity that Simon had counted on to push David to confront his high priest of the Falashian sect in Haifa about this alleged immunity. Sara filled in the holes in David's story and his reluctant quest to find the answers to the secret healing powers of the elixir of the High Priest, Yehoshua Gette...

CHAPTER 11

May 1999:

Davis rolled over, hoping it would be easier to catch his breath on his back. Sara's suddenly increased ardor was both exhilarating and sometimes exhausting. She was always very passionate, he had delightfully discovered, but the last few days she had been inconsolable. No, that wasn't the right word. *Oh yeah,* he thought between breaths, *it's insatiable. She's been insatiable.*

The room was dark but enough light reflecting from the street made movement possible without stubbing your toe on the furniture. They were able to explore each other without difficulty—and that was all that mattered to the smiling man breathing through his mouth. He thought that raising his head on a pillow would speed his recovery, but in his search with his hands he had failed to find either of them. After their last tryst, who knows where the pillows were now, he thought, giggling silently, lest he disturb his nude wrestling partner.

Initially, she had been the gentle recipient, hesitant to assert herself as they learned to explore their feelings, but then she became very physical, matching his every movement. He had never had a woman who could give as much as she got. Sara was no limp wallflower in his bed. He imagined the taunt muscles he felt in her back were akin to what a woman felt when holding on to her male lover. It was a turn-on, feeling her respond in kind.

He turned toward Sara in the dark room. She rewarded him with the back of her head. *Something is wrong*, he surmised. His sore, tired, but sated body argued against putting it quite that way. Although the last few days were physically draining, their every attempt had become an exciting adventure. Making love two or three times a day was wonderful, he admitted. He walked taller at work—on the days he went to work. More and more he was working from home, and the funny part? He was actually getting more done. He tackled problems now with vigor. Nothing seemed too big to solve. Something about when the woman you loved craved your love that made a man feel invincible.

As he rested between bouts of pleasure, he wondered why women, at least this was what he had heard, lost interest in sex after a while. In his bliss, he was sure the answer to infidelity in men was for their women to screw their heads off. After wrestling with Sara, temptations was the name of one of his favorite American singing group, not something he struggled with controlling. By the time, he thought about it, she had erased the "it."

But in his spirit, he sensed something was wrong with her sudden need for constant fulfillment. Then the cold wind of reason blew over him. As if it was a physical reaction, David pulled the covers up over his body. It was colder in the room, much colder.

"David," Sara said, responding to his nearness by pushing back until her hips touched his taunt abdomen.

Almost instinctively, he wrapped his arm around the smoothness of her waist and pulled her closer to him.

"David," she repeated while struggling to ignore the pleasure of his touch, "the end of our country is near. This damn plague is out of control. The government hasn't announced it yet because…" She hesitated, trying to find words that weren't too painful to say.

David listened to her but didn't really hear a word she said. The distracting fragrance of the perfume in her hair was awakening his interest again. He was the kind of man who could enjoy the simple pleasure of just being in the enticing presence of a woman. He nudged his face into her long, soft, black hair and indulged in the softness and warmth of her body.

Sara realized, too late, that her attempt to gain some emotional strength from him was mistaken for another attempt at sex. *Who can blame him?* She sighed as she thought about her obsession with the same the last few days. *I've been acting like a whore.*

"David!" she said in her I'm-getting-annoyed-with-you tone. When she felt his face move out of her hair, she knew he had finally recognized she was serious. "The plague will kill everyone in Israel unless Jehovah God intervenes. Official estimates say that in less than a month from today everyone in our country will either be infected, dead, or dying from this form of anthrax."

David sat up and Sara turned around to face him.

"Is the epidemic that bad?" he asked sincerely, his eyes wide with surprise.

"Worse. The government has nothing to stop it. No nation will permit those who aren't affected to enter their borders, and who can blame them for that? This variant is a murderer. It kills everyone who becomes infected with it, and it is highly contagious. Those who bravely administer to the dying soon catch the plague. Our hospital beds are now full of the same dedicated doctors, nurses, and volunteers who earlier tried to administer to the sick. And despite their illness, they continue to do whatever they can for the dying."

David stared at Sara as he struggled to make sense of her alarming words. When he spoke, he was very subdued. "I know this is hard to believe, but I've been so busy I haven't kept up on the news about this. I'm very sorry. I knew that there were many who were very sick and some were dying but I thought it was something that would run its course like other diseases usually do."

"No, David, this is different. One of our enemies launched this deadly plague from somewhere near our coast, our government believes. This wasn't a natural disaster."

"How?" he asked, concern etched on his face.

"We really don't know how. If they launched a missile

loaded with the stuff at us, we should have picked that up on radar. Maybe somehow they smuggled it across our borders. The worst part is the virulent properties of anthrax were deliberately altered to make it communicable and more deadly. Everyone who has contracted anthrax has died—everyone. David. The disease has already spread across our land and into the neighboring countries of Lebanon, Jordan, and Egypt. All air travel to the Middle East has been halted. No ship is allowed to enter or leave the Mediterranean Sea. We're isolated from the rest of the world. That will slow down the spread of it but they know that will not stop it. Who's to say Russia might not nuke the whole of the Middle East to eradicate the spread of the plague before it reaches their borders."

David could see the enormity of the fear that she was battling. In his joy of being the recipient of her loving, he failed to notice the depth of her emotional needs. Some of her passion the last few days, he now realized, was her attempt to hide from her fears in the mind-numbness of physical fervor. He could now hear the tremor in her voice and the catch in her breath that told of her terrible fear. Why hadn't he noticed it before? He wanted to say the right words to put the fire back in her spirit but couldn't think of any.

His silence baffled Sara. He sat there looking past her as if he didn't believe their country was sinking like the Titanic. "Do you understand what I've been telling you, David?" she asked, pushing the sheet off her and sitting up in bed.

David remained silent. He was staring off, as if trying to remember something just out of his reach.

Now his behavior bothered her. *Has the ghastly outlook that we face finally gotten through to him?* she wondered. She couldn't blame him for that. But the look on his face wasn't of fear or concern, but a look of wonder and puzzlement. Sara noticed that even her nakedness, when she sat up in the bed, had failed to break the stone face of her lover. There had to be something on his mind all right. He had never failed to respond to any opportunity to catch a glimpse of her in the buff. His eyes, she'd once thought, possessed some kind of magnetic attraction to her breasts. She reached out and gently caressed his face, trying to bring him back to her. It took a moment.

"Sara," he said, so deep in thought that his eyes looked through her as he spoke. "I need to tell you something but I don't want you to think that I've lost my mind. During the last few days, I visited most of the local *Masjids* in the area. I didn't realize it then but something very strange is going on."

David was talking to her, she noticed, but that puzzled look was still on his face, as if he was watching another scene playing out in his mind far away.

"Sara, there wasn't one sick person in or around the temples. That's why I wasn't too concerned about the epidemic until now. I thought, if the poor of Beta-Israel weren't feeling the bite of the plague, then the rest of the country must be all right also."

"David, are you trying to tell me that no one in the Falashian synagogues here in Haifa have taken ill?" Sara asked skeptically.

The biting tone of her words surprised him. "Don't you believe me?

"Not one?" she asked again. "Are you sure?"

"Honey, I don't know of any member who has gotten sick or knows of anyone sick. I know that sounds crazy, but it's true," David said defensively. "I would be one of the first to be notified because it's my job to seek medical help for the poor."

Sara stared at him, shook her head, then abruptly climbed out of bed, and walked over to the window. The cold floor sent a chill up her bed-warmed legs.

David was somewhat bewildered by her actions.

Standing behind the curtains, Sara looked out at the activity occurring down on the street. Everything was relatively quiet now, but she still shuddered at the memory of the violent riots that had almost destroyed the city. As more police became ill, the people looted stores for medical supplies to try and stop the plague themselves. Others just used the chaos to beat, murder, and rob the weak. Only the power of the army restored calm. Risking infection, these brave volunteers let their weapons be judge and jury, until their voices were heard above the calamity.

As if on cue, an army truck, filled with what she could see were bagged dead corpses, moved slowly past the window. She knew it was carrying them out of the city to a very secret burying site near Mount Carmel. There the bodies were being cremated to try and stem the epidemic. *Israel is dying, and he didn't know it. How could he not know it? It's all over the TV, the news.* There were angry words festering in her heart. The walk to the window saved her from choking the answer out of him.

"Sara," David asked, as he walked up behind her and wrapped his warm body around her, "have you seen or heard of any sick Ethiopians in the hospital wards or in the schools serving as hospitals?"

"What kind of question is that?" She tried to turn and face him, the stupidity of that question reigniting her frustrations with him, but he held her tight against his body.

"Just think about it for a minute, please," David pleaded.

Sara looked past her judgment of him and tried to remember. The television cameras had broadcast the misery for the world to see and there were the photos in the newspapers and magazines. "Sure, now that I think about it I recall seeing a few sick Black people in some of the crowded hospitals." But he didn't say Black people, she reminded herself as he hugged her close. He was speaking about the Beta-Israel, the Ethiopian Jews exclusively. Could they really be immune to the epidemic? Was it possible David was right?

"David," Sara said, finally able to free herself, turn around in his arms, and face him.

He kissed her full on the mouth and pulled her close to him. She involuntarily returned the kiss but her mind was wrestling with the possibility that she might have stumbled on something. She could feel her concentration wavering as her body relaxed in response to the warmth of his touch. When his hands started a much-practiced voyage down her body, she broke the embrace. "No," she told herself and then shouted at David.

Surprised, his mouth dropped open, as did his arms letting her go. *Darn it.* She was immediately sorry for her abruptness when she saw the little-boy-like hurt in his eyes. *After all,* she reasoned, removing him from any blame, *he was only responding to the mixed signals she was sending the last few days.* But she had little choice this time. How could she explain to the children that they died because she was busy making love again to her boyfriend?

Sara held him at arm's length, kissed him quickly on the lips, and then walked toward the bed. Picking up the pillows off the floor on her way, she fluffed them up, climbed in bed, pulled the sheets up under her arms, and sat up against the pillows. Envisioning those she had seen who were sick, no one person jumped out at her. They were all Israelis, she reasoned. They were all dying.

Now, it was David who was confused. Yet even in that confusion, he took a momentary respite to watch her naked backside as she crossed the room. That was one of her best assets, he decided, trying to remember where he had first heard that old line. She carried herself so gracefully. At five feet seven inches tall and about one hundred and thirty-five pounds of toned muscle, she was a full package but there wasn't any fat on her. Her curves were more curvy than most, as he loved to say. From the mane of black hair that fell down to her shoulders—when he could talk her into letting it down—to her cute face, she was a dream. Not as beautiful as some of the women he had met but with a beauty you knew wasn't created every morning in front of a mirror. With or without makeup, Sara Jacobs was simply good looking by anyone's standards.

"I need you to confirm," Sara said, bringing his thoughts from her body back to the crisis at hand, "that the Beta-Israel community is immune to the plague."

Once again, he didn't say anything. He turned and looked out the window like she had done earlier. Like a mist blown away by a strong breeze, he finally took notice of the empty streets. The look of death was everywhere. How could all of this of have happened in the few days he was down in the synagogue helping with the remodeling? David shook his head in disgust. The apocalyptic scene played out in his imagination like a grade-B movie.

"Call some of the other synagogues in the country and see if this is true," he heard her request.

David turned to face her and to tell her that wouldn't be necessary. He didn't say anything. Instead, he walked over to the bed and sat down next to her. He brushed a few wild hairs from her face and looked directly into those amazing eyes. "Sara, it's true," he said, appearing more confident and composed. "I remember now something I heard *Abba* Gette say. 'None of the Falashian in the synagogue would die from the epidemic. None of those who still worshipped according to the law of the prophets would take ill.' I thought he was just talking. You know how he likes to ramble on. But now that I look back, the last few days have confirmed it for me. None of the members of the church have taken ill, none of them. Three days ago the synagogue was full during worship and afterward the kids were running around playing like always."

"How is that possible, David? You must be mistaken." Doubt was written across her inquiring face. "The epidemic is killing everyone, Arab and Jew, Black and White."

"Sara, I don't know why, but it is true." He held her hand. "But I'm convinced that Rabbi Gette knows why."

Sara felt the mystical stirrings of hope. Twice burned, she was very reluctant to yield to it, yet. "Why didn't you say something to me about this before now?" Anger was seeping out of her every word.

David just shrugged his shoulders.

Annoyed, Sara threw the covers off and pushed him out of her way. Again, barely being able to resist the urge to vent her anger upside his thick head, she stormed into the bathroom.

David listened as the shower came on. He began to understand why she was upset with him and felt she had every right to be. He was acting as thoughtless and cavalier as the officials had who let Beta-Israel die in the desert of the Sudan. He knew there wasn't any intentional neglect on his part.

'*The road to hell is paved with good intentions*,' he recalled hearing someone say in Synagogue. While trying to come up with the words to explain that to Sara, he suddenly could clearly hear the shower water running.

Looking up, he noticed the bathroom door was now open and there was Sara with just her head stuck out looking at him.

"Sara, I'm sorry," he said to the lovely head wet with soap bubbles. "I didn't realize how serious the epidemic had become until now. I was so wrapped up in my job that I never realized life was dying around me."

"I know that, honey," she said softly. Gone was the abrupt tone and stern countenance. Having regained her composure, she explained, "There isn't anyone I know of more caring about others than you. Come on in and shower with me. I want you to go somewhere and tell your story to a friend of mine."

David jumped at the showery proposition.

"A shower only, knucklehead," she said to the gleam in his eyes and his purposeful strut. "Nothing else is going to happen." With that said, she disappeared into the steaming bathroom.

Stunned by her announcement, he stuck his head around the shower curtain, planning to plead his case. He watched as rivulets of white soapy water cascaded down her tanned shoulders, as she rinsed the shampoo out of her hair, and joined at the crease of her hips. He shook his head at the sight, took a deep breath, smiled, rubbed his hands together, and stepped gingerly into the hot shower.

"Sure," he whispered, doubting her resolve.

Minutes later, he grudgingly came to realize that this time no meant no.

Sara took David to a secret Mossad safe house in Haifa, near the Japanese Art Museum on Hanassi Boulevard. Before leaving, she called Simon and told him the story. The moment she hung up, the wheels were put in motion. Every member of the Falashian sect would be checked to determine if they were touched by the epidemic.

Simon hurried out the door, leaving word to call him at the safe house, or in his car, the minute any definitive information arrived.

Sara answered the knock at the door and ushered Simon into the living room. David turned to see a bearded man about his height and weight entering the room.

"David, this is Simon Levine, my boss."

"Hi, glad to meet you, Mr. Levine."

He was in his forties, David guessed as he shook his hand. They exchanged curious looks as each tried to read the other. Simon's cold analytical eyes were a match for David's smiling, dancing brown ones.

Each man had found it easy to make eye contact with other people, at times staring so intently they caused people to look away. A mutual respect immediately passed between them as they sat down on the couch.

Sara had explained to David that she worked for the local government as an accountant who traveled around Haifa, investigating foreign investors.

He expected that this Simon guy must be some big shot that Sara wanted to impress. He would do that for her, he decided.

David started telling Simon his story before Sara had a chance to sit down beside him. Simon listened without comment as David's words held him in awe. Only years of practice held back his questions as hope flirted with his imagination. *Could the story this Ethiopian Jew is telling be true?* Simon wondered. He watched him closely for any sign that he was lying. Misguided revelations and cures were as rampant in the country as the plague itself. Every nut had proclaimed a miracle cure—some even as their bodies vomited the truth.

David finished, confident he'd told all he knew.

Simon nodded. "Mister Yasuda, I thank you for being honest with me. I'm a government official who has friends in the minister's office. Sara called, in hopes I could pass this information to the right people. The Israeli government is desperate to find a cure for this epidemic that is killing our nation. There might be something in the genes of your ancestors, I'm just guessing, that's resistant to this bacteria. If that's so and we can isolate it, our beloved nation might survive after all. Forgive me for being rude," Simon explained, as he stood up and

offered David his hand, "but I must get this important information into the proper hands. Every hour thousands more become infected with this killer."

David stood shaking his head. "No problem, sir. I just hope
this information will help."

Sara thanked Simon for coming and walked him to the
door.

"Sara," Simon whispered in her ear as he hugged her goodbye, "I want to see you in my office as soon as you can get
away from him without raising any questions."

"That's no problem, sir," she said as she walked him to the
door. "We discussed it before you arrived. I explained to David that once you heard his story I would have to help you get
things started. I'll take him home and meet you at the office."

"Good. I'll see you then," Simon said, walking out the
door.

Sara watched him open his car door and then stop. She
knew him well enough to know he had thought of something
important. She walked toward the car as Simon turned around.
He shook his head in admiration when he realized she had
read his mind.

"Sara, stay with him for now," Simon said when she
reached him. "Stop in my office in the morning and we will
review our alternatives. He is far too valuable to leave alone
until we can be sure that what he said is true. I believe he may
be the key to our finding the way out of this pit our Arab
brothers have pushed us into. I can feel it. Maybe he's our Jo-
seph, and you're his 'Coat of Many Colors,'" Simon said,
smiling at her.

She blushed a little at his retort. *Are those seeds of hope in
his tired eyes?* she wondered. That wish warmed her.

Simon drove off as Sara waved good-bye to him. *Yes,
maybe God has finally shown us a way out of hell.*

"How did that go?"

Sara kissed David softly on the lips. She stepped back,
crossed two fingers on each hand, and then raised an eyebrow.
"We should know something tangible by tomorrow, honey."
She started to walk away and then stopped. "For some reason,

I'm starving," she said, turning around and rubbing her belly. "Let's go home and get something to eat."

David had another suggestion but wisely kept that wish to himself—for now.

CHAPTER 12

Despite the uncertainty of David's information about the Falashians, Sara and David shared a quiet evening together. She thought about calling Simon and asking how things were going but decided it might take all night to gather enough information to make an honest evaluation.

The dinner they cooked together was delightful and, surprisingly, nothing about the terrible crisis occurring outside his apartment touched them. Both lovers struggled with that cruel reality but managed to lose themselves in the bright eyes of the person beside them. Did they feel a little guilty? Yeah. The answer to that guilt was to concentrate more on the wonderful person in their arms. Concentrate they did, a few times, until fatigue ushered them into a world behind their eyelids that was minus the hate destroying their country.

By the time Sara reached Simon's office the next morning, the doorway out of hell had slammed cruelly in their faces. The deep lines on his sleep-deprived face said as much when she walked in the door. The voice that asked her to lock his door and take a seat next to him lacked any positive tone. That obvious fact drained the moisture from her mouth as she pulled a chair up to his desk. Sitting near him, she could see that the color had drained out of his face and he was wearing the same clothes from yesterday.

"Sara, David was right," Simon said, exhaustion showing in his listless voice and slumped shoulders. "Almost all of the Ethiopian Jews we tested were free of Anthrax. Some of them worked in the hospitals where the exposure is the greatest, and, Sara, they show none of the symptoms, none. Their work records indicate that they never call off sick. The joke around one hospital staff was that they must have found a cure for the common cold."

"Then there is something to their immunity," Sara said, softly clapping her hands together. "Good, I thought you were saying we were at the end of our rope."

"We are at the end of our rope, Sara. All night we have tried running tests on the blood of some wonderful Falashian volunteers who show no signs of the plague, and we have found nothing in their blood that is different—much to the chagrin of some of the bigots in this country—absolutely nothing!" Simon said, while pounding his fist on his desk. "We even gave ten of the sickest children blood transfusions from Falashian volunteers. Everyone was elated when the children's health immediately improved. You should have seen it, Sara. It was mystical how quickly they recovered. Some had had fevers as high as 106 degrees for hours. After the transfusions, their temperatures dropped to normal almost immediately. It was amazing, Sara. I finally thought we had the answer. Some were even sitting up, talking to their doctors..." Simon's voice trailed off on the last words. His head dropped down as he avoided looking her in the eye.

Confusion made her frown. Why was he—

"I got a call just before you walked in. All the children were dead by morning," he said looking up at her. He sighed heavily and placed his head in his hands. "Why, Sara, why? What the hell is going on here?"

She felt her spirit surrendering to this tidal wave of failure. The vision of the horrible deaths of those young children was a cold slap in the face. "I don't know," she finally answered, in a voice lacking any strength of purpose. "Whatever it is that is in them, must remain in them."

Sara sat back in her seat, staring solemnly out the window. It was as if this last gasp had stolen the soul from her body. For a few minutes, neither of them spoke another word. The busy voices of the people in the next offices filtered into their silence. Hope was the crutches that had helped them to go on. It was finally having to watch that thin thread of hope shattered by the stark reality of their situation that tugged at Simon and Sara's emotions.

"We're still trying to locate a possible gene or something in their DNA that would explain their resistance," an unconvincing Simon told Sara, now sitting with her head down, hiding the tears leaking down her face.

She surprised him when she suddenly sat up straight with a look of newfound confidence. After his failed attempt to implant some optimism into the conversation, he was caught off-guard. Wiping the tears from her face with the back of her hands, she stood up and walked to the window behind Simon. She then turned around and pointed at him. "Remember—" she said in a tone of renewed optimism. "—remember what David said, boss?"

Simon tried to figure out what she was talking about but drew a blank.

"He said that the high priest knew why they are immune to the plague."

Simon squinted, as he tried to see where she was headed with this. He had spent most of the night going over the conversation with David without seeing any other options. Had he, in his impatience, missed something?

Sara watched the puzzled look form on his face. She enjoyed her slight, momentary advantage over her very competent boss. She stretched out her advantage until she saw his patience was waning. "I think there's something else we don't know. If David is right, and he has been right so far, this Gette knows why they are immune."

Simon didn't answer her right away. He was trying to see the whole picture through eyes other than his own desperate ones. Was this the old, "grabbing at straws," syndrome that they were trained to avoid when under duress. *Reason out every move*, his past experience shouted. *Look beyond the beautiful fruit trees in the Garden of Eden and find the serpent, before the serpent finds you.*

"Sara, you've got to tell David everything," Simon told his

shocked young protégé as he sat up in his chair. He watched her battle with his reasoning. "There may be more to this than he is telling you," he continued before she could respond to him. "Hell! He may have answers that he doesn't realize he has. That might shock him into remembering or, if nothing else, reveal to him the importance of the slightest bit of information he may have overlooked. Maybe he is protecting someone or some religious secret."

"But it would crush him," Sara replied, surprising herself. *Stupid answer*, she scolded as she waited for his angry retort. Simon didn't answer her but the look his face sure did. She sighed. "Of course, you're right, Simon. Forgive me. I was thinking of one man and not a nation."

"If you would rather I did it, we could bring him here and break the news to him."

"No, sir, that won't be necessary. I'll tell him." She bit down on her bottom lip, walked to the door, and stopped. Pausing, she turned and gave her friend and confidant one long and emotional look.

He gave her a smile in return that told her he understood how hard this was going to be. What he held back was his knowledge on why that was.

She took a deep breath and returned the smile. Simon watched the door close on a woman who didn't realize she had fallen in love with her assignment.

The red light was a welcome respite from the mental battle raging in Sara's heart and mind as she slowed at the intersection. She stared at the red circle as if waiting for it to lash out at her and call her all the names she was calling herself. Reason and patriotism were the powers that drove her to David's house. A love she didn't yet understand made that drive twice as long as normal. Add to that the occasional stranger she spotted standing on a corner or in a yard with the blank face of one who looked into hell and realized the futility of their future.

Then on some corners, she slowed and looked into the stoic faces of heavily armed soldiers wearing gas masks that still patrolled the city. Well more like sat in their vehicles now and watched the few other vehicles on the streets. The plague had taken the starch and protest from the people. The streets were almost empty as she drove.

Another red light beckoned to her as she approached the next corner. She found that a small comfort. *It's strange how our relationship with objects or things can change as we need them.* In the past, the red lights on the way to David's house were demons that rejoiced in her impatience. Now they were friends that understood the painful decisions that awaited her and were giving her time to reflect. Today she silently prayed for them to maintain their strength long enough for the right words to form in her heart.

Green lights became the gremlins that were pushing her over the precipice. Rushing to destroy a relationship she placed almost as much value on as the love of country. Her practical side understood the importance of the drive to his apartment and the words she carried. Simon's edict was right on line—these were desperate times and needed desperate measures.

What slowed her progress was—she pushed those thoughts from her consciousness. To think was to acknowledge something her pride wanted to mislabel as duty.

"Hey, he has to understand, this is my job," she argued with herself as she slowly turned onto his street. "It's what I'm trained to do." She kindly let two parked cars pull out and race panickedly down the road in front of her. "We're both adults." Mentally, she counted down the blocks to his apartment. "I never intended to deceive him." She obeyed every stop sign, looking both ways twice before moving carefully into each intersection. Three times, she waited for the soldiers manning those intersections to wave her on before moving. "I didn't really deceive. I just didn't tell him everything. A woman doesn't have to tell everything."

Sara's real fear she hid from herself. It wasn't David she was afraid of losing—it was Sara.

She pulled up behind David's parked van. *Okay, girl, let's get it together. People are dying and he might be able to save lives. This is bigger than you and David. Duty calls.* This wasn't how she would handle this, but orders were orders.

She pulled down the visor and checked her hair in the mirror. Everything was in place. Inadvertently, her eyes met.

Looking down from his balcony, David confirmed the sound he heard was Sara's car. He watched for a moment as she pulled up and parked behind his van. "Yes!" Smiling, he hurried back into the apartment to make sure everything was perfect.

"She's early. Matches, where are the matches?" David stopped in his tracks. "Wait a minute. What am I'm doing? Oh no, how stupid. She may not want a romantic lunch after all the misery going on all around us. How stupid—stupid! She called and said she wanted to come over and talk to me about something, not to eat." David rushed into the kitchen that served as his dining room, snatched the chilled white wine off the table, and hid it in the refrigerator behind the milk. The china and wine glasses he dumped into the sink. Looking around quickly, he saw everything looked normal but—

He clutched the dozen yellow roses he'd been stunned he was able to find earlier and yanked them from their vase tossing them into the garbage can.

The reluctant eyes looking back at her in the mirror tried but they couldn't look past duty and the right thing to do. Sara shook her head, moved the rear view mirror back in place, and got out of the car. She locked it and walked around David's van to the steps leading up to his apartment. At the base of the steps, she stopped. That was as far as Sara the woman could go. The emotions that she had allowed herself to indulge in the last few months refused to die or submit to reason. She knew each step up would be like "walking the plank" for the new love that rose up from knowing David. That surprised her, standing there with trembling knees at the base of his steps.

She somehow knew each step up would erase the woman she had become in his strong arms. A woman she liked, a woman fully living her life now, instead of just surviving. Each step up signaled a goodbye to the passion, goodbye to his closeness, and goodbye to the man she had grown to need like breathing.

Part of her resented those feelings—a part of her that opposed submitting to feeling that way about any man. But over time with David, he had finally silenced those voices. Now fate, her boss, and reason had resurrected them, giving them a new and stronger voice.

"One step at a time, just lift your foot, Sara, let's go. There's no time for this."

That first tentative step led to another. The third came easier. She was half way up the steps when she raised her head. When she reached his door it was too late for the woman in love. The trained agent was now in control.

"Come in," David shouted to the person ringing his doorbell. "Hi, sweetie, glad you came over."

Sara smiled as David walked out from the kitchen and kissed her on the cheek. "Sit down David, we have to talk."

"Sure, babe. Let me turn off the oven."

"Were you cooking?"

"Well…yes. Nothing special," he lied.

"Okay. Go ahead and finish. I guess it can wait that long."

David kissed her softly on the lips and walked into the kitchen. Sara sat down on the couch and tried to relax. She grabbed both knees when she noticed her hands were shaking. His was a modest apartment that gave a visitor the feeling of comfort. It was easy to relax here because everything in his living room eschewed uniqueness. His place had the warmth of a comfortable motel. There were no pictures of family or friends on the furniture. The pictures on the walls were of beautiful land and seascapes. *Again, reaching out to the dreams we all have.*

"There," David said, walking into the living room. "Everything is turned off." He sat down next to her.

The joy written across his face didn't go unnoticed by the

lady searching for the right way—the best way—to tell him. He had that look, that look that always warmed her spirit. His dancing eyes left no doubt that the woman reflected in them was the light that chased away the darkness. No matter the intensity of a disagreement between them, he never let her fear where she stood with him. Sara's resolve sank to a lower level. She knew the words she had to say might forever cripple their dance.

She stood and motioned for David to say seated, needing the distance to say what was on her mind.

David began to sense whatever was bothering her was bad news.

"David, we need you to talk to your priest and find out why your people are immune to the plague. That is our only hope. Nothing else has worked. We—"

"Honey," David said, cutting her off, "the father gets back late today. I was going to ask him, anyway." *Didn't she know that?* David wondered as he watched her pacing the room. No, something else was wrong—he could feel it.

"I believe you, David, but you have to understand how important this is. You have to get the answer from him, you have to."

"Sara Jacobs."

Sara turned to face him. He only used her full name when he was worried.

"What is it?" he asked. "What is bothering you?"

She could only stare at him. She couldn't do it. She had to, she argued. *David, forgive me.* "David, I was sent here by my boss Simon. He isn't just a businessman. He's the head of the Mossad department assigned to a branch of internal security. More specifically, he is in charge of the investigation of the Falashian Sect." David stood up with a look that prompted Sara to hurry. "David, I work for—"

"*Wait!*" he shouted. "Sara, are you trying to tell me you are a—a—" He couldn't say it.

"David, I'm an agent with the Mossad. I was assigned—"

Again, he cut her off, only this time by walking over to the window where she was standing. The eyes she looked up at bore little resemblance to their dancing twins. Something in her responded negatively to the revulsion she believed she saw in them.

"I'm an agent, dammit, and a good one, at that. I won't apologize for doing my job. I would do anything to help our country. I also know you will do whatever it takes to save her. We are adults, David. Let's act like adults. Thousands of people are dying a horrible death. You may have the keys to save their lives. That's all that's important at this moment. We will have to worry about us later. There isn't time for that now. You have to hurry to the priest's home and talk to him. You do understand that, don't you? Every minute wasted another person gets infected, another person dies."

He didn't hear most of what she said. Only enough to figure out she had deceived him without explaining why. The pain in his chest grew in direct proportion to the coldness of her words—words without feeling.

Sara felt a strength of purpose when she inserted the despairing calamity that was Israel. The faces of the sick and dying was what fueled her engine. Sara, the patriot was now in charge having relegated Sara, the plaything, to some obscure place in her memory.

"I'll go over to the rabbi's home and confront him about the immunity," David said with a look on his face she had never seen. The light of life turned off in his eyes. "You are right, Sara. How could I have been so foolish?"

"What?"

"I lost track of what's important. People are dying and here I am making a romantic meal for another beautiful agent who climbed into my bed to get information out of me. You would think I would be use to that by now." He grabbed his keys off the hook near the door. "I'll call you if I find out anything. Please lock up when you leave. Oh—" he said, stopping as he opened the door, "Agent Jacobs, my personal papers are under my mattress if you need to see them."

The door slamming wasn't the only thing that startled Sara. What other agents climbing in his bed? Did Simon assign others to try to seduce him? How far did they—

She didn't want to answer that. Sara sat down on the couch and lowered her face into her hands. This plague was destroying everything. Sara rocked back and forth as she tried to comfort herself. Her thoughts kept returning to what David said. Unable to cope, she got up and walked out, leaving his door wide open.

CHAPTER 13

Flying over the Red Sea, June 1999:

S imon felt a firm hand on his shoulder. The distraction chased away the sordid nightmare that was his dying country. The copilot, Captain Aaron "Shooter" Kennet, knelt down in front of him.

"Sir," he shouted above the din of the aircraft, "the pilot asked me to inform you that we are approximately ten minutes from the African coast and less than an hour from touchdown. As you know, we plan on taking the shortest route. That means crossing the Eritrean borders to get to Ethiopia. We believe we can sneak past their radar stations before they know we were ever there. If they do pick us up, we will have to by-pass Eritrea and put down in southern Ethiopia from lack of fuel. That could mean a long walk for everyone."

"Then please don't get caught, okay?" Simon teased.

The copilot squeezed Simon's arm in agreement as the man stood up and staggered back to the front of the swaying helicopter.

David listened to Simon's short conversation with the copilot. Apparently, they were very close to landing. The pressure to find the "Messiah Drug" was starting to build. He thought for a minute about praying but held his peace. *It will be up to God if we're successful*, he resolved. *.I think the Heavens have been bombarded enough with supplications*. That revelation did little to lessen his growing apprehensions.

David believed he could find it. Now he would have to prove that he could. It was on his faith in the words of his high priest that had convinced Simon to attempt this risky mission. Abba Gette, David sincerely believed, was as honest as any man he had ever known. One had only to look past the hot rhetoric to see the truth. The man loved to talk, that was for sure, David remembered lovingly. Abba Gette's powerful voice reached past the vibrating hum of the helicopter blades into his troubled thoughts...

"We are the righteous descendants of the great King Solomon," Yehoshua Gette told the crowed *masjid*. His hands extended straight out. He then spread them wide to include his audience. "Jehovah led us to this promised land. We have no one to thank but him. We are gracious to everyone who helped us get here, but we will praise only Jehovah." A ripple of mumbled agreement reached him from the men assembled there. One of those men was David.

He listened to the sermon as he had many times over the last five years. Just being able to sit and listen to this man was a blessing. Sometimes he struggled to pay attention to Abba Gette when he was teaching because the stories of his life were even more dramatic than his messages. "He is a walking Holy Man," David had once described him to a friend, "One right out of the Holy Scriptures, a Falashian Prophet."

For the last year, David, along with eleven other young men, received the great privilege of sitting with the elders as they debated the Books of the Prophets. From that group of young men David was picked to receive personal lessons from the high priest in exchange for ministering to his daily needs. During these private lessons, David learned, in-depth, the long history of the Falashian people. It was during that last session, he recalled, just before the high priest left for a pilgrimage to the Holy City of Jerusalem, that he first heard the rabbi speak of God's "gift." The priest was incensed over the rude treatment he'd received from an orthodox Jewish rabbi as they discussed the history of Solomon and the Queen of Sheba.

After dinner that night, David, walking out on the balcony for a breath of fresh air, was surprised to find Rabbi Gette sitting alone in the corner of the balcony staring out at the ships in the dark harbor. Reverently, David walked over and sat down at his feet. Rabbi Gette didn't acknowledge him until David touched his arm.

"Abba, forgive me for disturbing you. Share with me the thing that troubles you."

The holy man looked down at his favorite disciple. It had always been a joy to teach him the Words of God. He was like a sea sponge, absorbing every word and blessed with the memory of an elephant. "David, my son, I was trying to understand the people who refuse to accept our place in the history of Israel. Rabbi Meir is a fool. He had the nerve to call me an African. Can you believe that?"

David shook his head. He had no idea why that was insulting to his rabbi but it seemed like the best answer to his question. He'd never seen his rabbi so angry. The whisper-thin white hair of his beard couldn't hide the wrinkles of an angry man. As David watched, the rabbi's face contorted more as he began to talk.

"We are the chosen of God!" he divulged after pounding his bony hand against his chest. "He has given us a gift that no other nation has ever received, the 'Sweat of Angels,' a powerful elixir that will protect us during the coming great tribulation."

David was stunned. Not as much by what he had heard as what he was seeing. There was something strange, something very strange about the expression on the elder's face.

"He has chosen us," the priest proclaimed loudly, as if addressing thousands from the twelve tribes of Israel who were gathered below his balcony, "and one day He will exalt us above these blind people. Jehovah God has joined us with the seed of King David." Rabbi Gette stood up, raised his fist to the heavens, and shouted over the balcony. "We are Jews!" He looked down at David—who sat flabbergasted at the display of emotion from his leader—then turned and stormed off into the house.

David stood up and looked in the window to make sure the rabbi was going to his room. Good, he was. What's this about an elixir, about sweat? *Should I dare ask him about it?*

David turned around and looked at the rabbi's chair. He had always thought it anointed. He wouldn't admit it but he felt more spiritual when he sat in the chair. It was as if some of the essence of the priest remained on its surface. He ran his hands slowly up and down the arms of the wicker chair. The main reason he thought the chair was special was because it belonged to Rabbi Gette. Silly or not, David felt more in touch with his spirituality when he sat in the chair. After looking in the window once more, he sat in the chair. In his enlightened state, he felt he understood Rabbi Gette's anger now. His words echoed through David's spirit. *'Solomon is our Father. Our bloodline runs to him, no one can remove that. No amount of hate can erase our history.'*

David was very familiar with the story of Solomon. It was sacred and very important to every member of the Falashian Sect. It was a story still told over evening cooking fires in Ethiopia and always in the synagogues here. David sat back in the chair and imagined it was a pulpit and he was the rabbi. From his pulpit, he preached to his imaginary audience.

"Solomon—from 961 to 922 BC—was made King of Israel by God. Early in his reign, because of his faithful service, God asked him to choose the desire of his heart and God would grant it. Solomon pondered on God's promise. Finally, he asked God to give him the wisdom to judge God's people fairly. Pleased with his unselfish request, God granted it and also blessed him with great prosperity. Tales of Solomon's great wisdom and wealth spread to the far reaches of the known world. Pilgrims from lands near and very far came to see the fantastic city of Solomon and to hear the extraordinary words from the great King.

"Yet, for all his wisdom Solomon couldn't see his own weaknesses. He had seven hundred wives and three hundred concubines, or mistresses, yet he never learned to control his lust. Even after God told the Children of Israel not to inter-marry with people who worshipped other gods, Solomon failed to heed God's warning. He took wives of all faiths and beliefs, even idol worshippers."

David stood up and looked out over the busy harbor from the porch. History recorded the vaunted wisdom of Solomon. Those were facts not myths. But how could such a wise man choose a woman over the law of God? He already had more wives than he could ever—

Memories of his own failures with women silenced David's judgment. He shook his head and sat back down in the rabbi's chair. Soon his mind drifted off as he tried imagining how captivating a woman was the mother of the Falashian sect to have so dazzled the King of the Jews.

David stood, looked out over his imaginary congregation, and continued his sermon. "One day, when pilgrims from around the world came to present gifts to the great king, an elaborately adorned ebony woman walked seductively down the main aisle of King Solomon's court. This queen came from the land of Sheba in eastern Africa—a dark woman so strikingly beautiful she stunned the court of Solomon. She came, like many other pilgrims, to hear the great words of the Ruler of Israel."

The strength of her presence, David reasoned, must have stopped all idle conversations as she strolled brazenly straight toward the king's throne. She must have been breathtaking to so capture the king's attention.

Mekeda, the Queen of Sheba, probably relished in the attention she was getting. She must have taken hours to prepare for that moment. The elders taught that her black hair was inter-woven with long strings of the purest gold. The yellow and black contrast was striking. Nothing, even the elegant, gold-laced pompadour could distract from the beauty of the face and curvaceous body that it adorned.

A body wrapped so tight in fine silk that she took their breath away. Every curve of her body was lined in colors that must have originated in the sun. Yellows that were so pure you wondered if bits of sunlight weren't trapped within. The stripes of blue that ran down and around her torso were so true that they must have been painted with pieces of the summer sky.

It had to be her eyes, David surmised as he thought about

the legendary queen. The body of a woman can ignite the fires of passion but the eyes of a mysterious woman can consume a man's soul.

"Queen Mekeda," David resumed preaching to his invisible audience, "had enough wisdom herself to bring King Solomon all of the things he craved. Behind her trailed a hundred muscular bearers arrayed in huge brightly colored ceremonial feathers. On their shoulders, they carried large vials of gold and exotic spices. Her private barges carried over four tons of gold and spices for the king. He was wonder-struck. She had given him golden gifts, but he now craved the gift-giver.

"Falashian legend says the queen realized the great king was very wise and very much a man. She cunningly resisted all of the attention Solomon lavished upon her. So enticed by her indifference, he was willing to give anything in his kingdom to have her. Her aloof attitude toward him so fired his passions that he offered her the desires of her heart if she gave herself to him. In a final act born of desperation, he took her to see the most private of his rooms of gold."

"'Behind this door,' the king proudly proclaimed to his mysterious visitor, 'is the wealth of Israel.' He slowly pushed opened the massive wooden door. The torch in his hand ignited the room in such a display of colors, at first, they had to cover their eyes. Solomon turned to receive her admiration. Sheba smiled weakly at him as if indifferent to the awesome spectacle.

"Solomon's spirit was crushed. Sheba, ever the seductress, knew when to give a desperate man a spark of hope. She sauntered slowly past the king into the room.

"She was awed by the magnitude of his fortune. With her back to him, the expression of wonder that bore the truth of her feelings was hidden. The riches and wealth she saw were beyond anything she had ever imagined. There were mounds of gold coins and jeweled chalices of the finest craftsmanship. Golden buckets of rubies and diamonds sparkled like a million fireflies. The walls were covered with the furs of exotic animals. From the ceiling dangled an exhibit of breathtakingly beautiful multi-colored silks. The brightness of the king's treasures, however, failed to unloose the fine threads woven around the ebony beauty that sauntered past the innumerable fortune."

David looked out at the harbor and shook his head. It was estimated that even by today's standards, he once read, that King Solomon's wealth reportedly made him the richest man to ever live. Yet consumed with lust for her, he broke a sacred vow. Blinded by his desire, he took her to see the most important treasure in all of the Israel. "Surely this will astound her," the lascivious king decided. The priest guarding the temple gate protested mildly—lest the king slay him—about bringing an unclean person into the inner Temple of God. Solomon ignored his priest and held the curtain open as the queen stepped into the inner chamber. The forbidden room was known as the Holiest of Holies.

The king led her to the center of the room. The chamber was empty but for a chest sitting on a table in the center of the room surround by seven candles. Queen Mekeda knew the significance of the chest-like structure. It was the legendary Ark of the Covenant. The stories had reached Sheba about an ark carried before the Children of Israel into battle. Legends told of the impossible victories they achieved. Word of their mighty deeds spread around the world. Yet, there it was, right in front of her.

"'That's our Ark of the Covenant,' the king needlessly explained.

"The Queen of Sheba was impressed and suddenly very afraid. She could actually feel the power of the ark radiating on her skin like sunlight on a hot day. She had never known such fear before, until now. Yet, the fear didn't stop her.

"King Solomon slowly walked the obviously frightened woman closer to the Ark and explained its history to the stunned woman. From the blessings upon the Children of Israel, to the curses on those who opposed them, the ark was their link with the Most High.

Sheba just stared at the exquisitely crafted chest-like structure with what for her was reverence. Solomon struggled to control himself. Finally, he thought, as the beautiful woman stood motionless before the Ark of the Most High.

"*'The ark,'* Solomon explained, *'was built by Moses and the Children of Israel to carry the two tablets of the Ten Commandments, Aaron's staff, and the manna that God fed to the Children of Israel in the wilderness.'* The most revered religious icon in the history of the world was less than twenty feet away from her. She was impressed!

"Before they consummated their relationship, Solomon, true to his word, inquired of her what she desired of him. She asked to be able to enter privately into the Holy Room and be able to worship at the *A*rk, in hopes that her poor country might also be blessed. Solomon agreed and had an entrance quickly constructed. It was a private passageway for his dark queen that led into the most revered section of the temple.

"When it was completed, she came to him. She became his queen. Later, the queen spoke to Solomon, revealed to him she was with his child, and wanted her child born in her homeland. He was so enraptured with her, he could withhold no gift. He agreed to let her depart. He secretly gave her more gold, in her departure, than she gave him upon arrival.

"When her barges landed in Sheba, she unveiled the Ark of the Covenant her people stole from Solomon's Temple. Her priest took the *A*rk and hid it in a temple reportedly near the city of Askum."

David had heard the rumors that it is there today, hidden away by priest sworn to silence and willing to protect it with their lives.

"It is believed King Solomon was crushed by her deceit, but unrelenting in his love for her. He placed his priests under a vow of secrecy with the promise of immediate death to all, should one word leak out.

"The Queen of Sheba had a son by Solomon whom she named Menelik, meaning son of the wise man in Arabic. Later, after he had come of age, she sent him to his father for his blessing. Solomon graciously received him as his son. He so loved the mother of Menelik that he never questioned him about the stolen ark, or its resting-place. Menelik later returned home and ruled the kingdom of Sheba."

Finished with his sermon, David sat down in the sacred chair and mulled over the priest's last words. What tribulation was he talking about? What was that about angels? He would have to question him once the great man calmed down.

CHAPTER 14

June 1999:

Minutes from entering Eritrean air space helicopter pilot Captain Benjamin "Benji" Mayer, a ten-year Israeli Army Air Corps veteran, looked out at the black, moonlit water rushing under them. Benji didn't want Aaron to see he was fidgeting in his seat in anticipation of completing the last leg of their mission.

Truth was Captain Aaron "Shooter" Kennet, his copilot and the weapons officer, had no idea what Benji was thinking. The reported death of Aaron's only sister from the epidemic had occupied most of his thoughts during the flight. He didn't share his pain with his flying mate, lest Benji insist he remain grounded and in mourning. Aaron had flown with Benji for three years and they had gotten to know each other very well. Both trusting in the flying abilities of the other without question.

Benji fought the growing urge to take over control of their helicopter. As ordered, they were flying over the Red Sea on autopilot. He knew this mission was too important to risk pilot error, but he had more confidence in his ability than in the autopilot. This was the type of mission he dreamed about since he was a kid, flying into battle with everything depending on his skills. Darting from one hot zone into another, with missiles streaking through the air, as he fought his way to complete his mission and then to return safety. His orders—and if nothing else, an Israeli pilot understood the importance of following orders—were to fly over the water in autopilot. According to those orders, once they neared land, the controls were his.

"Landfall in five minutes, Captain Benjamin," he heard his navigator indicate.

It was one of the few times, Lieutenant Eli Ben-Hon had spoken since they departed on this final leg of their mission. Benjamin wasn't sure if it was because this was Eli's first mission with Shooter and himself, or the understandable apprehension of trying to find their landing site in the dark without the aid of active radar or a satellite signal that kept him too busy to talk.

"Switching from auto to manual on my count, three...two...one. Okay, Shooter, I've got control," Benji said with an unmistakable hint of pleasure in his voice.

Shooter looked over at his commanding officer and just shook his head. He knew that behind the night-goggles Benji's eyes were wide blue circles. He had seen that look on his face before and knew how bad Benji wanted to feel the HH-60 Desert Hawk respond to his touch. Hell, Shooter knew that he was starting to feel the same rising excitement. *We share the same passions*, Shooter mused as the craft dipped slightly and then rose a few feet. He leaned to his right as he anticipated the next move. The helicopter swerved right and then left, as the pilot searched out the aircraft's responsiveness.

Shooter lowered his night-goggles in place and searched the approaching shoreline. He knew Benji was feeling the *burn,* as pilots called the burst of adrenaline they felt just before risking their lives. That feeling was mutual.

The red light above the ten passengers' heads started blinking. Major Yuri Steiner was suddenly awake and standing, Simon noted. Laughing to himself, he wondered if the blinking light overhead was wired to the major's ass. The tight quarters were now alive with the sound of weapon safeties being freed as highly trained soldiers prepared for war.

"We are over Eritrean air space," the pilot's voice echoed, silencing everyone. "We are less than a hundred miles from touchdown. If all goes well, that will be in less than twenty-five minutes. Stay buckled. The locals are reported to have shoulder-held anti-aircraft missiles. We may have to change direction sharply without warning."

As luck would have it, Lieutenant Ben-Hon spotted a Doppler radar station with passive radar, making a sweep in their direction, and gave orders to dip down beneath the horizon. Quickly Benji whipped the Desert Hawk around, erasing their forward speed, and then dropped down to thirty feet. At the same time, he worried that he didn't hurt any of his passengers with that quick maneuver.

"Did they pick us up?"

"I don't think so, Benji," Shooter answered, searching his radar scope. "Odd though, they were looking in our direction when they turned on, odd."

"Maybe not," Benji answered as he swung the helicopter around due west again. "We were coming in from the coast. If I were them, that's surely where I would search first."

"You both may be right," Ben-Hon injected, "let's play it safe. Stay under radar coverage for the next five miles. There appears to be nothing in front of us on my screen. The sun should be rising in a few minutes and, if all goes well, then we can then sprint again for the Ethiopian border."

"Roger," Shooter answered. "I agree. That will slow us down some, but it can't be helped."

Call it nerves or the deadly tension everyone was under, but the twenty-five minutes seemed only to take five. As Ben-Hon recommended, Benji patiently flew under the hundred-foot ceiling for about five miles, then rose up to a thousand feet, and floored it to the Ethiopian border.

Shooter searched repeatedly for another radar station that could triangulate their heading. Their path ahead was clear. That first radar station continued to sweep eastward as if looking for someone on a specific heading. Their five-mile slow-down had placed them behind the station.

Shooter continued to question their accurate search patterns. Were they looking for them? he wondered. Or following procedure?

"Eli, plot the location of that Doppler radar station. We want to avoid it on our return trip."

"No problem, Captain Kennet, already done. I figured you'd want to by-pass them."

"Good, thanks, Lieutenant Ben-Hon." The formal reference to Eli's name wasn't lost on him.

"You're welcome, Shooter," Eli answered with a little laugh, realizing it was time to become one with his crew.

Both Shooter and Benji turned and shrugged their shoulders in surprise. Their new navigator was finally opening up.

Shades of light blue fingers broke through the night sky as morning approached. A herd of giraffes were the first to spot the rays of sunlight bending over the horizon. They had spent a restless night on the move from a desperate pack of starving hyenas crying throughout most of the night. It was very early into the rising of the moon before they finally tracked, cornered, and killed their meal. The fighting noises and high pitch laughter emanating from the moonlit plains was replaced soon thereafter with an occasional lion's roar as they also hunted in the moonlight.

As the morning was born, the giraffes were eating as soon as the tree leaves became visible. The feathery leaves of the acacia tree were a staple for the giraffe. At up to sixteen feet tall and with superb eyesight they could easily spot any approaching predator, thus permitting them to feed in relative safety. They were also blessed with a great sense of hearing and smell. Usually, only the mighty lion posed any kind of serious threat to these tall sentinels. But rarely did the king—or, in most cases, the queen of beasts—hunt this early in the morning. The giraffes were safe to feed on the greenest leaves on the acacia trees.

It was during the morning meal that the herd stopped in unison at a buzzing they heard. The huge dominant male snorted at the disturbance and loped off in the direction of the rising sun. He sensed the sound was coming closer to the herd.

✝ ✡

"Look for a good spot to set down, Shooter," Captain Benjamin cautioned, surveying the rocky plains leading up to the base of Mt. Ras Dashen. "We need a place that offers protection from that road we passed over a few miles back. I spotted what could be a military truck that might have seen us as we passed over it. Wait a minute, look," he said, pointing at a break in the trees. "See that opening beyond those trees over there? Yes, that should do."

He turned the helicopter in that direction. When he reached the spot, he raised the helicopter to three hundred feet, high enough to get a view of the surrounding landscape, and completed a 360. That move was designed to surprise anyone hiding, by rising up over their heads and provoking a reaction from any ambushers. The only movement they saw was a startled herd of ten or twelve giraffes, about two hundred yards away, running off in the opposite direction.

"Setting her down. Shooter, signal our passengers to get ready to disembark."

Shooter reached over and moved a selector switch from stand-by to the ready position. The blinking red light in the cargo department turned green. The commandos quickly unbuckled and stood in unison. Major Steiner motioned for Simon, Sara, and David to do likewise and stand between them. Two commandos opened the side door and a gust of dusty wind poured in the cargo compartment. The early morning light seemed as bright as noonday after spending so much time in semi-darkness. The commandos understood this as an advantage, but their three charges simultaneously closed their eyes as if flashed by a camera. Quickly, they also adjusted to the dim morning light.

Whale stood ready to embark as he felt the helo slowing down. With the door open, he would be the first out followed by Dog. *Is this where we buy it?* he wondered. That thought prompted a quick look back at his friend. They silently shared that possibility together and then became deadly commandos again. The moment the wheels touched down, they were out the door and fanning out in a crouching position in the blowing high grass.

"Go, go!" Major Steiner shouted above the whipping sound of the copter blades.

The seasoned soldiers would have evacuated the craft in seconds during a normal drop, but with one inexperienced civilian, and two rusty reservists, it took longer. The veteran commandos quickly fanned out covering every direction with deadly intent. When the pilot saw Major Steiner wave, he lifted off immediately and headed inland. Their orders were to travel in that general direction for a few miles and then turn south to confuse anyone tracking them. Just before turning again, they would climb to five thousand feet to alert any radar looking for them. They would continue on their southern course then dive under the radar cover and turn east.

"Signal the *Seattle*, Eli, our Ten Little Indians are home, and we are returning."

"Yes, sir."

"Let's get out of here, Shooter."

While the commandos fanned out to secure the landing zone, Sara knelt in the tall, blowing grass and watched as their guardian angel winged out of sight and, hopefully, out of danger. She stopped for a moment when she realized *they* might be in more danger than the disappearing craft.

"Oh!" Sara groaned when a strong hand touched her shoulder.

A quick turn was rewarded with the man she recognized as the leader of the soldiers. He motioned for her to move out.

David followed the golden-haired commando up the ridge until they reached an outcropping fifty feet above the landing zone. The commando motioned for him to stop and kneel down. David watched as the commando used binoculars to scan the area ahead of them and then the zone behind their landing spot. David used that opportunity to catch his breath and take in the natural beauty of the awakening land. From where they stopped, nature offered up a great panoramic view of the surrounding landscape. A strange excitement gripped him as he realized he was back in the land of his birth. Back in a country of rolling grassy plains, surrounded by stark, majestic mountains and deep green ravines. The wind carried the diverse scents of wild life and the multitude of greenery that dotted the plains. The musty, grassy-scented wind was virginal to the man poised above the spreading plains.

Nothing about his native country was familiar to him. His family had departed for the promised land while he was a boy, yet, this was still his roots, his birthplace. And when he ran his fingers in the dirt, he sensed something. As if the earth was talking to him, welcoming him home. David stared at his fingers as he rubbed off the dirt.

Every tree had a story to tell. Rabbi Gette had taught him about the homeland, from the largest animal to the smallest insect, a place in the scheme of things. The path his family took was to migrate to Israel in pursuit of his heritage. Yet, nowhere on Earth was that same heritage more real than the plot of ground he was standing on.

David spotted a couple of giraffes feeding in a patch of trees a few miles away. Even at that distance, they were breathtaking. These strange new odors from nature were exciting to him. The wild grass triggered ancient memories and sensations that spoke in a language he was unfamiliar with but sensed he knew from childhood. It was like seeing a face that you were positive you knew, but you couldn't quite remember from where.

David turned to survey more of the land when he spotted Sara and another soldier moving up toward his position. All of the joy and awe he was experiencing in the land of his father was shattered by the image of the dark-haired woman climbing up the hill. The sun was up and the day had begun, clearly revealing Sara.

David inched his way closer to the edge of the cliff and watched her climb. There was a moment when he hoped she was climbing up to be with him. For that moment, he lost track of why they were there. For that moment, the intoxicating woman climbing up, around, and over the treacherous rocks was the only reason to be anywhere.

Forgiveness was so close it became words in his mouth,

gentle words, which would have removed the hurt and patched the cracks in their relationship. The same words that once burned his tongue to speak were now sweet in his mouth as he rolled them over and tasted their nectar. With the words came a pounding in his chest and a weak sensation in his legs. The fire blossoming in his heart was consuming him. Still he hesitated. David knew that forgiveness, however sweet, would be very costly. He would have to overcome his pride, and that he could not do—not without a bitter fight. Love and pride wrestled about in his heart as they had done in countless other souls throughout time.

Sara stopped to catch her breath and took note that she was starting to breath hard. Looking up, she noticed a lone figure standing exposed against the gray mountain staring down at her. He was to her a beacon in a fog. She felt an all-too-familiar rush as she watched him watching her. She sensed he felt the same and that he knew what she was enduring. The signals were clear, even though they hadn't said a kind word to each other since she walked out of his hotel room.

Don't just stand there staring at him, she scolded herself, fearing her inaction might send him the wrong signal. Wait! No. My life and the decisions made are my own. She directed her thoughts toward the man looking down at her. The pride she was able to muster up lasted for only a moment. Then those proud shoulders, that had thrust themselves upward in defiance to what she was initially feeling, sagged downward in defeat, as inwardly she pleaded, *Don't look at me that way*.

"Fool," Sara heard behind her.

She turned to ask what she was doing wrong now.

"He should know better to stand up like that," Major Steiner uttered between grinding his teeth.

Then she understood. David was unwittingly revealing their position to anyone looking for them. He was their beacon also. A searchlight may not reveal the object of a search but it always exposed the location of the searcher. Sara quickly caught up with the soldier after he rudely brushed past her. By the time they reached David, he was seated beside Simon and two of the other commandos.

"Mister Yasuda," Major Steiner cautioned David and any-one else so inclined, "please don't stand up like that again. We chose this spot because it offered cover for us with the high grass and provided a panoramic view for miles of everything on the eastern side of the approach to the mountain. Listen, everyone," he continued, as he wiped the sweat from his eyes. "We don't know who knows that we are here. Everything we do must be under the assumption that we are being hunted by the Ethiopian armed forces. We are violating the sovereignty of this nation, and they have a right to arrest us for that viola-tion. Under that assumption, we must remain as invisible as possible."

"I'm sorry, Birdman," David apologized. He looked around at all of those assembled, coming to Sara last. "I was caught up in the view." When she smiled and looked down, he con-tinued. "And the excitement of being this close to the Pond of God blinded me to all of your previous instructions."

"Yes, I understand, Mister Yasuda," the commando leader acquiesced. "That is why we're here."

Sara lowered her head to hide her smile. David, she knew, was talking directly to her. He was expert at turning adversity to advantage with only words. They had confronted the few people who disliked their being together with both wit and dry humor, many times turning those who quietly opposed their romance into open acceptance.

"Okay, people," Birdman said, back in charge again, "Lis-ten up. This time of year here the sun sets early at around sev-en p.m. so that gives us a little over twelve hours of daylight each day to search. We have already burnt up the first few hours.

"As you were previously instructed, we can't communicate with the ship until we have found this supposedly healing wa-ter. There are countries out there that would stop at nothing to keep us from doing just that. Each commando has a coded transmitter. Should any of you find the source of the elixir, to send that message just enter the letters W-A-T-E-R on the keypad, leave it turned, on and then hide the transmitter near the water. It will continue transmitting that bearing for a week or so, I'm told, or for as long as the batteries last."

Speaking directly to the three civilians, he added, "If captured, no one can know the real names of the commandos or where we came from. The Ethiopian government would try us and then possibly shoot us as spies if we were captured. The less you know, the better. On any mission here or at home, we have devised code names for communication purposes. If you haven't noticed," he said, pointing to his name tag, "they are sewn into our shirts."

That comment prompted a variety of snide observations and laughter about the truth of some of the names.

"Okay, people, calm down. This handsome man on my left is Snake. He will be the commando in the lead. He will often remain out of sight of the main party, scouting ahead of us. That robust young man over there is Hawk. He will always be stationed far behind us, keeping an eye on our rear."

Someone mentioned something about him volunteering so he could look closely at everyone's rear, evoking a stream of insults from Hawk. He looked embarrassingly at Sara and pleaded his innocence with a large grin. She smiled back, easing the awkwardness.

"Raven," Major Steiner continued, pointing to the golden-blond commando after the ruckus died down, "will cover our right flank, and Whale, kneeling next to me, will cover our left. I'm Birdman. The two other commandos are Weasel and Dog. Weasel will be between Snake and the main party in front and Dog will occupy the same spot in the rear. We will move out and make the next camp at the base of the mountain," the major said, pointing to the majestic, clouded-over Mt. Ras Dashen. "One more thing, remember you activate your radio-mikes—" He demonstrated for the non-combatants. "—by pulling it down in front of your mouth. Keep the earplug in one of your ears. Like I explained before we took off, there's a volume adjustment above the mike. The system is voice activated. Don't waste the batteries with idle conversation. If you want to talk without everyone hearing, push the mike up to shut it off. That will also turn your earplug off.

"Another very important rule, stay with the person in front

of you. Keep track of that person and the person behind you. Whatever you see them do, don't question it, copy it. If they suddenly start running, or stop and listen, or suddenly drop down and hide in the grass, don't hesitate—duplicate. Is that clear?"

Everyone nodded as he looked at each of them.

"One other thing, we don't know where this Pond of God or the Messiah Drug, as Simon likes to call it, is located, so keep your eyes open for anything that might contain or hide this pond. If it was easy to find, someone would have found it years ago, so it must be hidden in plain sight. So take a drink, a leak, or whatever you need now. We move out in five minutes."

Whale watched as Dog looked from Hawk to Raven and then shook his head.

"What do you see, Dog?" he whispered after walking over and kneeling down beside him.

"We won't be alone entering paradise on this mission. At least two of our brothers will join us. Makes me wonder if this mission was doomed from the start."

"Why do you say that?"

Dog didn't answer, just shook his head. He didn't have the heart to include David's gray face in his inventory of the soon to be dead. Even more so, when he noticed David and Sara making eyes at each other. But he wasn't certain about him. Dog had just caught a fleeting glance of grayness on him. He could have been in the shadow of something, Dog wasn't sure. He was about the other two, very sure.

Sara took a quick sip of the water in her canteen and took one last look up at the partly cloudy sky in the direction their helicopter had departed. The morning sky, earlier colored in deep blues, had grown bright as the sun gained strength. A spot in the bright sky caught her attention. She looked away but thought something was odd about it so she looked up at it again. It continued moving toward them and started to take on a familiar shape. She almost screamed when she realized it was their helicopter returning. Remembering her training, she crouched down and nudged Birdman who was kneeling in front of her studying a map. The what-do-you-want-civilian look she got from him almost angered her enough to tell him to shove that map in some place dark.

"Look Birdhead, I think that's our helicopter returning," she said, pointing over his shoulder and ignoring the urge to curse him out.

He just stared at her in wonderment. Had she just called him Birdhead?

Sara was so surprised at his action or rather inaction, that she lost track of her own warning.

Birdman looked over the tall grasses back the way they had come. He saw nothing. The joy of finally being able to humble Miss Smart-Ass tempered his usually unbiased assessment of the situation. The soldier in him finally took over as he carefully assessed the sky and all the terrain around them. He didn't see anything. *This broad is crazy.* Turning around, he looked her in the eye. A wicked grin cracked the corner of his mouth. "There's nothing there, my lady," he said derisively.

"*What*?" Sara looked around, ready to show Birdbrain that he was as blind as he was stupid. The sky was empty. She turned around in a circle and only saw a couple of small birds flying off in the distance. She sighed as the thought of apologizing to this gung-ho metal head sickened her. Why would their helicopter return for them so quickly anyway? she wondered. It didn't make sense to her either. She took a long look around again, but her inner prayers weren't answered.

"Sorry, Birdman," she said, pausing between each word for effect. "I could swear that—that what I saw was something that looked—like a helicopter."

"That's okay, missy," Birdman said, smiling too hard to be genuine. "It's easy to mistake a bird for a plane at this height. You know, thin air and all."

Sara didn't know if she wanted to scream or just punch him in his condescending mouth. She did neither. Her training tempered her anger. Throughout her mandatory military career, she had faced the same bias. Her ability to quickly learn and master very tough assignments soon endeared her to those same arrogant males.

"Okay, let's move it out." Birdman said, standing and using hand signals to communicate with the other commandos. The seven soldiers and three civilians set out in search of a miracle. It was a proven fact that it did exist, only no one knew exactly where. They could be heading in the right direction or standing right on top of it. One thing each of them did know, as they started walking toward the majestic mountain that dwarfed the horizon, was that thousands had died since they took off from Elat, Israel. And with each step they took someone, loved by someone else, was dying.

The first few miles were something right out of an encyclopedia. As they climbed, the natural beauty of Africa passed right before them. The base of Mt. Ras Dashen was an open zoo, filled with a wondrous variety of wildlife. Awed by the specter of nature's display, the "Ten Little Indians" found themselves frequently stopping to admire the show. The wild rush of a band of antelope caught their attention. Passing around binoculars, they watched as a quartet of lionesses stocked their prey. The beauty of the cats was enough to slow the steps of each of the "Indians."

As they climbed higher, they disturbed four ibex goats that raced ahead of them up the steep slope of the mountain. The sounds of birds caterwauling overhead were mixed with the trumpeting of elephants somewhere off in the distance. The varied sounds of Africa, they discovered, were as startling as the scenery. They heard lions roaring, the laughing bark of hyenas, and numerous sounds they couldn't identify. It was difficult to stay alert when so much of Africa was unfolding around them. As they climbed up the base of the mountain, the wildlife's natural calliope lessened. Each step into the thinner air produced more sounds of their labored breathing and the dry brush under their boots, and less of the wildlife.

Birdman ordered them to rest while Snake scouted a plateau that appeared as they climbed the base of Mt. Ras Dashen. The flat grassy plain would offer them little protection, while trying to cross it, and was too wide to walk around. Birdman radioed for Snake to start across. They all watched nervously as the lone figure weaved his way through the high grass.

Soon he was invisible as he melted into the tall grassy plain.

While the others used this respite to catch a breather, David looked up at the mountain, hoping for some clues that might lead them to the Pond of God. The story that the Rabbi told him on his last visit to his residence yesterday offered little hope of easily finding it...

CHAPTER 15

Having raced from his apartment to the synagogue, still angered by Sara's revelation, David stopped on the porch of his priest in an effort to calm down. Pacing he knew she was right about the nation's dire situation but that didn't ease his pain. Sitting in the chair of the priest also did little to erase his mood.

"Hello, my son, what brings you here on this beautiful June day?"

The priest had walked out on the porch surprising a sullen David as he sat in the holy man's chair, trying to make sense of what happened with Sara. It wasn't the first time David was caught sitting in the priest's chair, but it was the first time he'd sat there when the priest appeared. Still bridled with anger from his conversation with Sara, David avoided the usual pleasantries, stood up, and abruptly asked the holy man a question. "Rabbi, you once said we were blessed with the Sweat of Angels," he said after rising. "I need to know now exactly what you mean by that. This is very important."

Surprised by his outburst and the troubled look on his face, the priest walked past him and sat down, debating if he should reveal his secret to his favorite novice. David obviously knew something about the elixir and that was reason enough to give him a few bits of truth to get him to reveal just what he knew. After all...it was his rabbi's own loose lips, he was forced to admit, that had let that secret slip out.

"All that I have told you is true. We, the true followers of

God, are immune to the curse He has placed on Israel."

"What curse? This is the work of man, not God."

The rabbi looked away. Only his affection for young David prevented him from dismissing him. The boy had proven his faithfulness over and over again. Maybe Jehovah wanted him to share this burden, should something happen to him. Still, the man of God wondered about the reason for this outburst. He would have to pass on the secret in the basement to someone before his time was up, and David was trustworthy.

The priest ignored the terseness of his young trainee and motioned for him to come and sit at his feet. "I have a story to tell you that no one else knows but me. It's a story this poor farmer told me."

David continued pacing until the priest stopped talking and motioned for him to sit down.

Rabbi Gette started explaining to his unexpectedly rebellious disciple. "Apparently, the farmer was running for his life from some communist rebels. During those terrible days, the country was almost destroyed by various groups of anti-government forces, fighting and killing anyone they wanted. It was a terrible time. The farmer said he was trying to escape the bloodshed in his town when they caught up with him. He was robbed, shot, and left for dead. From what he recalled, he stumbled about the mountain in the dark for hours trying to get home to his family. Weak from loss of blood, he realized he wasn't going to make it. It was then that he looked for somewhere to die where the animals wouldn't eat his dead flesh before someone found his body. It was a popular belief in that region that they had to be whole to enter into eternity so it was an important last wish.

"He remembered climbing over hills and avoiding the many deep valleys on the mountain. Finally, exhausted, and after falling down many times, he couldn't go any farther. With the last of his strength, he crawled until he finally just collapsed unconscious and started tumbling down hill. But when he awoke, it was morning. He didn't die, he had just fainted. When he looked up, all he could see was a place that had a 'small sky,' the farmer said. I do remember him saying it was on the morning side of Mt. Ras Dashen. He thought that because, when he awoke, he was lying in a pond of cold water and the early morning sun was in his face. That would mean he was facing east.

"The amazing part of his story was that the two bullet wounds, one in his left leg and the other in his left side, had healed. Strangely, a deep cut in his right leg—he wasn't sure where he got that—was stilling bleeding badly. He was confused and couldn't understand why one leg would heal and one did not until he realized that the wounds in his left side were in the water and the bleeding one was lying on the ground. The farmer said he then put his right leg in the cold water. Almost immediately, the pain started to ease up. Within the hour, his strength had completely returned and his leg wound had closed. It had something to do with the cold water, he realized.

"Obviously worried about his family he felt strong enough to climb out of the little valley. When he returned home, he found his family had been murdered. Heartbroken, he buried his wife and young son. His family's murderers had taken all his animals and what little possessions he owned. He sat in his burned-out hut and wondered, what now? He said a voice spoke to his heart to climb the mountain, fill some containers with the miracle water that saved him, and bring it to the church. The determined farmer found two metal containers in his burned-out village and lugged the heavy containers down the mountain. Jehovah God met him half way when an old couple came by in a wagon, and he was able to induce them to give him a ride to the synagogue.

"When he told me his story, I thought he was just overcome with grief but when I gave some of the water to those who were ill, it cured every one of them. And during that time, there were many sick, wounded, and beaten who benefited from this holy water."

"Abba Gette, what did he mean he found it in a place with a small sky?" David asked.

"I don't know," the old priest told him. "I've thought about it a lot. I knew that one-day I might have to find the Pond of

Yahweh. You see so, I sent that farmer back to retrieve more of the healing water," he continued, "but he never returned. There was a lot of killing in that area of the country then. We were told he was murdered, trying to leave the city. After a few days of my people searching the seedy parts of town, they located his body, and I had him buried with honor on church grounds."

"Well, Abba," David said, standing to leave, "thank you, anyway. I feel I will have to go there and find it or our father-land will die."

"*What?*"

David quickly turned around at the rabbi's loud retort.

The old man angrily shook his head, raised a boney fist, and pointed a finger at him. "It won't die, my son. Yahweh has just opened the door for his obedient servants to inherit his promises. Most of the White Jews may die, but the God of our Fathers has spared us. The Israel that will rise up from the ashes will contain a strong Falashian influence. His will be done."

David was stunned. *Is he serious?* "That's crazy, Abba. God has not ordained that some of his children should live and some die. He doesn't divide those that serve him with a true heart."

"Sure, he does. Remember, David, His ways are not our ways. I think you're just blinded by your love for the seed of your estranged brother."

David was speechless. He stared at the old man in disbe-lief. Anger boiled up in his chest over the reference to Sara as the seed of his brother and over the rabbi's cruel judging of these people.

These same people had spared him the horror of Sudanese refugee camps and risked their lives to bring them to the homeland. A far greater need calmed him.

"Is there anything else that you can tell me that might help me find the pond of healing water, Rabbi?"

The priest rose up on trembling legs, stood nose to nose with his erroneous disciple, then walked past as David stepped aside. His actions said the conversation was over.

"Thank you, Rabbi," David announced loudly, "the God of our fathers will guide my steps."

"I pray not!" the priest answered him, never turning around as he limped into the house. His last words were clear to David. "You are on your own now and don't bother coming back."

That was how it should be, David decided. It was obvious that the bitterness of that hell Rabbi Gette had endured in Ethiopia had forever colored his opinion about the nation of Israel. David went into the synagogue next to the rabbi's residence, knelt at the altar, and said prayers for the dying children of Israel and the dead heart of his mentor. He couldn't help thinking that the rabbi's heart was even darker than their future.

"Father," David prayed, "we've been waiting for over six thousand years for the coming of the Messiah. If he doesn't come in the next few weeks, there may not be anyone to welcome him." *Maybe this Messiah is different*, David mused, while opening the doors to the synagogue and standing in the bright light of day. "Could the water from this pond be the Messiah we are waiting for? Is our Savior waiting in the mountains of Ethiopia? A Messiah Drug?" The words seem to come alive in his heart—a "Messiah Drug."

CHAPTER 16

"Okay, everybody up. Let's get ready to move out," Birdman barked. The small group gathered around him. "Stay down and move quickly when Snake gives the signal. We're sitting ducks until we cross this grassy plain and reach that section of rocks on the other side," he said, pointing to the other side of the plateau."

Something's not quite right, Birdman decided as he stood there waiting for Snake to signal. He tried reviewing everything they had done, in search for some flaws, but drew only blanks. Then there was that nagging feeling that someone was following them, watching them. Repeatedly, he stood up and panned his binoculars behind them. Only the plentiful wildlife of the eastern plains of Africa appeared below them in his lenses. He even searched for the crazy woman's bird in the sky.

"Dammit," Birdman swore, as nothing appeared to be amiss. The tightness he felt in his chest had always been a warning to him that he was walking into harm's way.

All nine other members of the expedition heard, "Birdman, the nest is clear," simultaneously.

"Good, all right!" Birdman shouted into his headset, relieved to hear that voice. "Where are you, Snake?"

"I'm at the base of a pile of rocks off to your right."

Birdman focused his binoculars in that direction and spotted Snake's hand waving at the bottom of a large section of boulders about three hundred yards away to the right of where

Birdman thought he should be. "I have you in sight, Snake. What are you doing way over there?"

"I couldn't find a way up the face of those boulders in front of you," Snake explained. "So I decided to try and find a way around them. This area has large rocks also, but they are more scattered. There is a well-worn path to ascend between them."

"Snake, climb up between those rocks and keep an eye on our rear," Birdman ordered. "I may be getting paranoid, but I can't shake the feeling that someone is following us."

"Okay, mother hen, I'll watch over the chicks."

Birdman gave a code over the microphone that started the commandos stationed around them moving cautiously forward with weapon safeties off.

"Okay, friends, let move quickly but carefully," Birdman said, while taking one last look behind them. "Hawk and Dog, watch your tails." A double click in his earplug signaled their response to his order.

Despite Birdman's concern, nothing happened as they made their way across the exposed plateau and up part of the slope to where Snake was keeping watch. Later, he would question if it were the relief of making it across that plateau without being ambushed that allowed him to relax his guard and not question some of what Snake said because if he had to choose a place for an ambush, he couldn't have found a better spot.

Having crossed the exposed area of the plains, they were bunched together as they were funneled into an opening between some huge rocks on this part of the mountain. Birdman motioned for the group to start up the slope to where Snake was stationed.

It had bothered David that, while they were waiting aboard the various ships, that the commandos never talked to him or tried to make eye-to-eye contact. David thought it was a personal affront at first, but he quickly realized they treated Simon with the same indifference.

They were professionals, he surmised, who were trained to always be on alert.

Humorously, he realized that didn't apply to the way Sara

looked in her form-fitting clothes—she garnered plenty of eye-to-body contact from everyone.

It was when he leaned back on a rock to catch a breather while the others climbed up the path and caught up that he saw a commando, the one called Whale, smile at him. That small act of friendship so startled David that he stood up and took a step forward, unsure if he should take it to the next level and say hello.

Providence was the entrepreneur of this mercy mission from the moment it was hastily conceived. Those same powers reached out to draw an innocent smile from a soldier who had lost the desire to do so since learning of his fate. From that common facial response, the life of David Yasuda was spared. Why Providence would take that road to save a life was a mystery. Today, a man took a step and the seven bullets that would have hit him from the nape of his neck to just above his eyes, ripping his head completely from his shoulders missed—by a step.

David never saw the seven-fingered hand of death swipe past his face. He might have heard it but his attention was on Whale. He was about to speak to him when suddenly everything seemed to be happening in slow motion. David first noticed that Whale's eyes took on a shocked expression and then a small geyser erupted on Whale's chest. It was like a smaller version of Old Faithful, only spewing out flesh and blood instead of hot ground water. Whale seemed as surprised as David. Another geyser erupted and then another, causing Whale to slowly look down at his exploding chest. The word "No," escaped David's lips but too late to help Whale. Just as Whale looked up at him, another group of geysers erupted, lifting Whale up into the air and slamming him back against the rocks. That was the last thing David saw, as someone shoved him down to the ground behind some rocks. He lay there, more out of shock than fear, as the image of Whale's death replayed itself in his mind.

"Get down!" Birdman shouted above the staccato music of deadly bullets whistling off the rocks around them. Instinctively, he had shoved the Black man to the ground as he dove for cover. If he hurt himself against the rocks, Birdman reasoned, it would still be better than getting hit by the hot metal rocks that were ricocheting everywhere.

Dog and Whale were killed instantly on the first volley. Both were shot ten or more times before they hit the ground. Raven, the one David secretly named golden hair, was shot in the stomach. Another bullet entered his back, as the first shot spun him around, and exited his chest throwing him against the rocks. Fighting blackout, he wedged himself between some rocks and brought his Uzi to a firing position. With his eyes closed and teeth clinched, and fighting back the excruciating pain, he fired a full burst up the mountain in a wide spread.

Hawk, the rear echelon, noticed that the group was bunched together starting up the only path leading through that rocky section. With them in such an exposed vulnerable position, he turned and checked the rear. Everything appeared normal. When he reached the base of the path and started up, he was surprised to see them up ahead and clustered close together as they climbed. It was a precarious position to be in. He was going to say something when his right knee exploded. The bullets that hit his knee saved the top of his head from being blown off when he lost his balance and dropped to the ground. His right leg felt numb. Being the farthest away, he was singled out by his assassins to kill next. An anxious gunman fired early saving Hawk from decapitation.

Ignoring the pain, Hawk hopped over and used a boulder for support as he returned fire. Assuming he was dead, the assassins stood up and aimed their fire at the other targets, trying to hide among the rocks beneath them. Three of them paid the highest price for that assumption. Hawk was up on his left leg and firing in seconds. He saw about ten men standing boldly above them, firing mercilessly at his comrades. Before the assassins spotted him, three died and two were wounded. Hawk dropped down behind the rocks as the air over his head filled with automatic rifle fire. He was sure one of those bullets kissed him as he fell. A trickle of blood slowly leaking down from his ear was confirmation.

The remaining commandos returned fire as they blindly aimed their Uzi in the direction of the assassins. It was a wild scene. Birdman tried to assess their situation. He knew that one and probably two of his commandos were dead or dying. From his position, he could see that David and Sara were unharmed. Fortunately, the rocks above them were larger than the ones they were hiding behind, thus affording double protection. He couldn't tell where Simon was. In his desperate dive for cover he had lost his helmet. Birdman blindly searched the surrounding grass for it as bullets ricocheted off the rocks. After a tedious few minutes and two close calls, as he heard rounds whistle past his ear, he located his helmet.

"Listen up, everyone," he shouted, while fastening the chin strap tight this time, "we are outnumbered and pinned down here. I need to know if anyone is hurt. Snake, are you all right?"

"I'm in a very bad spot skipper, but okay. Sorry for leading you into this mess."

"Not your fault, Snake. They were waiting for us, as if they knew we were coming. Weasel, are you hit?"

"No, Birdman, but I can see the back-stabbing yellow cowards from here. I think I killed a couple of them. For now, I have them pinned down but they are trying to work their way around me. We only have a few minutes before I'm exposed and I will have to shit or get off the pot."

"Keep an eye on them as long as you can, Weasel. If you get in a bind, bug out."

"Can do, Birdman."

"Ahh, Raven, are you all right?"

"Raven here," he said after a long pause. "Things don't look very good, guys. I've taken two hits. The shoulder wound is clean but I'm bleeding heavily from a gut shot."

"Did everyone get that? Raven, hang in there. We'll try and get you some help. Whale, are you okay?" Birdman asked, despite seeing him go down in the initial exchange. "Whale?" Birdman called out again.

The firing had slowed to an occasional sniper round every time someone tried looking up over the boulders they were hiding behind. He knew time was quickly running out and their assassins would be working their way down to finish the job they had started. Finally, Hawk answered Whale's page.

"Birdman, this is Hawk."

"Hawk, good. What's your status?"

"I think Whale is dead. Well, I should say I know he is. I saw him and Dog get shot up pretty bad on the first volley. Whale's lying face down in the grass off to my left and he hasn't moved. As for me, they shot up my leg at the knee. I have a tourniquet tied around it to slow down the bleeding." Hawk paused for a moment. "Skipper, I'm done for. That bullet ripped open my leg. I think it hit an artery. I tried, but I can't stop the bleeding."

Two are dead and two badly wounded, Birdman assessed, as he rubbed his hand on his chin. *Over half of my platoon wiped out and we haven't found anything but trouble.*

"Skipper, do you read me?" Hawk's plea finally got through the haze Birdman found himself sinking into.

"Yes, Hawk, I hear you. Sorry, I was trying to clear my head."

"That's okay, skipper. It's been that kind of day—uuuuuuuuuuh!"

"Hawk, are you all right? Hawk!"

"Yes, skipper, well, no really. I'm wounded pretty badly. It doesn't look good from where I'm sitting."

"Hang in there, buddy. We'll get you out of there!" Birdman vowed. He knew that it was time to take charge of the situation before the situation took further charge of them. "Look, everyone, hold your return fire as long as you can. We'll need to conserve ammo. Snake, Weasel, see if you can out-flank them and give them something to think about instead of killing us. We need to hold them there until we can get Raven and Hawk out of here."

"Skipper, don't bother," everyone heard Hawk say. "I'm wounded too badly to move, and I don't see any hospitals nearby. I think you can get around them and get away if you work your way back down the hill toward me. From the rock that I'm propped up against, I can cover your retreat."

"No, Hawk, you're going with—"

"Major," Raven interrupted. "Hawk has a good—" There was a long pause as Raven fought through a painful bout of coughing. After a deep breath, he tried continuing. "We are wounded too badly to move. Even if we did get away from here, we couldn't walk. The purpose of our journey is far greater—than two lives."

"Birdman, Birdman—listen to me," Hawk added. "Face it. You have little choice. The thugs that ambushed us are trying to out flank you as we argue. There's a large open field to my right that offers little protection to anyone trying to cross it. They know better than to try to come that way because I can kill anyone trying. I saw at least six of them move out to your left. They've been gone for a while so you may already be in some kind of cross-fire."

"Snake!"

"Yes, Birdman."

"Did you hear Hawk?"

"Yes, I did."

"Okay, look, umm…keep an eye out for any movement on our left. Give a holler if you see anything. Look, everyone, I'm against leaving anyone here," Birdman told the shaken group. "I don't know how many guns are trained on us or if we could make it out of here, anyway."

"Major Steiner."

Birdman hesitated. Hearing his name triggered fears that their secrecy had been compromised by their attackers until he recognized the voice.

"Major Steiner—sorry, Birdman, this is Simon Levine."

By this time Sara and David, hiding in separate locations, had turned on their mikes and were listening to the desperate conversations. When Simon finally spoke, it was enough to energize everyone.

"Simon," David heard a feminine voice call out, "thank God. Are you all right?"

"I'm fine, Sara. Are you all right and David?" She didn't answer, the voices of her fears too strong to assail. The answer to the last part of his question she was afraid to know.

"I'm here, Simon." David swallowed. "Shaken but not stirred."

Sara's heart leaped in her chest. *He's alive!* Hearing his dry sense of humor was so reassuring. During the worst of the fighting, after she realized she was still alive, she had tried looking around for him. Her first attempt was rewarded with a shower of bullets, pinging off the rocks where she was hiding. The second attempt was even more frightening when she saw the dead body of one of the commandos hit by another spray of bullets that split his head open like a ripe melon. She spent her next few minutes vomiting up breakfast.

"Simon, this is Birdman, where are you?"

"Birdman, I'm at the base of the trail leading up to where we were ambushed. When the shooting started, I ran for cover. By the time I stopped running, I was all alone at the bottom of the path. When no one followed me, I started climbing back to look for you."

"Did you see any soldiers?"

"No. I was able to climb back up without being seen or shot at."

"Birdman, this is Hawk. I hate to interrupt but I can see some armed men moving to our left, trying to cut off any retreat you may have. Major, we have maybe three or four minutes and our backs will be exposed. I'm sure that's what those killers are waiting for before they come down on us."

Hawk had brazenly reminded his commanding officer that it was time to make a decision.

"Snake, Weasel, work your way back here and take the civilians down the hill to where Simon is hiding. Simon, watch for them. Let us know if you see any of the ambushers coming from your left."

"Okay, Birdman," Simon answered.

"Hawk, keep an eye on our hosts. I'm going to try and work my way over to Raven."

"Dammit, Major, there's no time," Hawk answered. "Take the civilians out of here and find that damn water. Simon has found a way out of here, so take it. There is nothing you can do for either one of us. Raven and I will cover your retreat.

Don't say anything, sir, we know how you feel, just go."

"He's—right—sir," Raven said so slowly that his pain was obvious. "I'm dying and I know it, but—I can still shoot anyone—stupid enough to try sneaking past me. Please go, guys, and save Zion. There's—nothing you can do now—to save us."

Five bewildered souls moved carefully down between the large boulders. They crawled on their stomachs part of the way down. They were being as careful as possible to remain hidden from the deadly guns looking down at them from the rocks above.

Birdman reached where Sara was hiding and helped her down the hillside. He took what he thought was an easier way down for her. Unfortunately, he stepped around a large rock and right into the gun sight of a startled Ethiopian soldier. Quickly, Sara ducked down behind the rock before he spotted her. The young soldier put his rifle on Birdman's chest. Birdman slowly let his weapon drop to the ground. The soldier motioned for him to raise his hands.

"All right, all right, take it easy," Birdman said quickly, fearing the frightened, nervous young soldier might inadvertently shoot him. He seemed more nervous than the man at the killing end of his weapon. "Take it easy, I'm your prisoner."

Birdman hoped Sara had time to find a weapon of some kind or sneak away while he held the jittery soldier's attention.

Sara stepped around from behind Birdman before he could stop her. He watched the surprised soldier look her way. *No, Sara,* Birdman wanted to say to her as she moved beside him, but it was too late. Birdman started hoping that seeing Sara's face would distract the scared man enough to give him a split-second window. A window opened—just long enough for him to knock the rifle away and shove the young soldier's nose up into his brain. When the man's eyes suddenly opened as wide as his mouth, Birdman was so surprised, he almost waited too long. The young soldier never saw the hand that hit him. What he did see was Sara's shirt unbuttoned and her torn undershirt opened down to her bellybutton. The sight of most of her braless breasts exposed startled the young soldier.

For Birdman, it was almost too easy. When he knocked the rifle out of the soldier's hands, the man was still leering at Sara's chest and was dead before he hit the ground. Her beauty had captured the eye of another Ethiopian. Both had suffered a similar fate. Both were so captivated by her, they lost track of their mission in life and were rendered speechless.

Birdman turned around in time to see Sara starting to button up her shirt. She didn't see the sly smile of admiration on his face as she finished and tucked her shirt in her shorts. She looked up and was puzzled by the little boy grin on his face. *Oh, that's right. You Tarzan, me Jane.*

The grinning commando leader gave her a thumbs-up. "Let's get the hell out of here," he said as he looked around for other soldiers.

She never let on that she considered his blatant admiration to be sexist. Hell, he wouldn't understand that anyway, she decided. Sara smiled demurely back at him. She could take care of herself her look said. *And by the way, caveman—you were a little slow to react. You need to work on that*, she desperately wanted to tell him. "I am all for that," she whispered.

Her casual decision to wear a heavy cotton T-shirt instead of her uncomfortable bra under her baggy shirt in the African heat had probably saved their lives. Birdman's eyes said all the thanks she needed. After looking around and seeing no other soldiers, he gently grabbed her arm and pointed to the way down. He picked up his Uzi, took the weapon from the dead soldier, and followed her down the hill.

Weasel reached Simon first and watched anxiously as Sara and then Birdman finally approached from behind one of the large boulders at the base, carefully keeping their heads down as they moved between the rocks. Snake arrived a minute later with the Falashian. Everything was so quiet, Snake was wondering if the killers were gone. That thought evaporated when he saw three armed men climbing around the rocks to his left, toward the spot they had just vacated. He choked down a sigh of relief when he remembered that two of his friends were still up there. They were cut off from them as more of the soldiers appeared. As they encircled his wounded comrades Snake slowly raised his Uzi semi-automatic rifle until it was pointed at the backs of the soldiers.

Snake was the best shot on the team that had volunteered for a mission to save Israel. He had little doubt that he could take out most of the skulking soldiers, even with the poor accuracy of an Uzi at that range. What he was even surer of was that their position would then be revealed to the surviving soldiers climbing down the hill and trying to close the trap on their pinned-down quarry. He took their encirclement to mean their escape from their trap went unnoticed. Snake took a deep breath for that reason, exhaled slowly, and slid his finger off the trigger. His hand was stiff from gripping the weapon so tight. He wanted to kill those bastards who attacked them. Not firing was difficult, but not as difficult as having to leave his wounded comrades behind.

David knelt down in the tall grass, his mind awash with conflicting emotions. He was finally able to catch his breath. From the moment the world exploded in his face and he was baptized in the blood of the commando beside him, he had trouble catching his breath. Every time he tried to relax the sight of the chest of that soldier, collapsing from the volley of high-powered rounds hitting him, was replayed over and over in his mind. He never had time to worry about Sara as the chaotic scene erupted around him. All he could think about during his bout of panic and terror was that dead soldier. It wasn't until he heard Sara's voice that the cobwebs cleared.

Sara, he thought as he spotted her cowering behind one of the boulders, *so glad you're all right*. He was suddenly very angry. The knee-weakening fear that being near death could grip you with was replaced with an awakening desire to crush to death the men who would dare put this wonderful woman in harm's way. All thoughts about Whale's death were forgotten as David realized how close his Sara had also come to dying. He had to tell her that he still loved her the next chance he got, he vowed.

Sara had looked desperately for David when she reached the bottom of the path. When she didn't see him, her heart almost broke. She put her hand to her chest and swallowed down the erupting panic. She closed her eyes and surrendered to the certainty of his death. A scuffle of feet disturbed her solemn wake. She looked up and spotted David kneeling in the grass and watching her. *He's still alive! He made it down.* She rejoiced.

When she overheard everyone talking but him, she had resigned herself to the fact that he might be dead. When David finally answered Simon over the headset, her heart all but leaped out of her chest. Then after she climbed down the hill and didn't see him, those fears were re-ignited. Now there he was right across from her. She could see he was trying to tell her something when that was interrupted as they all overheard the wounded commandos talking.

"Hawk, can—you—hear—me?" a very weak Raven asked, interrupting David's vows.

"Yeah, I'm here—barely," Hawk answered.

The others had slipped out of the noose their ambushers had created, but none of them could move any farther as they listened to the dying voices of their comrades.

"Are—they gone, Hawk? Did they get away?"

"Yes, I believe so, buddy. I haven't heard any more shooting."

"I'm glad—I'm glad," Raven said. "Boy, you know what I was thinking?" When he didn't get an answer, he continued, "That Sara is a fox."

"She sure is," Hawk answered, without asking where that statement had come from. "I would—would die on this mountain for that."

"That's—very funny, Hawk, very funny."

"Raven, if you see or hear anyone coming, don't ask to see some identification, just shoot the bastards. I can guarantee it won't be me."

"That's—about—all—I can do—Peter," he said, forgetting protocol. "I'll be shooting so blindly, I just hope I—I don't—get you killed."

Hawk laughed painfully to himself at his friend's joke while a broken-hearted woman, listening to their conversation silently sobbed in her hands.

"Let's go," Birdman whispered to the crushed group kneeling in an impromptu, séance-like, circle. "We have got to be out of range before they open fire."

Sara's head jerked up and she was just about to curse the insensitive pig out when Simon grabbed her arm and shook his head. To Sara's surprise, he then started crawling after that heartless asshole.

Birdman led his disconsolate charges into the tall grasses and away from the ambush side of the mountain. It would have been better to have escaped altogether, but each of them understood, now more than ever, the need to complete the mission. The nightmares of the many deaths occurring at home were forgotten, for a brief moment, as they pictured two brave men, dying alone far, far from home.

They heard sporadic gunfire echoing in the valley below, as they made their way around the right side and up the mountain, but heard nothing more from Hawk or Raven. Each remaining member dearly wanted personally to say good-bye to the valiant men awaiting death's visit, but none wanted to intrude on the private minutes they had remaining.

Raven must be dead, Hawk figured, after he heard a volley of gunshots. He limped over, slowly looked to his left around the boulder he was leaning against, and spotted two soon-to-be-dead soldiers standing in the spot where Raven was. He steadied his weapon against a flat spot on the boulder. The pain had stopped in his wounded leg. He knew it was because the tight tourniquet around his thigh had cut off all circulation. It was just dead flesh now. He had no other choice as he took aim at one of the men standing over the body of Raven. He had to stay alive long enough to protect the others as they got away.

Hawk closed his eyes for a moment to clear his vision. The finality of his friendship with his comrades weighed heavily on his heart as he took aim and fired. The first burst blew the top off the head of one of the soldiers. It took more shots than Hawk had planned to hit the second surprised gunman before he could take cover. He then fired up in the direction of the soldiers he knew were working their way down the rocky mountainside. *That will hold them for a while*—he hoped.

Hawk slid down and closed his eyes. He was getting dizzy, he knew, from loss of blood. His thoughts went from his escaping friends to the one who just gave his life. Raven had been the newest member of their platoon. His humor, from the first day he arrived, endeared him to the tightly knit group right away. They became friends and partners on most of the missions.

Raven was only twenty-three, a year older than his sister, he recalled. He smiled when he remembered bringing the homesick rookie home to his parent's house for a weekend. One look at his dark-haired sister Sienna and the garrulous Special Forces soldier became mute and clumsy. After the rookie knocked over his second glass of water, Hawk thought it better to properly introduce them before Raven hurt himself or others. The thought of how quickly he lost his homesickness when he first looked into Sienna's dancing eyes lifted Hawk's spirit. He quickly became the odd-man-out with the two of them. He expressed that to both of them and was ignored, and he loved every minute of it.

Hawk shook himself from those memories and listened for moment. All was quiet. He didn't like that, so he painfully struggled to stand and look up the mountain. A quick peek over the rock he was hiding behind revealed someone moving off to his left. Hawk felt the dizziness return as he watched. For some reason, he didn't fire at them. It was if he wanted them to find him and put an end to his pain. A sharp stab of that pain cleared his head. He hopped over to his right to give himself a better firing position.

He grabbed the Star of David around his neck that Sienna had given him that last night they were home and squeezed it. When she placed it around his neck, she surprised him by whispering and asking him please to bring the blond-haired young man with him on their next leave. He hugged her and promised he would. The long walks they would take after dinner must have stirred something in his usually loquacious sister. "I'm not breaking my promise, baby," he whispered to his sister. "When next we meet, Raven will be at my side."

✝ ✡

In the twenty minutes since they escaped around the side of the mountain, the remaining six had put a half-mile between themselves and the soldiers waiting to finish them off. They moved very quickly now that they were out of sight. Finally, Simon halted their retreat.

"We've got to start looking for the source of the miracle water," Simon told the gathering. "If all we had to do was get away from those soldiers, that wouldn't be a problem. But remember, our comrades gave their lives today so we could continue the search. It's dangerous, but we've got to risk it if we're going to find the pond."

Simon waved off any further comments from Birdman. At this point, he was in charge of the mission. He motioned for them to move in closer. He avoided looking any of them directly in the eye, less they see how shaken he was. *Be the leader, be the leader*, he repeated as they closed the circle.

"We are going to have to spread out if we're going to find the 'Hope of Israel.' We all have read the report David compiled from the Falashian Rabbi. No one really knows precisely where this water is. All we have are some obscure clues to guide us." Simon stopped talking when he saw David put his right hand over his ear. David had inadvertently turned his earphone up to its max. That happenstance enabled him to hear Hawk's last words.

The look on his face puzzled Simon. "David, what is it?" he asked.

"It's Hawk. I can hear him again."

"I can't," Simon said.

"I can hear him now," an excited Birdman said, "turn up your volume control."

"If you guys can—still hear me—Raven is dead. I killed the two dogs who shot him."

"Way to go, Hawk," someone whispered.

Birdman put his finger to his lips to signal silence.

"I—just wanted to say—I know—you will find it. Maybe it's becau—because. I'm forgetting what I—because I'm dying—that I know this. Goodbye, they're coming now."

They strained to listen while also praying not to hear the sound of their friend's death. Each ignored the morbid fascination that stoked their curiosity. The silence was painful, as each of their imaginations created a picture of what was going to happen next. The sound of automatic rifles firing filled their earplugs and finally they heard—silence.

CHAPTER 17

At that moment, approximately seventy one hundred miles away, the President of the United States heard the stern and dire report read by the overly dramatic Deputy Director of the CIA, Robert Atworthy, but he wasn't really listening. It wasn't from lack of concern. What was occurring in the Middle East was of the utmost importance to him, the country, and the rest of the world. One of his largest voting blocks and wealthiest contributors to his election, he understood all too clearly, were people in this country with the same lineage.

President John Collage Martin, Democrat from Ohio, sat at the head of the table and listened to report after report about the heinous plague attacking Israel and her neighbors. He was suddenly more concerned about his own death in the polls than the demise of thousands of Jews.

"Robert, could you get to the point?"

"Yes, sir, Mr. President," Robert answered respectfully. "Gentlemen, the death toll in Israel and her neighbors have passed the 40,000 mark this evening." The loud sighs from his audience provoked him to continue. *That shook them up a little*. "With a majority of those young people under twenty, Israel may have lost its next generation.

"Sir, we only found out yesterday that this deadly plague has reached across into Egypt and Syria with a vengeance. Whole towns have perished as medical relief workers refused to enter the quarantine areas. There appears to be a lessening

of the severity of the plague as the circle widens from the epicenter—Israel. Reports are sketchy and unconfirmed, but apparently more and more people on the outer rim of a two hundred mile circle from the epicenter, are reported to be recovering from the plague."

Robert looked around at the five men in the room as he
read the last lines. None of the faces gendered the optimism
the president had counted on when he had him alter the last
section of the report.

"Thank you, Robert," President Martin said, motioning for
him to sit down.

The president scanned the tense, anxious faces of those he
had summoned to the White House. The air in the room was
bloated with the residue of expensive colognes and aftershaves
hastily splashed on in response to his urgent summons for a 6
six a.m. meeting. He couldn't smell it, but he knew the fear he
saw in their eyes also emitted a scent. For a moment, he was
distracted, wondering if dogs could really smell fear on people. Who was he trying to fool? He was just as afraid as they
were.

"Gentlemen," the president announced, "scientists and bi-
ologists around the world are suggesting that the repeated in-
fections might have weakened the plague enough for antibiot-
ics or antitoxins to enable the body's defenses to kill the bacterium."

The room was silent. The president looked around at those
assembled. He wondered if they were aware that he knew
about their secret meeting last night. Was it the source of their
hesitancy? Enjoying the power the good news gave him, he
took a pause before continuing.

"Mr. President, I strongly disagree," General Sentell said,
injecting his deep bass voice into the silence. As chairman of
the Joint Chiefs, it was his report, cynically labeled the "Final
Solution," that prompted a more private meeting last night
hosted by the Joint Chiefs. "Mr. President, are you suggesting
that nature is doing what we failed to do?"

You pompous bastard. President Martin stared in the coldly
serious eyes of the decorated soldier and stifled the voice of

anger swelling up in his chest. "The country is a democracy," he often told those assembled, "but not the Oval Office."

"Are you still advocating nuking the entire area, General?"

The general's face muscles tightened as he controlled himself. "Think like the leader of the free world," that James Earl Jones-like voice trumpeted, "and not someone from Ohio. I can guarantee you the Russians and Chinese are thinking about it."

"In Russia, China, and—Texas, they might nuke innocent women and children, but not while I'm sitting here."

General Avil Sentell, the third Sentell to reach the rank of general in his illustrious family's two hundred years of service to their country, wasn't about to take the bait. As chairman of the Joint Chiefs, the silver-haired soldier had proudly out surpassed his lineage. As a large, intimidating personage of a man accustomed to giving orders, he bristled at the rebuke of this...politician.

General Sentell pondered for a moment on his answer. His position was clear. Everyone in the room knew he favored burning up the deadly bacteria in a nuclear fire. Other than the president, he knew his suggestion had strong backing by the others in the room. Secretary of State Haskins had given him that half-grin of his, which usually signaled his approval. Vice President Oliver McCormick would agree with anything the group decided. That was why he was picked for the office.

"Deputy Atworthy, Secretary Haskins, Admiral Iversen, and Vice President McCormick all know my stance on this issue, Mr. President. This has nothing to do with the people who live in the area. If this was Texas, I would—"

"You would still advocate killing—no, murdering— millions of the people you serve, General?"

"This virus, left unchecked, will kill billions, sir," the general shouted, pounding on the table.

"Did you read the report, General? The epidemic has probably run its course and is dying out. I was right to be cautious. I also wanted to blast the hell out of it before it spread. But what would you do if the rest of the world decided to wipe us out to save the world? To nuke them would make us just another virus. Opps, it's a bacterium, not a virus. As long as the killing is isolated in the hot zone, we will only assist in the quarantine and fly in the special chemical units, and only when absolutely necessary."

The truth of that claim offered little hope for Israel. The "hot zone" was the heart of the country. The death rate was still close to one hundred percent. Apparently, a majority of the Falashian Ethiopians in that area were spared, but only a few in government knew that. Israel was a country with a diversity of people of color. The death of other men of color hid the secret immunity of the Ethiopian Jews. But one had only to stop and count the many volunteers to notice the abundance of Jews of color freely caring for the sick. The only two instances of public questioning of the apparent immunity of the Ethiopians were quickly covered-up. The country was so close to panic that no negative commentaries were permitted.

One positive was that Arab and Jew came together to try to help each other. Old hatreds were forgotten as this cruel monster didn't discriminate in choosing and devouring its victims. It killed Arab and Jew equally.

Temporary camps were set up in the desert for those unaffected. All of the healthy children were moved out of the cities. Anyone contracting the plague was removed from the camps immediately. The ravaged cities began to resemble the Polish ghettos of World War II. The shame of that war reared its ugly head among the same people who suffered the most from that madness. Now, another heartless invader had imprisoned them and was just as coldly putting them to death. Hunger and starvation started arriving as goods and services slowed to a trickle. Only the national strength, gained from living under the constant threat that marked their daily lives, prevented total chaos. There were many brave patriotic Israelis who risked and, in many cases, gave their lives to feed, clothe, minister to, and comfort their fellow countrymen. Once again, the world turned their backs on the Jews. Some even used the attack to say it was God's punishment on Israel for rejecting Christ.

Israel's only hope, their means of escaping the hell that had befallen them, had suffered a like fate. Death had reached out and touched their saviors, claiming some of them, and scattered those that remained...

CHAPTER 18

Snake was relieved to be taking point as they renewed the search. It meant he was doing something useful again. Hawk's last words seemed to drain the will out of everyone. Sara's gentle sobbing was a final song to the death of his comrades. On the move again, he was able to break the power of the guilt he felt for allowing them to walk into that trap. Regardless of what everyone thought or said he knew where the blame belonged. To him—only finding that damn water, if it existed, would avenge their senseless deaths. He wanted so very much to be the one to find it so he could look to the heavens and say he was sorry to his dead comrades.

Snake stopped climbing and scanned the landscape behind him. It took a few minutes, but he was able to locate each of the other five surviving members of their rescue mission as they slowly weaved their way up the mountainside. They were spread out about fifty yards apart as planned. Weasel was carefully guarding their rear as they searched in and under the trees and bushes for the hidden treasure. Snake's job, which he was determined to do right this time, was to prevent another ambush. Even as Major Steiner tried to temper his guilt, it was obvious that he had to protect them because they would be very vulnerable to another ambush while searching so relentlessly as the death knell from home echoed in their minds. As dangerous a situation as they were in, time had dictated they risk it all while there still was time.

Snake had tried to hide the hurt by looking everyone sternly in the face, but it didn't work. Especially after the woman, Sara, walked up and hugged him when he tried to take the blame. The pain on his face was as evident as cheap makeup. He held her much longer than he should have as the hurt from the loss of their friends threatened to pour from his eyes.

Snake stopped again and looked back at his friends. *Slow down, you are getting too far ahead*, he realized, when it took too long to locate them. Guilt was pushing him harder than the desperate, but tedious job of searching every nook and cranny by the other members of the group.

Snake climbed to the edge of a ridge to investigate a patch of dead trees and lost sight of the others. Standing too near the ledge, he slipped, lost his balance on some loose dirt, and stumbled down the slope. Thirty feet later, he grabbed hold of some protruding rocks, stopping his painful descent. He was up quickly and dusting off his sore butt. He kicked himself for wasting time, but every corner of the mountain had to be checked. Looking around, he noticed that the slope of the ridge continued downward for another hundred feet or more then dropped off again into a dark canyon. Snake took a deep breath after realizing that the rocks that bruised his butt probably save his life.

Five minutes later, he had climbed back up the side of the ridge. From the top, he tried but was unable to see his friends on the other side. He wanted to go on but decided to backtrack and make sure they were all right first. He was starting back when he realized he didn't have his canteen. Its whereabouts became clear. Snake kicked at the dirt in frustration. Climbing down and back up the treacherous ridge was the last thing he wanted to do but having water in this dry heat was a lifesaving necessity.

Carefully, he scooted down the steep side of the ridge until he reached the spot where he had stopped his slide. He found his canteen, stopped, and took a drink, then fastened it securely on his belt. "Ready or not mountain, here I come." The climb up was without incident.

Snake looked out over the beautiful plains that panned out from the mountain. It was an inspiring sight for one who grew up in the sandy, tree-less desert of southern Israel. He could just picture the wonderful wildlife that roamed under the green blanket below the mountain. Unable to enjoy the essence of Africa because of the desperate nature of their mission, he made a promise to himself that he would return one day. Return to enjoy this fertile land and see the many varieties of animal life that was abounding all around them in their natural habitat. That vow seemed to lift his spirits some.

"Okay, back to work." Snake took a deep breath and prepared to climb down the mountain and check on his friends. One last look around, he decided, stalling the inevitable tough descent. He turned and looked up toward the peak of Mt. Ras Dashen. It was clothed in low-hanging clouds and offered him no indication of how high its peak was. He had offered the suggestion to the others that the ice, frozen in one of the mountain's many ravines, might be the source of the healing water. Water frozen that only melted briefly during a severely hot period, thus keeping its existence a secret. After his treacherous climb along the narrow high ridge, he figured that neither man or beast would idly wander up here. It was decided that they might have to investigate that theory if they didn't find the water at a lower level. Not wanting to climb this area again prompted him to give the upper sections of the mountain a closer look.

Like the rest of this side of the mountain, the ridgeline he had climbed was full of boulders that must have tumbled down from farther up the mountain over the centuries. An army could hide in ambush, as he was well aware of, in a hundred different places behind those boulders. There were so many blind spots, cliffs, trees, and bushes on this mountain, which would have to be investigated, Snake started to doubt—

A dark area behind a large boulder caught his attention. It looked like some kind of opening. Maybe a small cave or something. He stared at the spot as his mind wavered on the question of what to do next. Should he investigate or should he check on his friends first? Curiosity won out. He climbed up the mountain for a closer look. The closer he got, the more this looked like it could be the answer to his prayers. He slipped on the loose stones and dirt a couple of times in his exuberance, catching his breath at the thought of falling over the side of the narrow ridge. It was a long way down.

The opening he spotted was shielded above by a jagged, over-hanging section of rock and was blocked in front by thick shrubbery that screened it from the view of anyone at the base of the ridge. Someone would have to be standing precisely where he was to have a chance of spotting the opening. The path to the entrance was a dangerous, narrow trail that wound along the edge of the ridge.

The picture of a pond of cold, healing water in that cave erased the concern he was feeling for his friends. A revived Snake rushed up d the narrow ridge. Carefully, he placed one foot in front of the other, as he walked along the narrow ridge-line. Death was a beautiful flower that bloomed in the jagged rocks below if he slipped and fell.

Snake charged between the bushes, getting his arms scraped by them for his troubles. The entrance was about waist high approximately four feet wide. Having to crawl into the dark opening gave birth to a multitude of fears. He hesitated. Thoughts of finding the healing water, and rushing down to tell his friends, had momentarily blinded him to the dangers that might loom behind the dark curtain that was the cave opening. He only had a laymen's understanding of the abundant wildlife in this area. That information offered little assurance of what could or did call that black opening home. He was the invader, his fear reminded him, and any creature attacking him was well within its rights.

With his heart pounding in his chest, he knelt down and surveyed the entrance. The ground in front of the opening appeared void of animal tracks. He tried sniffing the air around the entrance, uncertain of what that would tell him, but it seemed to make sense at the time. Nervously he knelt down and peeked in the entrance ready to flee at the slightest movement. Pulling his pocket flashlight out he aimed it at the entrance. He was pleasantly surprised when the entrance opened up into a large room. A large empty room.

Scanning the dark cave with his flashlight, he noticed there weren't any signs that man or beast inhabited the cave.

The ground inside looked remarkably flat and smooth, but unfortunately, there was no sign of water. The ceiling was from three to twenty feet at its highest point. The sides of the cave were relatively smooth as if they were polished. He had expected sharp, jagged stalactites hanging precariously over-head with vampire bats waiting to pounce on him. What he found looked too civilized not to be inhabited by something. With his Uzi ready, he slowly climbed into the small, dark hole.

The ground was soft and free of footprints, Snake noticed as he crawled into the cave. He slowly aimed the light around. There were no indications that an animal or bat had ever occu-pied the dusty lair. He did find an odd stain on the walls that was the same level, even though the ground curved downward toward the back of the cave. He surmised that the narrow path that ran past the opening was probably a conduit for spring water as the mountain ice at the crest started to melt. That seemed like a reasonable deduction and the soft floor could be sediment after the water drained or evaporated and the stain the water's highest level. With two or three feet of water in the cave, no animal would make its spring nest in here.

A horrible notion disrupted his train of thought. What if that mountain water was the healing water they were seeking? From what he could see, and smell, there weren't any signs of moisture. The air in the cave was stale but not dank. What wa-ter that may have accumulated in here had evaporated a long time ago.

"Maybe the water is buried." His voice sounded off the walls of the small cave. "I'll dig a little and check," he whis-pered.

His calm demeanor was swallowed up in his frantic dig-ging. Dirt was flying everywhere as his anticipation grew. Over a foot down, he uncovered a gravel bed that he knew would have drained the water even faster than normal. He tried three other spots with the same results. Snake sat up. He was panting and covered with dirt and sweat. He let out a long sigh and then wrapped his arms around his legs and buried his face in his knees. He remained that way for another ten minutes.

Snake knew he was quickly approaching burn-out. It had taken all he could muster to push himself to take this mission. Their last trip into Lebanon had stretched his nerves to the breaking point. There was a bullet with his name on it aimed at him, the voices in his head repeatedly warned him. Only the desperation of this mission gave him the strength to silence those voices. He would resign when he got home, he was sure of that. There was no way he could perform at the high level demanded of Special Forces personnel, worried that he was constantly living in a snipers gunsight.

One of the jobs of someone taking point was to either spot the enemy first or expose just enough of yourself to remove the target from those following you and have it aimed at you. Hopefully, that first shot didn't kill you but, even if it did, that would warn the main body following that danger was up ahead. Snake knew that as long as he sat in the small cave he remained invisible to that sniper. But yielding to his own survival instinct might prove deadly to the rest of his party. Four of his friends had already given everything for this mission, he acknowledged, and now it's his turn.

The urge to quit had found new life in the discouragement he was enduring. He shook it off and climbed out to find his friends, thinking that his redemption would have to wait. Maybe they had better luck. *Yes*, he thought as he started feeling a little better, *they may have already found it*.

CHAPTER 19

They were positioned the way Simon suggested. Snake was on patrol ahead of them. Weasel, was maintaining a watchful eye on their rear. He intentionally drifted farther back to give the others a better chance should he be attacked. If they were being followed, he would be the first one shot at. Birdman took the far right and Simon took the far left. Sara was placed in the center/left and David took up a position center/right. They were in a line two hundred yards wide, with fifty yards separating each of them, as they searched the mountain's many tree-lined ridges and deep green valleys for the location of the Pond of God.

For the next three hours they searched relentlessly for the mysterious pond. Just as mysterious to the commandos was the whereabouts of their attackers. Finally, under the torturous heat of the mid-day sun and the stress of jumping at every jungle noise, Simon stopped the search. They had covered a lot of tough, dangerous terrain, and they had to make a decision to climb higher or continue searching around the base of the mountain. There were perils associated with either decision. Birdman sent out a coded message to Snake and Weasel to close ranks.

Simon, David, Sara, and Birdman sat down to wait for the two commandos under the shade of three tall acacia trees—trees so green Simon thought they must have escaped the attention of those long necked giraffes they had seen earlier. He didn't consider that the terrain they had climbed would be too difficult for a giraffe. In fact, it was the beauty of the trees that first suggested to Simon's tired muscles that this would be a great place to rest.

David was grateful for the rest stop. It gave him a chance to catch his breath and finally to talk to Sara while waiting for Weasel and Snake to return.

David motioned for Sara to come sit next to him. "Sara," he said as he held her hand, "I need to talk to you. I'm so sorry about how I've been acting."

"No, David, you don't have any reason to be sorry. I should be the one apologizing to you. Oh David, I'm so glad you—"

"Everyone get up!" Birdman shouted, cutting Sara off in mid-sentence.

Weasel finally spotted them as he hurriedly climbed up toward their resting spot. He was expecting them to stop soon and rest because they had to be exhausted, so he wasn't surprised when he heard the coded message to close ranks. He was proud of the shape he was in but the climb had exhausted him. Numerous times, he had to stop and wipe off the sweat—and there were the bugs to deal with. Add to that the constant strain of expecting the soldiers to catch up with them.

Weasel continued turning around and scanning the area behind him as he climbed hoping to see soldiers behind them before they saw him. Snake was stationed somewhere in front them. The danger, Weasel figured, if it came, it would probably come from the rear this time as those soldiers they eluded found their trail and pursued them. At least that's what the seven-year veteran was hoping.

The way Dog and Whale died infuriated him. If he spotted their killers, he had already decided, as he dropped back farther and farther from his friends, he was going to avenge their murders in like manner. He didn't consider the Ethiopians as soldiers because this wasn't an attack on their country by the Israeli contingent, but a mission of mercy. But now he was joining in the battle that they started. He would die but they would pay a terrible price for his life. *A trained Israeli Special Forces commando will be their worst nightmare*, he swore. As his anger flared up anew, he stopped and, with his binoculars, scanned the horizon behind him again. Nothing.

Snake had already disappeared from sight over a high ridge on the eastern side of the mountain when the signal was sent. Birdman signaled again, when he didn't receive an answer from Snake. After five minutes, Birdman decided that if Snake didn't acknowledge him by the time Weasel reached them, he would go looking for him.

Through his binoculars, Weasel spotted the group sitting down under some trees. From the minute he received the message to join them, he felt something was wrong. That was the second time he had that feeling. The first time ended with the death of four of his friends. Weasel started running while trying to see through the psychic haze that was enveloping him. When Snake failed to acknowledge Birdman's coded message, Weasel at first thought he was just out of range or something. Now, he sensed danger was close by. *Is Snake in trouble?*

Birdman was also growing impatient, waiting for Weasel to catch up. It was taking him too long. Birdman stood up to spot him and try to estimate how long it would take for him to reach them. It took a tense few moments but he finally spotted him running up the slope toward them. "Everyone get up!" Birdman shouted. "Something might be wrong. Weasel is running toward us."

Birdman surveyed the valley behind Weasel and couldn't spot the source off his panic. Nothing was moving that he could see. He gave the green valley one more look through his binoculars but again he saw nothing.

"What is it," Simon asked when Birdman repeatedly scanned down the mountain.

"I don't know. Whatever is chasing him I can't—Wait a minute? Dammit! There, about a mile to his right, I see soldiers on foot heading this way. There's no way they could have seen Weasel or us at that distance, but they're headed right for us in a big hurry."

The group never had time to decide on a course of action. Birdman waved to Weasel to hurry up and was stunned to see him drop to one knee, raise his rifle and open fire in their direction.

"Hit the dirt," Birdman yelled.

A stream of bullets from Weasel sprayed over their heads and into some trees farther up the mountainside as they dove for cover. Birdman was the only one who understood what Weasel was shooting at. The others watched in surprise as Birdman rushed forward, took shelter behind some rocks, and started shooting up the slope toward a stand of trees. Then the return fire rained down on them, knocking leaves and branches off the trees over their heads. It was as if someone was in the trees with a dozen chainsaws as splinters of wood, leaves, and sawdust poured down, covering them. Their only shelter was the larger roots of the trees they were hiding behind as death whistled inches overhead.

"Sara," David shouted over the din of the war weapons.

She didn't respond. David put his arm around her and drew her closer to him.

"David, are we going to die?"

The fear in her voice strengthened the resolve in his own. "No, no. Birdman will get us out of this. Just keep your head down."

The accurate shooting from Birdman and Weasel soon silenced the hidden snipers.

"Birdman, can you hear me?"

"Yeah, Weasel, are you all right?"

"So far, yes. What's going on? How did they get ahead of us?"

"I don't know Weasel. But that's not but half our problems. Look behind you about a mile down the slope."

"Behind me, what could be behind—" He carefully turned an aimed his binoculars down the slope and, true to their bad luck, about twenty soldiers were climbing up as fast as they could. Once again, they would be in a damn cross fire. Weasel slowly removed the binoculars from his face. Boy was he glad he didn't say anything about Snake's goof up because it looked like he screwed up also. *Well, no use crying about it.* He replaced the empty clip in his weapon. *Time to go back to work.* "Look out for me, everyone," he said in his mic. "I'm coming up behind you."

He ran a zigzag pattern up the slope, trying not to give anyone a clear shot at him. His friends were in trouble and there wasn't time to be careful. He was almost able to reach them when three soldiers opened fire on him. Weasel rolled out of the way as a stream of slugs ripped into the ground where he was kneeling. Birdman responded in kind, as he emptied another clip into the rocks above.

"Birdman, we've got to get out of here," Weasel said, between gasping for breath after finding shelter behind some large rocks about twenty yards from Birdman's position.

"I know, Weasel. But if we make a break for it, we will have to cross open ground. You and I will have to stay behind to keep them from getting a shot at the others."

"Yes, sir, that's about how I see it."

"Okay then, that's the plan. Simon, Sara, David, can you hear me?"

No one answered. At first, he thought they were all dead but then he saw Simon's head look around from behind a tree.

Birdman waved, trying to get Simon's attention, but failed as the trio kept their heads down. "Simon," Birdman shouted across to him as he shielded himself behind the trees. Finally, Simon looked up and saw him waving. He nodded back when Birdman pointed to his headset.

When he heard Simon's voice, he spoke as calmly as he could. "Simon, is everyone all right?"

"Yes, we're shaken and stirred," he replied, remembering where he had heard that today.

"I bet. Simon, you will have to lead Sara and David through that tall grass over there on your right. It will shield you from them. Once you reach it, head up the mountain on the other side. The only chance you will have is to climb and hide above them."

"What about Snake?"

"He's probably dead, Simon," Birdman answered. "They

must have killed him before they found us. Get ready to run. There's not much time left before those other soldiers climbing up the mountain reach us. On three, Weasel and I will cover you. Run as fast as you can and stay low. Ready, everyone?"

Simon, David, and Sara repeated, "Ready."

"One, two, three!"

Weasel was up before the count reached three, running up the hill and firing into the tree line above them to draw their fire. Quickly Birdman joined him. First Simon, then Sara, and finally David made a mad rush across the open slope toward the safety of a thick patch of trees, tall grass and bushes on their right. Weasel aimed at two flashes he saw in the rocks. No other flashes appeared. *Maybe we got them all*, he hoped. "Shit!"

Suddenly, about a dozen soldiers emerged out of the rocks above and ran down toward them screaming and firing wildly. Five soldiers broke off and ran toward the fleeing trio. Birdman cut down two of them immediately.

Weasel sprayed a group of four or five men and all of them hit the dirt wounded or killed. He turned to take aim on the soldiers who were chasing after his fleeing friends. There was no time for a second shot. They were about to disappear into the bushes and tall grass after his friends. He would have to get them on the first try. He led the first man by a foot then squeezed the trigger. Nothing happened. Weasel pulled hard on the trigger, hoping it was just stuck from the heat generated from all the firing. Nothing! He must be out of ammo. He desperately searched his belt for another clip. When he found it, he took a moment to see where the soldiers were as he slid the clip blindly in place. They were taking aim on the last person to reach the woods.

"Nooooooo!" Weasel shouted as he raised his gun to shoot. Again nothing happened. The next instant the lead soldier stopped, took aim, and fired off a spray of bullets into the clump of bushes where David had just disappeared. Paralyzed, Weasel could only watch as three soldiers raced off into the bushes after them. Where was Birdman? he wondered. Weasel cautiously searched the smoking battlefield, finding him kneeling on the ground holding his bleeding left arm.

"I'm okay, it just winged me," Birdman said through clenched teeth. "Go after them. I'm right behind you."

"Right." The I-just-hope-they're-still-alive comment Weasel kept to himself as he drew his pistol and ran into the woods.

Birdman picked up his weapon, checked to see they weren't being followed, and ran after him.

Weasel couldn't see anything when he entered the tall weeds. He stopped and listened. He heard automatic weapon fire somewhere ahead but had trouble determining the direction. It was then that he heard someone running through the high grass behind him. He aimed his weapon, hoping. When Birdman caught up with him, he let out a deep breath. When the leader hurried past him, Weasel followed.

"Hold it." Weasel grabbed Birdman by the shirt and whispered, "Didn't that sound like one of our Uzi's firing?"

Both knew the civilians were unarmed and the soldiers carried rifles.

Slowly they moved through the bushes, trying to find their trail. For twenty feet or so the grass was so tall they couldn't see anything in front of them. Finally, they stepped through into a clearing and spotted the three Ethiopian soldiers lying on the ground, dead. There, standing on a hill overlooking a kneeling Sara, Simon, and a prone David, was an angry commando.

"I heard the gunfire and came running as fast as I could," Snake explained to his startled comrades after he ran down to meet them. "I tried raising you on my headset. All I heard was static. I might have damaged it when I fell. Unable to raise you, I raced back as fast as I could. I stopped to get my bearing when I saw Simon and Sara run out of the tall grass as if it was on fire or something. The sound of bullets whistling over their heads alerted me as they ran into the clearing. Then David staggered out of the bushes and fell down just as soldiers appeared. I guess they weren't expecting me to be there with their guns pointing down and all. I think they just wanted to take Sara alive for fun and games later. I shot them before they realized the error of their sexist ways."

Birdman and Weasel walked over to where Sara and Simon were kneeling beside David.

A brokenhearted Sara looked up at Birdman. "David's been shot. He has three bullet wounds," Sara explained. "One has punctured the meaty part of his right thigh from behind leaving a ragged, bloody exit wound on the front of his leg but, thankfully, it missed his femoral artery. The second shot cut a deep gash in his right shoulder, missing the bones somehow as it cut through his flesh. The third is the least serious as it just creased his head above the left ear. All three are very bloody wounds, requiring bandages we don't have."

Dog had been their medic and carried the medical supplies.

Weasel looked over at the dead soldiers. "Strip the shirts off our friends over there. That will have to do. Birdman get their shirts and we'll cut them up."

Weasel tied the impromptu bandages around David's head, shoulder, and his thigh. The remaining parts he used as a sling for David's shoulder.

"We have got to get out of here in a hurry, I'm afraid," Weasel reminded everyone after doing what he could for David.

"He's right," Birdman agreed. "There was a band of soldiers climbing up the slope of the mountain after us. They must have been alerted by radio when we were ambushed. They couldn't be more than ten minutes behind us, maybe less."

"How far can we get with David all shot up," Sara asked. She had already decided to die with him if she had to.

"Listen," Snake said. "Maybe our piss-poor luck is finally changing."

"Tell me you found the pond," Simon pleaded.

"No, but I think I found a place we can hide from those soldier chasing us. Come on, help me carry him."

David was unconscious from the blow to his head, thus the rough handling by his harried nurses went mercifully unnoticed and unfelt. They carried him very carefully over the narrow ridge edge that Snake had "stumbled" upon and into the cave. It was very difficult footing but after three or four slips they made it. Sara trailed after them, using a branch to sweep away their tracks and any blood drops.

It took three of them to uproot the thick bush blocking the entrance to the cave to allow them to carry David inside. Once inside, Weasel found a spot along the wall to place his army issue flashlight. It cast just enough light to see where you were going without revealing their presence to someone looking up the mountain.

They placed David on some soft dirt and put a knapsack under his head. Simon re-bandaged David's head wound while Sara tended to the more serious wound on his leg.

Weasel suggested taking the thick bush they uprooted and moving it near the cave opening. The bushy, green plant would make the entrance all but invisible and afford them a shielded exit until it was time to leave. Quickly, they agreed it was a good idea and pulled it very slowly into the cave opening, trying to prevent any sudden movement that could draw attention to them. With the rough terrain outside, each felt confident it would discourage the soldiers from looking here. Once the bush was pulled into place, Birdman used his belt to tie it to an out cropping of rock making it difficult for someone to pull it out. Weasel took first guard duty by the entrance while Snake explained how he found the cave.

"I was probably in this cave when you signaled for me Birdman," he said after hearing what had transpired in his absence. He spread his hand around in a circle over his head. "I was praying that this was the location of the Holy Water."

Snake could sense everyone turn toward him in anticipation.

"Sorry. I searched the cave thoroughly but found nothing. I was ready to give up on this mission when I stuck my head out into the sunlight and heard gunshots. Don't ask me why but now I believe we will find it. I don't know how or when, but I believe in my soul that we will. Maybe it's escaping that second ambush, I don't know. We should be dead and yet..."

No one came to his defense. With David all shot up, their

faith in finding the origin of the healing waters had more holes
in it than their comrade did.

"Has anything ever come easy for us?" Snake whispered to
those stunned doubters in the dark cave. "We had to struggle
to get our country, die to keep our country, and we took off on
this wild goose chase to save what's left of our country. Other
than the USA, whom can we count on as our friend in the
world? No one! We have shed our blood from the concentration camps of Europe, to this God-forsaken mountainside in
Ethiopia, yet still we prevail. It may cost each of us our lives
but we *will* succeed!"

"Quiet," Weasel whispered.

The way he pointed his rifle at the entrance let everyone
know there were soldiers in the immediate area, looking for
them. Snake turned off the flashlight, plunging them into
darkness. For what seemed like an eternity, they listened to the
search outside the entrance to the cave. It was an unspoken
fact that they were prepared to die and not surrender if they
were found. From the shouting they heard, someone was really
upset that they couldn't find a trace of them. Whomever it
was, Weasel could just make out their movement between the
leaves and branches of the bush.

Once they heard a helicopter pass overhead. There wasn't
any information in the pre-mission briefing about the Ethiopians having infrared equipment in their helicopters. If they did,
the cave would protect them as it blocked their body's heat
signature.

While sitting in the dark, Simon's training took over. *How
did they find us? Was it a coincidence or did their radar pick
us up?* Questions that he felt were important enough to ignore
what was occurring outside.

He replayed everything that had happened to them, in
hopes that he might discover a loose thread that he had overlooked. Did he slip up and tell the wrong person something?
He questioned. It was his job to leave no stone unturned in
preparing for this mission but because it was necessary to
rush, had he missed something? With the close brushes with
death they all had endured, he quickly brushed aside any be-

trayal by the battered group hiding in the dark cave. But the feeling that the Ethiopian government was tipped off was an ache that wouldn't go away.

The source of his "ache" sailed silently, fifty nautical miles behind the *USS Seattle* as the ship returned to her southern patrol lanes a few miles off shore in international waters. The message, sent by way of a satellite orbiting over the Indian Ocean, was about a helicopter that had taken off from a US warship and was racing east toward the African border. It was a normal flash message to Moscow that, once sent, also alerted the *Seattle* to their location. That was one of the reasons it was sent. The *Seattle*'s skipper and crew would now know that the silent hunter had again slipped undetected within lethal killing distance of the great ship.

The sub captain took great pleasure in writing that in his log as the submarine changed direction and submerged in the blue waters of the Red Sea before a helicopter, now being launched from the deck of the *Seattle*, could get a sonar fix on her.

It was a wasted effort. The *Seattle* was obeying orders to ignore the submarine as it approached. The unclassified range and listening ability of their improved sonar was judged far more important a secret than revealing that to the over-confident Russian hunter/killer submarine they had tracked long before it was in range to hurt them. It could have fired a missile-launched torpedo hours earlier, destroying the sub before it was able to sneak close enough to do the same.

The six team members sat in silence an hour after the soldiers apparently moved to search another section of the mountain. "They have been gone a while now so I think it's safe to move around but keep all conversation to a whisper," Birdman advised breaking the silence. "Snake use your smaller flashlight if needed," he explained. "The range of its beam would diffuse before reaching the entrance but supply enough light to see each other."

Sara avoided looking at Birdman. She could feel him watching her, waiting for her to rub it in. That had to be the helicopter that she saw earlier. It was probably how the soldiers were able to get ahead and ambush them. Snake might be right. Finding this cave could be the beginning of a change in their luck.

Birdman was thinking the same thing himself as Simon tied a knot in the piece of his undershirt he put around his wounded arm.

Sara changed David's bandages under the light of her pocket flashlight. The trip to the cave had loosened the old bandages soaking them in his blood. She took one of the bloody bandages, rinsed it with some water from her canteen, and wiped his face. *Damn*, she realized, *he's already feverous.* The leg wound was bleeding, and they had nothing to sew it up with or apply enough pressure to stop it. Who knew what other arteries were torn apart by the exiting bullet? she wondered, while checking his weak pulse.

In the waning few hours of daylight they remained hidden in the cave as the continued presence of the helicopter overhead, presumed to be searching for them, was heard as it passed hourly within earshot. As night came, the cave became very dark. Snake's flashlight died an hour later, so they sat around in the dark, saving the remaining flashlights to illuminate the cave whenever anyone had to move about or check on David. He was holding his own as the bleeding slowed, but he had already loss a lot of blood. The fact that they didn't have the chance to take more than a sip or two of water all day, much less eat a meal, was rewarded in their not having to dig out a latrine yet in the small cave.

"The soldiers must have moved off in another direction," Birdman suggested as the hours of quiet multiplied after dark. "We are safe for now. I don't think they would risk moving around in the dark on these dangerous ridges."

Each of them battled the lonely pangs of defeat, as

thoughts of their hiding while so many young children were dying at home was a common torment.

Their conversations were reduced to whispering short crisp recommendations or suggestions on the best course of action to take once they were out of there. Admitting failure wasn't an option for the brave "Six Little Indians" hiding in the dark, cool cave.

"How is David?" Sara heard Weasel's deep voice whisper in the dark.

"I don't know," she lied unnecessarily, because everyone knew he probably wouldn't make it to dawn's breaking. "He has lost a lot of blood."

"Harrrmmm," was his only reply. Weasel sat against the wall of the cave and fed a new clip into his Uzi. Even in the dark, it soothed him to know he was ready for whatever. Anyone foolish enough to try entering the cave would pay with their lives for that mistake. In his anger, he almost wished for the chance.

Sara sat close to David in case he needed her. No one in the cave would have expected anything else. Truth was, she was the one in need, because the words she wanted to say to him had never found release and now her audience wasn't listening.

Snake had little to add to the conversations. Killing their pursuers had given him a much-needed transfusion of inner peace. Where the cave was a prison or hospital to others, to him it was a place of rest and redemption.

The sound of Weasel loading his weapon triggered Birdman into action. The small flashlight beam signaled everyone without being alarming.

"We need to reconnoiterer the perimeter and determine the location of the soldiers. If they're gone, we can get out of here while it is still dark," he explained.

Weasel and Snake moved forward to volunteer.

"Do you think it's a good idea to risk losing anyone else?" Simon inquired.

"This is what we're trained for," Weasel answered him. "The way we were ambushed happened because we had to expose ourselves to look for the healing water. Now that you're safe, Snake and I can move at our own pace and wait for the right moment and opportunity. These soldiers are no match for a well-trained Israeli commando."

The dimmed light shaded but couldn't hide the angry looks on the faces of those highly trained commandos, Simon noted. God help anyone who crossed their paths.

He disagreed with Weasel but said nothing, as the two men stripped off everything but what was necessary for reconnaissance. They carried a sidearm, knife, and a few loops of wire that made Simon shudder when he remembered what it was for. Weasel was to work his way down and investigate the area to the west of their position. It was the same area they had covered climbing up the mountain. Snake had already traveled east of their position so he would return there and look for any soldiers. Cautiously, they slipped out the cave, under the bushes pulled up to the doorway, and into the star lit night.

Sara sat and listened to their conversation. She had nothing to offer because the only thing that mattered was the seriously wounded man lying beside her. After they departed, she did offer a prayer for their safety.

CHAPTER 20

In the deadly quiet of the ink-black cave, Sara sat huddled in a corner near where David was lying. Every time he would moan or breathe funny, she would aim her flashlight at him. Before long, she was able to distinguish the sounds of an unconscious, seriously wounded man, from a noise that was unnatural and might signal he needed her attention. That permitted her to relax a little in the dark.

"It will be hours before Weasel or Snake returns," Birdman warned her and Simon, "so try to get as much rest as possible. Each commando will cautiously search the assigned area for about two hours before turning back."

Funny things happened when sitting in the dark. Unable to see or be seen, Sara started to feel like she was completely alone. She let her imagination take her to a sun-washed, deserted, and very hot tropical island. Alone and free to wear the skimpiest of bikinis or nothing at all if she so desired, along a gorgeous white beach as the surf washed in at her feet. In her vision, beautifully colored exotic birds sang as they flew from tree to tree.

She pictured herself there as a carefree innocent nymph who carried no burdens or had to live by the concepts of others. Free there to do nothing, breaking the bonds of her normally tightly scheduled existence.

What David had given her, she decided in the dark of the grotto, was spontaneity. Well, there were other things. She felt a small grin appear at the corners of her mouth. One of his suggestions caught her completely off guard. There was no way she would have done it with anyone else. They were standing in his back yard late one night, looking across at his neighbor's pool. She was standing in front of him with his strong arms wrapped around her as they looked up at the starry night sky.

"Hey, beautiful, I've got this crazy idea."

"She reached around and grabbed his ass. "Oh, you do, what's that?"

"That too, but I was thinking, why don't we go swimming in that pool over there?"

"What? We can't do that," Sara said as she turned around in his arms and faced him. "That's your neighbor's pool."

"Sure, we can. Frank and his family are gone for the weekend."

"How do you know that, David?"

"He's my neighbor. We talk."

"Sure, you do."

"Come on," David said and started tugging on her hand.

When she hesitated, he smiled at her and then started walking off, unbuttoning his shirt.

She put her hand to her mouth and gasped. "David, you're not."

He let his shorts drop to his feet and was quickly down to his underwear.

"David!" Yes, it was dark out but if someone had looked out their window they would have seen him.

"Come on, girl, live. Take a chance, Sara. You have a beautiful body."

"David!" Sara said and started looking around at the windows of the neighboring houses after he finished undressing.

"I don't have a swim suit."

"Neither do I. We don't need one," he explained and, in one motion, stood there completely naked.

"David?"

"Trust me, Sara, it will feel so liberating. Trust me."

She did trust him, from the first time she looked in those brown eyes. She trusted him when she gave herself to him.

She trusted him more than she trusted any person she had ever known.

David thought he might be pushing her too far and looked around for his clothes. But when he looked up she was down to her underwear.

Sara stopped. She was only so brazen. If she went any farther, she was breaking the law—and her mother's heart if she was looking down from above. Worse than that, maybe her father was looking.

She wrapped her arms across her breasts and looked at David. He would understand when she told him her father might be watching, her conscience told her. That would have worked—had he not reached out his hand to her.

David watched as she stared at him for a moment and then reached behind her and unsnapped her bra. Her breasts were impressive but he searched her eyes. She smiled at him as she pulled down her white panties and stepped out of them. When she ran into his arms, they both started laughing.

It was one of her favorite moments, Sara recalled. The water felt amazing on her bare skin. Amazing. Maybe it was knowing they were breaking the law, but it felt so intense. A few times, they had to slip under the water and hide. First when someone came out to put some garbage in their garbage can, and the other time when an older man looked out his back door because they were making too much noise as they played in the pool. They were clowning and acting silly, Sara remembered, and laughing too loud. It wasn't the sensual joining she might have dreamed, but fun.

"Okay," Sara said when the coast looked clear, "time to get out of here."

"Okay, babe, I don't want you to wrinkle."

"We both know what is wrinkling," she answered, laughing.

David climbed out and lifted her out of the pool. He endeared himself when he shielded her as they walked back into his yard and picked up their clothes. After a shower, a cup of hot cocoa, they sat on his couch in robes, reliving the experience.

It felt like the right thing to do—with him, Sara recalled. But she was surprised she actually did it, the deed having awakened something in her. As she stood there in front of him, disrobing, she didn't even bother to look around and see if anyone was looking. For her, that was shocking as doing the same thing in the middle of Main Street at noon. All of her usual apprehensions reared their heads, but that was normal. What wasn't normal was the amazing feeling of release she felt as she slipped into the warm water. She didn't feel naked, but free. Not just free of clothes—no, it was much deeper than that.

We are born as free spirits, she once read. *As we learn to walk and talk, society ensnares us with a host of precepts. We learn to hold things within, to hide feelings that might mar the image we are supposed to display. Women tie up their bodies to hide their sexuality. Men flaunt their achievements to distract from their sensitive side.*

As the warm water washed over her skin, Sara felt those uptight precepts lose their meaning. It wasn't a sexual thing, even though when he pulled her into his arms in the water, both bodies responded as one might guess.

Making gentle love in bed later that night completed an awakening that gave birth to numerous first times in a variety of places.

Now in the quiet blackness of the cave, Sara began to take a good long look at herself. Up until she met David, she never felt she needed anyone. Sure, she enjoyed the company of others, but she never really valued it, until now. She wrapped her arms around herself—a movement provoked by the realization of how empty her life had been before David.

The emptiness that she felt when she learned of the death of her parents was resurrected in the darkness. Those feelings weren't born on the day they died. They just found sanctification. The wall of ebon did reflect some things back at her.

As she acknowledged it, she began to feel differently about herself. Blame it on their close brush with death, or the injury to David, but she felt a genuine concern for the wellbeing of all the men that she accompanied on this mission.

Sara felt moved by their sacrifice.

Isolated, and with most of her senses turned off, she was able to connect with a seed of emotion she never knew she had. From as far back as she could remember, no one really mattered that much to her. She was more into her career than she was with any of the men she met. Her family was important to her but there was always coldness between them. They loved each other but they never were an emotional, touching clan. Certain touchy-feely outward expressions like kissing and hugging were shunned, as if an unseemly act. Love was something you received and gave without demonstration. It was a noun not a verb or adjective with her family.

From that upbringing, Sara made decisions based on their value to her. She loved those who she was supposed to love and respected the same. That credo had worked well for her until she fell for the man she was assigned to get close to.

She suddenly started to giggle when she realized her eyes were wide open. It was so dark in the cave, she'd thought her eyelids were closed.

Where a bright day could cause one's spirit to soar, the dark cold refuge she found herself in quickly dragged her back down. "Emptiness, we were talking about your life of emptiness," the darkness seemed to infer, tormenting her with it. Sara remembered…

On the black screen that was in front of her, she imagined she could see herself standing over the graves of her father and mother. The hurt was enormous as she tried to reason out their deaths. No explanation offered her any respite from the pain. Even in a dry, dusty cave a thousand miles away from home, the misery of their deaths reached out to find her again. She had made peace with the fact of their deaths, but not with the loss. What hurt was her inability to show emotion as she stood at their graves. In her own way, she did love them, showing it or talking about it was an unborn child to Sara Jacobs. Regret over her inability to reach out to them started to drag her spirits down farther. Salvation was David touching her leg as he moved in his unconsciousness. Another sweep of his face with the flashlight reassured her that he was still alive.

Sara scanned the flashlight around the cave. Both Simon and Birdman were laying down with their backs to her. She turned off the light and lay down beside David. She listened carefully and could hear his labored breathing. At least it was a way of monitoring him in the dark.

She started to relax but, within minutes, she was remembering more of her past. The answer to the emptiness she had come to embrace in her life was just beyond the curtain of black that hung in front of her. "If you could just strain a little harder," the darkness seemed to say, "you would be able to see."

She started to question herself on the day that Simon gave her the assignment to infiltrate the Falashian sect. That was about the time she began to wonder why she never really felt happy. Oh, she had moments—like holding her own with other soldiers during her mandatory stint in the army and graduating from the Mossad academy near the top of her class. But not the joy of being that others had confessed to at the birth of a baby, or their son's first steps, or—or from falling in love.

Everyone thought she was being distant because of the shock of her parents' death, but she knew better. Her usual snobbish attitude had colored everything about her from childhood up until now. Mother gave up trying to change her "unhappy" child, as she called her. But never was it more apparent to Sara that something was missing than when she was standing over her parents' graves. She felt *something*—she remembered that. Pain yes, she would miss them, but where was the heartache, the emotion, the tears?

Sara reached out in the dark, blindly feeling for David. She found some unknown part of him and traveled over his body until she touched the soft skin on his face. He was warm but no longer feverish. She was surprised by her concern for his well-being. *Cold Sara*, she thought, using the painful nickname most of her roommates in school had hung on her, *is genuinely concerned about this shot up Ethiopian Jew lying beside her in the dark? Who would have believed this?* She realized, much to her surprise, that she was also getting worried about the heroic duo who were out there somewhere, putting their lives on the line again for all of them.

Was that really her, she wondered, crying over Hawk when he was killed? Sara's reflections were halted when she overheard Birdman whispering something to Simon that distracted her for a moment.

Why did she feel so strongly about this man? she wondered as she touched David in the dark. When she had walked out of Simon's office, he was only a face on a photograph. During that assignment, something changed in her. Sara turned over on her back in the cave and tried remembering...

CHAPTER 21

Walking out of Simon's office with her new assignment that April day it was raining outside, but she was so elated to be finally working on an assignment again she didn't bother to hurry to her car. Whoever this Mr. Yasuda was, she intended to turn over ever leaf until she knew more about him than his mother did.

After memorizing the data Simon supplied, Sara's next step was to follow this David Yasuda character and study his habits. Disguised in numerous outfits, from a neatly dressed white-haired old woman; a grungy vagabond; to an overly made-up, mini-skirt-wearing street hustler in net stockings, she was able to get within kissing distance of him on numerous occasions without his knowledge. After a week of studying his habits, she found her opening. She had to do it smoothly. Getting his attention without being obvious was the key.

At the Mossad training academy, every agent was taught the vital importance of establishing a solid first encounter without appearing to make the first step. If the subject was confident that they originated the encounter, they would more readily open up to a stranger. The successful agent learned to be a patient fisherman until the subject snared the bait. Sara was a natural fisher-of-men. She could bait her hook, sit back, and wait months for a nibble.

Haifa was a beautiful Israeli port city at the base of Mt. Carmel. The city was comprised of three tiers. The first section or tier was called the Old City or Old Town. It contained the harbor area, the coastal beaches, and ancient stone walls built by the Crusaders in the Middle Ages. Next was the middle tier or Hacarmel district. It comprised the downtown district with the scent of bakeries, the noise of the bazaars, mixed with the modern world of business. The top tier was called the High City. Up there were modern hotels, residential streets with posh homes jutting out overlooking the Mediterranean Sea. Farther up was the Carmel Center with parks, museums, and trendy cafés. The roads leading from tier to tier were often very steep and well-traveled.

David turned left onto Kish Blvd. "Where and what am I going to eat tonight?"

The question had more to do with the lateness of the hour than a choice. "It's too late to go shopping and then cook it at home."

Tired after visiting some of the Falashian students who were training at Elsha Hospital, he decided to eat whatever he found in the fridge. He was laughing at the growling sound that his stomach was making when a car hit him from behind as he slowed at a stop sign. The impact was enough to snap his head back. David looked at the person in the car through his side view mirror and saw a woman with her hands up to her mouth in surprise.

The light blue Volkswagen van he had struggled to purchase two years ago was now twelve years old. With over one hundred and thirty thousand miles, it still ran and looked as if it was new. David pulled over into a parking lot of some engineering firm and sorted through the mass of papers in his glove compartment for his insurance. The gray Fiat had followed him into the parking lot so David didn't expect any trouble with her.

He climbed out of his car and walked back to assess the damage. It wasn't as bad as it felt. The fender was bent in a little and the right taillight was cracked, or was that crack already there? Well, she was going to pay for it, anyway.

The woman pulled into the parking lot and circled her car around so that the driver's side doors were facing each other.

She watched him as he stood behind his vehicle assessing

the damage. *Oh, come on now*, Sara scolded silently, *I didn't hit you that hard*. She waited until she saw that she had his full attention before getting out.

Curious about the driver, David watched as she climbed out of her car. Dressed as if she was going out for the evening, she struggled to exit the car demurely in the short, tight dress she was wearing. The hem of the black silk dress slid up enticingly high over two very shapely thighs until she was able to stand up and tug down on the hem. She did that with such obvious embarrassment that David felt a little ashamed for staring. But the way she strolled toward him in that tight outfit overcame such feelings. Wow.

"Are you all right," the lady asked, walking over to him. Her caring voice, vetoing what her body was saying, seemingly demonstrated a genuine concern for his welfare. "I'm very sorry I hit you."

David took a minute to size up the driver. She was wearing a beautiful, shimmering, silky black dress and high heels. Her hair was pulled back in a bun and was as black as her outfit making her deeply tanned skin look radiant. *She's a very nice-looking woman*, he decided, acknowledging the obvious. Maybe not a ten, but she was *very* nice looking. The tight dress revealed a woman who was in excellent shape as there were no interruptions to her hourglass figure, which did as much for the dress as it did for her. The attractive lady's eyes were dark, probably brown, he noticed as she walked closer. She never, for a moment, took her eyes off his.

"I'm—fine," David found himself struggling to say, as he realized his mouth had somehow become dry. "My vehicle is a little beat up though."

"I'm terribly sorry. I was in a hurry to get to a function for my boss and I was trying to put on my make-up while I drove. I guess that was a bad idea, huh?"

When David didn't answer, the lady excused herself for a moment, turned, and walked back to her car. There were a few more walls for her expensive and tight-fitting outfit to break down. *If coming didn't shake the tree*, she abruptly decided, *then maybe leaving will*.

"Ah—ah, wait a minute, miss, where are you going?"

Sara stopped and turned around. She gave him a puzzled look and then pointed to her car. "Oh, ah, nowhere. I was trying to find my papers. I think my driver's card is in my other purse. I was in such—never mind." She walked up to him. "Listen, mister, my name is Sara Jacobs. I live and work here in Haifa. I'll get the information you will need for the insurance. I just don't have it on me," she told him then pretended to bend over and look in her purse again.

The "on me" comment garnered the desired result. His gaze found the deep cut of the top of her dress and admired the exposed fresh while she had her head down leafing through her purse.

David stopped staring and asked, "Can I have your address, anyway?"

She looked at him for a moment before answering. "Sure, that's no problem. You know what? I'm too late for my boss's party, anyway. Why don't you follow me home and I'll get the information for you? I really think it's in my other purse. I live on Hareef Road with my six brothers," she lied. "It's off of Pika Road, near Moria Blvd. It's not far from here."

David saw through the lie about her six brothers but understood her need to say it.

"Yes, I know the area. There's a high school nearby where some of my students attend."

"That's it. I graduated from there myself more years ago than I would like to remember," she said, smiling for the first time.

David didn't return the smile as she had expected. Sara quickly realized that it would take more than a tight dress and boobs to loosen up this guy. His river ran deeper than most men's. Sara turned and returned to her car.

David walked past her and held her car door open.

Well, well, is he a gentleman or does he want another look at my legs? "Thank you," she said and gracefully sat in her car. Sara was about to confirm her opinion about the lecherous man when she noticed he wasn't looking at her thigh-high hem but the mess on her seat. "It is always the little things you don't do that will catch you in a lie," she whispered to herself, turning her head. It was a phrase her instructors had pounded into her in training class. She was grateful that she took the time to dump out everything in her glove compartment in a genuine search for her driver's card. *That was what you were looking for when you held my door open, huh?* That thought was confirmed to her when he smiled back at her.

"I'll follow you this time," David said as he started to feel more comfortable with her.

That prompted a laugh from Sara who added that might be a good idea. Her smile had warmth to it that seemed to say everything is all right.

She reached over and gathered up the scattered papers and envelopes to put them back in the glove compartment. When she reached for the glove compartment door David couldn't help taking another look at her. *She is a good-looking woman.* Then he turned and walked away.

Sara watched him get back in his van. There was an uneasiness about him that triggered both caution and excitement in her. She wasn't frightened. He didn't give off an impression of someone who would try hurting her. Remembering some of the photos of him shirtless, she knew he was someone who could. But nothing in his bio indicated that he was violent. Still, there was something different about him, of that she was sure.

"Be careful, girl," she told herself as she started up her car and pulled out onto Kish Blvd. She didn't have to look back to see if he was following her. She knew he was as curious about her as she was becoming about him.

David wrote down her seven numeral license plate number. She seemed normal enough, but he wasn't taking any chances that this was a setup to get him arrested for harassing the woman. Her color wasn't a problem. Of the few women he had time to take out, some of them were White. As a coordinator between the Israeli government and the Falashian people, he was often required to do business with the opposite sex. What was unfortunate, David found himself remembering, was it was, often times, only business.

Normally, his religious leaders would have frowned on some of his romantic choices. But here in Israel, the color of your skin didn't always establish your true heritage. Some of the dark women he dated were later found to be Christians and not orthodox Jews.

They drove up Moria Blvd. and turned left onto Pika. She slowed down and then made a right onto a small road that didn't have a road sign anywhere that he could see. The naked pole on the corner, he guessed, must have once held a street sign.

David slowed as she signaled she was turning again. She stopped in a short driveway in front of a high wooden fence. There was only enough room in the small driveway for her car. David parked behind her in the street and started to get out when she motioned for him to stay in the van. For some reason he wasn't sure of, he felt disappointed. *Did you really think she was going to let some nut she bumped into with her car come into her home?* Feeling foolish, he sat back and waited.

From what he could see of her residence, it was a small two-story home with apartment buildings extended out on both sides and a high wooden fence in the back of her dwelling. Oddly, there were no windows on the side of the buildings facing hers and no balconies. She could probably sun bathe in her yard in complete privacy, he figured while waiting for her to return. He resisted the urge to visualize that thought.

Sara peeked out of her second floor bedroom window for a few minutes. He seemed willing to wait so she hurried and changed. The dress was to get his attention. Now she needed to get him to relax and be friendly. She left her nylons on but slipped into a pair of cut-off jeans. They were worn and gave the impression, she hoped, that they were everyday wear. She put on a pink shirt and tied it around her waist.

"Don't keep him waiting too long," she whispered as she took the pins out of her hair, shook her head a few times, and quickly brushed her hair back down her shoulders. One quick look in the mirror and she grabbed the papers from the table where she placed them earlier and hurried out the door. "Wait."

While David was wondering how many huge, man-eating dogs she had hidden behind that tall fence, the gate opened and a young woman, now dressed casually, emerged. She walked quickly toward the van. Should he get out and greet her? That would be the courteous thing to do. He didn't move.

"Here you are," she said, handing him the necessary papers through his window.

"Thank you." David was quick to distinguish the lack of rings on either hand. That was good. No crazy husband to walk out, shooting at him for ogling his wife. David quickly verified and copied the information. Sara Jacobs was her name and from her birthdate, she was…ah twenty-five. Okay. He wrote quickly because he sensed she was staring at him. He looked up from the forms he had nervously read for the third time into brown eyes that stared innocently up at him. Gentle eyes that promised nothing. But that was perfect with the man fumbling to write down her information.

She stood just far enough away from the van for her own safety, David noticed. That was smart, parked in an alley with a total stranger, very smart. But that also permitted him an overall view of her. His jaw had dropped open as he stared. Realizing that, he snapped it shut and swallowed hard, clearing his throat. *Didn't think it was possible, but she might look better in those shorts and shirt than she did in that dress. Damn, she is good looking.* Maybe it was the hair down, he guessed while stealing another quick glance when she turned to look up the alley. *Damn, she is good looking. Or did I already say that?*

David wanted to talk to her but couldn't quite get up enough spunk to look her in those friendly eyes. He felt naked under their scrutiny, as if she could tell the difficulty he was having and the thoughts he was thinking.

"Do you know how to get out of here?" she asked as she waited for him to finish writing down her insurance information. His delay was either a slow hand or a wandering mind, she surmised, the latter being part of the plan.

He paused as he searched for something deep and profound to impress her. "Sure do, Sara."

"Good. Oh, wait a minute; I didn't get your name and address."

David took a page out of the tablet he was writing on and wrote down his name, address, and telephone number. He reached out and handed the papers back to her. He tried to take advantage of the opportunity, while she slowly read the address he had written, to think of something witty to say to break the ice.

"David Yasuda, did I pronounce it correctly?" she asked, after taking note of the additional information he supplied.

"It never sounded so nice," he replied, surprising himself.

She looked up quickly and a smile slowly formed on her lips. With that, she turned and started walking toward her yard. Sara caught herself blushing as she stepped away from the van. And as he drove off, she congratulated herself. "Men." She chuckled. "Show some skin and they become boys again."

The outfit she was wearing was a first for her. Well, not quite a first. She wore a lot of shorts, but none two sizes too small and skin tight. She debated trying to scrape off the shorts, putting on something loose and comfortable, as was her style, and picking up his trail later.

"Oh hell," she decided as she watched him drive off, confident she had made the necessary impression on him.

What she hadn't counted on was the elation she felt. It bothered her somewhat that the feeling seemed genuine. She waited until his van turned the corner before running up the street and jumping into a dirty green pick-up truck parked a couple of houses down. There were sunglasses, a red/blue flannel shirt, and a large brimmed hat on the front seat. She put on her disguise, unbuttoned her shorts so she could breathe, and quickly drove off. She got within sight of David's van three blocks later as he turned onto Pika Road. Keeping her distance, she followed her mark.

CHAPTER 22

June 1999:

S ara sat up and leaned back against the wall of the cave, the sound of a now softly snoring Simon a welcomed distraction. *Got to shake this funk*, she thought while rubbing the ache in her sore thighs. Where did she leave off? she wondered. Oh, yes…

March 1999:

She followed him as he drove to his apartment on Vitamin Road. From his bio, she knew he lived on the top floor of an old three-story red-brick building that overlooked the harbor. Then she got lucky finding a spot a street over that gave her an unobstructed view of his apartment. She parked the truck just far enough away so as not to expose her position to anyone in his building who might be watching her as she was watching him. "Always expect the unexpected" was her motto then. For almost a week, she followed David all around Haifa, confirming the info in his bio. He worked for the Department of the Interior in a building on Balfour Boulevard across from City Hall.

From his Mossad files, she knew where he lived, worked,

played, and usually ate his lunch. Included in those files were the names of his friends and associates and where they lived. She memorized his hobbies, likes, dislikes, and even the amount of money he had in his bank account. As any well-trained agent knew, you never put all your trust in the information gathered by someone else, even other competent agents. In the following days, she discovered most of the information in his file was very accurate.

The Mossad had proven itself again, she thought proudly. Deciding that she knew enough about him, she determined it was time to bait her hook and land this Falashian flounder.

It was a day when the Balfour Restaurant was packed as the lunch hour crowd sought good food, a cold drink, and good conversation out from the oppressively hot April day. If one could get one or two of those, it was considered a great lunch break.

David arrived and was lucky enough to secure one of the small two seat tables, near a window, where he preferred to sit, that offered a super view of the patio deck outside and the harbor. He loved eating there and watching the massive ships sail by. Being a great tipper, he reasoned, kept his regular seat empty for lunch.

On the cooler days, he preferred to eat outside and enjoy the fresh air while watching the ships. The only negative thing about eating inside, David determined, was that the tables outside on the patio, when occupied, occasionally blocked his view of the sea.

Today it was so hot that only a couple of the outside tables were occupied.

Curious why anyone would try to eat outside in that bright sun and nearly one-hundred-degree temperature day, David took a more careful look at the people seated there while he waited on his order. Two youngsters, probably more caught up in the ardor of their fresh love for each other than the stifling heat, sat holding hands and cold drinks. Another person sat with her back to him, facing the harbor.

David's food arrived, halting his judgment of those tempting heat stroke.

"Hear ya go, David, I hope you like it."

"Maria, your food is always as delicious as you are."

With a bright smile, the veteran server was off to wait on another customer.

The third bite of his grilled chicken sandwich was so pleasing that he cheerfully wiped any lingering sauce from his mouth and looked out the window again. All the tables on the deck outside were empty now but one—and that person was getting up to leave. Thankfully, David hadn't started to swallow that next bite or he might have choked.

It was the lady's dazzling white pajama pants and halter-top that first caught his attention. She looked like a princess out of the Arabian Nights. Her black hair was loose and blowing across her shoulders as she stood with her back to him, looking out at the Mediterranean Sea. David looked around the restaurant and confirmed she was the object of attention for quite a few men, and even women, eating there. It was when she turned to leave that his mouth dropped open, losing some of his sandwich.

Sara placed the tip on the table, put her coffee cup on top to hold it in the breeze, and then stood and watched the ships out in the harbor long enough not to be too obvious. With her back to the restaurant, she was able to hide the silly grin on her face. Taking a deep breath, she walked—as sexily as she knew how—out along the walkway that took her past the windows of the restaurant and out onto the street. She didn't look directly into the window as she passed, but the man she saw out of the corner of her eye, with his mouth open and pieces of food hanging out, had obviously recognized her.

Sara had earlier found a waitress, showed her a picture, and asked her did she know him.

"Yes, that's David Yasuda. He eats here often. Why? Is there a problem?"

"No, no…ah…Maria," Sara said, reading her name tag as she placed some money in her hand. "David and I worked in the same building before I was transferred. I'm in town for a few days and I would just like to surprise him. Would you mind helping me?"

"What do you want me to do?"

She prepaid her for his lunch and gave her a nice tip to reserve that table for him. From past observations, Sara noticed he liked to sit there and the waitress confirmed that. Then, when Sara brandished another generous tip, Maria was more than willing to follow instructions and keep it a secret. By the time David had rushed outside, Sara was in her truck, putting on another disguise.

She watched as he looked up and down Balfour Boulevard but didn't recognize her or her truck. Figuring she somehow must have missed her, he walked back into the restaurant. Two minutes later, David emerged again, looking confused but this time with a piece of paper in his hand. That had to be the note she left with the waitress for him, Sara presumed, thanking him for being so understanding and telling him his lunch was on her.

She crouched down, waited until he left the restaurant, and watched him get into his car. He made a left out of the parking lot. Ducking down as he drove past hid her face from him, along with the grin she was wearing. Starting up the truck, she U-turned, and followed him, staying about five cars back. When he drove past his office building, she knew where he was headed. She made a left at the next intersection and headed back to the safe house to write up her report on David Yasuda.

When she returned home later that evening, after dealing with the jokes about her Aladdin outfit from other agents, she drove around her area without spotting David's van. Convinced she was alone, she climbed out her truck and walked down to the house.

When she opened her mailbox there, folded on top of a couple of envelopes, was her note to David. When she opened it, some shekels fell out. On the back of the note was a message:

It was very nice seeing you again. I had a great meal and the view from where I was sitting was…unbelievable. However, I can't accept you paying

for my lunch. I've returned your hard-earned cash. The
view was worth the lunch. Thank you very much, David

Sara beamed. Unbelievable view, huh? The note caught her
by surprise and even more so the message-in-a-message.
Thankfully, the evening shadows hid the smirk on her face.
She read the note again. She'd thought he might come by
that's why she delayed coming home. What she wanted was
for him to call her on the phone. People tended to lose their
inhibitions when hiding behind the anonymity of the phone, or
so her experience had taught her. The note threw her a little
off guard.

"Okay, Sara, what are you planning on doing now?" she
asked herself.

Her devilish streak rose up as she picked up the money she
had dropped while opening the note. She then ran up the street
to the truck, laughing. She had a great idea what to do next
and found it very exhilarating. *This is turning out to be fun*,
she thought, while climbing back into the truck and donning
her disguise.

David lay in bed, thinking about the crash lady. The past
year, he'd been so involved in his job that he had dated only
occasionally. There hadn't been anyone special in his life in a
long time. Relieving some of the pain in the eyes of the frightened refugees from Ethiopia had occupied his life. He was one
of them when, as a boy, he had come to Israel in the '80s with
his late father.

Now it was an occupational blessing because it elevated
him from a mundane desk job to a counselor/adviser to the
Ethiopian Falashian for the Israeli government. Most government officials understood that the sudden immersion of the
somewhat primitive Falashian culture into the Israel of the late
'80s and '90s would be a certain culture shock. David, an immigrant from Ethiopia and a practicing Falashian who had
excelled in the Israeli education system despite the bias he
faced, was a perfect choice to act as an advisor to the Israeli
government.

He was kept busy, finding housing, jobs, and explaining

the diversity of their adopted country to the excited Sons of Solomon.

David awoke to a full-day's schedule of problems to solve. There were several reported incidents of fighting at three absorption centers, which he had to investigate. There were several people in new jobs he needed to visit and review their progress. Then there was always the constant battle to get the government to help place more people in schools for training. So when David took a few bites of his P and J sandwich as he hurried to his van. The note folded under his windshield wipers went unnoticed until he was almost at work. At the first chance, he pulled over, got out the van, and retrieved the note. It read:

> *It isn't often that a kind gesture of mine is refused. This time, I'm determined to thank you for your kindness. I usually eat lunch at Balfour's when I can. I especially love their salads. I was pleasantly surprised to see you eating lunch as I was leaving. I didn't want to bother you so I paid for your lunch as an apology. Please accept it. I hit you remember?*
> *Love, Sara Jacobs*

David stood in front of his van, staring at the note as cars raced past. He wasn't sure if it was his imagination but he thought he sniffed a wisp of perfume. Embarrassed, he noticed his hand trembling as he held it. "'Love, Sara Jacobs,'" he quoted aloud. *Don't get stupid*—he scolded himself, banishing the seeds of hope before they could bloom. *That's a common ending to a letter.*

He looked at the second page and sure enough, the same shekels were taped to it. His mind went blank and all of the meticulously scheduled planning for the day's activities went right out the window. All he could think about was what to do next. Should he let this end here or keep it going? David struggled with that question as he walked into the Department of the Interior Building, thinking only of Sara Jacobs.

Tuesday, Sara watched as David entered the restaurant earlier than normal. He arrived around twelve, a good half hour earlier than he normally did. He came early each day that week for lunch. His dossier indicated he only ate there maybe twice a week. Sara smiled at that thought. On Thursday, she decided it was time to test the waters before her fish quit biting. Trying to blend in, she wore a conservative pea-green business suit, large sunglasses, a large sun hat, and carried a briefcase. She walked into the restaurant about twenty minutes before noon. She asked the waitress for a booth in the far corner so she could see everyone entering and leaving while affording her some privacy.

"I'll have a salad and ice tea."

It was the same waitress she had paid to give the message to David. And there was something about the grin on the woman's face that bothered her. She shrugged it off as the woman just recognizing her and remembering the nice tip she gave.

Sara ate the crisp salad and finished a second glass of weak ice tea, but there was no sign of David. *Of all the days to change your plans*, she chided her missing assignment, *why today?* An hour later, and after three strangers stopped to chat, she gave up and asked the waitress for the check. The woman stood there staring down at her and then broke out in this cat-that-ate-the-canary grin.

"Miss, the same gentleman has already paid for your lunch."

Sara stared at the woman. Her training took over as she sensed there might be more to the waitress than she realized. Sara sized her up as an average-looking woman, about twenty pounds more than she wanted to weigh. Her hair was pinned back off her ears, her dress uniform had that worn look only time can create. She appeared to be just what she was, Sara concluded, a woman waiting tables to earn a living. What gentleman was she talking—no!

The waitress nodded to her and smiled again.

"No!" Sara said, as that smile grew wider. "Was he here?"

"Yes. I thought that maybe you forgot about the other day. He was sitting over in that corner near the bar watching you while you were eating your salad," the waitress told her.

Sara stood and was rewarded with an empty group of tables when she looked in the direction the waitress pointed. If he was there, he was gone now.

"David is a very nice man. There are three people working in the kitchen who owe him a lot for getting them jobs when no one else would hire them. He's a nice man," the waitress repeated.

Sara was so surprised that she gave the waitress another large tip, said thank you, and walked outside. There wasn't the expected note on her car that she was looking for. This guy was more unpredictable than she gave him credit for and that annoyed her. She was the highly train agent, she told herself as she started up her car. The thought of being out smarted by a civilian hurt a little. She decided it was time to turn up the pressure a bit more.

David sat on his couch, trying to catch up on the work he had missed. All day at the Interior building he could only think of Sara. For two days, he had taken an early lunch, trying to get to Balfour's before her and staying late, in hopes she would show up. He had made up his mind today was the last day he was going to try. Because of a cancellation in his schedule, he arrived an hour earlier than planned. That proved advantageous when she unexpectedly walked into the restaurant. As luck would have it, his waitress blocked her view while taking his order. He remembered almost knocking over his water when he looked up and spotted her sitting down at a booth. He also remembered being so nervous he tried sneaking in the kitchen, pretending to want to chat with the workers he got hired, and slipping out the back door. Only finding another table behind her slowed his flight. From there, he could watch her unobserved. When he finally realized his change of tables had saved his plans, he took a deep breath and started to relax. Sara, he noticed, looked awesome in the green outfit she was wearing.

With her repeatedly looking toward the door, it became obvious she was expecting him to walk in any minute. He wasn't sure what she was planning, but he was glad he didn't walk into that trap. He would have been dumbfounded had she appeared out of nowhere. That thought triggered a foolish notion that maybe there was a chance that awesome woman liked him. Thankfully, common sense buried that impractical notion with the other wild ones his vivid imagination came up with while he was watching her eat.

Would he be biting off more than he could chew, he wondered, if he did ask her out? The lady's actions were so graceful and feminine as she ate her salad, everything about her screamed refinement and class. Even the smooth way she crossed her legs said sophistication. That prompted a question. What the hell was he doing here? He was more the down-to-earth person with little or no desire to prove anything to anyone. Yet, wasn't that what women like her expected? He was quickly losing the nerve to continue the game but what other choice did he have? Just the slim chance of getting a date with her gave him the confidence to at least try.

"There you are. I thought maybe you walked out and stiffed me," his waitress teased as she picked up his payment.

"No, Maria, I just changed tables."

"I think I know why."

David tried to look uninterested in her reasoning but she continued standing there staring at him. "Okay, what's the reason?"

She nodded in the direction of a certain woman seated in a booth. "How about the lady in green? I know, I don't know what I'm talking about," she said and then walked away.

"Maria, wait," David whispered. "I want to pay for her meal."

"Okay."

"When she asks for her bill, tell her I paid it before I left. Don't let her know I'm here."

"And what about her usual very large tip?"

"And I'll pay for her very large tip," David said as he reached for his wallet. "You robber with nice legs."

"I do have nice legs." She laughed, slipped the money into her bra, strolled over, and waited on another table.

David became anxious when the waitress finally walked over to Sara's table. He imagined she was telling her she was the one tricked this time. He loved Sara's reaction. Had she shrugged it off, he would have ducked out with his tail between his legs. But she didn't. It made his day when she stood and looked around the restaurant. He instinctively ducked down as she carefully scanned the room, looking for him. When he peeked from behind the many plants in the restaurant, she was walking out.

"Okay, lover boy, the lady in green was completely surprised," Maria said when she walked over to where David was hiding. "I'm not sure she was too happy that you played the same trick on her."

Maybe she was, David thought, but either way he was pleased with both reactions. "Thank you, dear."

"Yeah." She smiled and headed for a table of a man waving at her.

It was the joy of turning the tables on Sara at lunch that prevented him from concentrating on the work he brought home. He tried turning off the TV, but that didn't help. Turning the radio on and then off—the same results. Three hours later and twenty minutes of actual work accomplished, he gave up and went to bed.

No relief was found between the sheets either. While his body sought sleep, his mind replayed the events involving Sara over and over. After battling the sandman until early morning, a tired warrior arose, showered, shaved, and headed for work an hour early. This time, he looked at his windshield wipers when he approached his van. The small, white piece of paper immediately caught his attention. He stopped and looked around. His street was crowded with parked cars as usual, but nothing was amiss. David could hardly breathe as he slowly approached his van. Again, he stopped and looked around. He didn't realize that he was now holding his breath. There was little doubt what it was and who had placed it there. He was more afraid that it might not be from her. It was.

Dear David, the note read. *Since I can't pay for your lunch, can I offer to take you to lunch? I still owe you and I hate to owe people. Please let me off the hook. Can you meet me for lunch at Gan Ha'em Park on Hanassi Blvd. a week from this Saturday? Say about noon? I'll be there looking for you. Please don't stand me up. Sara*

David was stunned by the offer. While re-reading the note, he noticed that she ended it with only her first name. Suddenly, his sleepless night had lost its bite. Tired and groggy evaporated in the warming light of the rising sun. *A week from tomorrow, and I'll get to see her again.* David danced a jig in the empty street, oblivious to a pair of eyes watching him from a dark lot across the road. The owner of those sleepy eyes felt something also. She couldn't quite understand why she was so pleased with his obvious joy after reading the note. *He's just an assignment,* she told herself as she headed back home to get some rest. It would be much later before the muscles in her face relaxed.

June 1999:

Sara remembered those feeling as she sat in the dark cave. Looking back, she was sure now that it was when she first started falling for David. His expression of joy at getting her note touched a virgin cord in her heart. She warmly recalled the way she felt as she watched his celebration. It felt wonderful to see someone that happy for the chance to get to know her. No matter what the rest of the world thought of her, it said, this guy was delighted.

After checking his vitals again and finding him stable, she wondered why it had taken so long to come to grips with her feelings. The answer became plain the more she thought about it. But when she awoke that day, David was once again just an assignment. Denial had reentered and stolen the spark that their note trading had created. It was business as usual, as she stepped out of her shower and blow dried her hair, she remembered, looking back on that day. The old, cold, and calculating Sara smothered any thoughts of enjoying the repartee they were having.

"He's just an assignment," she kept repeating.

The joy she was feeling wasn't emotions, she convinced herself, but because of how smoothly this black widow spider had enticed the fly into her web and was about to suck him dry.

CHAPTER 23

March 1999:

By the next weekend, everything was set up for their meeting. Mossad agents, against Sara objections, were planted in the park as tourist and vendors. She had voiced her opinion that David wasn't a threat to her or anyone in the park but was overruled by an overly cautious area chief.

Sara had mics hidden under her collar and in her purse that would record their conversations. By Saturday morning, she was ready to reel in the fish that was nibbling on her baited hook and catch her Falashian flounder. She parked her car two blocks away and walked to Gan Ha'em Park as instructed. A block away she received a signal from a "taxi" driver that David was there waiting for her.

Being one who abhorred being late, she hurried to the meeting place. Sara had spent more time than usual getting ready for this lunch date. She tried to ignore that fact, and her growing apprehension, when she realized she would be late getting there. The words, "This is just another assignment," had been repeated all week and several times Saturday morning as she put on her makeup. Her hair was back up in a bun, a concession to her pride for wearing her tightest jeans, her most revealing blouse, and purchasing the tiny lace underwear she was wearing. Four different outfits were tossed across her bed for failing to satisfy her changing moods. The two faces of Sara Jacobs were warring for control of the situation. The two

"D's," *desire* and *duty*, were both preparing to meet and dazzle David. It was yet uncertain which one would rule the day.

As she walked into the park, she spotted David with his back turned, looking at the crowd of people enjoying displays and beautiful greenery. He was dressed in tan slacks and an open cream-colored silk shirt. He had broad shoulders and looked handsomely comfortable. Sara surprised herself when she realized she was nervous about meeting him. *Okay, he is the fish and you are the fisherwoman*, she reminded herself. *He is the one with the hook in his mouth. Just reel the poor man in, girl.* The apprehension she felt eased when she spotted two other agents walking around being loud and obnoxious, just like tourists. The park was crowed, but safety wasn't a problem. Still, until they could get a read on David's mind-set, she was told, the Mossad would continue to supply her with protection—some seen, and others unseen.

"Hi there." Sara walked up to him, her high-pitched voice evidence she was genuinely nervous.

David turned around and, for the longest time, said nothing. His eyes, however, revealed the little-boy happiness he felt as he looked at her.

That felt good. Also, the fact that his eyes only looked at hers and not any other feature she was advertising.

"Hello," he said a little louder than he wanted to. "I thought maybe you changed your mind or something."

"Well, you know a woman is entitled to do that if she so pleases."

"That's what I hear," he said, finally smiling.

Sara felt her heart jump when he did. Something about the sincerity of it stirred her. What apprehension she might of felt melted away in the warmth of the look on his handsome face. His round eyes spoke volumes about what the man was thinking. As a woman, she couldn't resist the fascination she saw reflected there.

"May I add, you look lovely?"

"You may add that any time you want," she answered with a wink.

They started walking toward the zoo in the park. Neither

seemed willing to leave the fresh air for either the Museum of Biology or Pre-History Building located in Gan Ha'em Park.

"Have you ever visited the zoo?" she asked.

"A few times. I admit I find the zoo's famous white tigers my favorite part."

"I love the giraffes."

"Yes, the best part is you can get very close to them."

They looked at the assorted zoo animals but never really noticed them.

"Would you mind sitting down?"

"Not at all."

"Good." Sara walked over and sat on a bench shaded by trees and away from most of the flow of the crowd. David followed her without comment.

"So, pretty lady," he said, after sitting and staring into her eyes longer than he intended, "tell me something about you other than your great driving abilities."

Sara laughed. "I'll have you know I'm a great driver."

"I believe you. Your driving is great. It's your stopping that needs work."

"Very funny," she said, smiling at the man seated beside her. "What would you like to know, David?"

Hearing his name did what she intended.

"Tell me about you growing up. You said you attended school here."

The idea of taping his conversation was to get him talking. Sara started by talking about growing up in a Kibbutz, her life in the army, and her present boring job tracking foreign investments. "Okay, I've talked enough. Tell me about you. Are you married, have any kids?"

"No—no," a surprised David answered emphatically. "I'm very single and no kids. Actually, I have no immediate family here in Israel. My dad died a few years ago."

"Sorry," Sara said, while looking down at her feet. "So did both my parents a few months ago."

"Now, I'm the one sorry."

"Thank you."

They sat in silence as old pains stole their joy.

"I came here as a boy from Ethiopia with my father. My mother died a year earlier and that was when my father decided to leave."

When Sara sat back and looked at him, he continued. He stole the show with his stories of his voyage here, the Falashian refugees he worked with and their perilous struggles to get out of Ethiopia. The tales of their bravery and sacrifice genuinely awed Sara.

David continued expounding on the heroic Israeli missions to airlift his people to the promise land. At first, Sara repeatedly tried to get him to talk about the present Falashian movement because she knew their conversations were being recorded. But every time she tried, he brought the conversation back to the salvation of the Falashian people by the heroic Israeli government.

Sara was quick to realize that David was sincere in his appreciation of the rescue of his people. From what she could garner, he had only admiration for the country and people who saved them. Fascinated, she sat back and let him talk. The message she was recording in her purse would answer any questions of whoever had authorized the covert spying on the Falashian people and one David Yasuda.

"Well, Mister Yasuda, where do you want to eat?" Sara said when David was winding up the history of his people's fight to immigrate.

"You know what, Sara, I'm not hungry. I've talked so much I forgot about lunch."

"Oh, no, you don't," she said, pointing her finger at him.

"What do you mean?" he answered, smiling again and holding his hands up in defense.

"You're trying to get out of lunch again."

"No, no." He chuckled. "That's not true. I've thoroughly enjoyed sitting here under this shade tree, just talking away. This spring day is beautiful, you're beautiful, even the animals look beautiful."

Sara sat back with raised eyebrows.

From her response, David knew he had screwed up—just not how.

"Mister Yasuda, are you comparing me to some smelly animals?"

David laughed heartily as he realized he was fighting a losing battle. "No way, my lady, and please, call me David."

"Good, David. These are my best pair of jeans," she said as she stood and turned a perfect pirouette. Her hands slid seductively over her hips. "I was hoping," she said demurely, "that they looked better on me than they would on those monkeys."

"From where I sit, that's no contest," David answered, looking a little longer at those jeans than might be appropriate. Try as he might, he couldn't hide the grin on his face. *Come on, David*, he scolded himself. *Don't let her see you grinning like a schoolboy. Be aloof. Yeah, fat chance.*

Sara turned and walked slowly over to the fence overlooking the beautiful pond with dancing jets of water in the center. She liked Mr. Yasuda—David—she decided as she adjusted her purse on her shoulder. He seemed very confident and at ease around her. She wondered what he was really like once you got to know him.

David watched her for a moment before strolling over and joining her. Everything about the woman was impressive. Other people—women—walked past but she stood out. He took a deep breath and blew it out, as if symbolically forcing his nervousness out on the waves of his breath. Staring out at the pond after joining her, he sought the correct words to say to this lovely lady. Although he had practiced a dozen lines while getting dressed, none seemed appropriate now.

With him momentarily distracted by the view, Sara read his features more carefully than was prudent when she was the center of his attention. His skin looked very smooth, as if he never had to shave or had a much better razor than the one she used on her legs. She thought that fact to be amusing. His hair was a rich black and soft looking. *Soft looking? What the hell does that mean?* she questioned. *Oh, well, he is very attractive, but not a pretty-boy; muscular, but not bulky; and he's athletic looking.* She liked that in a man. *Let's see...hmmm, nails are manicured and clean. No hair hanging out of his nose. He is too neat. He has to be either gay or married,* she decided, snickering to herself at that old joke. Sara looked into his eyes when he turned as if to say something, but he didn't.

"David," Sara said to the bemused look on his face, "let's take a rain check on lunch," she suggested as she tried reading his body language. "I've got to be going soon, anyway. Give me your number please," she asked as she reached in her purse for pen and paper, "and I'll give you a call whenever I get the chance this week. I'll be out of town for a few days on business, but I promise to call when I get back." She wrote down his number. "Do you still have mine?"

"No," he lied. "I turned it in to my insurance company and—"

God, she is enticing. David watched her dig through her purse until she found something to write down her phone number on. *Gee, get a grip, boy.* He acknowledged he needed a woman bad, and she was definitely all woman. *Talking to yourself again, that's not good, David.*

Sara handed her number to him. For a moment, as both held the slip of paper, something passed between them. Neither of them recognized it for what it was. David came the closest   hours   later   when   he   admitted   he   liked her...personality.

"Did you drive here?"

"Yes, I did."

"Then may I walk you to your car?"

"Yes, I would love that. Thank you."

Sara shrugged off the ebullience, equating his walking her to her car as part of her successful assignment to seduce him. As they walked and chatted she marveled at the ease in which she was able to enjoy his company. He never mentioned himself in their conversation yet he talked with a confidence that said he was proud of his accomplishments. When he asked, and she permitted him to open her car door for her, it was all she could do not to laugh out loud. *Poor David,* Sara decided as she drove off, *he really wants me bad.* For the sake of her assignment, she graciously conceded, she just might let him. Maybe granting him that privilege, she teased, for-the-good-of-the-country. Sara denied herself the truth of what she was feeling. The emptiness of her childhood was gone, and she didn't recognize the joy that replaced it. The short relationship with David had resurrected the young woman in her that the weight of life had buried.

CHAPTER 24

June 1999:

Sara turned on her flashlight and aimed it down at the groaning sound from the wounded man she loved lying next to her in the dark. He was still unconscious and a little feverish to the touch. His bandages were wet with blood but didn't appear any worse than the last time she checked. He was holding his own—for now.

Leaning back and closing her eyes, she worried about David. There were very few options. Soldiers were out there searching for them, and then there was the mission. The beginning of a headache made her rub her temples. She said another prayer for him, for them, and tried again to relax. As she did, the good feelings from that wonderful time of getting to know David reached out and found her sitting on the hard ground in the black cave.

That was the day it had begun, she finally was able to admit to herself. She was so full of life after meeting him. Like a movie in fast-forward, the memories raced past her mind's eye. They met four days later for a real lunch date that lasted into the night. On ensuing dates, they visited most of the scenic treasures of Haifa. From the Museum of Mane Katz, where her sculptures were on display, to enjoying the old ships in the Marine Museum on Allenby Street. They walked barefoot through the Bahai Shrine and took a boat trip around Haifa harbor, acting like tourists.

For some reason, the city never looked more beautiful to them.

Their first kiss came on a canceled date. David was hastily summoned to Rabbi Gette's residence just as he was walking out the door to pick her up. On the way, he stopped to break the bad news to her. She answered the door lovelier than he had ever seen her. She had finally given in to his plea to wear her hair down off her shoulders instead of her always-predictable bun for work or ponytail at home. Tonight, of all nights, she had surprised him. Her glossy black mane decorated a soft, perfectly made-up face that adorned a peach-colored shoulder-less summer dress. This time he didn't try to hide the effect she had on him. The blind would have seen his stunned expression.

"Sara, you're—you're beautiful."

She remembered thinking how proud and feminine she felt at that moment. She did look great, felt great, and he confirmed it. But hearing him say it was a new sensation. Sure, other guys had hit on her but, with him, somehow it seemed…genuine.

"Thank you, kind sir, won't you come in?"

David hesitated then stepped just inside the door. "Sara, I have to cancel our date tonight."

"Why?" she asked.

The obvious disappointment written across her face moved David. Her hazel eyes searched his face for the truth. "Rabbi Gette called me as I was leaving," David told her as he held her hand. "There are some serious problems with two of the absorption centers. Some of the men are fighting again with their wives and neighbors. The unemployed there are growing restless and frustrated because they can't earn a living."

"What can you do about that tonight?"

"Well, Rabbi Gette wants me to drive him to the centers and support him in front of the men. They seem to trust me more than the rabbi, I think."

"I would think so," Sara added. "You've earned their trust."

"Thank you."

"I'll wait for you," she said, surprising him as she walked him to the door. "If the meetings don't take too long, come by and see me. I can heat up something for you and we can eat here."

He felt her eyes were saying something her lips did not. "I'll try," he finally answered. He turned to walk away then stopped for another look at her. "How late is too late?"

Sara just beamed. She then walked up to him and put a hand to his chest. Looking up into his eyes, she slipped her arms around his neck and kissed him.

David squeezed her tightly to his chest as they kissed, while caressing the soft material of her dress. She felt wonderful in his arms as her body moved into his. The delicious scent of her had him swooning. The power of their kiss was the need each felt for the other, and it sent a message. David broke the embrace, looked her in the eye, and nodded. Her intentions were very clear, and he passionately concurred with them.

"I'll hurry," he said as he kissed her again and hurried toward his car.

Sara picked up her phone. She dialed all but the last digit then put the phone down. Duty called for her to report any potential problems with those whom she was assigned to monitor. She only questioned her actions for a moment. Further evaluation would have certainly revealed her reasons to be selfish. Maybe it was the kiss and her expectations that prevented her finger from hitting the last number.

It was late that night when David parked his van in front of Sara's house after dropping off the priest. For an excruciating ten or twenty minutes, he had to park and listen to the priest expound, as he had numerous times while driving him home, on solutions to the unrest before he permitted him to escort him to his dwelling.

"Is this too late?" David whispered as he climbed out his van. "She did say she would wait."

He returned around midnight. Standing at her door, he hesitated before ringing her doorbell. Was it too late to be here? he wondered. The last thing he wanted to do was to presume, or worse yet, have her think he was being presumptuous. David turned and took a step away before stopping again. "I promised I would return. I should keep my word even if it is too late."

It was more than his word that prompted him to ring her doorbell. The feeling of her in his arms and the touch of her lips had occupied his thoughts all night. Even the rabbi asked if he was feeling all right because he seemed distracted.

When Sara opened her door in only a satin nightshirt, he stood there with a bouquet of yellow roses in his hand. This time, Sara was stunned. The sight of him at her door, holding her favorite flowers, with that look on his face that she loved so much was enough to trigger something she had been holding back for the weeks of their casual relationship and the last few years of her life.

All the doubts that David had let fester, after hurriedly dropping off the rabbi and running a few red lights rushing over here, were answered the moment she opened the door. His fears had painted scary pictures of a woman behind that door who was now bored and angry with his extended absence, or a woman tussled from falling sleeping on her couch from his tardiness and no longer in the mood for a late night visitor. Those frightening pictures were erased the moment the door opened and soft brown eyes looked lovingly into his. She no longer had every hair in place, but that didn't matter. She no longer wore make up that accentuated her bright eyes and tanned skin, but that didn't matter. The beautiful off-the-shoulder peach-colored summer dress she had been wearing was back on its hanger and, again, that didn't matter.

Yes, the woman standing in the doorway had changed. To the man with the flowers in his hand—that he had seen in a florist window as he stopped at a red light, because a car was in front of him—flowers he paid three times their value for when the vender saw he was desperate and allowed him to continue slipping money under the door until reaching his price. He had begged the owner of the closed florist shop to open up for him, while berating himself for leaving her. And he couldn't have been happier with the change.

From her hair, now banded up in a ponytail, to her clean

and bright face, to the cream-colored plain silk mid-thigh night shirt, the message came across that they were no longer just dating. They were no longer required to cut their pizza up in small pieces and eat it with a knife and fork. They could now use the other's bathroom. Their relationship had progressed to another level. It was okay now to pick up a delicious slice, covered with pepperoni, sausage, and dripping with extra cheese with your hands. David realized, at that moment, Sara preferred holding her pizza with her hands. The same hands that took the flowers from his, closed and locked her door, wrapped them around his neck and then...

Their clothes lay scattered where they had tossed them and the roses on the floor by the front door. After deep and longing kisses, they found themselves in bed, searching out the pleasures each held in their bodies. She was everything he dreamed she could be, and he touched her in places she thought were only a fantasy in the romantic books she read. They came together so smoothly it was as if they had previously practiced until they got it right for the big unveiling. Just to make sure it wasn't a fluke, they happily tested it again and again.

Awakened in the early hours of the morning by his closeness, Sara tried but couldn't recall any of the men in her life giving her flowers. She also wondered where he was able to find them and how he knew yellow roses were her favorite. They were absolutely beautiful flowers. Then she wondered where they were. The answer made her chuckle.

When David awoke, she was lying on her elbows, staring adoringly at him. He turned onto his side and returned the muted praise. "Hi, beautiful."

"Too late for platitudes, my friend, you've already taken my best."

David smiled at her. "That's true. It was wonderful but, like they say about eating Chinese food, a half hour later, one gets hungry again."

Sara moved over and allowed him to wrap his large hand

around her ass and pull her even closer. As he stared into her eyes, she gently kissed his lips.

David pulled her into his arms and massaged her back as they hugged. He was aroused but sensed the next move belonged to her. When she laid her head gently on his chest, he got his answer and was pleased with that.

They had experienced the wild, physically draining side of intimacy—twice. Like clean air after a sudden spring storm, there was a peace that now settled on them. No words needed to be said. Words, though thoughtful, could never truly elucidate the honesty of what their eyes were saying. Those words were yet unlearned between men and women.

They spent the day together wearing little more than they were now. And even those garments found their way onto the floor—often.

The days melted together as they rejoiced in the wonderful intimacy they discovered. Sara's reports to Simon obviously spoke well of David and the job he was trying to do. She also covered her ass by reporting that she was beginning to get closer to the leaders of the sect. David took Sara with him whenever he could, she reported, and it wasn't long before the rabbis realized they were an item. She was then able to sit close enough to listen in on their meetings, without raising any alerts. The respect they had for the hard work David was doing tempered their opinions of her.

Sara gained insight into her feelings as she became involved with her assignment, but she never acknowledged to herself the truth of what she felt for David at the time. It was as if the nights with him permitted her to totally indulge herself in whatever emotions emerged, only to have her hot morning shower wash them off as completely as it did the soap on her skin—theoretically flushing them down the same drain between her feet, exposing the cold, calculating agent, Sara Jacobs.

Each day, David began to put some of the problems he faced, with trying to blend his Ethiopian brothers in with Israeli customs, on other people and began to relish his and Sara's time together. He knew he loved her but couldn't quite see past their differences to tell her. But the joy of being together slowly made both of them forget those differences. Who they were lost significance as only the days that they were together became important. Unlike an addiction, that drove people once thought to be sane and rational to sell their bodies and soul for a fix, the pressures of societies norms held no influence over them after the joy of being together was experienced. If society dictated, you must color them, then color them happy.

For the next few weeks, they were almost inseparable. During their time together, Sara began to gather a better understanding of the plight of the Falashian in Israel. She was able to suggest some brilliant ideas to David for circumnavigating Israeli red tape. Passing on those suggestions to Simon didn't hurt any, either. In his position, he was able to remove a few roadblocks.

The future of their relationship looked bright with promise. He was now more than an assignment to her. That changed when people started getting very sick and dying. Sara received the top-secret information twenty-four hours after the plague started killing Israelis. A day later, the entire world knew that the country was under attack again. As medical science failed to stem the tide of death, Israel faced complete annihilation. David's random suggestion, that maybe the Falashians were somehow immune to the plague, set in motion a frantic search for an answer to his assumption. It was the failure to find an answer, and the escalation in the spread of the plague that led Simon to order Sara to tell David everything and then ask for his help.

Then she discovered, to her surprise, telling David that he was her assignment was akin to a woman telling the man who loved her that she'd been having an affair—with every friend he had. He knew it was more than an assignment now, but how did you convince someone who you have willingly lied to that you were now telling the truth. Sara knew that it was the right thing to do. Hell! It was the only thing left to do.

At first, he took it better than she thought he would. The verbal tirade she expected never materialized. He only looked like she had cut open his chest and ripped out his still-beating heart. Her dramatic explanation failed to impress the shaken man. David listened impassively as she tried convincing him of her motives.

He raised his hand to stop her. "I'll help, Sara," he said, as he got up off the couch and walked to the door, "not because of how I feel about you but because I also love this country. If there's a reason for our immunity, I'll find it."

Numbed by his response, Sara slipped back into her shell. After a long moment spent forcing down the emotional eruption that threatened to ruin her mascara, she called Simon and reported their conversation.

David did confront Rabbi Gette with his allegations and refused his simplistic explanation on why he kept secret the healing water from the "Pond of God."

From the first day of the outbreak, Israeli scientists had struggled to find a vaccine to halt the spread of the epidemic. Their efforts, and those of other scientists around the world, met with the same failure.

When David surprised them by returning with some of the healing water from the priest, their hopes were buoyed. They confirmed the rabbi's claims were true. Everyone who took the limited amount of elixir given them completely recovered. Some in minutes and others within hours, depending on the severity of their condition.

When Simon told her about getting secret permission to sneak out of the country and to enter Ethiopia in an effort to try to find the source of the elixir, she began to have hope.

"Sara, this is hastily planned but I'm assembling a squad of commandos to secretly enter Ethiopia and find this water on that damn mountain. I talked David into coming. After talking with the priest, he might be an asset."

"That's great, sir."

"I want you to come along."

The reason was obvious and she felt insulted. But with people dying she swallowed the angry words bubbling up in her. "I'll do anything I can, Simon."

His reasons for her accompanying them were shallow and,

being a trained agent, he knew she knew that. But it was a hunch he was playing. Something he never could get past his superiors if there was time for evaluating the mission. There wasn't, and he knew he would take St. Nick along if he thought it might help.

David and Sara didn't speak to each other until she went to his hotel room later that day before they were scheduled to leave for Ethiopia.

CHAPTER 25

It was said that each of us at some point in our lives had an opportunity to see ourselves clearly, and a like opportunity to accept or deny what we clearly see. At twenty minutes to midnight, in a place as dark as midnight, that opportunity occurred for Sara. She looked at a woman who had obviously fallen in love with David. She did love him, she finally confessed in the dark. Probably from the day she bumped into him, she surmised. All the strange, silly feelings she fostered when they were together now made sense.

As she looked back at that woman now, she couldn't understand why it had taken until now to see how deeply she loved him.

"How did I miss that? Even if I was blind and missed the look in his eyes, I should have acknowledged that truth just from the wonderful way I felt in his arms," she whispered to herself, forgetting she wasn't alone. She brazenly smiled at the next thought that filtered her into her mind. If she didn't love him, she admitted, she damn sure loved the way he mastered her body until it yielded over and over again to his touch, his lips, his tongue, his—

She was very inexperienced in surrendering to the emotions she felt. Her body wasn't virginal when she met him, but emotionally she was. Sara had dated sporadically and was intimate on a few occasions, but nothing that stirred her desires to take things to the next level with her lovers.

Sara had impressed everyone in the Mossad with her work

habits and the results she was able to obtain. Those who might have doubted her quickly learned she was a tough, intelligent, and a determined agent who got results.

David was the third client she was instructed to befriend for information. According to Simon, their superiors in the Mossad were very pleased with the information she was able to obtain or confirm with the other two. Thus, she had no reason to suspect that her latest assignment would be any different.

But none of those assignments had affected her like David. None of the others had been able to seduce her with just their smile, although each had tried with various expensive gifts. But all three, she acknowledged, as that fact massaged her ego, did fall victim to the tight dress she wore for catching her fish.

Sara slid down until she was lying beside David. Her hand touched him and carefully worked its way up his body until she found his face. She leaned over and gently kissed him on the lips.

"I hope that's you, Sara," she heard him whisper, "or I'm in real trouble."

"David!" she shouted, as she quickly sat up.

"What's wrong, Sara," Simon asked after suddenly being awakened by her shout.

It took her a moment or two, while fumbling with the flashlight, but she found hers and aimed it at David. He was trying to sit up as the light hit his face.

"David, how do you feel?" Simon asked when he saw what was transpiring and crawled over next to him.

"Horrible," David mumbled as his dry mouth slurred his speech.

"Don't try to get up," Sara said. "Where does it hurt?"

David looked up at her in the dim light for a moment before relaxing back on the knapsack. He started to comment on the tears leaking down her face but thought better of it. "My leg hurts and my right shoulder feels numb," he said as he looked at her. "Oh yeah, who hit me in the head with a pipe?"

It worked. She smiled.

"You were shot as we ran from the troops," Simon explained. "Luckily, the head wound was superficial and the bullets in your shoulder passed through you without hitting any vital organs. We're not sure about your leg wound yet," he lied.

"I—don't feel—very lucky, Simon."

"Well, you are," a very feminine voice added.

David again looked up at her. In the dim light, the shiny streaks running down her dirt stained cheeks were clearly visible. She leaned over and kissed his forehead. One of her tears hit David's face and rolled down over his lips.

"I guess I am," he mumbled.

Elated with his progress, Sara placed her light on the wall behind them. Its beam turned the cave into a den, softening the harsh contrast from the smaller lights.

Simon filled David in on what had happened to them and that they expected Weasel and Snake back in a couple of hours.

"If the soldiers have left the area, we will have to continue the search in the dark with flashlights if we have to," Simon continued. "We don't have time to wait for daylight."

"What about David?" Sara asked, crawling over toward Simon. "He can't possibly keep up with us."

"I know that, Sara. He will have to stay here. We're running out of time."

"Then I will stay here with him, Simon."

"No, you won't," David told her. "I will follow you whenever I can, but you must use every available person to find the pond. Unfortunately, Simon is right. Israel is running out of time. Too many people are dying, my love. I could never forgive myself if I took you away from the search. With the loss of our friends, we are already critically undermanned."

"How can you follow us? You can't move or you'll bleed to death."

"That's not true. My leg hurts but I can still move it, and the bleeding has stopped. By morning, who knows? I might be able to stand up."

No one believed that.

"I don't care what you say, David, or you Simon. I'm not going to leave him here alone to die."

"Sara, don't be stupid, we need you, your country needs you," Simon said, growing a bit angry at her stubborn attitude.

"Simon, I understand how you feel, and you're right. Please don't be upset with me. Hawk and the others died for something they believed in. I finally found something I believe in and he needs me now more than ever. I love my country but I just couldn't live if—if I lost h—him," she said as her emotions broke through.

Simon lowered his head and shook it in disgust. He never would have believed that Sara Jacobs would let her emotions rule her actions.

Birdman sat quietly by the cave entrance. He listened to the argument but his thoughts were on the men he had lost, and the two still out there in the dark.

Sara wiped her eyes and looked down at David. She knew he was desperately trying to be strong for her, hiding the pain he must be feeling. She wanted to be strong for him but she also knew her career in the Mossad was over with that outburst. The memory of the emptiness she felt in her soul before she met him was something she never wanted to experience again, at any price.

It was more than just David. She understood that all too clearly if they did not. She couldn't blame them because she wasn't that sure about everything she was feeling herself. It was more about finally finding herself, and she could never explain that to anyone. Losing her career was painful, but she felt so alive now. For the first time in her life, she felt alive. David was just the catalyst that brought forth her butterfly from its cocoon. She couldn't see it yet, but he was her first love.

While the two of them quietly talked, Simon moved over to the cave opening where Birdman was guarding and sat down.

"Birdman, when we leave do you think we should split up?" Simon asked.

"Yes! I was thinking the same thing. We have a lot of ground to cover and we are behind schedule. When Weasel and Snake return we will have to take more chances, I guess. We should have come here in force and secured the entire damn mountain."

"You know that's not possible," Simon told him. "Our country is under United Nations quarantine. They would have every right to nuke this whole damn mountain. I know I would. And what if we carried that plague into this country? It could spread across this third-world continent like wildfire. The more troops we use, the greater the chance of that happening. Hell has already claimed the poor in this God-forsaken place with AIDS, drought, and war. God forbid that we bring them another plague. No, it had to be a small, clean, covert operation."

Birdman just nodded in frustration. He looked over at David and Sara lying together talking. While he understood Sara's feelings but he disagreed with her decision. David, on the other hand garnered nothing but admiration and respect from the hardened veteran.

"Let's get some rest," Birdman suggested to the others in the cave. "Snake and Weasel should return in a couple of hours and, if the way is clear, we can all get out of here."

"All of us, Birdman?" Sara asked, hoping she heard him right.

"All of us, my lady. I could never leave you or, as you so eloquently put it, *your reason for living* behind. If he's feeling up to it, we'll build a stretcher and carry him if we have to unless someone has a better idea."

No one spoke up.

David struggled, against Sara's objections, and was able to sit up on his elbows. He turned and looked over at the powerful leader of the commandos.

Birdman's words of hope caused Sara's heart to race. "Did you hear that, David?" she asked. .

With everyone's eyes on him, Birdman crawled to the far side of the cave and curled up on the ground. His actions were like a sedative to the others as Simon, and then a very tired and happy Sara, killed their lights and followed suit. Sara struggled to stay awake, until she was sure David was sleeping, before she dropped off into the deep sleep of the physically and emotionally exhausted.

Within a half-hour Sara, Simon, and Birdman were asleep. David listened to their deep breathing. It was now or never. He wasn't sure how he was going to obey the voice in his head but he knew he had to try. It was the reason he was spared, the voice claimed. The reason he was here back in his homeland. The earth would direct him, the voice explained.

He gave Sara a soft kiss on her cheek and tried to get up. The pain in his leg was so great that he blacked out for a moment and just caught himself before he fell on her. Sara was sleeping so soundly, she never heard or felt him drop back onto the ground. He lay there, gritting his teeth so hard to stifle his scream, it wouldn't have surprised him if they had shattered into little pieces.

He wasn't sure how long he lay there until the pain became bearable, but everything seemed quiet and no one the wiser. He tried sitting up again. The stabbing pain in his leg centered his thoughts on what he had tried to do. He squeezed his eyes shut and gritted his teeth until the pain subsided. Again, he was barely able to stifle a scream when he tried to move, as shards of stabbing pain rippled through his body. Beads of sweat ran down his face in the dark as he fought to control his breathing. He felt as though someone had just stabbed him in his sore shoulder with a red-hot poker.

David lay on the soft, cool ground, his breaths coming in short gasps. He had to rethink his plan, he was forced to concede. Taking that moment to think gave his good left leg time to stop trembling. Finally the rest of his body relaxed and he was able to breathe normally again. He looked up in the dark cave and tried concentrating on something other than the pain he knew awaited his next attempt.

Man up, he berated himself, *people are dying.* After trying to think about his family, his love for Sara, and the God of his faith, David failed to muster enough courage to face that wave of agonizing pain that surely awaited any serious movement. He wanted to sit up but his muscles refused to help, knowing what awaited their effort. As he relaxed, his memories painted a reason to try again. It was the vivid images of the suffering children he saw in Israel. Their innocent tears and bloated bodies gave him the resolve to at least try again.

David thought of another way to move, hopefully less painful. He crawled slowly away from Sara. Should he fail again, he didn't want to fall on her. He then clinched his teeth and rolled over on his left side. Using his left arm, he pushed up on his left knee, leaving his right leg straight. Just before he could no longer hold back the screams, the pain eased enough for him to swallow and catch his breath. He became worried his grunting would wake up someone.

His head was spinning. The blackness was an advantage to him because he couldn't see the room whirling. He took a couple of deep cleansing breaths until the pain lessened. His plan was to get up on his knees and crawl out of the cave, but reality painted a different portrait. Any weight on his wounded leg would most certainly cause him to blackout again. Crawling out on the one leg just might be a better idea, he decided. He found he was able to move on his good knee and left hand.

He was going by memory as he looked back toward Sara. The urge to say goodbye was overpowering. In the dark, he was unable to make out her silhouette. Hell, everything, including the exit was blind to him. He guessed at the direction and figured on feeling his way once he got close.

In the quiet of the cave, they had apologized for their behavior before going to sleep. Sara was finally able to admit to him that she loved him. Nothing in his life, he realized as he looked back to where she should be laying, had ever sounded better.

Making small moves and resting every so often, he crawled toward where his best guess said the cave exit was. When he stopped and held his breath, he could hear what he thought was the rustling of leaves. After the pain eased, he moved in that direction. Miracles of miracles, he thought when he actually found the opening on his first attempt. David struggled through the small opening on one knee after he, trying to be quiet, slowly pushed the bush out of his way.

The night air was fresh and warm as it blew over his sweating face. He touched his right leg and wasn't surprised when he found it wet with his blood. The effort to escape, though successful, had drained him of his strength. He slowly lowered himself back on the ground just outside the cave entrance, his body welcoming the cold ground like a wet towel on a battered prizefighter.

Birdman listened to the struggle going on. He knew what was happening and battled with his conscience on what to do about it. His heart went out to David when he heard him groaning in the dark. He almost got up to help him but decided to wait. David appeared to be all right as he listened to him continue the struggle. When he heard David start crawling toward the cave entrance his chest swelled with emotion. He knew the effort would have opened up his wounds again and he was risking his life, yet the man crawled on.

At first, Birdman didn't know what David had in mind when Sara and Simon were arguing, until after he made eye contact with him. When David nodded to him, Birdman decided to give him his lead and see what transpired. On a hunch, he announced he was going to try and get some rest then crawled over and pretended to fall asleep. Birdman had removed the belt tying the bush to the entrance and made sure it was loose enough to move. Now, while listening to the man struggle to crawl outside the cave, Birdman's assumption proved correct. David was giving them the freedom to search the mountain. He knew they would try to drag him along, slowing down the search. He was probably also saving Sara's career and giving them another pair of eyes to search with.

"Goodbye, friend," Birdman whispered after hearing David push the bush back into the opening.

CHAPTER 26

The night sky was a mix clouds, the moon, and stars. The beauty of the Milky Way Galaxy was spread out above like a million fireflies. The thin mountain air magnified the brilliantly dotted display, revealing starlight usually hidden from the naked eye. David felt as if it was God waving his hand to him, beckoning him to try again.

He fought the seductive urge to close his eyes and sleep as he lay on the cool ground. He knew that, if he did, it might last longer than he would have hoped—a lot longer. He struggled on a trembling arm but was able to lift up off the ground, using his left hand to push himself. Gritting his teeth, he ignored the pain and looked around, surveying the mountainside. Nearly everything below him was clothed in a blanket of dark. In the starlight, he could see the top of a deep canyon that began as a ridge, only a few feet to his left, and dropped off into the darkness.

"I've got to get moving before they discover I'm gone," he whispered up at the night sky. With an effort almost as strenuous as the first time, David turned over on his left knee and started dragging himself up the edge of the ridgeline, holding on to whatever he could find and, when not, he lay down and crawled forward. An hour later, and a half-dozen stops to rest and stifle his screams, he had labored valiantly but crawled only a hundred feet up the steep slope of the mountain. Reasons to keep going were the push that carried him another few yards and then another yard. Those same valid reasons pushed him on but now his effort was measured only in feet before he plopped down, completely worn out.

Exhaustion finally pushed him face down in the dirt, breathing so hard he honestly thought they must be able to hear him in the cave. The way his shorts and shirt were sticking to him, he knew he was bleeding again. *This spot will have to do*, he decided as his only good arm was trembling from the effort. "If they find me here, then they find me. Lord, I can't go on any farther."

His head lay on the very edge of the ridge. The updraft blew warm over him as he looked down into the dark mountain canyon. He knew he was in bad shape. There was something draining out of him with the blood he was losing.

Is this Rabbi Gette's curse? he wondered. David looked down into the blackness that was the bottom of the ridge and remembered the words of the angry priest. He had vowed nothing good would come of their attempt to find the pond.

"How come you kept this to yourself?" David had asked his indignant mentor when he surprised him by returning from his room before David could leave.

Rabbi Gette just stared up at him after he walked past and sat in his chair on the balcony. David stood with his arms crossed, waiting. He realized the rabbi might not answer him but he had to try. Too much was at stake to permit the man to remain silent about this secret.

"Let me tell you something, son," the priest said with obvious annoyance, "you have no right to question me like this. Do you know the mind of God? Do you know his purpose in all this? Well, my young friend, I believe I do."

"No, Rabbi, I don't." David took a few steps closer to the man in the chair. "But I do know it's not the Father's will that his children suffer needlessly. A cure for one is a cure for all. Is there a time to do good and a time not to do good? The God I serve asked me to do good all the time. Thousands outside the masjid are dying, and you say you have the means to stop it. You have taught many times on our right to be here in the promised land, the *aliyah*. We fought to get here, now we must become worthy of the right to stay."

"Worthy!" the rabbi screamed at David as he stood up and pointed his bony finger in his face. "We who eat every day and sleep on soft beds can never become worthy. The worthy are those who died in those accursed camps in the Sudan. The worthy had their bones picked clean by the vultures and ants after they fell in the desert heat, trying to get here. Those are the only people worthy of the Grace of God. The soft people who brought us here aren't worthy. What have they endured to make them worthy of the Healing Water? Nothing! Those who suffered during the war in German concentration camps are worthy, but they are dead. Are their children worthy, no! They are to blame. They only rescued us after thousands had died needlessly."

"But they did rescue us. No other country cared enough to try."

"I think you are blinded by the light, my son. Your heart is with another and not your people."

"Maybe at one time that was true, Teacher, but I've broken off that relationship, and I can still see the error of your judgment."

Both statements shocked Rabbi Gette. He was mildly surprised to learn of the breakup of his favorite student and that white Jewish woman. But even more so that the student dared to stand in judgment of his teacher's decisions.

"Do you think it was by chance," the old man said, waving a finger in his face, "that the farmer found that healing water before he died? By chance, that he walked down that mountain, carried that miracle all the way to the church, and found me? By chance, that he survived the shooting and I survived to reach the Promised Land of our ancestors with the Healing Water? No, my young friend, not by chance. Jehovah God ordained it. Before the worlds were formed, he ordained it. We endured the wilderness of Zin like Moses did thousands of years ago, and now it's our turn to sit on the throne of David, David."

The old man smiled at his pun. David didn't.

"It is God who has anointed us," the rabbi continued as he paced the porch, "and who has chosen us to rule." He turned and studied his misguided protégée. "I administered small portions to the flock in the cities I visit each year to preserve Yahweh's people. You have unknowingly partaken of the elixir yourself. But why are you questioning me? You never did before."

David was silent. The look on the face of the elder who he had trusted without question these last few years demanded an answer. A rebuttal raced from mind to lips but nothing was spoken.

The rabbi sensed David's inner struggle. He had proven himself a worthy servant and student. "What do you want of me, my son?" the older man asked as his pupil maintained the stone face of one convinced he was right. Like the son he never had, the holy man saw himself in the stubborn young man and reached out to him with compassion.

David sighed, reached out his arms to plead with the priest. "Help me, Rabbi. Little children are dying all over our country. I remember your stories about the bad times and how you had to pile the bodies of the dead children in separate tukuls because no one had the strength to bury them."

"Yes, but—"

"Open your eyes, my priest," David said and pointed out toward the city, "that same terrible demon that butchered those children is outside your door, ravishing the innocent. It doesn't care about the color of the children's skin, or their religious beliefs, or the amount of money their parents have in their bank accounts. All it knows is killing. Because of that vicious demon children are dying so fast they are dumping them in a valley and burning their little bodies. Remember what that was like, my priest. I'm here for the children, not for those who let us die in the wilderness."

David thought he saw remorse in the lines of his mentor's face, as if something reminded him of his past. Maybe the vile memories of those *horrible* deaths in the refugee camps would soften his heart.

"No, I won't help," Rabbi Gette said, surprising David. "I still believe that Jehovah God has unleashed his wrath on the stubborn people of Israel for hardening their hearts to the plight of their brothers. The plague will run its course, and those who are righteous will survive. Those who turned their backs on us will perish. It's our turn in the sun. We, the descendants of Solomon, will have to take over for King David, our departed Father."

The slanted reasoning of the Man of God dumbfounded David. Couldn't he see his own hatred had colored his actions? *Why do we always insert God into our biases?* he questioned. There was a lot of pain in the words he had heard his teacher speak. David had sat at his feet on many occasions and listened to the terrible ordeals that he had personally endured. The old man wept as he told about the terrible sobs of the many little children who cried into the night and were dead by morning. Of the pile of rotting bodies stuffed into the straw huts under the inhumane heat of the sun. On occasion, the rabbi told him, he could still smell the repulsive scent of the rotting flesh of the dead. Of those who had once been his close friends and their innocent children. Then there was the wave after wave of maggots that oozed out of the walls of the huts.

Yes, the world had forsaken the Ethiopian Jew. Did the priest have a reason to hate? Probably hundreds. But David knew that if the rabbi didn't come to see the light beyond the darkness in his heart, there would be thousands of other terrible memories occurring right around him to torment him forever.

"Rabbi, I only want two things from you. One, give me the healing water from the Pond of God I believe you have, and second, if you don't have enough, tell me where to find it in Ethiopia."

His pushy student surprised the old rabbi. How could he be so certain about his having the elixir? *He must be guessing,* the old man decided. *Smart boy, that David.* The priest started to walk away when he stopped and looked back at his indignant novice.

With a wry smile, he asked, "I will give you one of your wishes. Which one will it be?" The priest was again surprised when David didn't take the bait. "Now what will you do, my pompous young friend? Will you choose to save some of those dying now or sacrifice their lives for the good of the many?"

The gulf between them widened.

"Have you replaced God?" David shouted and pounded his fist down on the small table next to Rabbi Gette's chair. "Neither you nor I have the right to do either."

"No, but in my position, it is my responsibility to read and understand what God's will is. And someday, my young angry one, you will discover his will and yours or mine sometimes conflict."

David held his comments, quickly realizing the wily old man was maneuvering him down a path that would feed the anger in him, making his emotions more important than his convictions. Taking a deep breath, David smiled then walked toward the holy man. Now the old rabbi was puzzled.

"Rabbi," David whispered, leaning within a couple of inches of the old man's face. "I will return to Ethiopia and seek the Waters of God for the dying children all alone if I have to. I ask, one last time that you help me."

The elderly priest stared up at him for a minute. He felt a twinge of empathy, moved by the sincerity of the rebellious pupil standing up for what he believed. *What if he's right?* he wondered, after looking away from two very determined eyes. "David, my son," the old man said, acquiescing a little. "I will give you all but a little of the Healing Water that I have. I will also tell what little I know about the location of the Pond of God. But the water I give you—" The rabbi punctuated his point by placing a finger on David's forehead. "—must be for the children only. You are right. They are innocent before God of abandoning His people in hell. You must pledge that to me."

"I cannot. I can only ask that your request be honored."

The old man motioned for David to sit down with him as he retold the story about the farmer deciding to bring the Miracle Water to a priest and the death of the man when he sent him to relocate the Pond. Finally, he told him the few clues he was given about its location on Mt. Ras Dashen.

"Help me up, David," the old man bade his student.

David grabbed him firmly by the arm and helped him walk

into the house. He followed the old man down into the basement. He then lit the lantern at the base of the steps. Holding it
up, he noticed that the priest stopped and pointed to some
boxes in the far corner of the dark basement and asked him to
move them aside. Behind them, David found a small wooden
door about two feet high in the wall. The priest held his hand
out in a fist. David watched him skeptically.

The old man then smiled and opened his hand, revealing a
key. "Open it," he said in a manner that was both threatening
and challenging. "The Healing Water of The Most High is
inside, just behind that little door." He tossed the key to David.

David caught the key and stared at it in his hand. There
was nothing special about it. It was an old-style skeleton key
pitted with rust. All he had to do was use it to open the door
and get the water but he couldn't move. David stared at the
piece of metal in his hand but that wasn't what halted his
steps. Behind that dusty door, he knew, was a miracle from
God. Something touched by the hands of the Creator himself.
David found it difficult to breathe. What did Rabbi Gette call
it? Oh, yes, the "Sweat of Angels."

David could feel his heart pounding in his chest. He was
starting to get dizzy and wanted to ask the rabbi to help him
but he couldn't speak. He began to wonder if the rabbi
planned it this way. A wave of anger passed over him when he
realized the Man of God was testing him, teasing him. David
knelt down and placed the lantern on the floor. He slowly put
the key in the lock. A quick turn to the left and he heard the
lock pop open. Slowly he opened the door. His heart almost
stopped when he heard the door creak as it moved, like something right out of a scary paperback novel.

David heard the chilling voices of fear as they warned him
about the indescribable horror that awaited him once the door
was opened wide enough for "it" to get out. Was his life pure
enough to touch the Sweat of Angels? the voices asked. He
tried not to listen but he found himself questioning his worthi-
ness. He only stopped once to consider it then threw the door
open. Slowly, he knelt down to look inside the opening. He

held up the old lantern and it illuminated two dusty, five-gallon silver cans.

"Well that's something, anyway," David heard the priest say from behind him, "you're the first person who's found the courage to unlock the door. I know of two priests who were so shaken at the thought of opening that door, they ran out of the house in terror. But don't fool yourself, that just means you're brave—not smart.

David didn't turn around or comment.

"The one on the right is full. You can take that one. The other only has a few cups worth in it. I'm saving that for God's people."

David grabbed both containers and lifted them out of the little closet. He handed Rabbi Gette the nearly empty can.

"Thank you for your help," David told him sarcastically.

"Wait a minute," the old man said, showing a little more life than David thought he had in him. "You—you think this is going to endear you to them, don't you?"

"I don't care about their opinion of me, or yours anymore!" he shouted at the priest. "What I care about are the innocent children who are dying in Israel." He turned to leave but yielded to the anger boiling up in him. "You have sacrificed them on the altar of your hate and vengeance, just like the people you blame."

"Like I told you, David," the old man said with a sneer on his face, having finally cracked the demeanor of his student. "God's will be done on Earth as it is in Heaven. Take your treasure and go. This will not change what Jehovah God is doing. I'm warning you, son, if you resist the will of God, He will break you. He doesn't need you to fulfill his word."

"Or you, my priest, to judge his people." David stared angrily at the high priest for a moment then turned and hurried up the steps.

"I'm warning you, David," the priest shouted up the empty steps, "if you get in the way, Yahweh will crush you and everyone around you."

As David hurried out of the basement, the elder's words of warning echoed off the hollow walls. He took another few steps, stopped, and went back to help him up the steep stairs. David thanked him again when he helped him to his chair on the porch. "Rabbi, may I use your phone?"

With a nod of his head, the priest gave his consent.

David stopped in the rabbi's private office and called Sara.

"The priest gave me the miracle water. It only five gallons but it will save some lives."

"That's great, David. Can you bring it to the house where you met Simon?"

"Yes," was all he said before hanging up.

Sara was taken aback by that but quickly called Simon to tell him the good news.

When David pulled up in his van, Sara, Simon, and three other men were waiting. David handed the five-gallon can to Simon.

"Rabbi Gette said this is the source of our immunity. He gave it out to those who worshiped at the synagogues without their knowledge as he traveled around the country. Its power to heal is unlimited in most people. According to him, it only takes about a half a teaspoon to heal the sick and its effect lasts for months, he said. Oh yes, he also asked that this be given to the children first. That's all the elixir there is. I checked."

David wasn't sure why he lied about the small amount the rabbi kept for himself. He wanted to believe it was to protect the old man's life.

"Thank you, David. I'll pass on his request. Hopefully, we can make enough of this for everyone," an excited Simon said as he handed the valuable container to the men beside him. "This may be the answer to our prayers."

"I hope so." Then looking over at Sara, he said, "Because it cost me enough."

She called out to him, but her words were lost in the sound of David's van racing away from the source of his pain. Simon put his arm around her as they both watched him drive away.

"He'll come around when he realizes the truth."

"No, Simon, you don't understand," Sara said, turning around and looking up at him. "He understands why I was ordered to do what I did. What he can't accept, is why I couldn't tell him before this."

Simon thought it best to leave it at that.

The Healing Water was divided into over seventy five hundred one-half-teaspoon-sized portions as David recommended. Five hundred portions were rushed to the hospitals. Two hours later, Simon received a scheduled call from the Falashian nurse at Elisha Hospital who he asked to keep him informed about the conditions of the patients receiving the elixir. She was so animated that he had trouble understanding her accent. What he was able to determine was that none of the people they gave the drug to had died. "Some," she said between bouts of crying and laughing, "were as close to dead as possible and now they are awake and responsive."

The results were the same everywhere. The prime minister had the dubious duty of dividing the remaining portions of Healing Water. His decisions were kept secret, lest a certain area of the country, or group of citizens, felt neglected.

Some of the solution was given to scientists to analyze and try duplicating. Their results were a complete failure. They found nothing in the water, absolutely nothing. A bright young biochemist suggested that maybe the reason it worked was the purity of the water. Hours later, they had purified cups of water down to about a few tablespoons of the cleanest, purest water humanly possible. None of the people that they gave it to recovered. The same people quickly improved after being given the "Sweat of Angels."

The power of the elixir was undeniable. It was a fact that medical scientists were forced to admit. They couldn't recreate it or explain it, so very reluctantly they accepted it. Thousands of recovering Israelis knew why. This clear, plain, basic element's power wasn't in the chemical balance of the water. The Healing Water contained something invisible to the naked eye. Something their God, whoever that was, had placed in the water. As illogical as that was to the learned community of science, not one of them could find an answer to its one-hundred-percent recovery rate, regardless of the deplorable, hopeless condition of the recipient.

The "Elixir of God" saved over seventy-five hundred of the most ill people, leaving over two hundred thousand who were infected with the plague to some degree in Israel alone. It did buy the nation some hope.

Sara's suggestion that David's priest might know more about the location of the elixir had set in motion Simon's plan. First, David had agreed to return and see if there was anything else that Rabbi Gette could recall that might help in locating its origin and then he agreed to join them on a secret mission into Ethiopia to recover all that they could. That desperate, secret mission had cost them the lives of their friends and chased them until they were forced to hide in a dark, dusty grotto in the eastern side of Mt. Ras Dashen, Ethiopia.

CHAPTER 27

Birdman aimed his weapon at the entrance to the cave. A whistle signaled that it was Weasel. When he climbed in, they both heard the second whistle minutes later as Snake approached the opening. A whistle from Birdman signaled to him that it was okay to enter.

Simon heard them enter and sat up. He turned on his small flashlight and aimed it at them.

"Birdman," Weasel said while taking off his helmet. "The troops that were following us have turned around and are making camp at the base of the mountain. I followed them until they reached the spot where their helicopter is stationed." He paused then shook his head. The cave dwellers knew then his next words were painful. "They have the bodies of our friends. I think they want to claim the bodies of our fallen comrades for political reasons. The coast is clear for over five miles."

"Good," Simon said, ignoring the distasteful part. "We need to get going." There was a sadness he felt over the loss of the remains of the other commandos, but this wasn't the time to mourn or dwell on their fate. Simon looked at Snake.

"Yes, Simon, the way east is also clear to get the hell out of here. But what are we going to do with—" Snake stopped after looking over were Sara was sleeping. In the shadow of Simon's flashlight he was able to make out only one body lying there. From the size, it was obvious who that was. David should have been lying next to her, but he wasn't. "Where's David?" Snake asked.

Simon turned and aimed his flashlight in the direction of Sara and David. He was gone! Everyone was stunned, save one.

Like an alarm going off, Sara's eyes popped opened, alert and searching. She spotted Weasel and Snake and smiled at them. Her prayers were answered. She started to lie down again but wondered why they were aiming their light in her direction. When she noticed the look of concern on their faces and realized they had bad news, she sat up. *Well, what else is new?* Sara thought as she turned around to check on David. She just stared at the knapsack, laying there with the same indentation his head had made. He was gone. Sara fumbled in her pocket for her miniature flashlight and illuminated the area behind her. He was gone. Like a lost child, she slowly looked up at Simon for an answer. Her puzzled, little girl expression moved everyone watching her.

She opened her mouth to speak but nothing came out. Turning again, she looked at the last place she had seen him, as if that empty space was a mirage. Voices in her head proclaimed that Simon was going to say he had died and that they had buried him while she slept. No. She turned and looked at Simon. He would never rob her of the chance to say goodbye to David. She tried to wish a positive answer from Simon's tired face by smiling innocently at him. He didn't return her smile. Her spirit dropped so suddenly, it should have echoed around the cave. A terrible pain raced through her chest and her hand clutched at it. That look of panic did finally induce a response from Simon.

"Sara, David is—" Simon started to say.

"No, don't tell me he died while I was sleeping," she said, cutting him off.

Simon crawled closer to his favorite young agent. "No, Sara, I don't think so, not yet."

"What do you mean, Simon?" she said as she reached out and grabbed him by the arm.

"Sara, David is gone."

"David is dead?" she asked, placing her hands over her mouth.

"I don't know that, Sara. I don't think so, anyway. We just realized ourselves that he was missing. We believe he left on his own while we were sleeping."

Sara shook her head in disbelief and then started crawling around the cave, searching for him.

"Sara," Birdman said, grabbing her and stopping her futile search after she pushed Simon out of her way. "I've already looked. He is gone."

"Then we have to go out and find him," she shouted at everyone, "in his condition, he couldn't get far."

"Wait a minute, Sara," Birdman ordered. "Why do you think he left?"

"I don't give a damn why, let's go and find him," she replied and started to crawl toward the opening.

"No, Sara, think about it," Birdman said, moving in front of her. "He knew what he was doing. He didn't want to be a burden to us and understood the time constraints we are under. Every hour, the plague spreads to more people. I think David left so that you could help us search for the Pond of God."

"Listen to me, Bird-whoever! I don't care what his reasons are. I won't leave him. He needs me. Without him, there wouldn't be any search for that damn pond. For all we know, it may not even exist. I won't let him die for a dream. His life means nothing to you. To me, it is everything, so get the hell out of my way!" She screamed the last few words at him.

In the dim light, Birdman looked over at Simon for help. Restraining her would be simple for him, but Simon motioned for him to move.

Sara noticed him looking over her shoulder and figured he was questioning Simon on what to do. Her anger told her he couldn't stop her. Her common sense vetoed that foolishness. When he moved out of her way, thankfully she didn't have to find out. Sara kicked the bush out of her way and climbed out of the cave into the night air, followed by her four escorts.

Weasel walked over to Sara and pointed up the mountain.

"From these tracks and blood drops on the ground," Weasel explained, "he must have climbed farther up the mountain."

The five of them stared up the ridge line but didn't see David.

"Sara, wait!"

She ignored Simon and started climbing up the mountain.

"Sara, it's too dark. We need to use our flashlight, or we might tumble over the edge of the ridge."

Sara took another few steps and realized it was a very dangerous climb. But if an injured David could make it surely—

"Okay, Simon, let's use the flashlights."

Weasel led the way with Simon lighting his path from behind him. Slowly they followed Weasel along the more dangerous part of the ridge until he stopped and looked around.

"What is it Weasel?" Simon asked when the commando surveyed the ground around his feet.

"This was as far as he got."

"What do you mean as far as he got," a panicky-voiced Sara asked.

As they crowded in the small space near the ridge he explained. "There are no foot prints past this spot."

Simon aimed his flashlight where Weasel was pointing.

"The ground past this spot isn't disturbed," Weasel pointed out. "See where his blood pooled here by the edge. Maybe he got dizzy or fainted and—"

"No!"

Each of them knew why Sara screamed. Weasel was the closest to the edge and he joined Sara in looking over the ridge at the dark valley below. And, like her, he prayed not to see a broken body amongst the rocks far beneath them. Only the shadows of the night welcomed their search.

"Simon, where is he?"

Simon turned and aimed his flashlight at Snake. "I don't know, Sara."

Snake shrugged. "I didn't see any sign on him as I climbed up from the valley below."

All eyes turned toward Weasel. He just shrugged his shoulders in the light and then shook his head. The other possibility was something they didn't want to consider. But as each stood there contemplating that, Sara's cry started them.

"Oh, no," Sara cried, walking around in circles with her hands in tight fists. Suddenly, she came to a decision, moved quickly toward the cliff, and jumped off. Weasel turned in time to see her rush past him and lunged for her. He came within fingertips of losing her. He lay on the rim of the cliff with his arm over the edge and only a handful of Sara's shirt keeping her from jumping to her death. Before he could shout for help, the others had recovered from their shock and were reaching down to grab what they could of her. They were able to pull a very hysterical, fighting woman back up over the edge of the cliff.

"No!" she screamed as they held her down. She kicked out at them and punched at whatever her arms could reach. "Let me go, I don't want to live without him. Please, let me go," she started to beg as she realized she couldn't break free. Her face was covered with her tears and dirt. Her shirt was open as the buttons popped off in the struggle. The men tried looking away as her chest was exposed in the struggle to hold her down. Although, at one time, each had fantasized about being with her, none felt that way about the broken-hearted woman now. She was a sister who had her love taken away from her and needed the strength of a brother to go on.

Sara sobbed like a child. Simon was the only one holding her now. One by one, the other men had let her go as her broken heart drained the fight out of her. Each of them had to come to grips with David's sacrifice. As abhorrent as suicide was to each of them, the courage and conviction of the crumbled man lying somewhere down there in the night, moved each of them to some degree of admiration. *Truly, this man was a Jew*, each thought, as they said their goodbyes to David.

They sat quietly on the ground around Sara as she prayed and talked to God about her David. Her sobbing plea for his soul was a moving entreaty. Simon made no effort to hide the tears that filled his eyes as he held her. Weasel, Birdman, and Snake just kept their heads down until their own pain had eased. After her crying subsided, Simon helped the limp woman stand to her feet and led them back down the mountain to the cave.

CHAPTER 28

The object of the five cave dwellers' mournful consternations had earlier chosen another course of action.

After sneaking out the cave and crawling up the mountain, an exhausted David had to stop and rest. With his body growing weaker, he fought the strong urge to sleep. He envisioned it as a sweet pleasure that would erase the agony his body was enduring. The loss of blood was draining him of what little strength he had. He was running out of time. He lowered his head to the ground as the question of what to do next troubled him. Slowly he felt his eyes closing and couldn't seem to muster the strength to resist. It felt so good when his lids closed over his dry, burning eyes that he felt himself starting to drift—

David jerked his head up and looked around. Did someone called him? He listened. Silence.

"Was I dreaming about hearing someone call my name?" Struggling to sit up, he knew he had to make a decision. If it was up to him to find the Messiah Drug, he had to start searching. But he no longer had the strength to climb and, looking up, he saw that the ridge line became even steeper ahead. Down. He sensed he needed to go down the mountain. That should be easier anyway.

When David stopped climbing and lay on the ground, he was very close to the edge of a ridge with a steep drop-off. Leaning to his right, he looked over the ridge at the shadows of the valley far below.

"Man that's a long way down. Okay, let see if I can stand. Can't hurt much more than it already does, I'm guessing."

Crawling toward a large rock, he used it to stand on his good leg. Taking a second deep breath, the first failing to motivate him to try and move, and leaning against the rocks, he slowly made his way down, hopping on his one good leg. Stopping at the entrance to the cave, he took a moment to say goodbye to the sleeping trio before continuing his arduous trek, grabbing hold of plants and rocks as he descended.

David found it easier to transit down the mountain as his wounded leg hurt less. Reaching a pile of boulders, he stopped again to rest. Thankfully, the moon had peeked out from behind the clouds, making it a little easier to see. Laying his head against a cold boulder gave him momentary relief. He hugged the stone, growing reluctant to continue his painful journey, then suddenly stood up when he heard something.

"What was that," he whispered.

Straining to identify the sound, he came to the realization someone was climbing up the mountain ridge toward him. The only avenue open to him was to either expose his position by trying to climb up again or down, and that wasn't much of an option.

David decided to try hiding from the Ethiopian soldiers in a large cleft between two huge boulders. The moon, that he once thanked for its help, he now prayed would go back into hiding. Quickly looking around, he resolved this was the only refuge available. Squeezing between the boulders until only the toes of his shoes offered evidence of his presence, he tried to fold into the space between the rocks.

David held his breath and listened as a soldier, breathing heavily from the climb, missed him in his hiding place. David waited until he could no longer hear him before relaxing.

"Thank God," David whispered. He hesitated a moment and lowered his head to give thanks. It was that silent prayer that prevented him from stepping farther out from between the rocks and into another soldier climbing up the mountain ridge. Quickly slipping between the boulders, he could only hope the soldier climbing the ridge didn't turn around. David was more exposed this time. The soldier, like the last, moved past, seemingly more concerned with looking for his friends farther up the mountain.

"Maybe I should give myself up," he questioned, feeling guilty. "That way, they might forget about the others hiding. Taking me might be enough to allow the others to escape when the sun comes up and continue the search. The next soldiers," he resolved. "Maybe I'll surrender to the next soldiers."

As the minutes rolled past, he came to realize he was alone. The two soldiers who climbed up the mountain hadn't returned. Were they hiding waiting on his friends to appear? he wondered. Or had their hidden cave again stymied the soldiers search and kept his friends safe.

"Damn, giving up is not an option. Simon wouldn't give up," David admitted as he stood up. "Hell, I know Sara wouldn't. The reason I'm here, Jehovah sent me to find it." Feeling renewed and stronger, he decided to continue his search.

Like the staff given to Moses, David spotted a stick lying against one of the boulders. "Thank you," he whispered when a use for the stick crossed his mind.

Working his way down, he found that the treacherous ridge widened, allowing him to make better progress. But as he reached the lower tree line, the tall grass and bushes hindered his progress. When the moon slipped behind the clouds, he was all but blind. "Well, stupid," he said as he pushed his way through some bushes, "this was a great idea, going it alone and in the dark yet. Me thinks mine ego has got the best of me," he joked. Limping along with his arms extended in front of him proved futile as branches scratched him and he stumbled and fell three times.

"Lord help me," David pleaded after tripping over something in the dark and falling hard on his wounded shoulder and leg. The pain was so great he lay on his back, gritting his teeth until it ebbed. His spirits fell a little each time he did. "I can't quit. I can't quit if it's meant for me to find the water," he muttered. This time, he didn't get up but lay in the weeds where he fell. *You have no idea where you are*, his negative thoughts pointed out. That was so true, he had no upbeat response. He could be walking—ah, falling—toward the soldiers and away from the hope of Israel. He had no way of knowing.

"Lord help me," he entreated, covering his face with his hand.

Staring up at the night sky, a despondent David, trying to get back in the search, watched as the full moon again slipped out from between some clouds. The forest around him was still dark but the moonlight offered some help in avoiding the shadows. Reading that as his answer, David struggled to stand. Closing his eyes while his body recouped, he heard something that made his blood run cold. Spinning around he searched the woods in the direction of that sound. He heard it again.

"My God!" David started limping in what he hoped was the other direction. Although he couldn't see very well in the forest, if that sound was what he thought, the owner was nocturnal.

Now the bushes and branches scratching and hitting him in the face as he fled were ignored. He heard it again and it was much closer. "Oh God, oh God," David said as he panicked and changed direction again, moving to his left, after hearing that sound, to his right this time. He was being skillfully herded in that direction. In his fear he never considered why?

This time, the growl was so loud David tripped and fell, trying to turn around and see how close whatever was stalking him was. David fought through the pain and with the help of his staff, hastily stood, envisioning that the animal growling was about to pounce on him. Wide eyed and panting, he looked around, searching for his stalker. He heard something in a patch of bushes but couldn't see anything.

Walking backward, David almost fell again when he saw something moving in the shadows. "My God!" he shrieked, his body paralyzed with fear. He quickly looked around, the hair standing up on his neck. In the dark shadows, he imagined a monster stalking him, as the warnings of his priest labeled his fear. David turned and tried running away on his one good leg.

Stumbling out of some tall grasses, he found a mound of rocks and boulders blocking his escape. Standing there panting and panicking, he looked up at the maybe thirty-foot-high mound of stones and dirt, feeling trapped. It looked like a wall preventing his escape but it could also be a wall he deduced, that could save his life if—

He ignored the pain in his injured shoulder and leg and started to frantically climb the mound of rocks. Like a cold breeze on his neck, he sensed Death was stalking him in the woods. This avalanche of stones seemed to be his only salvation. Hurriedly, he climbed the rocks, repeatedly looking behind him as he went. His clothes were soaked in his sweat and blood. Half the way up his injured right leg gave out. Gritting his teeth, he tried pulling himself up and over the stones. When he ran out of gas, it only took a vicious growl from something close behind him to drive him to the top of the mound.

"Thank you, God," he exclaimed, exhausted, kneeling on one knee at the top of the mound. Even the air seemed fresher at the top. But hearing something moving toward him, David panicked and stood on his shaky leg, trying to put more distance between him and the pursuing animal.

A snarl behind him was so loud it signaled that it was too late to run. His time was up. Terrified, David knew he had to fight for his life. Reduced to desperation, he picked a large stone, and, as he turned his head, he only saw a blur of black before it hit him hard in the back, knocking him and the stone tumbling down the other side of the mound of rocks.

Dazed, David landed on his back and winced in pain. His spine was on fire. As his head cleared, he looked up at the stars. Questions floated across his mind but no answers. The roar from an angry predator resolved one of those questions. Although weak, David slowly turned his head toward the sound and, in the moonlight, spotted a huge black panther stalking back and forth along the top of the mound of rocks. Its jaws were open and huge fangs glistened as he growled. But it was its eyes that provoked the most fear. They were bright yellow against its black pelt and seemed to project hate and death, as the animal paced back and forth atop the wall of stone, taunting him.

As David lay staring at that angry beast snarling its contempt for the stupid man lying on the ground, the Lord's Prayer came to mind. "The Lord is my—" was as far as he got when the panther started down the mound toward him. A terrified David stopped praying, ignored his painful shoulder, and started crawling away from the beast as fast as he could. "Oh God," he muttered as he scuttled backward. Feeling his arms growing weaker, he knew this was only a momentary deliverance. The panther stopped, raised its head to the night, and roared in anger. After staring menacingly at David on the ground, it returned to stalking along the top of the mound.

David couldn't see where he was crawling, unable to take his eyes off the large animal. Exhausted, he stopped when the animal resumed its pacing. Starting to believe he was somehow safe, he felt that feeling of hope quickly evaporate when the black panther was joined by a spotted leopard. Already resigned to being killed by the yellowed-eyed demon, David swallowed hard when it's mate showed up for dinner. As if on cue, both animals started moving down the mound toward him. Everything started to happen in slow motion. He could feel himself beginning to blackout as he started slowly crawling away from them.

"Noooo," he said in a weak whisper as his body became heavier and his arms kept slipping out from under him as he crawled. The blood curling growl from the duo approaching him seemed to echo in the valley where he fell. "Lord have mercy," were the last words uttered by him as they charged and he blacked out.

David opened his eyes, feeling no pain. But everything around him was black. He couldn't hear anything, see anything, or feel anything. He wasn't food for the leopards, so that was a good thing, he decided. *I'm between life and death,* he reasoned. He felt at peace with that knowledge. Suddenly his life flashed before him, racing from birth to now. But Sara was the one memory that stuck with him in the void between life and death. David didn't know where he was, but it wasn't...where he was. He remembered his heart beating slower and slower until he started to black out and, seeing the leopards about to attack him—then he was here in this void as his life was played out before him.

One image, thankfully, he was able to retain. And even in death she looked beautiful. Surprisingly, even in death, he still yearned for her.

"Sara," he called out in his spirit.

From the moment he saw her, she'd touched something in his heart. In the beginning, he was too busy with his job to recognize it. *Or is deep, abiding love hard to recognize because we tend to ignore its grip on us until we are snared?* The one thing he had to acknowledge was that she touched a part of him he didn't know existed.

He was thinking how great they were together when he suddenly felt himself falling in the void, yet nothing was moving past him to give an indication of where and how fast. *So this is dying.* He started falling faster and faster. Then the sensation of falling started to ease. He somehow knew that some strange power had found him and was struggling to hold him here. "Why, why is it taking so long to face my eternity?" he shouted in his spirit as, again, he sensed he was floating in a weightless black void.

It seems as if there is no hurry in this place, he reasoned, *no such thing as time.* He pictured an eternity clock as one with hands but without numbers, and eternity as a day with endless hours, hours with innumerable minutes, minutes with uncountable seconds.

Well, he had no one to blame but—

He remembered that death didn't come for him. He called it from wherever it hid with his singular act of searching in the dark in one of the more dangerous jungles of Africa, for the Messiah Drug. Or was this God's curse for those so foolish as to question his holy men? Now am I doomed to float in this nether world forever? The void he was in didn't stop the feelings of depression that idea garnered.

Then another possible explanation crossed his thought processes. Maybe it was because the many thousands of those dying from the plague had delayed his entrance into Heaven, or worse, Hell. He pictured a long procession of people waiting in lines at the Pearly Gates because of the backup. No answer or the dumbest answer carried the same weight when you were alone in total, absolute blackness.

The only light he could see were the pictures of his life that he created by his thoughts. Here, in this way station to eternity, the mind was free to recreate clear and colorful memories. David resumed where he left off. Sara appeared in his mind's eye in all her glory. He wasn't sure where they were in his imagination but there she stood dressed in a long, white flowing negligee. The wind blew it against the curves of her body, the same breeze blowing her hair behind her. It was a picture formed in his imagination from something he had seen in the movies.

His mind took him on a visual trip from the dinners they ate on the beach some nights, to their many tourist-like fun tours of the sights in Haifa that they both seemed to be enjoying. And then a picture formed in front of him of the night when they finally made love. *Oh, God.* Like a voyeur, he watched as they came together. Void of his body, there wasn't the fire of physical passion he'd felt then. It was the beauty of their caring that he sensed. But his memory recorded the fact that he found her an amazing lover that night. Each time afterward was an improvement on the last, and the first time was magnificent.

"But into each life a little rain must fall." The words of that song had reached out and touched them when the plague floated into Israel and infected their lives. Sara's desperate confession hurt him so deeply that he thought about quitting his job and leaving the country. He had made up his mind to do so after helping discover why the Falashians were immune to the plague.

His conversations with Rabbi Gette were very disheartening. He had such a deep respect for the elder that it hurt to see his weak human side. But after what happened with Sara, nothing the priest could say could make him feel any worse. Was it because of what happened with Sara that he found the nerve to not only confront the priest but to demand he tell him what he knew? he wondered as he floated in black nothingness, awaiting his fate. Would he have ever confronted him, had she not? David deliberated on that thought for a moment. He knew it wasn't the first time God had used the beauty of a woman to further his plans.

As if he was gazing through a telescope, her face zoomed in closer. The woman owning his soul then looked at him, as if she knew something he didn't. David wanted to ask her…what? Suddenly, the face of the woman who stole his heart evaporated into the blackness, her eyes being the last thing he saw as they stared lovingly at him.

David sensed her sudden departure signaled something new was starting to happen He began to feel an odd change come over him. He felt both weakness and great strength. What was surprising to him was how his body had fought so hard to hold on to life after the massive injuries it must have suffered. He began to worry that the slow metamorphosis was Death, unable to make up its mind. To die was scary, but to somehow survive the attack of the leopards and maybe live as a vegetable—far worse.

Is my punishment for angering God, as my priest warned, to dangle here forever between these two worlds? he shouted in the silence of his mind.

David was wrong. Like a heavy steel shade dropping down, he died.

Passing over, David discovered, wasn't painful or frightening. The blackness cleared away like smoke in a breeze and he found himself lying on his back. When he raised his head up, he was surrounded by a beautiful green forest. It was night but he could see as clearly as if it was day. Then, without much effort, he just stepped out of his prone body and stood up. He looked down at his limp body with neither joy nor sadness. He felt as if this was a natural occurrence in nature. A birth void of the struggle, pain, and bloody mess of the first. Looking around, he saw the two powerful animals that had probably sped up his demise returning to the top of the mound of boulders.

Then without warning, he was gently lifted upward into the air. Again, he wasn't afraid because he now understood this was what happened when you died. He surrendered to the power that held him and soared upward even faster.

As the clouds passed under him, he saw a sight reserved for only astronauts and dearly departed souls, the sudden explosion of stars as he entered the blackness of space. Billions upon billions of bits of light, unhindered by the pollution of our atmosphere, danced naked before him. Looking around, David spotted the moon off to his right. Very pleased with himself, he looked down and was awestruck by the beauty of the blue-white orb shrinking quickly beneath him.

He knew he had died, but "physically" he never felt better. There was a power surging through him that seemed to have a purpose. His body had died but he wasn't dead. *To all those who lied to themselves, thinking their existence ended with their last breath—surprise! Your body has limitations, your soul, the essence of who you are, is eternal. The "where" of your eternity is the question.*

A peace had come over him that transcended Death's power as David soared upward toward whatever fate awaited him in the Heavens.

The awesome beauty of the Earth deserved one last look before it faded from sight. It was during this farewell glance that he spotted a long blue cord of light that snaked upward from the Earth. In the brightness reflecting off the beautiful blue marble beneath him, he had missed it. But as he moved away from the blue-white sphere and entered the absolute blackness of space, it became visible.

"What is that?" he said, but never heard his words. He trailed the dancing blue cord upward and finally realized it was attached to him. Like a child at birth, it was his umbilical life-cord. That prompted him to examine his body. It was void of sexual organs or clothes and that seemed normal.

The blue life-cord emanated from the area of his body that would have been his navel. As David soared toward the heavens he realized he was still attached to the Earth. Trying to reason what that meant, he became panic-stricken. As the fear built up in him, he started to tumble around at the end of the cord. The more he tumbled, the more frightened he became. The more frightened he became, the more he tumbled. He began to understand the tumbling was related to the fear. He tried to relax. Immediately, the tumbling slowed until he was once again soaring toward the stars. This time, he slowly looked at the life-cord attached to him. It was as thick as his wrist and, like a loose rope, it looped around in S-shaped spirals downward to the Earth.

As he watched and questioned its purpose, the loops began to straighten out as he continued to soar faster and faster into the Heavens. Before long, he would be out of cord, and then what would happen? Was this cord some kind of a measure of his good deeds? What if he didn't do enough good deeds to get into Heaven? Would he then be stranded between worlds like a ghost or like a kite floating on the winds of space? Oh, no!

He could suddenly visualize millions of people together dangling on the end of their cords, their different distances from Heaven a marking stick of their lack of good works. Would he be one of those poor souls falling just short of the necessary good deeds and forever dangling just short of Heaven's rewards? Now *that* would be hell.

David felt himself starting to flip over again.

"No," he shouted into the void of space. "I won't be frightened anymore." Again, he stopped and continued to move away from the Earth. The life-cord was now a straight line down into the darkness. He no longer could see the blue-white orb sitting in the sea of black and stars. David expected to stop at any moment but he continued on even faster. As he did, the cord began to stretch. It became narrower and narrower as he ascended into the Heavens. Before long it was only a fine thread that reached through the black ink of space toward a small blue world hidden somewhere in the ebony pool below him.

David couldn't feel any pressure from the cord stretching

as it surely approached its breaking point. The understanding of what that probably meant became clear to him. Once broken, he could never return to the Earth. *That life-cord is the umbilical that attaches us to Mother Earth. When it is broken, we are born into another plane, another realm of existence. Cutting of the life-cord is the last step into eternity.*

Although David desperately wanted to continue his journey into the Heavens, he still felt the love he had for Sara. A powerful love, he realized, that reached past the black walls of death. Here, in the nothingness of space, her image was as bright as the brightest star. Yet the love he had for her couldn't satisfy the longing he felt for what awaited him beyond the stars, hopefully at the end of his cord.

Tighter and tighter, the cord stretched until it was almost invisible. Ahead, he noticed this speck of light brighter than anything he had ever seen before. In his spirit, he knew that was his final destination. That speck started to grow in size as he neared it. His anticipation soared as he awaited the momentous event. "Just a little more," he said to the hair-thin cord, "just give me a little more."

David felt himself starting to slow down. He tried to ignore it but very quickly it became obvious that he was slowing down. "No!" he shouted into the void of space. "No!" He even tried reaching out, as if to grab hold of something and pull himself along.

He came to a stop. David looked around, wondering if this was his destination. There was nothing around him but the blackness of space. He looked at the super bright star ahead of him. It was now so bright it illuminated his body. But he was alone in the vastness of space. There weren't millions of other souls in the same predicament, as he feared, just the emptiness of space. For as far as his eyes and imagination could see, he was surrounded by nothing. In his panic, the words of the high priest came back to him. "God will crush you if you get in his way."

"Did I get in your way, Lord?" he asked prayerfully. "If I have, please forgive me."

David had closed his eyes during his prayer. Then he felt

himself moving again. "Thank you, oh, God thank you."

When he opened his eyes, he saw that the Earth was a tiny dot beneath him. He stared at it for a moment in shock and bewilderment, and then he screamed. He continued screaming as he was being reeled in like a prized fish.

His religious teaching explained clearly that the rewards for a good and faithful servant were in the Heavens, somewhere beyond the stars. Another reward awaited others in the molten, burning, bowels of the Earth, another kind of eternity.

David screamed in the silence as he tumbled wildly toward an Earth, now rushing upward to embrace him.

CHAPTER 29

Simon helped Sara to the cave. She crawled in and dropped down in a corner. The other men crawled in and each found a spot to sit apart from the others. The death of David had divided them as each inwardly questioned the insanity that had enveloped their mission of hope. No one bothered to leave on any of the flashlights. The darkness was a coveted blanket that kept out reality.

But even that shield was punctured as they heard Sara whimpering. None of the men could find the words needed to comfort her. Simon suffered the most, as he felt the blame for everything that had gone wrong. This was all his idea, he berated himself. He convinced the prime minister to risk sneaking into this God-forsaking country. Another Entebbe, he told him. They would be in and out before anyone knew they were there.

Simon was told that Prime Minister Shamir had asked the Ethiopian government for permission to search for a vaccine that was believed to be in their territorial borders. Their ambassador said he would forward the request as hastily as possible. After two days of dragging their feet, Shamir called the ambassador into his office and threatened to use force if necessary. The ambassador from Ethiopia spoke eloquently about his government's absolute refusal to permit any of the diseased Jews to cross their borders. Shamir threatened to invade Ethiopia and find the vaccine by force if he had to. The ambassador then informed him that they had already appealed to the United Nations for help to protect their borders. He then played his ace in the hole. The Russian government promised to send ten fighter squadrons to protect their sovereignty. Privately, the ambassador revealed to him that there were countries debating the annihilation of the disease by nuclear means. Shamir was ready to call their bluff when Simon presented his covert plan to find the source of the Messiah Drug.

Simon explained to Shamir the information David was able to get from Rabbi Gette. His medical staff had already confirmed the proof of the power of the drug. Their inability to duplicate it was the drive that powered this desperate attempt. If the location was accurate, Simon explained, it would only take a small group of commandos to find it. Shamir had no real choice in the matter, as the deaths would soon number in the hundreds of thousands. Shamir gave him a free hand but vowed to come and get it by force in three days if his mission failed.

Simon quickly assembled the best commandos available. When David agreed to accompany them, he had his crew. The last minute addition of Sara would be some insurance that David would give it his all. *Man, did that plan work*, Simon thought, *too damn well.*

The candidates were isolated and given a battery of tests. None of them displayed any symptoms of the suspected Sverdlovsk strain of anthrax. Quickly Simon assembled his group and placed them in quarantine in a hotel until they were ready to depart.

Was it a place in history that motivated his reasoning? Simon questioned as remorse pounded him. If so, he should be the one dead, not David. He came here trying to help a country that only grudgingly accepted him. He jumped off that damn cliff so they could continue the mission and here they were, hiding again. The reality of their failure to capitalize on his sacrifice bothered Simon, but not enough to motivate him to drag the stunned group out of the safety of the cave. Sara's whimpering and his assumption she needed this time to mourn her loss was the glue he used to cement them in that dark hole.

The cave became ghostly quiet, as everyone was lost in

their own interpretation of the failure of their mission. The four men reasoned that they were only there to give the distraught Sara time to recover from David's crazy suicide. In reality, they were themselves drained by the thought of his body bouncing cruelly off the mountainside. In their quiet reflection, a flashlight, unexpectedly aimed in their faces, suddenly blinded them.

"Okay, guys, let's get out of here," the holder of the light ordered. "We've been in here too long. We damn sure can't find the water sitting on our asses."

The tone of the voice was apparent. The owner of the voice was obvious. The abrupt change in her startled them. While they were busy feeling sorry for her, she was gathering herself together.

Sara aimed the light in her face as an indicator of her seriousness. While they watched, she tied her torn shirt in a knot under her breasts, gathered her knapsack, and started crawling out the cave. When she stood up and looked around, she noticed the eastern sky was a little brighter. The morning of another day was coming. The men quietly followed her out the cave, unsure of her emotional state. All four men studied her for any sign of the hysterical woman they had to drag back from the precipice.

Sara sensed their genuine concern for her. She turned around and took a minute to look at them. "I'm okay now. The Sara that loved David died with him. There was no way any of us could have stopped that. The old Sara Jacobs, an agent in the Israeli Mossad, has returned to this damn hell hole. We've got a job to do, let's get on it. Oh, and I need a gun. The next person shooting at me is going to catch hell."

The coldness of her voice disturbed Simon. The dead serious glare in her eyes was enough to convince him she had blocked out her feelings for David. Simon resisted the seed of regret he felt because she was, again, the callous Sara of old. There was a world of pain between the new/old Sara and the old/new Sara.

Painful memories that needed to be resolved before she could be whole. Maybe now wasn't the time or the place, but he vowed to get her some professional help to deal with her loss when they returned.

Birdman handed Sara his sidearm and she stuck it behind her back under her belt.

Snake led them down and then east below the canyon wall where David had fallen. In the early morning's dim light, they searched the trees and bushes for the Pond. Systematically, they covered every possible foot of ground where water could accumulate. Six long hours later, exhausted, they had come full circle and found themselves at the bottom of the canyon where David's body might have fallen. What they discovered in searching this area of the lower section of the mountain was that from eruptions, earth quakes, or other reasons, there were numerous piles of boulders of infinite sizes that had tumbled down from the mountain over the centuries. They literally had to circle some mounds of rocks and climb others in their search for the hidden pool of miracle water.

The U-shaped ravine they next approached had high, sheer walls that circled a patch of trees at its base. The lush green foliage hid the ground. As they climbed down and neared the opening of the ravine, they discovered another mound of rocks and boulders, blocking their path. Trees and plant were growing between the rocks, suggesting to Birdman that this rockslide must have occurred a long time ago.

"Hold it, everyone, let's take a break before we try climbing over that barricade," Simon suggested, his own legs throbbing from the trek. He had watched them stagger down the last hundred feet or so. As confirmation, they dropped down where they stood.

"Anyone interested in making lunch?" Silence followed Simon's request. "Never mind."

"Later," Weasel volunteered as he laid his head down and curled up in a shaded spot. "I'll whip up something later."

"I'm going to take up watch on that little hill over there," a tired and guilt-ridden Snake told Birdman, pointing to a spot about fifty yards away. "Someone has to stand guard."

The tired group readily agreed with his summation and his choice as watchman.

Sara leaned back against a tree and looked up at the wall of the canyon, trying to find the spot where David had fallen. It looked totally different from below the ridgeline. She couldn't believe how high it was. What was plain to see was that a fall from that height had to have certainly killed him. She swallowed hard to keep down her emotions and that violent picture she imagined of her lover's body being thrashed and slammed against the mountain side and cruelly tossed into the darkness. Sara gasped and quickly looked away, lest the others see the pain she was feeling. They were all watching her, she could just sense it.

As they rested, the fact that David's body might lay just beyond that rockslide wasn't lost on any of them. He was only twenty minutes of tough climbing away, but none of them really wanted to see his broken, bloodied body. Simon's suggestion they rest carried more weight for that reason than their tired bodies had.

Sara lay back on the ground and closed her eyes. The three men seated near her, trying not to be obvious, watched her from the corners of their eyes and did the same. They wondered as one if she should be allowed to enter the ravine and have to see the broken body of the man she loved. None had the heart to tell her she shouldn't, or the wish to be the one to bring it up. Maybe someone else would think of a way to tell her, each of them hoped.

Snake pulled himself up a steep mound by grabbing hold of the branch of a tree. It appeared that part of the rockslide reached this far, burying the large tree without killing it. The perch he finally settled on gave him a view of the canyon and the area leading up the hill toward it. With the trunk of the tree to lean against, he was able to rest and stand watch at the same time. The branches also offered some shade from the hot sun and cover to hide behind.

The only movement he was able to detect with his binoculars was a herd of frightened wildebeest apparently running from one of the many predators occupying the plains at the base of the mountain.

Snake put his Uzi down beside him. He finally felt his

friends were safe near the rockslide. After resting, they would
have to climb over that huge mound of fallen rocks, search for
the body of their friend on the other side, and give him a proper burial. From the cliffs above, they couldn't see the ground.
The canopy of tall green treetops that filled the valley hid it
from view. Like a green umbrella, it might also shield the broken body of David Yasuda.

This was the only area they hadn't checked on this part of
the mountain, Snake thought as he took a long deep breath,
leaned back against the tree, and looked up at the clouds overhead. That was also the last spot he wanted to search. They
had scoured this section of the mountainside in search of the
Pond, consciously avoiding the place where each knew David's body lay. Hours later, exhausted by the climbing, searching, and most of all, the failures, they stumbled down toward
the little valley. The plan was to rest, bury David, and continue searching up the mountain. For the next half hour, they
rested their tired bodies and listened to the demons of anxiety
tormenting their thoughts.

The quiet of his shaded spot helped Snake to relax. After
scanning the area around them for the umpteenth time and seeing no one, Snake's eyes drifted down to the ground. The
movement of some ants seemed to relax him as he studied
their daily grind searching for the crumbs of life. Their hard
work, and the quiet of the valley below, held his attention. He
never saw the squalid native shuffling up the slope of the hill
toward him until, growing bored with the ants, he looked up
just as the man stumbled behind some trees.

"Who in the hell was that? Dammit!" Angry with himself
for allowing another possible threat to come within striking
distance of his friends, he grabbed his weapon, jumped up, and
actually ran down the steep mound of stones toward the man,
risking breaking an ankle—or worse. Thoughts of his friends
being harmed again because of his negligence fed his chaotic
pursuit.

Snake quickly ran through bushes that snagged his clothes
and scratched his face, but he didn't stop until he was positioned between his friends and whoever was approaching.

Thankfully, he counted only one unsuspecting native. And the way the poor man struggled to walk he didn't appear to be a threat but the way their mission had deteriorated, the old guy could still be leading others toward them. Snake cursed himself because he didn't check the valley below them while he was on top on the hill to see if the old man was alone. One screw-up after another, he lamented.

A very thick dead tree, felled by age, storm, or some other act of God, offered him a perfect camouflaged blind. Peeking out from between the broken branches, Snake watched the man as he battled his way up a path between more of the scattered rocks and boulders that time had shaken loose from above and rolled down the mountainside. The whole area was strewed with boulders that had rolled down from the heights above over the centuries, an area of frequent earthquakes in the early history of the region.

As the native drew near, Snake was able to get a better look at him. He felt a growing rage to lash out at the Ethiopian for the anguish they had endured in this beautiful, but deadly land. Finally, Snake had to acknowledge the error of his feelings and the thoughts that were teasing him as he watched the man struggling to walk, then stop and take a breather.

"My God," Snake said almost loud enough for the stranger to hear.

He was surprised when he noticed the poor ragged man was covered with dirt from his muddy brown hair to the one shoe he was wearing. The man had sat down and rubbed his obviously sore bare foot. Then when he stood and stumbled closer, Snake saw he was completely covered with mud. Apparently, he couldn't wipe it off or didn't give a damn about trying. Maybe getting away from whoever cast this poor man off, alone and battered, was far more frightening to him than his shoddy appearance.

Snake's anger ebbed as he realized this indigent soul was no threat to them. Life, he decided, had already pummeled this lonely traveler. He would probably flee in fear if he spotted any of them.

Snake noticed blocking the stranger's path was an enormous boulder that cut off the trail he was following. If the man took a right, he would be walking away from the valley and the resting-place of his comrades. If he made a left turn around the boulder, he would pass within fifty feet of where Snake was hiding and walk directly to the spot they were resting. Snake watched him as he resumed his climb. Go right, he silently prayed as the Ethiopian disappeared behind the boulder. The bad luck of the mission continued as the dirty native approached the dead tree. Snake put his Uzi down and pulled out his pistol. He couldn't just let him walk into camp.

The Israelis were noted for taking a good invention, redesigning, and improving its capability. The pistol he pulled out and aimed at the head of the squalid mud-man limping unaware toward him was of Israeli redesign. It is a twelve-shot automatic 9 mm with a ten-shot silencer built into the barrel. The muddy Ethiopian's head would be blown off his shoulders by a deadly force that he never heard coming.

Snake took aim, slowly squeezed the trigger, and fired a four shot round at the head of the stranger. He then closed his eyes and slid down behind the trunk of the tree. Disconsolate, he tossed the pistol on the ground at his feet. *Is it the air here*, he debated, *that makes you shoot first without thinking?*

Shake rolled over and slowly peered over the tree. The target of his anger was very still. His eyes were opened wide and staring skyward. *Why murder that poor soul?* he berated himself. *He's probably only trying to get home just like we are. My friends are dead because someone else decided to settle a grudge by shooting at us from ambush. That poor unarmed man in no way presented a threat to us,* he acknowledged sadly. But he knew he was a soldier and had a soldier's job to do, regardless of his opinion of the sanctity of that job.

Snake watched the man until he started walking again. He had changed his mind about killing him at the last instant. The bullets that whizzed over his head had sounded like insects to the tired man. He looked around, hoping that he hadn't walked into an angry swarm of killer bees. Then he started walking again, all the while talking to himself. He had considered the mud he had repeatedly fallen into as the final insult in a long, horrendous day full of them. Now that same mud, he believed, was probably a shield against most insect bites.

When the Ethiopian staggered past him, Snake took a different path back to camp. At the speed the old crippled man was walking, Snake figured he would have no problem reaching the camp first. He didn't kill him but he was certain the others would shoot first. He was both right and wrong. The man started walking a little faster as he neared the camp. He was recovering from whatever catastrophe had befallen him. Snake was amazed when he walked around some bushes and spotted the man just up ahead of him. From behind, he seemed taller, stronger, and steadier than he was earlier. And there was something about the way he walked now. Snake shook those thoughts from his mind and tried to determine what to do next. Unless he shot him in the back, the man would reach his friends a few moments ahead of him.

Weasel was looking for another cup to pour the stew he was heating up into when he noticed movement out of the corner of his eye. Without giving it away, he watched the Ethiopian standing at the edge of the woods about ten feet behind Sara. When the intruder took a step, he dropped the cup in his hand and in one quick motion drew his pistol. The stranger raised his hands and froze. If he had moved another muscle, he would have had a small, bloodless hole in his forehead. Birdman spotted Weasel taking a firing stance. He rolled over on his injured arm, got up on his knees, gun drawn, aiming in the same direction. Birdman didn't hesitate—he pulled the trigger and fired. Both Weasel and Birdman heard Snake shout the order not to shoot, but for Birdman, the order came an instant too late. Thankfully, he only wanted to scare the man, not kill him.

Sara and Simon didn't notice anything until Birdman fired in their direction. The thought of another ambush had cruelly stolen the little contentment the rest had given them. Death, they both feared, was back to claim the ones he'd missed. Simon jumped up and looked around, his heart pounding in his chest. He quickly spotted a frightened beggar standing at the edge of the encampment, staring wide-eyed with hands raised.

Simon decided that this poor soul couldn't be the source of Birdman's deadly force.

Sara was a little slow to respond to the commotion around her. Her desire to fight or run had waned since she looked up at the spot of David's suicide. More than ever, the pain of his death was crushing her spirit. Her breathing became labored as the realization he was gone forever sat heavily on her chest. She was too deep in her own self-pity to care anymore. But when Birdman fired off a shot behind her it shook her out of her malaise. With angry intent, she gritted her teeth, growled a lethal threat as she jumped up, and reached for her weapon. The urge to kill those who had caused David's sacrifice gained strength. But it was the curious expression that she noticed on Simon's face, who was now standing and looking behind her, that slowed her hand. She just turned and looked.

Snake quickly walked in front of the stranger, waving his hands at a group of mannequins frozen in the spot where fear had first touched them. He stood between them, turned, and looked into the eyes of the tattered, mud covered Ethiopian. "Don't shoot," he said as he shook his head in surprise, "I think the prodigal son has returned."

Weasel held his weapon aimed between the eyes of the stranger until Snake walked between them. Snake's panicky voice almost startled Weasel into doing what his words pleaded for him not to.

"I think it's David," Snake told the shocked group.

Sara watched Snake turn his back to them and confront this tattered-looking beggar. She let out a sigh and released her grip on the trigger of the pistol in her hand. *Is this the threat?* she wondered. *Are we that paranoid now?* She was about to say something to that effect when she noticed Snake was staring oddly at the stranger from the woods and then said something that she heard, but it didn't quite register at first.

"I think that's David," she heard him say the second time.

Snake then looked at her and pointed to the intruder. This time she did understand him. The why of his cruel attempt at hurting her she didn't understand. That was somewhat baffling coming from him. He was the quiet one of the group of soldiers. Had she done something, she wondered while looking at Snake, to provoke him to say something that mean?

She looked deeply into the eyes of the target of Snake's insensitivity. The man she saw was covered in what looked like dried mud. His face was hidden in a thin covering of dirt. The dirt-covered tattered clothes on the poor beggar must have weighed a ton. Only the savage rays of the sun, in this ungodly hot country probably prevented him from discarding them. Unprotected skin of non-natives, they were told in their pre-mission briefing, suffered a painful fate when exposed to the piercing African sun.

Sara looked at his face. Snake's cruel words were quickened in her mind again. Why would he think this pour soul was David? No one could survive that fall, no one.

Sara noticed that the stranger was now staring at her instead of the armed men aiming guns at him. At any moment, he could be dead, yet his eyes—

When Sara looked deeper into those eyes, a trembling raced up her arms leaving goose pimples in its wake. Her pistol slipped from her hand and fell at her feet. She opened her mouth to breathe, but nothing entered. Her lungs failed to co-operate. The shock of recognition froze the muscles in her chest. Fighting to stay erect as her head started spinning, she took a feeble step toward him. "David," she whispered softly with the little air that she was able to inhale. "David, it is you, isn't it?"

Simon looked from the stranger to Sara standing behind him. The tears running down her face conflicted with reality. David was dead, Simon told himself. *No one could survive that fall. His arms and legs had to have been broken in a hundred places, yet Sara is acting as if this poor soul is our David. This man standing here is virtually unhurt under those filthy clothes. Where are the broken bones?*

Its Snake, Simon remembered, *this cruel fabrication is his doing. He was the one who first said this poor native man was David. His stupid statement provoked this very vulnerable woman to think her David had risen from the dead.* As Snake moved away from the stranger, Simon grabbed his arm to ask him if he was crazy when Sara stepped past them and walked closer to the stranger, preventing Simon's grilling of Snake.

"Sara."

Sara ignored Simon and took another step toward the stranger.

The mud-man had stood silent and perfectly still the moment he stepped out of the bushes and into the encampment. As the guns aimed at him dropped, his shoulders sagged in obvious relief. The closeness of his death had turned him into a statue. He knew, before Birdman fired the shot over his head, not to move, not to even blink, and he didn't. Even when he saw Sara's tears, he maintained that pose. When Weasel, and then Birdman, holstered their weapons, he finally was able to speak.

"Saaarrra," he said dry mouthed. "Sara, it's me."

"Wait, Sara," a cautious Simon called out to her as he stepped between them and raised his hands to stop her. "That can't be our David. He died last night, remember? This must be another person named David."

Simon looked to the others for help. As one, he could see they had accepted the man as David Yasuda. Birdman and Weasel were on their feet now with a smile of recognition on their faces.

"No!" Simon shouted. "No, my friends," he said, looking each of them in the eye, "there's someone else under that coat of dirt. There—has—to be."

Sara ran to the stranger and wrapped her arms around him. He held her tightly as they turned in a circle hugging, laughing, and crying. Snake, Weasel, and Birdman joined the two in one big hug-a-thon. Simon stared, unbelievingly, at his friends. How could they be so easily deceived into thinking this filthy man was David? David was dead! No one wished this were David more than Simon did, but it wasn't him. It couldn't be him.

David saw Simon watching them and pulled away from the group. The others noticed and stopped the celebration. The five of them turned and smiled at Simon. When David took a few steps toward him, their eyes met. Then Simon knew, as a lone tear leaked down his face, Simon knew. The shock of seeing David alive was still fresh on Simon's face when David took another step toward him and extended his hand.

"Simon, I've returned."

A heavy weight of guilt fell off Simon's shoulders and he broke down and cried where he stood. Everyone knew he shouldered the blame for every death they had encountered and none more painful than the apparent suicide of his friend David.

Sara led David and the others to Simon as she held him until he forgave himself.

"Come everyone and sit down. I want to hear how David got away."

Listening to Snake, they sat down around a very overcooked meal in rapt anticipation. They had a thousand questions each wanted to ask. Just as they started to question him, Sara stopped them.

"Excuse me gentlemen," she said as she stood up in the circle of men. She picked up her canteen and motioned for David to follow her. "Be back in a minute." That said, she took David's hand and led him into a wooded area out of their sight. An embarrassed David turned and apologetically shrugged his shoulders. The four men watching grinned at him, increasing the awkwardness he felt.

Simon shook his head at the unambiguous display from his young agent. Everyone figured that, after their emotional reunion, Sara wanted some time to be alone with him. As one they gave their sister room to heal. They were surprised when, a few minutes later, they returned with David wiping his face with a white towel. As the duo sat down they guessed correctly where the silk 'towel' came from. She had needed the privacy to remove it for her dirty friend. Apparently, she could no longer take looking at the face of the mud-man. In their absence, David had shaken off most of the dirt/mud from his clothes and was buttoning up the few remaining buttons when they stepped out of the woods.

Sara sat David down and poured some water from her canteen over the few spots he missed on his face, arms and hands.

The bright smile that appeared after she finished was the final touch. She had blocked the others from seeing him as she stood in front of David. When she finished drying him, she turned around, carefully blocking his face. Seeing she had everyone's attention, she stepped aside to reveal the man behind the dirt mask. Simon recognized it immediately. Snake, Weasel and Birdman were seeing it for the first time. It was the look on David's face when the love for Sara filled his heart.

"I know you guys have a lot of questions. I don't blame you. I'm as shocked to see you as I'm sure you are to see me."

"David, what happened to you? How did you survive that fall?" Simon asked.

Simon's trained mind registered the snicker behind David's smile. *He's up to something,* Simon surmised.

Sara sat close to David, doting over him, and using her "towel" to wipe places he had missed interrupting him as he attempted to explain the last twelve hours to them.

"When we were in the cave, I realized I was holding everyone back. With my injuries, I knew there was no way I could travel very far. So when almost everyone fell asleep—" David looked over at Birdman and smiled. "—I crawled out, trying to get away and force the issue. I was so weak I couldn't get very far. I knew Sara would insist on staying with me, reducing the search party by one fifth, and that—" he said, looking at her, "—was unacceptable."

She frowned at him but only momentarily when she realized it had little or no effect.

While Weasel removed their well-done meal from the fire, David explained. "Crawling out the cave, I tried climbing up the mountain but became so exhausted I had to stop and lay on the ground to recuperate.

"Laying in the dirt, I seemed to actually get stronger, as if Mother earth was giving her prodigal son an injection. A much need injection because I was very weak. I crawled near the edge of the ridge and peered down at the valley below. Then standing up against the rocks I made my way down the ridge past the cave were you guys were sleeping. I was working my way down when two soldiers almost caught me hiding."

"Soldiers?"

"Yes, two soldiers, Weasel."

"Snake and I were on patrol and we didn't see any soldiers."

"Well, I was able to hide until they walked past and then I continued down the mountain."

"David, why didn't you come and get the rest of us if you were able to continue the search?

David looked at Simon and then the others. "My ego, Simon, my ego. While I was lying in the cave, voices kept telling me I was spared to find the pond. Not us, but me. Stupid, I know."

Sara leaned back and stared, surprised by his confession. Ego was never a fruit on his tree.

"Let me explain. While lying in the cave, I started to believe I was the only one who could find the miracle water. Delirious from loss of blood? Who knows? But that's what I started thinking. So as I began to feel stronger that only underlined my fantasy."

"Okay so you made it down the mountain, right?"

"Right.

"Well, we thought you took another path down."

Sara and another commando chuckled at Simon's revelation.

Puzzled, David stared at Simon then continued. "So I'm walking the woods blind and tripping over everything with my one good arm and leg. Each time I fell, it hurt like hell and all my wounds started bleeding again. I'm not sure if it was the scent of blood that caused what happened next, but I suddenly realized I was being hunted by a jungle cat."

"No shit!" Snake exclaimed.

"No shit. When it started growling behind me, I started running on my good leg."

"Hell, I bet you did," Snake said and Sara clinched David's arm to her chest.

"How did you get away, David, climb a tree?"

"No Snake, it was a—"

"Don't tell me, a leopard." Snake clapped his hands and

laughed. "Maybe," he tried explaining to the group. "Maybe you might climb a tree and get away from a lion. But leopards live in trees. When they kill other animals, they are strong enough to carry the animals up in the trees to eat."

"It was a black panther."

"Stalking you at night—damn. So how did you get away?"

"I didn't. It chased me up this mound of rocks and, just when I thought I had escaped, it leaped at me—" David stood and turned around, revealing that the back of his shirt was slashed. "Ripping my back open to the bone and knocked me down the other side of the mound."

The five gasped, seeing the shredded back of his shirt. It looked as if it was slashed with a knife, numerous times.

"I lay there, bleeding to death. Well, I was already bleeding out. But that wasn't the worse part," David explained to a rapt audience. "A second leopard arrived and the two of them came down the mound to finish the job."

"Now, wait a minute," Birdman demanded. "You didn't die, they didn't eat you, so why are you telling us this shit?"

No one spoke up either to defend David's wild tale or Birdman's practical interpretation.

David motioned for Birdman to sit back down. "Birdman, you are right about the second part. They didn't touch me. But I did die. I think from the loss of blood. But I remember leaving my body and standing there looking down at myself, and I was lying in a pool of water. Anyway my soul started to float above my body. I was on my way to Heaven. Don't ask me how I knew I knew. Then suddenly I was back on earth again—alive."

No one spoke for a moment.

"What about the cats?"

"Oh, yes. Strangely when I was standing above my body the leopards were sitting harmlessly in the grass like—like kittens, Snake. They looked at me and then stood and climbed to the top of the mound. Crazy, huh?"

"No. I meant after you returned."

"Thankfully, they were gone. Believe me, when I sat up, they were the first thing on my mind."

"So you didn't die."

"I'm not dead. I stood up and my clothes were soaked," David continued, ignoring Birdman's claim. "My only thoughts were about you guys. Dripping wet, I decided to climb out and find you. One thing I did know is I wasn't going to climb out where I saw those leopards. I found another way out and as I climbed down I slipped and fell in this deep mud puddle. It was at the end of a stream and probably the last section to have water. Man, that mud was deep. I don't know if it's because hippos played in that mud hole, but it was so deep I thought it was maybe quicksand. If it wasn't for a branch I grabbed to pull myself out, I might have still been there."

A frowning Birdman stood up, as if waiting for David to acknowledge the truth.

"David?" Sara said when he stood to confront the accusing commando.

The others stood up fearing a confrontation.

"Do you remember my injuries, Birdman?" he asked the scowling soldier.

The object of his question remained silent.

David started to unbutton his shirt and held it in his hand. "Do you see the wound where I was shot in my shoulder yesterday?" Staring at the unimpressed soldier David unbuckled his shorts and allowed them to fall to his ankles. He didn't have to say anything as the five saw his thigh, like his shoulder, was unblemished. Before anyone could ask, he turned around. "Remember I told you that panther ripped my back open to the bone."

Where the other injuries were completely gone, they noticed his back was still healing and carried the healing scars of numerous slices. Five faces looked on, as if seeing an apparition. Even Sara stood, open-mouthed, staring at him.

"Lady and gentlemen, not to delay our mission any longer. But that snarling black panther, following the voice of its Creator, herded me to the top of that mound, and then knocked my crippled ass down the hill and right into the pool of the— Messiah Drug!" David shouted, raising his arms.

Sara let out a high-pitched scream.

Snake repeated "Yes! Yes! Yes!" over and over again.

It took a moment for the others to join in but quickly the five were dancing with the man in his underwear like they did when Moses led their forefathers out of Egypt.

"I died, Birdman," David explained when they hugged. "And the Healing Water reached up to the doors of Heaven and pulled me back. Being submerged in the elixir, I guess I swallowed enough to heal and to fan the last spark of life in me until it was a roaring flame." He turned to Simon. "God has finally heard us. Signal our countrymen, if there is any left in that hell, that we've found the "Sweat of the Angels."

While Birdman sent home the news that would send helicopters swarming down on their position, the other men rejoiced. Finally, they were ready to get back to the business of being soldiers.

Birdman positioned Weasel and Snake on each side of the high canyon ridge. From their positions, they had an unobstructed view of miles of territory. Nothing could approach the valley by air or ground without being seen.

David led Sara, Simon, and Birdman around the far side of the avalanche of rocks and into the valley the way he had climbed out. Well, to be honest, he had to tell them, he really fell out.

"When I finally decided I was strong enough to leave and look for you guys, I knew I was still very weak but decided to risk it anyway because I just couldn't wait any longer. The voices of the dying were telling me to hurry. I stumbled around until I found the easiest way over the mountainous pile of rocks."

"The easiest way?"

"Don't be a smart ass, Simon," David said, nudging his friend. "Okay, another way out, away from where those friendly panthers roamed. Jehovah might have used them to guide me the first time, but I wasn't taking any chances on what they would do the next time we met. Anyway, like I told you, I was almost down the other side when I tripped and rolled down the hill, landing in a deep pit of mud. It must have been a watering hole during rainy season but was only mud now. But, as I found out, it was a very deep mud pit, and I sank down in it like it was quicksand. After getting submerged up to my neck, I was finally able to crawl out of that pit by grabbing hold of a tree root and pulling myself out. For a while, I was so weak, I thought I would drown in that mud hole. In fact," he told them, pointing to his one muddy foot, "I did leave something behind. Exhausted, I lay in the hot sun for hours before I felt strong enough to get up and look for you guys."

David led Sara, Simon, and Birdman past the area of the lake of mud, around enormous boulders and thick shrubbery, over a smaller pile of fallen rocks, and then through a narrow passageway into the valley. On the other side, they stopped and looked up in awe at the tall trees that had shielded the tiny valley from inquiring eyes above. David stopped and pointed out a sparkling pond nestled against the mountainside surrounded by those tall trees. The three wayfarers stood in shock as they took in the picturesque scene unfolding before them. It was a Middle Ages painting brought to life.

When they reached the Pond, the water was so clear you could count every stone or pebble on the bottom, and it reflected the shimmering light that streamed down between the lush green trees. It was a small version of what the Garden of Eden must have looked like, Sara thought.

Simon looked up and understood the parable the farmer had told the Ethiopian priest. This was the valley of the short sky. The tall, sheer walls that surrounded the small valley blocked out most of the sky. The direct sunlight could only reach in for a few hours, early in the day, before it hid behind the walls. The indirect light that made it through the trees illuminated the valley with sparkling reflections as the rays played off the surface of the pure water.

The water had a depth of about five feet at its deepest spot, they discovered, and spanned outward for about twenty-five yards at its widest.

"I think this is as close to God as a person can get on Earth," Simon told his friends, as he looked around, awed by the spectacle.

The valley had a virginal air about it that touched the visitors.

Without comment, Sara sat down at the edge of the pond and meditated. There was something holy, serene, and deeply moving about the valley that none of them could quite figure out, but each sensed the power there. They spoke very little and then only in whispers as they walked around the pond.

Birdman had little to say once they entered the valley. No one took notice of the strained look on his face. He grudgingly realized that his life as a warrior seemed insignificant when compared to the power of the presence they felt in the quiet, shady valley. He drifted away from the pond, away from his companions. "I'd better stand guard at the entrance," he announced. "You never know when those leopards might appear."

Only Simon took note of his sarcasm and turned to watch him leave, but no one objected.

David sat down near the spot where he crawled out of the water and reflected on the miracle that was his life. He somberly acknowledged that this was the place where he had died and was resurrected. It was the why that he questioned. The real power of the valley was revealed when, in a cool breeze that waved past his face, he heard the answer to his "why."

The weight of that answer was painful as he considered how much it required of him. He accepted the answer with a sad but willing heart and was resolved to fulfill the new commission in his life.

The sereneness of the tiny valley moved Sara in a disparate way. She heard a different voice. The essence that touched her, she directed toward her noble goal to make David her life's work. It was her way of thanking God for giving him to her, she rationalized. The deeper voices of commitment that whispered to her spirit were ignored when they offered to guide her to a higher level of social involvement and consciousness. She discounted any voice as foolishness that suggested a life where David wasn't the center.

Simon watched first Sara, then David, surrender to the power radiating from the sparkling water. *There is something here, something greater than we are,* he acknowledged as he walked around the pond. No wonder the savage beast was becalmed when they entered this serene valley. Death is forbidden here.

He looked back at the two lovers. They were seated near each other but it was apparent that they were oblivious to the other person. Simon felt the tugging of his spirit to let go and allow the peace of this Eden to cleanse the soul. He resisted, unwilling to let go of the shame of past failures.

He walked around to the far side of the pond to get away from his friends. The peace he felt only stirred pangs of guilt. His heart was very heavy as he mourned the deaths of the commandos.

"History has taught us Jews," Simon prayed to the presence of someone greater than himself, "that there's a price to pay for everything. It is said by the elders that the millions of gallons of our blood shed in Nazi German concentration camps was the price we paid to be granted our country. The wars we have fought with our neighbors, the price to keep it. But the value attached to this quiet pond is almost too great to pay. Yet, it wasn't your hate that has killed hundreds of thousands of people. You didn't kill the children, we did. You have helped us, oh, loving God, to find a way out of Hell.

"You prepared this place of deliverance before the plague. Would it not of been better to just slay those responsible, before they *were* responsible?

"It is the price of your help that causes me to question why it is so expensive. Have we drifted so far that the cost of our journey back to you is a hundred thousand lives? I know, I know, we have brought this on ourselves. I just pray, my Lord," he said, looking up at the bright rays of light filtering through the green canopy over his head, "that you will intervene quicker next time before we annihilate each other." With that off his chest, Simon retreated and joined Sara and David at the edge of the pond.

Birdman watched his new friends sitting together. He felt the pull to join them but resisted. Feeling a strangeness he couldn't explain, he retreated to the entrance of the valley. He would explain later that he wanted to climb the mound and check on Snake and Weasel.

Sara watched Birdman as he slowly walked away. She knew the pond frightened him. There was a power to it that you either respected or feared. His violent world had no place here, so he felt out of place.

Birdman stopped and took another look back at his friends kneeling at the water's edge. They were so child-like in their trust of the powers that anointed the water. He, on the other hand, was a little suspicious. The farther he got from the pond, the better he felt. He would rather trust in his own fate than commit to something unseen and spooky. The power of the water could have nothing to do with a God. It probably contained some mineral or something that destroyed the bacteria. Yes, that was it, just an act of nature compensating for another act of nature. Satisfied that he had properly defined the problem and found the only practical solution, he climbed the mound of rocks. Reaching the top, he stood proudly, looking out at the green valley below, once again, a competent, dangerous, and powerful Israeli commando.

CHAPTER 30

Upon receiving the signal from Simon, the evacuation plan was put into action. Unbeknownst to Simon, the Israeli government had made a covert deal with the Sudanese to place rescue helicopters and tankers in the desert near the Ethiopian border. They quickly fashioned a makeshift runway in the sand. It was in a very isolated area, diminishing the probability of infection. Truth was that the cowardly Arab government was hoping it might eliminate some of their non-Arab countrymen in the southern part of the country that they were systematically murdering. The Israeli government used that hatred to their advantage.

That site was very important because it would enable them to fly the elixir directly to Israel by plane, cutting the transport time down to a few hours.

Helicopter gunships took off from that covert base in Sudan and slipped unseen across the Ethiopian border. The gunships destroyed every radar station in a fifty-mile-wide path. Four additional gunships flew constant patrols in that corridor to persuade others of the danger of approaching it.

Three hours later, the first three of ten helicopters arrived over the valley. The three were heavily armed gunships that patrolled the designated area for ten miles on either side of the mountain. Next to arrive were five helicopters refitted as tankers to transport the precious fluid and one as a pumping station. The final helicopter arrived with supplies and to remove the victorious discoverers.

They made it clear in their broadcast that they were not leaving until the job was finished.

Two engineers were off the first chopper as soon as it touched down. The chopper fitted as a pumping station was directed as close to the hidden valley as possible, the tall trees preventing direct access by air. Fortunately, they had enough hose to reach the pond from outside the valley negating the need to blast out a landing zone in the small valley destroying its beauty. The hoses stretched over two hundred feet from the pumping station helicopter to the "Pond of God."

Within thirty minutes, three of the specially fitted helicopters tankers were filled with gallons of the elixir. Forty-five minutes after they arrived, the first of three copters was airborne and leaving under the protection of one of the gunships. The two remaining tanker-helicopters landed and began taking on the miracle water. When they were finished loading, the second of the gunships escorted the two tankers and the pump-station helicopter back to the base.

The third gunship remained overhead protecting the Pond and the copter waiting to escort Simon, Sara, David, Weasel, Snake and, of course, Birdman. They were adamant about refusing to leave until last.

Unfortunately, the fifth tanker-helicopter was less than half full when the last of the water was drained from the Pond. What remained of the Pond was a bowl of solid rock. The engineers siphoned every drop of water they could find. The rocky bottom was vacuumed until nothing remained but a dry waterbed.

Simon, Sara, and David watched from a quiet, grassy corner of the valley as geologists poured over the dry pond bed, looking for clues to the origin of the healing water.

"They won't find it," David volunteered as he held Sara close to him. "I know they will not leave a stone unturned, but they won't find the source of the elixir."

Simon remained silent as he pondered David's words. Only after failing to see David's reasoning did he speak. "What makes you so sure they won't stumble onto something? It could be God's will that they do to cure some of the victims of the multiple diseases, plagues, and illnesses around the world."

"Simon, this was a sign to the world that God is not dead and that we are his chosen people. If there was an unlimited supply, man would soon worship the water and not the water's creator."

Sara smiled at Simon as he thought over David's treatise.

"They will return, you know."

"I know, Simon. If not us, then another government, maybe the Americans. None of them will find it. This valley has been here for probably thousands of years. Only the grace of God allowed us to find it."

"Maybe those leopards you saw are the reason no one had found it."

"True, Sara."

There was some truth to David's words as the geologists explored the valley in the time allotted to them but couldn't find the source of the water.

From the water line on the rock walls, the Pond had maintained the same level for a long period of time. There wasn't any stream that fed the pond, above or underground that they could locate.

When the three helos lifted off and headed west under the protection of the second gunship, Simon signaled the young captain of their rescue helicopter that they would be leaving as soon as they said goodbye to their fallen comrades. In fresh clothes, Simon led them to an opening in the trees that gave them a panoramic view of the grassy plains.

"Somewhere on the other side of this mountain, our comrades gave their lives for this moment," Simon said as they gather around him. "I'll never be able to forget them but since we, or rather David, found the water, at least they didn't die in vain."

"Here, here," Weasel added.

"I received some messages I'm sure you'll want to hear," Simon told the huddled group. "First, two gunships discovered the Ethiopian soldiers' landing zone and was able to pick up the bodies of our friends. It appeared they were being kept there by our friendly hosts who were more than willing to give them back when the gunships appeared."

"Yes," Birdman shouted, as he shook the hands of the surviving commandos.

"Yes, is right," Simon added. "Also the navy picked up the captain of the ship that launched the attack on our country."

"Kill that murdering bastard slowly," Snake shouted above the growing roar of the warming helicopter.

Simon motioned for them to follow him farther away from the noise of the copter blades. After a couple of minutes, they stopped at the top of a rise above the helicopter landing zone.

"You can tell me what you would do with him, Snake, after I finish."

"You don't have to say anymore, Simon," Snake answered. "If I had him here, I would kill him."

"Let me finish. The captain jumped ship after launching the bacteria. Seems he had a touch of conscience—"

"I'd like to touch him," Snake growled, interrupting Simon again.

"Anyway," Simon said after staring at an unrepentant Snake, "this captain is from Libya."

That surprised them because the leading villain was believed to be Iraq or Syria.

"This captain said the attack was the brainchild of Libya. It seems that old Colonel Qaddafi's replacement, somebody named General Ahmade, concocted this to provoke us into attacking Iran or Iraq. United Nation troops, led by American planes, have invaded Libya. This general, if he's found alive, will stand trial before they fry the bastard."

The copilot climbing up the hill interrupted their meeting. As she approached them, she signaled they were ready to take off. Simon gave her an affirmative wave and told the group to move out. He led the way down the hill toward the idling copter. For some reason, he turned around and saw that David hadn't moved a step and Sara was in front of him pulling on his arm.

Simon told the others to board the helicopter while he investigated what was keeping David and Sara. He climbed back up the hill and overheard them arguing. Sara was kicking the pile of empty canteens they had left behind.

"David, Sara, is something wrong?"

"I'm not leaving with you, Simon," David said.

"Then I'm staying to," a stubborn Sara added crossing her arms.

A stunned Simon looked from face to face without satisfaction. Finally, he asked. "Why do you want to stay here, David? Our country is waiting to hail you as a hero. Your courage has saved the lives of millions."

"What I've told Sara I was planning to tell you, my friend. I understand what your telling me and I hope it will make the lives of other Falashian Jews more bearable when our story is told. But what I failed to tell you is that while we were sitting around the pond I saw the pain that the AIDS virus is causing in central Africa. Whole generations will disappear in the next five years. In some countries, half of the children will die from AIDS alone, not to mention from other diseases and starvation. As we sat around the Pond of the Most High, I began to understand what God requires of me. I filled six canteens with the Water of God. What I plan to do is take them into the center of hell and save the children."

"That's very noble, David, but can't we do it better from Israel?"

"The power of the elixir will prevent a government from sharing the last of it with other countries. Take my advice, give all of it to those in need. Don't save any of it, or people will hoard it, fight over it, and probably kill for it."

Simon nodded in agreement, as the picture became clear. *This young man is special*, he acknowledged.

"Well, I don't care what either of you say," Sara told them. "I'm not leaving you, David, not now, not ever. 'Whither thou goest, I will go,'" she said, quoting Ruth from the bible.

"No, Sara. Where I'm going is no place for a woman. You will draw too much attention to us. If word gets out about what I'm carrying, our lives won't be worth the dust in the wind. Please try and understand that."

"Listen to me, David," the animated woman from earlier in

the cave said. She got in his face, her bright eyes alive with indignation. "I'll say this very slowly; I'm—not—leaving without you. Not now—not—ever!" She screamed the last few words at him.

Steely determination was chiseled across the enchanting face of the woman he loved. He nodded at her in agreement. David shrugged at Simon, as if to say, he tried. Then he walked over and picked up the canteens. He tied them together in a string and placed them over his shoulder.

Cautious, Sara stared at him from a distance. She had decided she would tolerate no trickery from either of them and no macho male bull droppings were going to change her mind. She would die if she had to, but he would never leave her sight.

"Come on, honey, let's walk Simon to the copter." David walked over to her. He put his arm around her and rubbed her back. "Our friends are anxious to leave, and I want to say our goodbyes."

Sara didn't move. Even when Simon motioned for her to join them, she didn't move. It was evident she didn't trust either of them. David shook his head and started down the hill toward the landing zone without her. Simon looked sternly at Sara and motioned for her to please accompany them. She looked at him as if he was insane or had a horn growing out of his forehead. That look told Simon all he needed to know. He turned around and walked away. Sara watched them until they were a safe distance ahead and then reluctantly followed them down the path to the awaiting helicopter.

The pilot shouted out the window at Birdman as David and Simon approached. He heard him but couldn't make out what he was saying. Birdman saw him point to his watch. Birdman raised a fist and opened it. The pilot returned the five-minute signal. Simon motioned for the three commandos to join him a short distance from the chopper.

David quickly explained his vision to Snake, Weasel, and Birdman. If there was any possibility they could respect him anymore, his vision sealed it. They hugged each other unashamedly. Sara was caught up in the emotion and joined in kissing goodbye the brave men she had come to love and respect. They weren't surprised that she was staying with David. Each kissed her goodbye, shook David's hand, walked over to the helicopter, and climbed aboard.

"Goodbye, Sara," Simon told the obviously happy woman. "Take care of this man."

"I will, Simon, I promise."

"I know you will."

"When our work is done, Simon," David said while hugging him tightly, "we'll return to Israel and not for some dumb parade."

They shook hands passionately. David put his arm around Sara as they walked Simon to the helicopter. Simon climbed aboard and waved to them. David stepped back behind Sara and signaled to Simon to wait a minute. The other commandos on board saw him motioning something. Sara noticed that her friends were looking over her shoulder. The look on their faces alerted her that something odd was going on. Worried that more soldiers were approaching from behind them she turned around to make sure David was all right.

Sara saw the amateurish punch coming in plenty of time to normally block it and counter-punch. She was a highly trained agent who excelled in self-defense. The fact it was being thrown by a man that she loved more than life confused her. She paid for that momentary hesitation.

The men watching were stunned as David sucker punched Sara. Not one of them doubted how hard it was for him to do that. Sara dropped to the ground like a rag doll. David had telegraphed the punch but it was a solid one. Weasel and Snake started to climb out the copter to help but David motioned for them to stop. He walked over, placed his canteens in the helicopter, and then knelt down, kissing Sara gently on the forehead. As he wiped her hair from her face, he noticed that there was an ugly bruise growing on her chin but she appeared to be breathing normally.

He slipped his hands under her and picked her up in his arms. He started to walk to the helicopter and then stopped, looking at the woman in his arms. Other than the bruise, she appeared to be sleeping. The love he felt for her swelled up in his chest. The tears he swallowed burned his throat. He would always love her and, at the same time, doubted he would ever see her again.

"Goodbye, Sara," he whispered as he kissed her cheek, all the while knowing this goodbye could be forever. He placed his face against hers and hugged her close to him. "I do, and will always love you."

Leaving her was a pain that echoed throughout his being. This drastic measure was a momentary thought, a deed done because he just couldn't find the words or the strength to say no to her. With his face in her hair, he inhaled her essence for the coming lonely cold nights ahead. The scent of her, he was afraid, might be all the comfort he would receive as he walked through the remote plains of central Africa.

David carried her to the helicopter and placed her in the arms of Weasel and Snake. The sadness in their eyes surely mirrored his own. They carried her tenderly into the helicopter. Simon and Birdman observed silently as David watched them buckle his love into her seat. They were speechless. What could one say to someone who tossed away happiness, in the arms of this wonderful woman for the hell that was central Africa? What could they say to someone who tossed away the adoration that awaited him at home for the diseased, murderous countries that lie ahead for him?

Embarrassed by the water swelling up in his eyes, David turned and walked away. He heard the whine of the helicopter blades increase as he climbed the hill but he couldn't bear to watch them leave.

The sound grew louder as the helicopter lifted off. David acknowledged that fact by walking faster. His blurry vision caused him to stumble a couple of times as he struggled up the hill. Finally, as he reached the top, he stopped and listened as the noise from the helicopter abated. Minutes later, all he heard was the sounds of nature.

Suddenly David had a wild thought. What if Sara came to and got off that copter? She was stubborn and feisty enough to do that. She could be waiting for him at the landing sight. He tried not to let that thread of hope drive him to dream. He took a few steps then stopped. Overcome by her loss, he ran back to the landing zone.

"Sara," he shouted as he ran.

With each step, he began to picture her waiting there with her arms outstretched. Every branch in his way was another attempt to keep them apart. He fought through the bushes and trees as if they were part of the conspiracy. With each step, he could sense he had to hurry. Something was wrong he could feel it.

He ran recklessly down the hill and through the tall grasses. The dangerous predators of the countryside were forgotten as the need for her overcame his fear. He burst through the bushes. There, in the spot where the helicopter took off, was nothing. David screamed out her name and ran around frantically looking for her. Reality slapped him out of it when he had to sit down to catch his breath. *She's gone, they're gone, deal with it, David*, he scolded himself.

Okay, okay, that's over with. If Sara could have gotten off the helicopter, she would have, he thought, consoling himself. She was strapped in when they took off, he remembered. He took a moment to catch his breath and then stood up. It was time to get out of here. Those soldiers were sure to return here now that the world probably knew what the Israeli military had done.

David walked back to where he had placed his knapsack. He had secured all the rations he could carry in it and thankfully the shoes that Birdman volunteered. The picture of walking all over Africa barefoot didn't sit too well. The 9 mm pistol Snake gave him he placed in a hidden compartment in the knapsack. If he ran into trouble, Snake explained, his best option, with his background, was to avoid it and not shoot at it.

He placed the soft cap he was given by one of the engineers on his head. Looking around, he said his goodbyes to the valley of the "Angel's Sweat." It was then that he had a most troubling thought. David glanced around frantically. A voice told him where they were but he refused to listen to it.

"The voice is wrong—it has to be," he mumbled.

Fate couldn't steal his love and vision from him at the same time. David retraced his steps, again and again.

There was something about the truth that was unmistakable. No matter how you reasoned with it, twisted it, discolored it, it was still the truth. David found that out when he searched every foot of ground and found nothing. The picture of the canteens lying on the floor of Sara's helicopter was true. The "Messiah Drug" was gone.

Dealing with the suffering of the Falashian people they encountered traveling through the Sudan had depressed him. The battle with an indignant Rabbi Gette had made him very despondent. When Sara told him her assignment was to use him to investigate the Falashian sect, that almost destroyed him. The loss of the precious canteens stripped him of the last of his strength.

"Why, God?" David cried as he dropped to his knees in utter despair. "What have I done wrong? Please forgive me if I've angered you somehow. Surely you aren't angry at me for sending Sara home." David buried his face in his hands as his frustrations threatened to burst out of him. '*His will may not be your will.*' The rabbi's words pummeled him. He had sacrificed Sara to do what he thought was God's will, yet that same will was lying on the floor of the medal bird carrying his heart. Had he let her remain here, he acknowledged, he would still have the elixir. Was that God's will then for them to be here together? he wondered. Did he screw up, worrying about her safety, and misinterpret His will?

He knew in his soul that God was on his side, despite the hell he had endured. So he didn't want to tempt Him with the anger that surged through his soul. His Lord didn't take kindly to human judgment of his handiwork. History taught him well the very sad endings for men and angels who had tried.

Kneeling on the ground, David felt lost. The sudden, violent change in the direction his life had taken had badly shaken his confidence. The strength of his character was his ability to rebound from defeat or rejection. On behalf of his displaced people, he had encountered plenty of both lately without throwing in the bloodied towel. The seed of that strength took root in his hopelessness and whispered a possible direction out of his dilemma.

He got up off his knees and took the two extra canteens of drinking water he had borrowed from the departing engineers from his knapsack. Maybe if he poured some of his drinking water from one of the canteens, his desperate mind wondered, on that sacred ground, the power of The Most High might reenergize the water.

This new vision started to make sense as he climbed over the rocks and back into the hidden valley with the canteens of water. *God is just testing me*, he concluded, unconvinced but fearing to admit it.

David walked slowly between the tall trees as he approached the remains of Pond of God. From a distance, he could see something was different. The valley seemed much darker and more foreboding than he could remember. It was more than the time of day that shaded the valley. Something was awry. Even the air in the tiny valley felt like it had lost its savor. The why of this omen became clear when David got close enough to look into the pond.

After getting slapped continuously, one began to expect the next one. Although it hurt just as much, the body usually adapted enough to endure the barrage. Such was the case with David. It didn't surprise him that his plan evaporated before he had the chance to try it. "It is just the way things are going with my life," he said, as if seeking pity from whoever was listening.

In their sincere desire to save as many sick people as they could, the engineers had broken up the rock floor in search of the water's source. What awaited David was a deep hole of dirt and rocks. He took a deep breath and shook his head, realizing that the water from the canteens would only soak into the dirt if he poured them out.

This time he didn't let the pain of another failure crush him. Defeated, yes, he accepted that. But in this defeat he remembered something from, of all people, Rabbi Gette.

"'The battle is the Lords, and he will give them into our hands.'" *1Samuel 17:47.*

"Stop fighting for God." The words of the rabbi reached out to him in the hidden valley on the face of Mt. Ras Dashen, "He will fight your battle."

A peace came over David, and a new strength. Whatever path he took, he decided, then and there, it would be up to God to fulfill the purpose in his life.

David dropped the canteens and sat down in the grass. He prayed for God to forgive him for being weak and faithless. "It is your will that I deliver the healing water to those afflicted with the AIDS virus, not mine," he said to God with renewed confidence. "It's your battle. I'll get there. You, my Lord, will put it in my hands by hook or by crook."

He meditated there until he found peace in his spirit.

CHAPTER 31

David stood up and wiped the dirt off his knees. It was time to stop feeling sorry for himself, he acknowledged, and formulate a plan. He was alone with enough food for a few days, a hand gun he had never learned to use properly, three canteens of water, and other than the mountain he was standing on, he had no idea where he was exactly.

It was getting late in the day. Night was coming and he had to either get moving or find some place to sleep for the night here in this mountain.

"I've got to head inland soon or get caught in the jungle below the mountain after dark," David admitted. Memories of being there at night added weight to his decision.

He started walking and stopped when he had a thought. What if he could get to a phone and call Simon to send his canteens to him? Better yet, once they discovered that he left them onboard, they would surely come back with them. "No they won't," he argued, and under the circumstances, neither would he. "They can't risk exposing themselves for one man's dream."

How to get the water from off the helicopter was God's problem, David decided as he brushed off his clothes. At that moment, a beautiful butterfly buzzed past his face as he turned around. Instinctively, he slapped at the dancing bug. The blue, red, and yellow insect dropped like a stone. David watched as it fell onto the soft overturned earth.

A twinge of remorse and guilt nipped at him. He was sick of things around him dying. Death was every—

David stopped thinking about the butterfly when he noticed a very shiny blue stone in the dirt turned over by the departed Israeli engineers. He reached down and picked it up. There was nothing special about it, just a smooth pebble with a blue tint to it. His curiosity abated, he was about to throw it away when he noticed another a few feet away, then another. The angle of the remaining sunlight, sneaking through a small opening in the tall trees, illuminated the shiny stones making them sparkle in the dark and rich soil. The trail of pebbles led across the destroyed pond to the wall of the canyon in an irregular pattern. Had they been larger, he surmised, they would be stepping-stones across what was left of the pond.

David walked around the pond to the base of the canyon wall. Some massive trees blocked his path. He stuck his face in the narrow space between two of the trees and studied the wall. For the first time, he saw that there was a small trough or channel worn into the face of the wall. It protruded outward about five feet and was approximately twenty-five feet high over his head. With the branches of the tall green trees blocking it, and unless one was standing exactly where he was, the channel was virtually hidden from view between the branches and leaves.

David tried to climb up behind the trees and failed. The sheer angle of the face of the wall made it impossible to climb. Curious, David studied the wall for another way up or even more important, a way down. He knew he was wasting traveling time but felt he had to satisfy the question in his mind about where the channel led. He couldn't bring himself to hope. Hope was a cruel, vengeful lady in this bitter land. It was best not to disturb her. Once awakened, she dished out cruel and unusual punishment.

From where he stood, David could see that the trough appeared to originate at some rocks protruding out of the wall face. *That's odd,* he thought when he spotted a small bush thriving in a crack in the wall at the same spot. If he could climb up one of these trees, could he reach those rocks? He backed away to get a better look. There was a way, but it would be very dangerous. If he could climb up around the outer canyon wall, maybe he could slide down or lower himself down the wall to the channel.

It was this hope that delayed his departure down the mountain. He gathered the knapsack and canteens and hid them under some bushes. Climbing out of the valley, he looked around for something he could use as a rope to lower himself down the cliff face.

The vine he found wasn't quite strong enough to supplant all his concerns for his health, but it was all he could find. He coiled it up around his arm and started climbing up the right side of the canyon.

The path he took was littered with loose rocks that threatened to toss him back down the slope of the canyon. More than once, he had decided to turn around and get off the steep cliff with his pride and life intact. Then each time a little success would give him the determination to go on a little farther. David was forced to stop when he reached a particularly difficult spot on the cliff. A large, jagged boulder blocked his path. To climb over it would be very dangerous. If one of the narrow, sharp edges he would have to hold on to broke off, he would fall over the side into the valley below.

Unable to climb any higher, he looked for another way around the barricade. While carefully climbing back down, David saw what looked like an opening in the cliff about a hundred feet away from the valley. The uniform symmetry of the round opening shouted man-made. While staring at the opening, he remembered reading that some of the native religious sects dug holes high up in the mountains in Ethiopia to bury their high priests. It was a hazardous but effective way to prevent animals from digging up the bodies of these revered holy men.

These slopes, he imagined, were probably studded with tombs dug into the hillsides. As treacherous as the climb up the cliff was, he couldn't imagine who would risk their lives digging into the face of such a steep precipice. Looking down, he couldn't see any evidence of a trail people would use to climb up to that tomb. He guessed that was the point of putting it there.

David faced a dilemma. Time was running out for him to start climbing down Mt. Ras Dashen. Yet, that perfectly cut opening called out to him to investigate it. The tomb won. He carefully climbed down and over the steep hillside. It took him over a half-hour to climb back up to the opening. As he neared it, he realized it wasn't as inaccessible as it first appeared. The smooth narrow flat path he encountered that led up directly in front of the cave was a surprise. The path up was hidden by bushes but it was obviously man made.

The narrow path widened as it reached the tomb and the then continued past the opening and farther up the mountain and out of view. Cautiously, he peeked into the mouth of the tomb. The small opening revealed little that he could see. He tried sniffing the air inside the opening for an indication of the occupant but didn't recognize any odor of animals or rotting flesh.

"Is anyone in here?" he shouted into the cave in Amharic, the main language in Ethiopia.

No one answered and he couldn't hear any animals moving about. David searched his pockets and found that the small flashlight hadn't fallen out of his pants while he was climbing up the jagged mountainside like he feared. *Lady Luck smiles on everyone sooner or later,* he mused sarcastically. Without it, he would either have to climb back down the mountain or enter the tomb blind.

David entered the tomb very slowly, prepared to run out at the first sign of trouble. He aimed his flashlight in an ever-expanding arc around the tomb. It was the size of a very small room but empty. There were, however, some very old writings carved on the walls in a language he didn't understand, mixed in with some words in Amharic. The words he could make out in the dark tunnel all warned not to go any farther and to flee this holy resting-place. There were frightening references to angry demons that guarded the entrance to the secret place and dire warnings for anyone foolish enough to take another step.

This must be the burial tomb of someone very important if

they went to all this trouble to scare people away.

As he aimed the small beam of the flashlight around, he noticed that there was an opening behind a very large rock in the back of the tomb. As he approached, leery of what might be in that hole behind the rock, he realized that it was a passageway that narrowed and veered sharply around to the left, shielding whatever lurked back there. David swore. He knew he would have to move farther into the tomb to see what was around that bend. The opening was only four feet high. He would have to stick his head in first. Frightening thoughts of someone with a machete, lying in wait to separate his head from his shoulders when he stuck it in, froze his feet to the ground.

After a deep breath and rebuking himself for being frightened, David aimed the small light around the opening, leaned down, and entered the passageway. He wasn't able to completely stand up but the passageway was wider than he first thought and veered again around another bend. He took a couple of very quiet steps and then stopped and listened. Only the wind blowing past the opening could be heard mingled in with distant voices of the varied wild life outside.

Encouraged, he started to move farther along in the passageway when he sensed something was hurtling toward him. He couldn't see or hear anything but sensed something was coming around the bend. He listened intently but he still couldn't hear anything. The flashlight, quivering in his hand, only illuminated a few feet of the curved tunnel ahead and what lay beyond the darkness remained hidden.

David summed up all the courage he could muster, took a deep breath, and then stepped farther into the channel.

Like being caught in the middle of a dark train tunnel and then suddenly having a train racing headlong at him, David was suddenly inundated with a surge of fear so powerful and real that it froze him in his tracks. He had faced death before, but this was stronger than the tall black robed man with the sickle. He wanted to run but he was too terrified to turn his back on whatever was approaching, preventing a frantic dash out of the tomb.

David couldn't move. He felt the cold arms of panic holding him tight. He had violated this hallowed ground and now
the powers that held reign here were determined it was time
for him to pay for his crimes. His heart beat so violently in his
chest he thought he was going to have a coronary. Despite his
chest heaving and his frantic gasping for breath, he couldn't
breathe. He was so terrified he couldn't budge and didn't
know what he was so frightened about. There was nothing in
the beam of his light but dust balls, yet he felt waves of numb-
ing fear emanating from somewhere in front of him.

Was it death waiting around the next bend in this cave?
Did the next step forward drop off into hell? Was it some vicious wild animal lying in wait for him if he continued? He
wasn't sure of that, but what he was sure of was that he wasn't
going to leave. When he survived the initial thundering burst
of absolute terror, he resolved to stay. All the suffering that he
had endured had honed a determination in David that surprised
even him. He had died once, so the fear of death had lost its
sting. He was alone, so death couldn't threaten him with the
life of a loved one.

"Okay, okay, okay," David mumbled. "We can do this."
That did little for his confidence but he was still there. After a
deep breath, he slowly took a small step then another, as he
turned another corner and walked farther into the tunnel. The
confidence he built up dissolved instantly when a horde of
white phantasms, in the shapes of everyone's nightmares,
charged out of the blackness and ferociously assaulted him.
Physically, nothing much happened. His clothes waved violently on his body as if caught in a wind tunnel. He felt the
real presence of the specters. The shaft echoed their horrible,
shrilling screams as they raced toward him some with claws
and sharp fangs open for the kill. The voices of doubt hollered
above the din for him to "*Run, run for your life!*"

David never moved. He never even blinked. Looking back
on that moment, he didn't feel particularly brave or determined. Later, he thanked Yahweh for gluing his feet to the
ground.

The phantoms were horrifyingly disfigured creatures with

long claws and mouths of sharp teeth—savage-looking crea-
tions from the dark depths of his fears. As they passed over
him David realized he was still alive. Specters of every possible frightening description came at him, trying to drive him
out of the tomb. David mumbled a prayer but never took a step
back.

Just as suddenly as it started, the shaft was quiet again. Dry
mouthed and trembling, David noticed everything was very
dark. He tried aiming the flashlight around and nothing happened. When he slowly looked down, he realized his hand was
empty. In the frenzy that had occurred he had dropped it. He
looked around quickly, lest another adversary leap upon him
unawares. He spotted the light a few feet away. Mouth dry,
knees weak, he slowly bent down and felt around for it, picking it up while nervously keeping his eyes on the wall of
black. David aimed it down the shaft. After another deep
breath, he started moving forward again, only more deliberately this time. The fear continued to bombard him but it had lost
its tenacious grip. What it had threatened to do to him, he had
already endured. He cautiously looked around another bend in
the cave and, again, nothing happened. The shaft continued to
curve around out of sight. He took a step forward, and another.
In reality they were very small steps. But in surviving them, he
felt as though he had walked the "green" mile.

David took a deep breath. He might have to face the unknown again, only now he was more confident. The feet that
felt as if they weighed a ton only moments before now were as
light as a feather. He sensed there was a difference, an assurance that nothing was going to stop him. Like stepping out
into sunshine, he felt a warm calm come over him. He had
survived.

The beam from the little flashlight illuminated only a small
area of the wall of pitch black so David had to weave it back
and forth, while taking small tenuous steps, as he slowly
walked forward. There was a reason for his being here, he
tried convincing himself while peering carefully down at the
floor of the shaft. He continued walking slowly forward until
the walls of the narrow shaft suddenly opened up into a large

room. He aimed the light around the room and spotted dust covered torch holders along the walls near the entrance. The room had to be very large because the beam from the flashlight disappeared into the darkness without illuminating anything in front of him. His fears whispered that it was a large hole surrounded by slippery moss and that he would slip and fall into if he continued moving forward. David laughed, mocking his fears, but he swept the light across the floor in front of him as he walked.

A feeling of disappointment replaced the dread that he had battled as he fought his fears to get here. The large, dark, empty room was a small reward, he scornfully acknowledged. *How much time have I wasted exploring this stupid tomb?* David lowered his head and shook it in frustration. He turned to leave, took a few small steps, and stopped. *Might as well see who is buried in here*, he decided.

He walked over to the nearest wall and followed it around the room. He found additional dusty torch holders on the walls, but little else. Bored, he gave up continuing the search but instead of retracing his circular steps around the room, he started walking across the room toward where he guessed the exit was. After about ten small steps the beam of his flashlight reflected off an object sitting on the floor in the middle of the room. If he had continued around the walls of the large room, he would have missed it completely.

As David moved closer, the light illuminated an object sitting on a table of stone. At first glance, the beauty of the object was stunning. *What a magnificent casket*, he first thought, *but small for a—*

It was about a four-foot-long box with two small golden angels on—

"Oh!"

David started walking backward until his back hit a wall and the object was again clothed in darkness. He felt dizzy and his legs buckled. His breathing came in short gasps, as if the air had been sucked out of the room.

It can't be, it just can't be, he kept telling himself. *Relax, think this thing out.*

He tried hard to remember the biblical description of what he thought he just saw.

Two and a half cubits long and one cubit and a half high.

That's about right, he guessed as he mentally converted cubits into feet. He stepped forward until it reappeared. From where he stood, it was about four feet long and over half that high. There were two long staffs running the length of the box and two figures on top.

"And thou shalt make two staves of shittim wood and overlay them with gold. And thou shalt put the staves into the rings by the sides of the ark that the ark may be borne with them. And thou shalt make two cherubims of gold. The cherubims shall stretch forth their wings, and their faces shall look one to another," David whispered.

In bits and pieces, the teachings of the scriptures came back to him. The object in front of him fulfilled every description that Moses wrote about thousands of years ago. "Could that terror that I felt when I entered," he whispered as he stared at the object, "could that be a direct result of being in the proximity of..." He was afraid to even call it what it was.

David found breathing difficult as he came to realize what he had stumbled upon in the tomb. Feeling dizzy again, he sat on the ground and leaned against the wall for support. The Holiest Shrine of Judaism was only a few feet away from him. Inside that over-three-thousand-year-old chest was believed to be the actual tablets of the Ten Commandment made by the hand of God; manna from Heaven, the food of Angels; and other priceless religious treasures.

David recalled the stories of armies that had been destroyed as that gold-inlayed chest was carried with them into battle. From his childhood, he had heard the story of the death of Uzza. When the ox that was carrying the Ark stumbled, he reached out to stop the precious Ark of God from falling off and touched it. God forbade everyone but the high priest from touching the Ark at the cost of their lives. Uzza's goals were noble but God's word was the law. Uzza died.

"Don't touch the Ark," he whispered as a warning to himself. "Even if it falls, don't touch that Ark."

David stood up and walked around the stone table that the Ark sat upon. What he found on the other side offered another surprise. There, reflecting in the beam of his light was a small pool of water. He aimed his light up at the ceiling. There were cracks overhead that ran the width of the room. In those cracks, David spotted glistening brown water stains. While he was staring up at the ceiling three drops of water fell and were illuminated in the beam of his flashlight. As if in slow motion, they drifted downward until they hit the Ark and then something amazing happened. Each drop exploded into thousands of tiny bits of very bright light and floated up over his head like fireflies. David turned off his flashlight but the droplets held their glow. The cavern became the night sky on the clearest of nights. Each time the bits of floating light would fade out, two or three more drops would strike the Ark renewing the show. Sometimes it continued for minutes before the cave became completely dark as the bits of water-light slowly lost its sparkle and drifted down to puddle on the floor under the Ark. *What a manifestation of God's power it must be in here when the water flows in a stream over the Ark.* Years later, when reflecting on the incident, he realized the wondrous light display was just for his benefit.

His joy was short lived when an ominous thought crossed his mind. After being hidden for thousands of years, the weakened ceiling looked as if it was ready to cave in, burying the Ark forever. The fate of Uzza determined that he couldn't remove it himself. He would have to leave and get help. The excitement of seeing the Ark returned to the Holy Temple in Jerusalem blinded him to the mission he was called to do. Only after the golden glare of the Ark wore off did he remember his vow to God and the sick children of central Africa. That conflict troubled him as he sat in the dark. Why would God put him here if not to retrieve the Ark? *Did he change his mind? No, Yahweh doesn't change his mind. Maybe it was His plan all along to get me here.*

In his reflections, the region's troubles came to mind. Starvation had almost destroyed Ethiopia over the last twenty years. Why? Drought, famine, plagues of insects, diseases, and deadly viruses were common to those who lived in Central Africa, yet Israel prospered above every nation in the world when the Ark was in their homeland. Why?

An answer came to him that eased the weight of his inquires a little. The continent of Africa, and Ethiopia in particular, was blessed with some of the most beautiful, scenic areas in the world. Nature had given this land everything it needed to support itself. Compared to the rocks and desert that the Children of God inherited, this was truly "a Promised Land." It was the people of the continent that appeared to be cursed. Was it in response to the cruel treatment that the Falashian people had endured over the centuries on this continent that brought about this curse?

Another possible answer drifted into the quiet of his thoughts. "The Prophet Jesus," Rabbi Gette often preached, "said the good servant takes his talents and puts them to use. He risked losing them. The bad servant takes his talents and buries them, lest someone come along and steal them. What God gives you, he gave you to use, not to save in some safe place. The bad servant lost the talents he had and was thrown out into the fires of hell."

Falashian lore accused Queen Maqeda of stealing the Ark from Israel and hiding it somewhere in Ethiopia. The truth of the fable was a few feet away. But could this "hidden talent" be the cause of the curse on the people of Africa? David sighed, as another reason to remove the Ark became clear. The weight of his dilemma caused him to lean back and close his eyes. He didn't want to use up the batteries in the small flashlight anyway so he sat up, took a quick look around the room, then turned it off. The darkness was welcomed as it delayed any decision he had to make. Unfortunately, no answers surfaced as he wrestled with his conscience about what to do with this world-shaking discovery.

What would the world think of this? he wondered. Would they rejoice? Would it bring about world peace, a return to common values? David visualized people rejoicing and dancing in the streets as the proof there was a God was flashed around the world on TV. A rebirth in religious fervor maybe or peace. He pictured a world at peace, the trillions spent on war machines now directed at places like the hell of central Africa. He shook his head. No.

Somehow, someway, mankind would find a way to screw up this discovery. Or turn the Ark into a weapon of war.

The late afternoon sun reached a spot where the rays of light came through a crack in the wall at floor level. He only noticed it because he was sitting on the floor in the dark. The thin beam of light ran across the floor and illuminated the pool of water. Curious, David leaned down and put his hand in the water. He pushed some of the water toward the crack. The water pooled around the crack for a moment before draining out. He did it again. Soon the act became a distraction from the decisions he was forced to make. The game grew old as his hand started to get cold in the water.

A tired, very lonely and troubled man stood up and departed the hiding place of the Ark of the Covenant. The answers he sought, he finally realized, weren't in the dark musty tomb, but in the light of day. The answers about what to do with the Ark would come, he felt in his spirit. They always did. The dead and dying weren't in that cave but out in the real world. He sensed it was in this real world where he would find the answers to the questions that troubled him.

The climb down the narrow ridge went quickly and was uneventful as David found an easier way down toward the valley. He climbed over the lowest section of the avalanche-caused rock pile and walked into the hidden valley. Gathering his knapsack and the canteens, he started his climb back out.

The decision on what to do with the Ark was put on hold when he walked out of the secret tomb. He had plenty of questions but no answers. Sitting on his butt in the tomb had accomplishing nothing. If he started soon he could find the road to the Ethiopian city of Aksum and be near the city before sunset. From there he could call Simon or Sara and maybe get their opinion on what to do with the Ark.

The urge to take one last look at the dug up Pond of God tugged at him. He could not silence the voices whispering that maybe he missed something—a hope all men had when things went bad. "Okay, I'll take one last look and then I'm out of here," he said to his doubts. That should finally put to rest the nagging voices that offered false hope of some miracle. "The pond is dry" he said to whomever was listening, "and stupid left the canteens on the helicopter, those are the facts."

Finally, after swearing under his breath, he put down the knapsack and walked back toward the pond, surrendering to his curiosity. The sooner he got this over with, the sooner he could forget this and get on with his life.

A pile of rocks and dirt now replaced the shimmering beauty of the serene pool. Man had passed through the hidden valley and the pond carried the mark of his footprint. This time, David could honestly testify that the destruction wasn't from man's usual greed but an honest concern for the health of other people. The act was noble, even if it was environmental rape.

Only a tiny mud spot remained from the clear, sparkling pool, the weary climber noticed when he walked around the scar in the earth that had been the pond.

David said a prayer for his friends that they arrived in time to save the country from annihilation. After taking a deep breath, he turned and walked away.

He tightened the chest harness on his knapsack, tied the three canteens together, and tossed them over his shoulder. Looking around, he figured the walk across the dangerous plains of Ethiopia would be easier than climbing up and down this darn mountain. He was about to start another climb, but this time over the wall of rocks that blocked in the little valley, when he remembered something. It was like an itch that that wouldn't go away. David shrugged it off and started his climb out of the valley.

Five steps later, he was backing down the pile of rocks. The itch had to be scratched. David dropped the knapsack and ran back to the pond. He did remember seeing a small puddle. He was sure of it. Standing there catching his breath, he frantically searched among the rocks and dirt. "There it is!" he said out loud.

Only now it appeared larger than he remembered. Questioning a memory, he looked around for the butterfly he'd slapped to the ground. There was no sign of it anywhere.

Could they have missed that wet spot in all the confusion going on here hours ago? he wondered, ignoring the missing insect. The Israeli engineers, David recalled, removed every inch of wet soil in an attempt to capture any trace of the miracle water. Could they have overlooked this? It was possible, wasn't it?

David knelt down, putting his finger in the muddy spot. It appeared to be freshly made. While he was running his finger in the dirt, something landed on the rocks in front of him. The butterfly waved its wings back and forth at the kneeling man. A sigh of relief passed from him as he realized he didn't kill the pretty insect.

David took off his cap to wipe his head when something hit him in the back of his neck. He gasped and jumped back as if struck by lightning. Turning around, he half expected to see soldiers pointing their weapons at him, but saw nothing. Then he remembered that his head was down, and whatever hit him had dropped down on him. While looking up, he wiped the spot on the back of his head. He saw nothing threatening above him. But when he looked at his fingers, they were wet.

Confused, he studied the trees and rocks above him. He had missed it the first few times he looked but when he placed his face between the trees he noticed a narrow piece of rock jutting out between the branches of the two trees about twenty feet over his head. His next question was answered as a drop of water hit him in the face. That was the final piece to the puzzle.

David was able to climb up the nearest tree until he could to see the wet line leading down to the rock. The water seemed to originate from out of the sheer cliff wall. The answer replayed in his mind like the coming attraction of a movie. Climbing back down, he knew he was the cause of the wet spot. The source of the water's power became clear to him.

Gathering two of his canteens, David rushed back up the mountain. He paused for a moment at the entrance, gathered his courage, and walked back into the tomb. Much to his relief, none of the guardian specters appeared to frighten him this time.

His faith was so high now he truthfully didn't care what jumped out at him. Nevertheless, he was glad nothing appeared.

He carefully poured a small stream of the water from one of the two canteens over the Ark and used a cup to gather up the water that ran off from the pool underneath the Ark, being very careful not to touch the chest. The power of the Vessel was never more real to him than it was at that moment.

While filling the two canteens, he surmised that the winter snows probably melted in the spring and drained down through the cracks in the ceiling, dripping onto the Ark. When the level rose it drained through the cracks in the wall and was diverted down a channel into the pond. David felt redeemed.

He put the canteens beside his knapsack and sat down before the Ark. He was dumfounded. Everything, the accident with Sara, their love affair, meeting Simon, the deaths in Israel, the deaths of the commandos, his forgetting the elixir on the copter, was it all part of a plan? Was this some complex conspiracy that the omnipotent forces of the universe had played out at his expense? Well, not really at his expense, he decided when he recalled those who paid the ultimate price.

Whoever was pulling the strings meant for him to be here at this moment in time. It was predestined. What did all this mean? Did some powerful spirit decide the poor brown child, growing up in a poverty-infested land only a few miles from the Ark's secret resting place, would travel over a thousand miles to Israel, grow up, and then return years later in a desperate flight to find a miracle, and then stumble upon it? Those thoughts both comforted and amazed him.

David felt small before the only physical symbol of God's power left on Earth. Would touching it cause his death? He wondered if God's word concerning the Ark was still valid. Could Africa's curses be a direct link to their having stolen the Ark and hiding it in this mountain? Closing his eyes, he meditated on those and many other questions for a long time.

He felt the unwanted pressure to be worthy of something

he could never measure up to. It was that realization that led David to kneel before the Ark of God and pray.

"Lord, lead me to the souls you commanded me to give the Elixir to. Forgive me for doubting you. Help me not to judge your choices or to yield to my own."

An hour later, exhausted, David stretched out on the cool floor and quickly fell into a deep sleep. A sleep alternately punctuated with the bright light of Sara's smile and the cold, dark despair of this diseased and dying region. The night moved on as he slept quietly in the cave. Other spirits he couldn't see watched over him lovingly.

CHAPTER 32

D avid awoke to the shrill sound of birds calling out to each other as they passed the cave opening. The morning sun was at a level that reached into the cave and reflected just enough light to be able to see the way out.

"I shouldn't be in here," he said as the light revealed more of the hidden treasure. David removed his shoes. "Forgive me, Lord, I didn't mean any disrespect." Gathering up his canteens, he moved to the outer part of the tomb. After returning to the valley where he hid his belongings, he took out most of the food from his knapsack and put the two priceless canteens in it. He had plenty of money to buy food with, thanks to the generosity of his departed friends. Weighed down by the water, he felt as light as a feather. God had blessed him to be the first man, maybe in centuries, to see the Ark of Yahweh. He was at peace with his decision to leave. He would report to Sara the location of the Ark. Should something happen to him, she would tell Simon about his find. Even the threat of the cave collapsing didn't bother David. If it happened, God would have had to sign off on the bottom line. And if it was his will, so be it. Taking one last look, David climbed out of the valley of his death and resurrection.

A host of wild animals punctuated his walk through the plains. David knew that God was leading him when he absentmindedly stumbled upon a rouge lion. The powerful beast looked up at him from his shaded resting place under a tree and let him walk by without so much as a growl. The fact that he had probably just eaten didn't enter into David's equation of God's power to stay the savage beast.

After that encounter, he wisely avoided the lower valleys, keeping along the ridgelines where he could keep an eye out for the more dangerous wildlife. Four hours later, he spotted a dirt road that he hoped led west to the Ethiopian City of Aksum. Two jeeps passed him without slowing as he frantically waved them down. The clouds of dust he had to eat did little to dampen his enthusiasm. Ride or no ride, he was content knowing that God was directing his path. He understood that didn't mean everything would fall into place for him. If anything, the way seemed to become more difficult when He guided your path. The Creator seemed to require one to avoid the easy road and directed you down the tougher path.

David heard the next vehicle approaching before he saw it covered in an onrushing cloud of dust. A rusty old pick-up truck sputtered as it stopped beside him.

"Hi there, son. Do you like walking or can we offer you a ride?" an elderly man asked from his cab. "You'll have to ride in the back though, there's only enough room up front for Mother and me."

David thanked them for stopping and offered to pay but they politely refused. He climbed aboard and was just about to sit on a pile of old rags, when the truck lurched forward without warning. It took a moment but he was able to lower his feet from over his head and sit up.

"Whoa, old man," an embarrassed David said when he regained his composure and his seat. "We are never going to make it at these speeds."

Twenty minutes later, he felt the bouncing truck slowing down. He raised his cap off his face, looked around, and saw the old man was driving around the half-eaten carcass of a deer. The killer, he thought while carefully scanning the brush, must of left it when confronted by the loud noise of the approaching truck. David carefully scanned the plains around the bouncing vehicle. At least that was what he hoped had happened—that the carnivore had ran away.

Later, the vehicle stopped again, waking up a bone-tired

David. This time he saw a woman standing at the side of the dirt road with two small children. One was sleep in her arms, the other held on to her skirt and a toy wooden soldier. David graciously climbed down and helped the woman and her two little boys into the back of the truck. She thanked him as she sat down holding the smaller boy in her arms. When David helped her up, he noticed the thin emaciated condition of the small child she was carrying. His tiny face was marked with ashy white splotches. One small arm, like a twig from a dead tree, hung down out of the dusty blanket he was wrapped in. It was obvious death would be riding along with them in the back of the truck.

The rest of the ride, though punctuated with numerous bumps and potholes, was uneventful until the young child in the beleaguered woman's arms woke up and began spitting up blood. The thin, tiny woman gazed lovingly at her son. Her eyes looked past his pain and must have seen him in another light on another day, David thought, watching the caring way she touched him. She gently wiped the blood from his lips until he stopped coughing and relaxed again in her arms.

The weak little boy's face searched out his mother's. They passed thoughts between them that David felt he was intruding on, but he couldn't take his eyes off the sick child. She looked over at David as if to apologize for her son's illness. He, in turn, just smiled reassuringly back at her after sensing God's will for the child.

There wasn't a voice that spoke to him to minister to the child. It wasn't because it was the right thing to do. If that was the case, he understood the canteens of elixir would be empty before the day was over. "The poor you have with you always," the prophet once said.

David just sensed that their paths had crossed for a reason.

She hugged her little boy to her frail chest.

First things first, he decided, reached into his knapsack, and took out a canteen. He poured some in a cup and gave it to the other little boy who drank greedily and finished with a large grin on his dusty face. The little guy politely gave it back to him. David offered it to her. She declined for herself but took the canteen cup for her sick child. David grabbed it from the surprised woman's hand before she could give it to her baby.

She stared at David for a moment, puzzled by the swing in his actions. Her facial expression changed as she realized he was fearful of the child contaminating his water.

David acknowledged her confusion as he screwed the lid on the canteen of water and placed it carefully in the side pockets of the knapsack. He then opened the largest compartment and pulled out a similar canteen. He took the cap and poured a measured portion of the water in it and offered it to the woman for the child.

"*B'ezrat hashem*," David told her questioning dark eyes as she hesitated before taking his offering.

"With the help of God," she repeated to him. Her tiny black fingers reached out slowly and wrapped around the cap. She took it from his hand never taking her eyes off his. Very slowly, she poured the water into the child's mouth. The first few drops ran down his face as he failed to swallow. Then he seemed to acknowledge the cold water's presence. David was very relieved when the child finally started to drink. His mother thanked the stranger for his prayers and the water.

He replaced the canteen, nodded at her, then sat back, and closed his eyes. Pictures of another woman returned to steal the moment. He knew he would take her with him every mile of his journey. Yes, he would call her, he reasoned, and tell her about the Ark. Should something happen to him, someone should know where it was. The fact that he just wanted to hear her voice again was ignored.

An hour later, as the rusty, antiquated truck neared the outskirts of Askum, the young child abruptly sat up in his mother's lap. He was so animated and clear eyed that even his older brother noticed the difference. David just stared at him. The other little boy stopped playing with his toy and watched his bright-eyed little brother. The mother's face brightened as if she had received a transfusion of the child's new spirit. Her sad, forlorn countenance was tied into the hopeless condition of her child. As the young child's eyes sparkled with life, his mother's heart healed. One tear rolled down the dust covered, under-nourished face of the mother.

She looked up at David. "Thank you stranger."

"It was God's will, Good Mother, it was God's will."

The truck slowed and then turned right on the first paved road David had seen in this country. Twenty minutes late, the truck pulled over at a busy intersection. David had asked the old man to drop him off near a bus stop. The elder directed him to a gas station across the street that served as the local bus station.

"Sir, let me pay you for the ride. I would still be stranded out there if not for your kindness."

The old man laughed. "You already paid for your fare. Your weight kept me from running off the road. Ha, ha, ha."

David tossed some money on his lap and walked away. "Then give it to your other weary passengers."

The old man shouted that he would.

David ran across the road, turned, and waved goodbye.

The tired old truck rumbled to life again and moved back onto the road. The little boy waved at him as the truck pulled away. David returned the wave. He now had confirmation. Whether the power of the elixir came from it running over the Holy Ark or if it was just faith, he wasn't sure. The water healed, that was a fact.

He watched until the truck disappeared over a hill before turning and walking toward the gas station. The weight of the canteen filled knapsack was a wonderful burden as he pictured other children waving at him as Death passed them over.

There were about a dozen people standing around who, David figured, were waiting for the bus. He hurried inside and purchased a ticket to the capital city of Addis Ababa. From there he could get transportation into the interior of Central Africa.

"You are indeed very fortunate," a young lady with dancing brown eyes told him. "The last bus today is due in thirty minutes and you have one of the few seats remaining."

He thanked her, bought some gum and a soft drink, and turned to leave. He almost dropped the bottle when he spotted the pay phone near the door. As the coins dropped into the slot, David's heart raced in anticipation. After five minutes of delays and numerous operator switches, he heard it.

"Hello?"

CHAPTER 33

"Hello, Sara."

"David—David, is that you?"

"Yes, baby, how are you?"

"I'm fine, how are you, where are you? Oh David, I miss you so much."

"I know, baby, I miss you too."

"Are you coming home, do you need our help?" Sara held her breath as she awaited his answer. *Please say yes*, she silently pleaded.

"Soon but not yet." David knew that wasn't what she wanted to hear, at least he hoped so. "I still have some work to do here, babe."

"Please stay safe."

"I promise. Will you wait for me?"

"Until hell freezes over, or another nice-looking guy refuses my lunch date."

She heard him laughing and smiled.

"My bus is coming, Sara, I have to go. I can't call too often or people might figure out where I am, but know that I love you wherever I am."

"Ditto." Battling her emotions, Sara heard the dial tone and knew he was already gone.

✝ ✡

David worked his way west giving the elixir to the sick in local towns and hospitals. The magnitude of the "curse" on the people of Central Africa was a cold, staggering slap-in-the-face. Hopelessness, the callous fiend that stole the spirit from people, was the most disheartening disease he encountered and for which he carried no cure. It was invisible, but the results from its effect on the people of Central Africa were very evident everywhere. Life, to its victims, had become nothing more than just another means to an end. A life spent just existing in a world they wished they never were born into, until mortality's inevitable invitation to leave. After walking from country to country in this disease-riddled land, David knew that it was a merciful God who sent him into this hell.

From one small cesspool to another, he stepped in the dung of humanity, in search of a person or persons randomly chosen to swallow a sip of Messiah Drug and survive Death's fatal grip. He carried "Liquid Life" in a few canteens for people he had never met. Where that chosen person resided was as vague as his/her face, their anonymity requiring him to travel to places where his own life carried little or no value.

He found those in desperate need of the Life he carried everywhere he traveled. He could have dispensed all of the Elixir of Hope in the first village he entered in Uganda. Stunned by the living conditions and despair he saw, he found himself asking, "Is this the one? No," he said when spotting someone in even worse condition, "it has to be for you. Surely your broken body is next," he murmured as he tried reasoning his purpose in Hell and the next recipient of God's grace. The toughest part, he would learn, was realizing that there were only a few among the thousands who desperately needed his help who were chosen to receive the miracle.

He tried not to let the extent of their suffering influence his opinions, but he had a heart, and seeing people so ill they were lying in their own waste, touched that heart. Those he could help, he helped. He couldn't give them of the miracle water but he could help with washing them in nature's water, leaving what little money he had for their care.

Days later, broke and having traversed only a few miles into hell, he had to look into the face of despair and walk away, leaving more of himself than he realized. What saved David's sanity was when he realized he wasn't the one who decided who was worthy, who lived or died. He just prayed he gave the precious gift to the right persons.

The key was always their eyes. Their eyes, when he studied them, would lock on to his and then he knew. Just like that, no matter how old or young, he knew. No matter how sick or injured, he knew. It was like a light came on in their eyes. A feeling of peace would descend upon him and he knew he had found the next part of the puzzle. A peace that enabled this caring man to find the strength to step over the bodies of dying infants and give Life to their mothers, or to be able to choose one frail, human bag of bones over another.

Soon he became adept at reading the faces of the people he met, this gift also saving him from countless encounters with danger. Again, sanity was in following the leading of the Author of the Messiah Drug. He, the Author being the only one capable or worthy of judging the worth of the souls David met.

Still, he struggled under the awesome burden of the misery he saw. He only had enough elixir remaining to reach a few hundred of the very ill, he reasoned, his effort but a grain of sand on a large beach.

"This is God's plan not mine," he chanted as he staggered under the enormous weight of the misery around him.

Who knew what those hundreds would do with the second chance they now had? That thought triggered one he wanted not to remember. Not a day had passed that he didn't chastise himself for leaving those other canteens of elixir onboard that damn rescue helicopter. Oh, the many others he could have helped, his troubled spirit lamented.

From town to town he traveled, dispensing liquid hope to those most ill. Only to have to sit and wait for God's direction on where to go next. He knew where he wanted to go but that, and she, would have to wait. But in every town he traveled, he found himself looking into the sea of dark faces for Sara. In their brief conversations, he had expressed how much he missed her. It was all he could do to keep his feelings from pouring out when he talked to her, knowing that would have been disastrous. There was no way he could continue this mission with his love for her in control of his judgment.

To Sara's credit, she was desperately trying to understand what drove him to leave her and resisted the urge to beg him to return home. She was more forgiving than he had dared hoped. She did threaten to return the favor and punch his lights out when she next saw him, the joy in her voice unmistakable.

His mention of the Ark sent her into shock. He refused to tell her where it was because he wasn't sure yet if that was what God wanted from him.

Sara explained that she would have to tell Simon. David had known she would feel obligated to when he told her. She was very loyal to her boss in the Mossad. He also knew, or rather secretly hoped, that might provoke them to come looking for him. Possession of the Ark, to a devout Israeli, was a far greater goal than even finding the "Elixir of God." Sadly, he knew he couldn't help them until he had finished the job God had entrusted to him.

David was pedaling the old bicycle down another no-name dusty backcountry road in Rwanda. Calling it a road was more of a misnomer. It was more of a bike path with two bumpy ruts in the weeds. The sun was out in its fullness, baking the "road" and the sweating rider who dared to venture out in midday. Exhausted, he started reciting out loud the directions he was given as he tried avoiding some of the rocks in the road that would ruin his thread-bare tires.

"Somewhere along this very bumpy road, about twenty-five miles outside the Rwandan town of Kigali, is a hospital filled with AIDS cases. Who knows," he said doubtfully, "this could be my last stop."

"It's where the sick and banished people of surrounding villages are discarded," the ragged little priest explained, elated with the healing of his own sick child by the mysterious stranger's potion, as he offered David food and water for the trip. "They are discarded there to die by a cruel, cowardly, and corrupt Rwandan government that steals all the aid intended for them."

An overworked nurse at the last clinic he'd stopped at for directions confirmed the location and the desperate situation of the people there. With the last of the Elixir, he set out to find it. Just before dusk, exhausted and hungry, David located the hospital or what was serving as a hospital. It was a small brick building set at the end of a dirt path. Crumbling walls encircled the compound.

Hearing the groans of the very ill, he approached the clinic cautiously. Inside the crumbling walls, bodies lay on sheets in the courtyard as the building over-flowed with the dead and dying. The arid smell of death had assaulted him long before he could approach the entrance. There was a loud buzzing in the air as he neared the compound. As he entered the open gate, the buzzing question was answered. Flies by the thousands were feeding off the misery laying in the yard. Like a black cloud they hovered over the dying as some of their bodies lay in their own maggot-filled waste, many too weak to move as the filthy flies covered their faces. David struggled to hold down the meager lunch he had eaten and wept, as he took in the misery of the abandoned.

His days in this Hades had viciously schooled him in the depths man's inhumanity could reach. He had seen ten lifetimes of misery in this tour across Africa. What he didn't see personally, others had told him of the unbelievable tales of cruelty they had witnessed.

Shock after shock eventually numbed one's senses. The mind developed walls to protect itself from repeated shocks. At some point, people just tuned out the misery and became numb and unresponsive to the suffering as their protective wall isolated them from their emotions. Others, denying what they saw, acted as if they were removed from it.

People sometimes turned their noses up at their ignorant indifference but what did it take to push them to that callous

edge? They all had their limits. He had heard stories of captured children from a warring village released in a field to be
used as target practice by another warring tribe, of old people
run over by jeeps as they were chased for sport. Young girls
savagely raped by groups of animalistic males as they plun-
dered helpless villages. Women crippled so they couldn't escape the village and their rapists could return whenever they
pleased. These were just a few of the floors his elevator
stopped at on its descent down into this man-made hell.

But this—this scene—was at the lowest level. Here, Death
had shed what little consideration it had for humanity and
spread its victims out in the scorching hot sun to spite God, as
if they were pieces in a heartless mosaic puzzle laid out for the
gods to gaze down upon. This lesser god stood on shaky legs
as he looked out at the field of dying and struggled to keep his
sanity, to endure the terrible gut-wrenching smell, and the
cloud of biting flies.

The horrible exit these valueless souls were exposed to
threatened to wrench his spirit from his body. David wept.

Getting a grip on his emotions, he took some deep breaths,
wondering if the nearly empty canteen would be enough for
these poor people. Hell couldn't paint a bleaker picture. Thin,
wasted, and partially naked bodies lay everywhere. In their
emaciated condition, there was little to determine their sex or
age.

Where were their dreams? All people dreamed about finding love and living a good and happy life. Where were their
dreams? For people who never had the pleasure of lying out
on a sunny beach maybe sipping wine coolers, why should
their exit be so inhumane? Who were they? Someone bore
them into this world in love. Where had that love gone? Who
loved them now? Did anyone give a damn? People treated
their animals better.

He had to stop thinking, he realized. His anger served no
one but himself. The facts were that the consuming fire in
their immune system had destroyed all evidence of their per-
sonality, leaving in its wake a collection of thin black skin
covering bones.

Clouded eyes, which had long ago surrendered to death's call, watched as a broken-spirited stranger parked his bike and opened a knapsack.

The moans and cries of the dying burned through the haze David was in. The stench of the dead and dying was so strong, it took on a life of its own. It was a rabid beast that attacked him the moment he drew close and sought to crush him under its awesome power. He took a deep breath through his mouth and forced himself to ignore hell and see life.

Quickly, he spoon-fed about ten of the people lying about the courtyard a portion of the Messiah Drug from his canteen, while constantly fighting off the hoard of flies biting him. Could they know he carried life?

A haggard old nurse, attending to some of the sick children she mercifully kept inside out of the brutal sun, happened to walk out of the hot building and, seeing a stranger doing something to the poor souls in her keeping, tried to stop him.

"Hey, you! What are you doing?" she shouted as she waved her hand to get his attention.

"I have something here that will help them," he answered, holding up his canteen.

"Or it could kill them. Their bodies can't handle some foods."

"This is water, gentle caretaker, blessed water. It will either heal them or, at worse, sooth their parched lips," he explained as he stood up. "Either way, they will be blessed."

"Just leave," the old woman pleaded, as she limped up to him pointing toward the gate. "These retched people have very little dignity left. Don't offer hope that doesn't exist."

David tried explaining to her that he carried the cure for their illnesses in the blessed water from his canteen but gave up when she threatened to get her gun and shoot him if he didn't leave. The fire in her tired brown eyes touched something in David.

She was a frail little woman dressed in a filthy uniform peppered with blood and who knew what else? What was obvious was her determination to protect the dying souls in her keeping from this ignorant stranger. Again, his healthy countenance labeled him as an alien, an outsider, in this land of death.

Reluctantly, he backed off, picked up his bike, and started walking toward the road. He had just reached the gate of the hospital when one of the sick he had given the elixir to sat up and called out to him. The speed of her recovery staggered the exhausted nurse. Two, three, and then four others began to show signs of renewed life.

"Wait!" the old caretaker shouted and then walked up to him, grabbed his shirt, and tearfully pleaded with him to stay and help with the others. "Don't leave, man," she cried, "They—I—need you."

The only doctor, she revealed, had taken ill and lay on the floor in the clinic very near death himself. The old nurse helped David administer the healing water to the sick patients and the doctor.

As if acknowledging defeat, Death moved away on a suddenly strong, fresh breeze that now blew through the encampment. Carried off with the breeze were the pungent smell of despair and the stench of hopelessness that permeated the tiny way station to eternity. It was as if the breeze had washed the filth from their bodies in its passing and scented their parched skin with the fragrance of the living and the essence of life returned to the worn-down sanctuary. With it, the air became fresher, the sky brighter, and thousands of fat, black flies moved on with Death in search of other victims.

"I could use you help, mister…"

"David."

"…David, in caring for my patients."

"Whatever you need, kind mother."

"Careful what you ask," she answered, smiling, her tiny face alive with hope.

David learned she was correct about that as he helped clean and dress the recovering males. The resilient nurse helped the females. Surprisingly, the clinic had a wonderful well with a deliciously cold and clean water supply. The small clinic had compiled clothes donated by the families of other unfortunates who lost their lives there. The clothes she had washed by hand, and she was able to offer them to some of her recovering patients.

After administering to each of the sick, David was amazed to find there was a very small amount of the Elixir remaining. He asked the nurse if she had anything smaller he could pour the healing water into. She located a dozen small plastic vials with lids in one of the medicine cabinets that would each held about a teaspoon full of liquid.

He carefully filled each of the containers half full and had eleven vials containing the last of the Messiah Drug. He held the vials up to the sunlight.

"The most powerful substance in the universe is in the hands of a nobody," he whispered. "Sure, there are more dangerous substances in the world, but they are created to do harm, hurt, and damage. Can the atom bomb heal a broken bone, cure cancer, and close an open wound?"

About a dozen more people would be able to taste of this miracle of God. David put the priceless elixir away in his knapsack.

"My name is Elle," the nurse told him as they sat eating some potato soup.

It was thin and watery but hot.

"I'm just one of five nurses who work here," she explained as they ate. "Three others are either off today, or sick, or just couldn't deal with the misery any longer," she said without an ounce of indifference that he could see.

Who could blame someone who decided they couldn't take any more of this suffering? Later, a younger woman arrived to relieve her and watch over the place at night.

"This is Alia," nurse Elle explained when she walked into the building where they were eating. "She comes in the evenings to allow me some time to go home. I have family in the village."

Alia was a small woman, maybe in her thirties, with a manly looking, but kind, face. She spoke little but nodded a lot.

"I've worked for three doctors in my years here," nurse Elle continued after Alia went to check on the others. "Two took sick and died and I thought the third would join them.

Doctor John Abume will recover, thanks to you."

"Not me, caretaker, it's the grace of God that has saved him, as well as the others."

"Yes, it would take a God to deliver us from the curse. What did you give them?"

"Like I told you, blessed water is all."

"Is that all you have?"

"Yes, I'm afraid so. When it's gone the miracle is over."

David finished the soup and placed his head on the table.

"Are you all right, my son?"

"Do you have a corner that I can use as a bed? I'm bone tired and could sleep through an elephant dance."

The grateful nurse laughed and apologized for her poor manners. "I have a small room in the back you are welcome to have."

"No, no, I don't want to put you out."

"You aren't, my son. I stay in the village with my people."

That said, she led him to a small room in the back where he could sleep for the night. The nurse lit a candle. The room consisted of a small window, a cot with a pillow, and a small table in the corner with a chair. It was stark but clean and functional.

"Thank you, this will do just fine. I didn't expect a bed." As he lay back on the soft pillow, he knew that by morning the patients would be making complete recoveries from their various illnesses. He also expected morning would find a happy David many miles away from this hospital, pedaling down another unpaved dusty road, which eventually would lead east toward a certain beautiful woman.

After she checked in and kindly covered him with a thin blanket she'd found, he heard the nurse lock the door to the room for the night. He waited until she left then tried to find another way out.

"That old witch," he whispered when he discovered the window didn't open, "am I your prisoner?"

If he was her prisoner, he knew his life might be in danger. Maybe someone had found another value for the rest of the Healing Water. When it came to the Messiah Drug, he was under no illusion that, to obtain it, people would kill. That was the underlying reason he put his *heart* in Simon's helicopter and watched her fly away.

Awakened in the night by a stone or something hitting his window, David discovered the door to his room cracked opened. He grabbed his knapsack and quietly sneaked out of the hospital. Someone had arranged for his escape. The courtyard was now empty as the less ill patients were soon healthy enough to leave the hospital grounds. Those closer to the other side when he arrived would need more time to heal so they moved them inside out of the sun.

Even as he pedaled out the front gate in the darkness, he knew a friend was watching him leave. Was it the old nurse having a change of heart? He didn't know or care. He was just grateful to be free again, thank God.

Alia had waited patiently for the young man to realize his door was unlocked and flee. It would be morning in a few hours, and she was sure Elle would return with the men from the village.

"There are others sick in the village," Elle told her, after locking the door. "They could use the medicine this man carries."

"That is true," Alia argued, "but I don't think it's right to take it from him, not after all he had done for the sick here."

"Well, I disagree. We won't harm him as long as he listens to reason," Elle retorted and took the only key with her—the only key she knew about.

It took three stones against the window to get the man to realize he was free. Afraid he might be angry, she decided that was the safest way. She watched as he hurried from the building, looking around anxiously. His exit through the front gate was reminiscent of her brothers, one of the last to recover, hours earlier when she arrived and learned of the miracles.

Over the next couple of months, David was continually on the move. Eleven people that God apparently wanted to save were scattered across Africa. David had no way of knowing who they were, or where they were, or how long it would take to find them.

He also sensed that word of this priceless cargo had some-how gotten out, and he was a hunted man as he traveled across Central Africa, trying to locate the last of eleven souls for the Messiah Drug. There must be something special about the last eleven, he figured, as he spent many lonely days and nights, traveling across some borders and sneaking across others. *They must be going to play a pivotal part in Africa's future.* Those travels had taken him through many areas desperate for help, yet he never felt led to stop. The minute offering he carried was no dam for the flood of misery he saw.

Knowing that pursuers might be hot on his heels, he prayed for the wisdom and strength to give out the last of the Elixir.

David had survived the ambushes that killed some of the commandos when they first landed in Ethiopia in search of the Messiah Drug. The world had learned about their sacrifices. Now, while riding in the back of a rusted old truck that he thumbed a ride in, David made a decision to start a journal about the search for the recipients of the "Last Eleven Portions," should something happen to him. After the miracles he witnessed, he wanted to make sure the world learned and acknowledged the glory to God for the wonder of his healing power. When he finished a chapter, he mailed it to, Sara, who had almost given up hope of ever seeing him again after joining a six-week exhausting and futile search for him in the chaos that was Central Africa.

David was sitting in the grass at a local crossroads in one of the many nameless towns he'd visited in the last few months, trying to decide where to go next. The road on his right led north and eventually to Israel and the woman who colored his dreams. The other road snaked east back across the barren Hell that was Central Africa toward Ethiopia. Until this morning, there was little doubt where he was going.

Yesterday, after searching for a week and traveling over a hundred treacherous miles, he gave the last portion of the Healing Water to a teacher dying of cancer in an old run down school house. "Mother, can I enter," he had asked as he peeked his head into the two-room school house.

"Yes, son, are you one of my old students?"

"No, kind Mother, but I have heard from one of them. He said you were the reason he believed he could be president or pope someday."

David heard the old woman laugh from behind the curtain to the back room.

"Come in, my son."

David moved the curtain and stepped into a small room with meager furnishings. Other than the small bed the frail older woman was sitting on there was a table, two chairs, and a small dresser.

"Come sit with me. Forgive me if I don't recognized you. My eyes, like everything else, are failing me."

"Well, kind Mother, your God has sent me with holy water to give you more time to change the lives of other children like you've desired."

"That would be my prayer."

David placed the small container in her trembling hand. "Drink, kind Mother."

As he sat with her, she told him it had always been her dream to teach the children in her village. "I feel strong enough to make us tea. Would you like some tea, young man?"

David accepted her offer and sat at the table with her as she continued expounding on her mission in life.

"Listen to me, talking the day away. A young man like yourself doesn't want to listen to the stories of an old teacher. But would you help me outside. I haven't been able to walk that far in a long time."

As the dedicated woman struggled to her feet and walked out of that building for the first time in months, a burden that weighted a ton fell from his shoulders. With the chains of his promise to God broken, he danced the dance of the free with a teacher just as happy to be alive.

He didn't know the teacher's name, but as they danced he whispered "Sara" under his breath. That night, David made his bed under the stars, anticipating an early start back to nirvana.

He was up before dawn, awaiting the first bus headed north. Wonderful expectations filled his heart with delight at the thought of a future with his Sara. He sang "their" song for the first time in months. That changed and he suddenly lost that tune when a rusted old yellow bus pulled up to the corner. He jumped up but kicked at the dirt when he realized it wasn't his bus. He nodded to the twenty or so children who stared at him as the driver struggled to put the road-beaten transmission in gear.

The Sara-generated bliss, that had given him his first good night's sleep in months, was slowly erased by the sadness in the eyes of the children. David was stunned and took a step back when their faces seemed to blow up like balloons. He desperately wanted to look away and retain the giddy joy that was seeping out of him under the piercing stares of the children. The vision expanded until the bus was filled to the limit with their faces. The bus started to screech as the metal frame bulged under the pressure of their expanding heads.

The bus backfired and finally started to move. He blinked and the vision cleared. Only one child continued to watch him as the bus drove away. Somehow he knew the little girl staring at him was dying. He wasn't sure how he knew, but he knew.

"Sorry, sweetheart, but I'm all out of miracles."

He watched the bus until it was out of sight. He found that picture so depressing, he turned and walked away. About fifty feet from the road, he found a flat rock, sat down, placed his face in his hands, and tried to come to grips with what he saw, or thought he saw.

The only answer that made sense was the only one he didn't want to hear. For hours, he sat in the heat of the morning sun, trying to reason away the guilt, but there was no antidote for feeling selfish and no reasoning that gave equal weight to his self-pity.

No amount of explaining could wash away the picture of the deaths he'd seen. He watched as his bus and two others drove past and he came to grips with his future.

"All I ask Lord," the subdued man prayed as he walked in

the direction of the sunrise, kicking stones along the road, "is that I get a chance to see her again."

David had expected no answer and received none. He grudgingly accepted that as a gust of wind blew road dust in his face. He did, however, feel good about getting another chance to help ease some of the misery and pain he had seen. But in the deep places of his heart, a voice of longing cried.

As David walked toward the sunrise, another man in another place hid six full canteens in a dusty cellar, awaiting the return of their owner.

EPILOGUE

United Nations troops invaded the nation of Libya, looking for the author of the plague released on Israel and the Middle East but were unable to find General Ahmade's camp. It was only a matter of time, the Israeli Mossad believed, until they flushed him out of hiding—if he hadn't killed himself.

The good news was that the "Messiah Drug" had saved Israel from annihilation. The death toll from the epidemic unleashed on them had reached 90,000 when Simon led the victorious team of commandos back home. It was estimated that approximately one million people in Israel were infected in some degree with the plague. The people of Israel, given a second chance at life and voiced by a huge majority, gave the remaining vaccine to their death-riddled Arab neighbors. Jordan and Lebanon had suffered the most of the countries that bordered Israel. Estimates ranged as high as half a million dead in those countries as the close proximity of the population allowed the plague to spread faster. It was proven true that the percentages of those infected dropped rather significantly as one moved away from the epicenter—the Israeli coast.

At first, the Falashian Jews who had migrated to Israel did not learn of David's invaluable contribution to the success of the mission or that the young Falashian immigrant had remained in Ethiopia. Simon had asked that David's name be withheld from the public until he could be found. He had assigned agents to search the surrounding cities of his last known location. From his calls to Sara, it was clear David was on the move. What he was doing there now that the canteens of elixir were here waiting on him he was uncertain. Knowing David, Simon confided to Sara, he had found some way of helping the unfortunate there. And when he was ready to leave, Simon would be there personally to help him.

David was in danger. The Mossad learned that there were mercenaries hired to hunt him down in Africa and force him to reveal the location the source of the Messiah Drug. Its value was reported to be worth millions of dollars for just a tea-spoon. What dying millionaire, Simon explained, wouldn't pay a king's ransom for a cure for his cancer? Some would even kill for it. Word, as it usually does, leaked out that David was the real hero and had remained in Africa to give the drug to some of those afflicted with AIDS.

The object of their interest was headed in search of more of the Messiah Drug to complete the new mission on his heart, and then home to—Sara.

The End of Book 1

About the Author

According to author, E. Lessly Taylor, "Looking in the mind of a writer can be a scary place depending on what he or she has to say." He started writing as a hobby, putting to paper the characters he saw in his mind. A place where he could take his vivid imagination, all the while presenting a calm face the people around him could be comfortable with.

Working twelve- to fourteen-hour shifts, sometimes every day for three weeks at a clip, when an inspiration strikes, he would scribble notes on any piece of paper he could find. Riding the bus, he would get an idea and, afraid he might later miss the true meaning, scribbled notes on the inside of gum wrappers or on bus schedules.

His over a dozen novels cover a variety of subjects. "It's said great writers steal ideas from other writers," he claims. "My inspirations came from every day people. The words I've put to paper are meant to reach a variety of intellects and place them in situations they can relate to and with sensitive characters that energize their emotions."

Taylor's wish is that, when reading his novels, readers are taken to a place where the weight of life is lifted for a time, and, once again, that naughty you hiding inside can breathe.